ROSE PETAL SOUP

Recent Titles by Sarah Harrison from Severn House

A DANGEROUS THING
THE DIVIDED HEART
THE NEXT ROOM
THE RED DRESS
ROSE PETAL SOUP

ROSE PETAL SOUP

Sarah Harrison

This first world edition published 2008
in Great Britain and the USA by
SEVERN HOUSE PUBLISHERS LTD of
9–15 High Street, Sutton, Surrey, England, SM1 1DF.

British Library Cataloguing in Publication Data

Harrison, Sarah, 1946-
  Rose petal soup
  1. Domestic fiction
  I. Title
  823.9'14[F]

  ISBN-13: 978-0-7278-6662-2   (cased)
  ISBN-13: 978-1-84751-074-7   (trade paper)

Except where actual historical events and characters are being
described for the storyline of this novel, all situations in this
publication are fictitious and any resemblance to living persons
is purely coincidental.

All Severn House titles are printed on acid-free paper.

Typeset by Palimpsest Book Production Ltd.,
Grangemouth, Stirlingshire, Scotland.
Printed and bound in Great Britain by
MPG Books Ltd., Bodmin, Cornwall.

For Patrick

One

Successful sex in later life is like crime. You need means, motive and opportunity.

In our case, 'means' included a tolerably comfortable situation (we had done floors and tables in our time, but that time was past). As to 'opportunity', if time were all, we had unlimited opportunities – trickier by far was finding that *snap!* moment when everything else fell into place. Nico was by nature a *cinque-a-sept* man whereas I saw the early evening as a good time to watch competitive cookery programmes on TV; I was at my most receptive (as Sir David says of lionesses) in the early morning, when Nico was more likely to be aroused by coffee and marmite toast.

That leaves 'motive'. You might very well ask: does one need a motive for sex? After all, if your name doesn't appear on the sex offenders' register and you're not in the business of selling your body (scarcely an option past sixty), you engage in it for its own sake – for pleasure. And, increasingly as the years go by, for consolation, reassurance and mutual support. Sex is the simplest and most effective reminder that you are not alone.

When I was eighteen, London and everyone in it was swinging. My motive then was to shed my cherry as soon as possible and get on with the serious business of being hip. The youth who obliged probably imagined that I'd never forget him, but the only recollections I have of that long-ago shag in his crummy hall of residence were of his hairy nipples, and the wet-shrapnel sound of a student two floors above being sick out of the window. By my early twenties my bedpost had more notches than Woody Woodpecker's tree house, none of them any more memorable.

It was Nico who changed all that. He homed in on my G spot like a heat-seeking missile and was so hopelessly susceptible to my charms, and I to his, that I felt I could have given

Julie Christie a run for her money. Sex ceased to be the blurry and slightly uncomfortable coda to an evening's partying and became the main event. For the first time I experienced burning desire.

Nico lived in a grotty shared flat in World's End. I in a marginally less grotty one in West Hampstead. I was a student. He was an assistant stage manager with an experimental theatre group south of the river. We conducted a peripatetic relationship based around inexpensive cultural dates, parties of the BAB and hash-cake variety, and lashings and lashings of sex. We never lived 'in sin' as it was then sweetly called, because I fell pregnant and that seemed like a good excuse to get married.

At our wedding breakfast in the Brouhaha bistro on the King's Road, a twice-married actress called Myra (long since excised from my address book) took it upon herself to tell me that I could expect a lull in that side of things.

'Not to be gloomy or anything, it goes with the territory. Once it's on tap a lot of the excitement goes.'

'Thanks for the tip,' I said, 'but I don't think so.'

She shrugged and patted my arm. 'Don't take my word for it, poppet. I'll buy you lunch here, a year from now and you can fess up. Nico . . .! Can I claim my last kiss . . .?'

Nico, justifiably wasted, but ever the world's most delightful and engaging drunk, obliged enthusiastically. Notwithstanding his free hand making 'don't worry' gestures at me and slopping Italian red down the back of Myra's dress, I couldn't help wondering what she meant by 'last'? That, and her use of 'poppet' can take at least some of the credit for the longevity of our marriage.

A little later we danced to Mama Cass's 'It's getting better'.

'What's she on about?' he growled amorously, his hands firmly on my buttocks. 'We had rocket ships and poetry from the off. Still have . . .' He squeezed my bottom. 'In fact I've got a ruddy great rocket ship right now. How soon can we get away?'

I decided not to mention Myra. If she and Nico had history, then history it should remain. I wouldn't have had lunch with her if she were the last woman on earth, but if I had done I'd have been able to hold my head up, look her in the eye and say completely truthfully that Nico and I still had plenty of fireworks.

We were slowed down temporarily by the babies. Not so much Hal, who popped out like a cake of soap, thrived and was sunny, and whose infancy I remember as rather a sensual period, all late-night shared breastfeeding and dreamy doting amid the domestic chaos. The late arrival of Elizabeth was a different matter, but we made our way back from that and had continued, with the odd hiccup, to this day. (Incidentally, you may well be sceptical, as I was, about the hiccup's ability to spice up activity in the marital bed, but if so take heart from our example. A jolt, albeit a small, low-voltage one, proved therapeutic.)

The sex life of the long-time wed is like their conversation. Ours, viewed from the outside, may have looked as though very little was happening, but that was because the shorthand had long ago kicked in. Beneath the surface we were a seething hive of intuitive erotic exchanges. A little forward planning was required, but that was titillating: the shock of the new replaced by the slow burn of anticipation.

One Saturday afternoon in early spring I felt it coming on when England were twelve up on France in the Five Nations at Parc des Princes. (Nico was the embodiment of the feel-good factor engendered by sport.) As the half-time whistle blew he hurled himself on me in a sort of seated tackle, crushing me in a grizzly-bear embrace and subjecting me to a voracious kiss through which, God knows how, he managed to warble: '"Swing low sweet bloody chariot . . .!"' *A bas les Frogs!'*

At that stage, I was on a promise. But rugby is a game of two halves and we hadn't got the green light – yet. We adjusted our dress, and I made us some tea.

At the beginning of the second half the French came out with all guns blazing and nearly ruined everything with a try and a conversion six minutes in, but after a sticky half hour the Golden Boot (returned, Lazarus-like, from repeated injury) sent over a soaring drop goal to keep our lead healthy. Ten minutes later matters were back on a knife-edge. England had the put-in on the French ten-yard line. Nico, glass of Scotch clasped in a white-knuckled fist, was leaning forward tensely, shoulders bunched with the effort of playing all fifteen positions.

'It's nip and tuck here.' He didn't so much as glance at me. '*Merde!* Cheese-eaters have regained their form.'

'Oh dear.'

We watched, frowning in concentration. I may not have been lying back, but England was certainly uppermost in my thoughts.

'Yes!'

It wasn't the most cultured try in rugby history, but there was no disputing the four, then – 'Yesss!' – six points that put England beyond the clammy reach of defeat. Seven minutes plus injury time later I was subjected once more to Nico's boisterous embrace, and half-stifled though I was, I could pinpoint the moment, a few seconds in, when the nature of the embrace changed from one of general jubilation to determined amorousness . . .

On the screen the action had moved from pitch to studio where a triumvirate of tieless pundits sat ready to deliver insightful analysis of the famous victory. Nico pulled his head back to the point where our mutual long-sightedness brought us within focusing range.

'What do you say?'

'We hung on grimly, the back row were rock solid and in the end our tenacity was rewarded . . .'

'Not that! Fancy a lie-down?'

'Maybe.' I was trying for insouciance, but it was impossible to shrug flirtatiously when pinned down by a large husband with congress on his mind.

'Come on then.' He sat up, swigged the rest of his Scotch, doused the pundits and rose to his feet. 'Catch me while I'm ready. When it's gone, it's gone.'

He bounded awkwardly up the stairs, with me following, and went into the bathroom. I undressed, lay down, and listened. A torrential pee and a lot of energetic splashing was accompanied by his spirited rendition of the opening stanzas of Alfred Noyes' 'The Highwayman'. Along with the popular music of several decades, the great swathes of narrative verse Nico had committed to memory at school provided a kind of soundtrack to our married life.

'"Riding, riding, riding; Over the hill in the moonlight; Up to the old inn door!"'

This brought him, as intended, naked to the door of the bedroom, where he paused for effect.

'Look at you,' he observed appreciatively. 'My Bess.'

'If the troopers show up, don't expect any heroics.'

'Don't worry,' said Nico, advancing. 'I'll hold them off.'

'Nice and easy does it, every time,' crooned Nico, to himself as much as to me. His eyes were half-closed as though looking into the sun. I ran my hands over his head and shoulders and down his back, every inch of which was as familiar to me as my own body. Further down my fingertips found the long, scimitar-shaped scar from his recent hip replacement. We had both been impressed, and even a bit shocked, by the size of the incision.

'Struth, I'm amazed my leg's still on!'

'I suppose they have to create a pretty big aperture in order to rummage around.'

'Stop, enough, I don't want to think about it,' he said, but still peered glumly at the operation site. 'I hope I'm not vain, but that's a fucking enormous blemish in anyone's book.'

Nico had his little indulgences – his hair, his eccentric clothes and hats – but they were more in the nature of opt-outs, statements of independence, of distance from the herd, or at least the tribal markings of the smaller, wilder herd to which he belonged; he was not a man who spent much time on his appearance, let alone checking it in front of a mirror. He was largely without vanity (a deplorable thing in a man), but the hip replacement had activated the little he had.

Now he fixed me with enormously dilated pupils.

'Go on,' he growled, 'Garbo me.'

I took his face in my hands and adopted a slightly predatory attitude to kiss him. We had once watched a documentary in the Hollywood Greats series in which it had been pointed out that Greta Garbo, being tall and of an independent cast of mind, had been the first female star to be proactive and dominant in the clinch. In other words she had done the kissing. Nico happily admitted to finding this titillating.

'Screen goddess takes the initiative . . . That's so bloody sexy.'

'"A jug of wine, a loaf of bread and thou . . ."' he intoned, keeping the pace as slow as possible while he still could. I braced my hand against the bedside table on Nico's side. Contrary to popular prejudice, he was the one with the clutter: a small radio and pillow-speaker, a personal CD player, a glass of water, a watch, a pile of change, a Bart Simpson alarm clock, a Moleskine notebook and pencil, a crumpled handkerchief and assorted dog-eared tinfoil sheets of tablets – paracetamol and milk of magnesia. He had also balanced his reading lamp on a pile of books, forming a teetering structure that began to wobble dangerously as our pace quickened. Now, as he hit top gear with a cry of '"The Assyrian came down like a wolf on the fold; And his cohorts were gleaming with scarlet and gold!"' the table rocked violently before crashing to the ground, sending the contents flying in all directions.

After a breathless, recuperative moment Nico peered over my shoulder.

'Fuck me,' he said in awed tones. 'Did I do that?'

Two

That was just over a year ago, when life was tranquil, on the whole. If asked at the time, I'd probably have described it as having its ups and downs, but what did I know?

We were getting older, of course. By which I mean that apart from a few creaky joints we were unchanged, while the financial advisers, the doctors and the government ministers, let alone the policemen, became mysteriously younger. And like most of our circle we were grandparents. We still worked, but a substantial minority had taken early retirement in order to expand their horizons and develop their interests. In other words to frolic, unfettered, wheresoever they pleased. They fitted in Disneyland and Center Parcs between trekking in Nepal, white-water rafting on the Colorado and unfeasible quantities of culture. We had seen all the latest CGI animation features and the Christmas show at the NFT. Those of us who continued to work, did so from choice. We were the lucky generation; the world was our playground.

That said, we abhorred labelling. The terms baby boomer and the horrid SKIER – Spenders of the Kids' Inheritance – were taboo, not to be spoken by us or anyone of our acquaintance, but they nonetheless hovered in our collective consciousness. Roger, the first of us to go on a Saga cruise round the Black Sea had returned declaring it fucking amazing and rife with opportunities for a single gentleman of artistic temperament: a civil partnership was imminent. After years of fretful computer dating following her acrimonious divorce, my good friend Denise had enrolled for a degree course in archaeology with U3A. On a dig in Herefordshire her trowel and that of a retired detective inspector had clashed over a submerged hypercaust and they had embarked on a shagfest that would have shamed the most libidinous legionary. She had never looked better, or back, and (this was interesting) had become instantly, magically desirable, to all the other men around, the living proof that everyone loves a lover.

Weird, then, that in a time of eternal – or at least reclaimed – youth, our generation celebrated significant birthdays with such brio and at such vast expense. The acquisition of a senior railcard, free prescriptions and a winter fuel allowance was marked in our social circle with egregious events ranging from marquee-and-Moët bashes on the lawn to week-long villa parties in Umbria. There was an undertow of irony to these rites of passage – we were shaking our fists and (where a band was present) our booty at Old Father Time to show him we gave not a tinker's for his relentless march. But there was no denying his presence first thing in the morning, especially when wine had been taken the night before.

We were conscious that no other generation of sixty-somethings had had it so good. Work, play, romance, travel – all were there for the taking.

As for me – I was going to be mayor.

The appointment was no surprise to either of us, least of all me. When I told Nico I'd accepted, he congratulated me, declared himself chuffed to monkey's on my behalf and then added, shaking his head as he speared another new potato from the dish: 'I still can't quite picture it.'

'Why not?'

'Well, to be candid –' he cut the potato in half – 'I realize you could scarcely refuse, but I'd have thought you'd simply loathe the idea.'

'What you mean,' I said, 'is that you would simply loathe it.'

'True,' he agreed equably. 'Thank Christ there's no chance of that, for everyone's sake. No, Joss, it goes without saying I've no objection whatever to your doing the job. You're exactly what they need. I'll be proud as punch.' He illustrated with an expansive flourish with his fork. 'If this is what you want, bring it on!'

I watched with mixed emotions as my husband cleared his plate, using the last mouthful of potato to mop up his hollandaise sauce. Dr Atkins had been wasting his time in our house. It didn't help that Nico's wardrobe of choice, running to loose collarless shirts, kaftans, colourful baggy waistcoats and unstructured drawstring- or elastic-waisted trousers was both stylish and perfectly suitable work-attire for the business manager of a successful provincial theatre, so he was rarely confronted with the discomfort of creeping weight gain. It was only when (under protest and usually as my escort) he had to attend formal dinners and realized that successive chain-store dinner jackets failed to do up, that he became disconsolate, and then only briefly. His sanguine nature was one of the reasons I loved him. And he was handsome at any weight, open-faced and brown-eyed, and blessed with wavy and luxuriant hair, which he kept quite long. For the dreaded black-tie occasions he would wear it pulled back into a sleek queue tied with a narrow velvet ribbon, the better to display his maverick credentials. Who gave a flying fuck about suits? said the hair. Suits were for wearing over stuffed shirts.

Now he placed his knife and fork together and raised his glass. 'Cheers. That was sumptuous.'

'Very simple.'

'That was the best thing about it.'

He beamed, eyebrows raised, hands resting, fingers spread, on his stomach. What could I do but smile back? It's not overstating the case to say that Nico's ability to make me smile is what's kept our show on the road for the best part of four decades. He knows it, too. After our infrequent spats he shines that searchlight smile on me, and the more reluctant my reflexive grimace the more he points and says gleefully: 'There – gotcha!' And for some reason I am not irritated by this triumphalist crowing. I give in and laugh.

Aeons ago, on planet youth, over a post-coital joint on the sagging sofa bed in World's End, Nico announced expansively: 'You know, Joss, there's no reason in the world why you and I shouldn't have it all. Always. All that heaven will allow.'

And I agreed. Why wouldn't I? It was the sixties – the dawn of all dawns, in which it was bliss to be alive and very heaven to be young, liberated and on the loose. Allowed everything? We were owed it! No effort was required to achieve this sense of laid-back entitlement. Nico and I were just going with the flow. I was in my last year studying English at London and Nico's job at the experimental theatre meant we had absolutely no money; we made half pints last for hours, and hash was an occasional treat. I could have written a cookbook: *One Hundred*

Ways with Mother's Pride and a Teaspoonful of Blow. On Sundays, as often as not, we pocketed our cool and went for lunch with my parents in Potters Bar, returning with carrier bags full of foil-wrapped swag. No two people whose parents approve of them to the extent of parting with valuable leftovers can be fully described as rebels.

Our marriage prospered. Hal was a good baby whom you could take anywhere, and we did. Why, we asked ourselves, did people make such a fuss about child-rearing, when it was a piece of piss? Over the years we were in danger of becoming complacent. But complacency invites a good shaking, and all in good time, we got it.

When I told Nico about the mayorship we were having supper in the kitchen of the house where we've lived for the past twenty-five years. We've never been rich, nor destined to be, but we'd been lucky to find the house at a moment when an upsurge in our finances coincided with a dip in the housing market. Like most of our friends we were sitting on a good investment and our greatest asset, but we loved 7 Dover Terrace too much to think of it in those terms. It nearly broke us when we bought it and thereafter bound us to it with hoops of steel. The house was Georgian, and we accepted that the day would inevitably come when five flights of stairs would be too much for us, but that day was some way off yet. We still junked the Stannah Stairlift catalogue, and Nico even took a certain pride in causing a bleep at airport security, because he imagined that the official with the electronic wand would be amazed at someone so youthful having a stainless-steel hip. One of the defining characteristics of advancing age was the widening gap between self-image and reality.

The kitchen is what estate agents call 'double aspect' – basement at the front, ground level at the back. In summer, with the double doors open, the walled garden is like a leafy and scented extension of the room. On the first floor, beyond the hall is a rarely used dining room, which is gradually, like a weather front, losing its identity. Above are three more floors with a drawing room, bedrooms, bathrooms and a study. The study used to be Hal's bedroom, but Elizabeth still has one we think of as hers. Something subconscious on our part to do with marriage, perhaps.

'Anyway,' I said, 'we'll have a while to get used to the idea. Mayor-making isn't till next April.'

'Mayor-making – sounds like something feudal involving a stallion.'

'My secret is out.'

Nico, who loved a new subject, leaned his folded arms on the table. 'So is this a trial period? I mean, in the very unlikely event of your changing your mind, can you dip out?'

'I don't know. I suppose so. I'm not sure it's ever happened.'

'Presumably there are instances of people having to move house.'

'I suppose.'

'Or die.'

'Yes.'

'That presumably would be flogging a dead mayor . . . Is there any of that rum and raisin ice cream left?'

I nodded. 'There is.'

'Do you want any?'

I shook my head.

'Mind if I do?'

'Go ahead.'

He pushed his chair back and began collecting our plates. 'Allow me . . .' He transferred the plates to the side, and then kissed me warmly. 'Congratulations, darling. Richly deserved, and you'll be fantastic. I shall be the envy of our friends.'

Six months after that conversation we were lucky to have any friends left, and I barely saw the house or my husband. The smallest bedroom had been given over to two rails of new clothing and thirty hats, almost none of which I would ever wear again once this year was over. Those could always go to the dress exchange and charity shop, but I had an enlarged big-toe joint on my left foot from standing in high heels, and a strange little callous below my little finger, from shaking hands, both of which were to be a more lasting legacy of my year as mayor.

One evening in mid-May, a few weeks into my year in office, Nico got home early and I had no meeting, a conjunction that had assumed the status of hen's teeth in our life. In fact it was so rare that we experienced a real sense of occasion and

did not, as in pre-mayoral times, go upstairs after supper to
watch the television news. Instead we took our drinks – Nico's
single malt and my "chimps' tea" as he called it – out into
the late spring dusk. We sat on the edge of the soft pool of
light from the kitchen. It was a little cool, but the air was
sweet with early flowering honeysuckle and the promise of
long summer evenings ahead.

'This is the life,' said Nico. 'Happy days.'

The phone rang.

'Bugger,' he said in the same affable tone. 'Is there to be
no peace?'

'I'll get it.'

He didn't demur. 'It's bound to be for you, toots.'

I picked up the handset in the kitchen.

'Seven three nine?'

'Hello, seven three nine, this is your daughter speaking.'

'Elizabeth – hi, darling, how are you?'

'Good, thanks.'

'Splendid.' I'd never quite got used to the *Friends* generation's use of 'good'. I had no idea whether Elizabeth was
good, though I naturally hoped she was well. When had 'good'
superseded 'well', and when had 'well' taken over from 'very'?
These questions preoccupied me as I walked back into the
garden. Nico blew an indolent kiss in the direction of the
handset.

'We're just sitting—' I began, but she cut briskly across me.

'Is it OK if I come up this weekend?'

'Of course.' I ran through a high-speed mental inventory of
the next few days. 'I've got a couple of things on Saturday,
but that doesn't mean—'

'Sunday lunch?'

'Sunday . . .' I closed my eyes. No church service, no drinks,
a blessed oasis of calm, until now. 'Sunday?' I flashed a look
at Nico who spread his arms in an attitude that was both
welcoming and a surrender to the inevitable. 'That would be
wonderful.'

'And Mum . . .' I heard the warning even before it came.

'What?'

'For goodness sake don't go to any trouble. No fuss. I'll
only be dropping in.'

'Sure, fine.' I forbore to point out that a drive of seventy miles was scarcely consistent with 'dropping in'; she hated to be corrected. She wanted loose? Loose I could do. 'Don't worry, darling,' I said. 'The fatted calf will have nothing to fear from me.'

'See you Sunday then. Love to Dad.'

'He sends his.' Nico nodded vigorously. 'Look forward. Bye.'

I put the handset down on the grass. 'She's coming on Sunday.'

'So I gather. And in good spirits?'

'I think so.' Our daughter's interpersonal style was notoriously tricky. 'Yes. Hard to say.'

'Best not get our hopes up,' said my husband comfortably. 'Her ways are not ours.'

When we first got married, the 'all' that we imagined ourselves having definitely included a great brood of children. Nico in particular nursed a dream in which, as part of some future sun-kissed family holiday, we would sit at a rustic trestle table groaning with peasant fare in the shade of a gnarled olive tree, he at one end and I at the other, with our laughing, voluble offspring between us: at least three to a side, maybe four.

Fate mocked our hubris by giving us first Hal, to lull us into a false sense of security, and then leaving us strictly alone for six years. The olive tree fantasy began to fade, we were adjusting to the idea of being the Three Musketeers, a sort of tight-knit Team Carbury, when (and they say this always happens when you accept it's not going to) I fell pregnant again. The fantasy – God help us – reignited.

Eight months later, not long after my thirtieth birthday, our daughter was born: Elizabeth Jane Carbury – early, undercooked and scaly, a miniature Gollum absolutely livid at being propelled from her warm and watery niche before the appointed time. When I looked at my daughter I saw not my crowning achievement as a woman, but Nemesis.

From day one Elizabeth seemed to know that I'd had it too easy for too long; that my experience with her older brother, and even my foreshortened pregnancy this time round had been a quite undeserved doddle. She made her feelings plain by taking a full twenty-six hours to arrive, and doing so feet first and writhing like a cat in a bathtub. My most private erogenous zones were first torn to shreds, then stiffly cross-hatched with the junior doctor's inexpert needlework. For six months thereafter, oblivious to all but her own overarching needs, Elizabeth gave us gyp. We became shadows of our former selves. Even if the houseman's sewing had allowed for sex, we wouldn't have been up to it. Nico, the man who had dreamed of a trestleful of young, did his best to make Elizabeth a daddy's girl through near-clinical bafflement and exhaustion. Whenever we caught each other's eye it was with the wild, unspoken surmise: if this was what it was like to have two children, what would it be like to have three? Or four? Let alone . . . Jesus!

What in the name of all that's holy can we have been thinking of?

Hal, in his second year at the local C of E primary, watched as his easy-going parents turned into twitching, red-eyed nervous wrecks. He did so with an air of growing disillusionment, as though we had been deliberately deceiving him all this time, and were now revealed, through the agency of his tiny, ferocious sister, to have been shams all along.

As to Elizabeth herself, he was unsure what to make of her. He'd been well prepared during pregnancy. He was the first, we assured him, he'd always be special. The new baby would be special too, of course, but in a different way. Hal was going to be that majestic, heroic thing – a big brother. But the reality wasn't like that. In our small Edwardian terraced house in north London, Elizabeth, yelling day and night, permanently unsatisfied and enraged, ruled the roost. So, his look seemed to say, was he still supposed to love her? To feel senior, stronger, superior? And if so, how?

I found him one early morning when none of us had had a wink of sleep, sitting on the edge of his bed in his pants, pulling his socks on. They were yesterday's socks, which somehow pinched my heart, and I grabbed them off him and helped him with clean ones.

'Is she all right?' he asked.

'Oh, yes, she's fine. All babies cry.'

'When is she going to smile?'

I bought time by threading his head and hands through his T-shirt. We'd told him about smiling, how it was a big thing for a baby, and would happen at around six weeks. But in our situation the question seemed to have a slightly different meaning.

'Any day now,' I said with a brittle hopefulness.

'Will you tell me?'

'Of course! And anyway –' I picked up his trainers and loosened the Velcro – 'you'll see for yourself.'

'Will she smile at me?'

'She'll smile at everyone,' I said. 'Promise.'

Really?

It all goes to show that the personality is formed much earlier than we think. To this day our daughter's smiles are rare. I like to think we appreciate them more because they are bestowed when she feels like it and not when they're expected of her.

But in my darker moments, I can't help wondering whether in some way the course of Hal's commitment-phobic life was set back then when he witnessed first-hand and at a tender age the fearsome attrition of family life.

Our big-brood fantasy was dead in the water; the prospect of a repeat performance was just too petrifying. From that moment on we made sure it was never going to happen and got on with our lives.

As for our daughter, she continued to run us ragged, but in her own peculiar way. She was so . . . different; from us, from other people's children, from just about anyone we knew. Where, we wondered, had she come from, this precocious, sardonic, self-contained creature? Dismissing – but only just – the changeling myth, we still from time to time wondered in all seriousness whether there had been a tagging mix-up at the hospital. Hal was no angel – he was bright but lazy, did his fair share of flunking and bunking off at school, and embarked on a social life which on the whole we were glad we didn't know too much about – but his were faults of omission. There was never that sense of closely guarded privacy, of deliberate exclusion, that we experienced with Elizabeth.

Nico had a line on it. On those nights when we sat, sleepless and strung out with anxiety, when she was a baby who wouldn't sleep, a teenager who was late, a young woman travelling alone; when she wouldn't grant us eye contact, let alone an explanation or the time of day; when we sat there with books unread, the nervous adrenalin chugging round our exhausted systems, our eye sockets like sandpaper; when we would have happily killed for any of half a dozen of the less challenging, more communicative daughters of friends, Nico would fold his arms, look up at the ceiling with a reflective smile, and say: 'I tell you what – isn't this interesting?'

Yeah, as they say these days – right!

Now Elizabeth was over thirty and had announced her intention of coming to visit. My mental scanning of the diary had been a formality; the truth was that nothing short of major invasive surgery on the day itself would have been considered sufficient grounds for refusal.

On Sunday morning I was twenty minutes into preparation of my not-the-fatted-calf lunch of fish pie, and Nico was playing with his computerized flight simulator in the study when we heard her loud, peremptory knock. She was early, and I'd forgotten to take the front door off the latch. She'd never have dreamed of ringing the bell – the knock expressed her irritation and impatience at being locked out of the family home. I yelled up the stairs.

'Nico? You're nearer!'

'I'm beginning the descent into Changi! Isn't she early?'

'Yes, but she still needs letting in!'

The knock was repeated, yet more thunderously. Nico came thumping down the stairs. 'Landing aborted, I'm there, I'm there . . .!'

I spread mashed potato over the fish at speed – the last thing I wanted was to be caught making the proscribed fuss – and put the dish in the oven. As I took off my apron and ran my hands under the tap, I heard the front door open and close, and our daughter's commanding, slightly nasal voice mingling with Nico's as they greeted each other.

'Lizzie,' cried Nico, the only person licensed to use the diminutive, 'how the devil are you . . .?'

I ran up to join them in the hall. When I say 'them' – there was Nico, Elizabeth, and a handsome, elderly man in chinos and a dark blue shirt.

'Hi, Mum.'

'Hello, darling.' We exchanged a kiss. No hug – Elizabeth didn't do hugs.

'And who's this?' I asked, peering round her at the stranger. My broad smile was intended to convey inclusiveness, an open mind, liberty hall . . . Behind it I did a quick mental divvy up of the fish pie.

She said crisply: 'I was just about to introduce you. This is Edward Chapman.'

No explanation, nothing. She could so easily have rung and said she was bringing someone with her, but that would have implied 'fuss', her own and other people's. My smile stretched to breaking point.

'Edward, hello.'

'How do you do?' His hand was lean, warm and dry, but the handshake, though far from limp, had something tentative in it. At least he didn't say it was nice to meet me, an American affectation which always grated on me.

We stood there for a moment, like a glee club waiting for someone to give us a note.

'Jocelyn,' I explained, since Elizabeth hadn't.

'I know, yes . . .'

'But Joss is fine,' I added, wondering what else he knew. 'And this is Nico.'

'Actually we've been introduced.'

'Terrific,' said Nico, slapping his hands together and bouncing on his heels, 'Splendid. Come on down. Or – actually it's not particularly nice, is it warm enough for drinks in the garden, what do we think?'

'I'm game,' said Chapman. 'Sounds delightful.' His preppy elegance contrasted sharply with my husband's weekend ensemble of a mattress-ticking kaftan and frayed jeans. Thank heavens the jeans' waistband, the button eased with a length of knicker elastic, wasn't visible. The contrast wasn't lost on Elizabeth, who skimmed her father with a glance like a razor blade.

'If it's chilly,' she said, 'I reserve the right to move us all indoors. I know you two, and your obsession with alfresco eating, and Edward will be too polite to say.'

'It won't be cold,' I said. 'It's so sheltered.'

In the garden Nico made rather a business of getting out another two chairs from the shed. Chapman relieved him of one and Elizabeth waited serenely while he placed it behind her, holding the back like a waiter until she was safely seated.

'Right,' said Nico, 'what will everyone have? We've got a spot of fizz, gallons of beer, wine of every hue . . . whatever you'd like, really.'

'Mine's a vodka tonic, please,' said Elizabeth.

'V and T it is. Edward?'

'Fizz would be nice.'

'Not the real McCoy, you understand. Chateau Superstore.'

'Please, that's great . . .' Chapman raised a hand to show he absolutely didn't care. As Nico went in for the drinks, I wondered what Elizabeth had said to her friend about today. Had he any idea that he'd not been expected? His old-fashioned good manners suggested that he probably hadn't, otherwise I was sure he'd have made some self-excusing remark. By keeping us all in the dark Elizabeth had retained the whip hand. I decided he should definitely have the benefit of the doubt.

'So tell me,' I said. 'How do you two know each other?'

Elizabeth was busy scratching something off the side of her wedge sandal, so it was left to Chapman to say: 'Actually, we're colleagues.'

'Oh?' I waited for more, but it wasn't forthcoming. This would have been standard practice for Elizabeth, but I sensed he was a more naturally communicative being, holding back. 'So you're a journalist.'

'Yes, but not of a glamorous kind,' he said, humorously rueful. 'Not like Beth, feature-writer at large. I'm financial.'

I was glad Nico wasn't there, so I could get over that first 'Beth' without the need to avoid his madly questing eye. And I certainly wasn't going to look at Elizabeth to see what she thought of it. Instead, I remarked: 'I thought money and glamour were pretty closely allied.'

His face folded in a brief chuckle that made him look older, but sound younger. 'Good point. Still, how do you square that with the poor image enjoyed by accountants?'

He was rather nice. I did hope that (a) he liked fish pie and (b) he wouldn't think it was what I always cooked for Sunday lunch. A man of his age would probably have a fondness for a traditional English roast with all the trimmings, just as we did under normal circumstances. As to his status in Elizabeth's life, 'colleague' sounded about right. Our daughter had no boyfriend, let alone partner, that we knew of and she didn't do lame ducks. Her personal life wasn't just private it was a closed book and one that we were not invited to open. She could have been living like – or with – a nun or selling her body on the mean streets of Camden Town for all we knew.

Now she said: 'I'll go and help Dad,' rose abruptly, and disappeared into the house. There was no point in saying Nico didn't need help, because she so clearly wanted to get away from us. It occurred to me that, uncharacteristic though it would be for her to get lumbered, Chapman's presence might be a source of embarrassment. Perhaps some work-related contingency had made it impossible to avoid. On the other hand, he didn't present like a sponger.

'You have a gorgeous garden.'

He was gazing round appreciatively.

'We love it, I must say.'

'I bet it takes a hell of a lot of work to achieve this appearance of casual abundance.'

'Well, yes.' I found myself liking the poor chap more and more. 'All Nico's. I can take no credit whatsoever.'

'You provide the back-up.'

'Not really. I'm the one lounging in the shade with the chilled white wine and the encouraging remarks.'

'I'm sure that's not true,' he said with a gentle, automatic courtliness.

'Do you have a garden?' I asked.

'Sadly not – not that I'm any sort of gardener, never have been. I'm renting at the moment, in Bloomsbury. The closest thing to outdoors is the living room window sill, and even that gives an uninterrupted view of the town houses opposite.'

I skipped to the safe bit. 'Bloomsbury though – how wonderful. I lived in a flat behind Goodge Street tube in my bachelor days, over what used to be Kooks coffee bar, and we used to regard the other side of Tottenham Court Road as a parallel universe, starting with Heals, then Dillons, UC and the British Museum, all those literary associations . . .' Chapman wasn't to know that my nostalgic shake of the head was less for these cultural splendours than the memory of the pouting, booted, mini-skirted, philistine bird I'd been at the time, who in spite of a creditable Eng. Hons. knew the inside of the Marquee Club better than any museum, whose area of specialist study was the boutiques and bistros of the Kings Road, and who spent more time ironing her hair than reading.

'It's certainly convenient,' he agreed, 'for many things – ah, here they are.'

He stood up as Nico and Elizabeth approached. Nico carrying a tray with drinks and Elizabeth a single dish of olives. They placed their respective burdens on the plastic table; Nico poured and distributed and we sat down.

'So how are things in the fourth estate?' asked Nico, as if he hadn't already asked her how she was and spent five minutes alone with her in the kitchen. 'Any scoops we should know about?'

'Not bad. I've got a nice byline feature in on Tuesday.'

'We'll look out for it, what's the theme?'

'It's part of a series we're doing on transgressive love affairs,' said Elizabeth. 'Teachers and pupils, age differences, cross-cultural marriages, in-laws in love, kissing cousins. Nothing heavy or illegal, no incest, just against the social grain.'

While she spoke, Chapman's gaze rested on her admiringly.

'She does have a flair for drawing people out,' he said.

I digested this before asking: 'So which one's first?'

'Marrying out. Jewish princess and English toff.'

'Ah,' said Nico, 'but who's "out" in that particular mixture? Discuss.'

While they did so, I reflected that one of the many anomalies of our relationship with Elizabeth was that we now subscribed, out of loyalty, to the hugely successful but risibly right-wing tabloid she worked for and had it delivered along with our liberal left-leaning broadsheet. Hers was a paper with a statistically proven appeal to women, and I had secretly to admit to a certain guilty pleasure in reading it. In fairness to myself I didn't do so for the news – delivered with a siege-mentality spin that managed to be both sanctimonious and salacious – but for the double-page spreads on topics like cellulite, Botox, which shorts to wear and girls whose mothers were like (and often taken for) their sisters. Not that this last group was one in which my daughter and I were ever likely to be included. We maintained a distance; we respected boundaries; quasi-sisterly intimacy was not an option.

'And presumably,' Nico was saying to Chapman, 'we can

then turn to you for advice on what do about this blasted Emeritus Life cock-up.'

'You've been affected, I take it.'

'Robbed blind.'

'Not much anyone can do except limit the collateral damage.'

I took this as my cue to retreat and check on the lunch. I'd only just got the water boiling for the peas when Elizabeth joined me.

'Anything I can do?'

Two offers of domestic help within half an hour were unprecedented, but I kept my surprise to myself.

'Keep me company if you like.'

She added another splash of vodka to her half-full glass. 'Smells nice.'

'Fish pie.' I glanced at her. 'I hope that's OK, only you said—'

'Oh, Edward will eat anything.'

Not exactly a ringing endorsement, but then I'd learned not to expect one. 'Fine.'

There was a brief silence during which I took the peas from the freezer and Elizabeth leaned against the dishwasher, her glass resting against her mouth, her brows drawn together in an expression that might have been pensive, or irritable.

'Did Edward just—?'

'We wanted to—'

We both spoke at once, but it was Elizabeth who repeated herself.

'We wanted to see you.'

My parental antennae trembled. Something about those five simple words made the atmosphere trip – I breathed a different air, saw things in a different light, attempted in the split second that followed to ready myself for whatever was coming.

'Oh?'

'We wanted to tell you – we're going to get married.'

'Are you?' I chirruped. I was surprised I could speak at all.

'Yes,' said my daughter. 'Wednesday, in London. No fuss.'

With a furious hiss and a sweet, scorching smell, the peas boiled over.

Elizabeth was back in the garden first, and when I got there all three were standing up, Nico holding the cava. His knuckles were white, but his face had a hectic flush that I was pretty sure matched mine.

'Well!' he said, with a kind of wild joviality. 'Joss! It appears we have something to celebrate.'

Chapman came over to me. 'I'm so sorry to spring this on you, but it seemed the simplest way.' He put his hands on my shoulders and kissed me on both cheeks. 'In fact Beth was all for presenting you with a fait accompli. She thought you'd find that easier, but I'm afraid I wouldn't have, so we settled on this somewhat awkward compromise.'

'It's not a compromise,' said Elizabeth. 'It's a sensible solution.'

'Yes,' I said. 'No – this is fine. It takes a bit of digesting, that's all.'

'Sorry,' said Chapman again.

'Speaking of digesting,' said Elizabeth, 'Dad, aren't you going to propose a toast?'

'Of course,' said Nico, 'I was waiting for your mother.' Without meeting my eye he topped up my glass, Chapman's, and his own, and set the bottle back on the tray. Then he came back to my side and put his arm around my shoulders. My head span, it took all my self-control not to shrug his arm off; I was being traduced, bounced into a response I wasn't ready for and couldn't own.

Just as well then that Nico, always quicker than me to adjust, was getting into it.

'It's not often I'm lost for words – remember you saw it here first! You'll excuse us if we appear a little shell-shocked, but don't imagine that we're anything but absolutely one hundred per cent delighted, yup?'

'Fantastic.' I grinned and nodded dazedly like one of those dogs in the rear window of a Cortina. 'Amazing.'

Nico raised his glass. 'To Elizabeth and Edward! We wish you all the happiness in the world.'

Robotically, I followed suit. Chapman – Edward, as I should now have to think of him – lifted his glass, took a sip, then kissed Elizabeth on the lips. With the announcement over, he certainly looked like a man in love – warm, bright, radiating an unforced happiness – but our daughter was less readable.

I went over to offer my maternal congratulations, kissing her on the cheek and even risking a cautious embrace to which she submitted but did not fully respond; her hand touching my back as if it were a bed of nettles.

'Darling . . . wonderful news. Such a surprise, but so lovely . . .'

I heard her murmur 'Mum . . .' Her voice and manner may have been cool, but her face was hot.

With the worst, for the time being, over, the ground intact beneath us and the world still turning, Edward and Nico became voluble with short-term relief. At lunch Elizabeth and I sat on either side of the table, avoiding one another's eye, following the ball of conversation as it bounced back and forth between the two men. Cricket, finance, house prices, travel . . . I gleaned that Edward would be quitting the rented flat and moving in with Elizabeth in Camden while they looked for something 'mutual', and that he was indeed a little older than us – looking at retirement or at least going freelance in a couple of years' time.

We'd reached the rhubarb crumble before I'd regained enough composure to confront the elephant on the sideboard and say as light-heartedly as I could manage: 'You'll have to bear with this interrogation, Edward – you're still a man of mystery to us. We face a steep learning curve.'

He pulled a mock-rueful face. 'Me too.'

'It was a whirlwind affair,' said Elizabeth. Her expression was deadpan, but Edward laughed, so I smiled uncertainly.

'That's not far off the truth,' he said. 'We've known each other since before my wife died, first as colleagues, then friends, but the actual, shall we say, romance—'

'Must we?' Elizabeth pulled a sardonic face.

'All right, we only became an item – how's that? – a few weeks ago. And I suddenly thought –' he took her hand firmly in his – 'hang on. I want to spend the rest of my life with this woman.'

I could only assume that 'item' meant sex. Child of the sixties though I was, my imagination still flinched at the idea.

'Bloody good show,' said Nico, who'd been doing full justice to the Kookaburra Creek. 'Spoken like a gent.'

Elizabeth allowed her hand to rest in Edward's for a moment, and then withdrew it and picked up the cream jug. 'Happily,' she said, pouring, 'it was mutual.'

In this exchange only one word, apart from the uncomfortably freighted 'item', stood out, and was impossible to ignore.

'You said your wife – I'm so sorry – when did that happen?'

Edward answered with the matter-of-factness born of years of setting people at their ease on a delicate topic.

'September 2002. After a long illness, as they say – which of course –' he looked round, taking in the others – 'means you are expecting it, but no less unprepared when it finally happens.'

'Of course.'

He went on: 'Your daughter was an absolute stalwart, a rock, when I needed one.' He smiled, lightening the tone. 'So since sound friendship is an essential prerequisite of marriage, I know we'll be OK.'

Stalwart? Rock? But that would explain the tender, womanly (and, I had shamefully thought, inapposite) 'Beth'.

It appeared I knew nothing.

We were outside, about to see them off, and the men were admiring Elizabeth's black-on-black Mini Cooper, when she took an envelope from her handbag and passed it to me.

'What's this?'

'A couple of photos for you to look at. Me and Edward. Him and his family.' Her hand shot out restrainingly. 'Not now, though.'

'OK.'

'More relaxing for the two of you to study them on your own.'

From experience I inferred that she meant more relaxing for her. 'I think that's right.'

'Sorry about the flying visit.' She opened the car door. 'And the surprise.'

'Not at all.' I longed to embrace her, to keep her there, to understand, to know. 'At least it was a nice one.'

'Yes.' She had one foot in the car now, and one hand on the side of the steering wheel. 'And please don't take it the wrong way about Wednesday.'

I was choked; not 'the wedding' or even 'us' – just 'Wednesday'.

But: 'We don't,' I said. 'You don't want anyone there, all very quick and simple.'

'It's nothing personal.'

'We understand perfectly.'

She sat, closed the door and spoke through the open window. 'We've been together for quite a while, so this is just a rubber stamp. We want to get it done and carry on as normal.'

Normal?

'Still, do let's get together again very soon,' I said. 'We'd so like to get to know Edward better.'

'Sure.'

She blew me a kiss and I blew one back. Edward made his farewells charmingly, his thanks warmly expressed, his cheek pressing mine with respectful affection, and they were off. At the end of the road the Mini seemed to lean into the corner in its haste to get away.

'Darling . . .?' Nico dropped his book on the floor, and rolled to face me. 'Hey, Joss . . .? Don't cry.'

He was wasting his time. It was weep or explode. I wept.

After they left I'd been angry – furious and humiliated – until Nico had talked me round, to his satisfaction at least, and we'd polished off the second bottle of Kookaburra. I was fairly pissed when I rang Hal in New York, but it was noisy his end, he and Lili, the latest squeeze, were having brunch out with friends.

'You're kidding!'

'That's what we said.'

'No, we didn't,' said Nico, from next to me on the sofa, 'we took it on the chin.'

'What did Dad say?'

'That we took it on the chin.'

'But – hang on, I'm just . . . did you know anything about this guy?'

'Not even that he existed.'

'And he's how old, you reckon?'

'Our age . . . a bit older if anything.'

'And forgive the stock question, but how do you feel about that?'

'Completely shell-shocked.'

'I don't blame you . . . Fuck me, it'll take a bit of getting used to!'

'We'll bond in no time,' put in Nico.

'What was that?'

'Dad said we're bonding.'

'Jesus . . . Anyway, look, Mum, I can't really talk, there's a bit of a social situation going on . . . But thanks for calling, thanks for telling me. Should I call her?'

I looked at Nico. 'Should Hal call her, do you think?'

'Of course. If he wants to, he should.'

'Did you hear that?'

'If I want to? I wouldn't go that far, but I'd better get it out of the way.'

'Good luck.'

'I might well need it. Bye, Mum.'

'Let us know how it goes.'

A couple of hours later, with the benign effects of the Kookaburra draining away, he reported back.

'What can I say? What you'd expect really. All very businesslike.'

'I'm glad you spoke to her, anyway, Someone has to act spontaneously around here.'

'Steady on,' said Nico, 'I was spontaneous.'

'And Wednesday's the big day?' asked Hal.

'Not big, exactly.'

'The day, then.'

'Yes.'

'We'll try and send something . . . And you're not invited?'

'No.'

'Seriously, I cannot believe—'

'Hal – sorry, darling, I think I need to leave it there.'

'Mum, you OK?'

'We'll speak again very soon.'

'Sure . . . Mum?'

'Bye, darling.'

That had been bad enough, but now my secret was well and truly out. Nico pulled me into his arms.

'I repeat, I genuinely liked him,' he said, kissing my hair absent-mindedly as he talked. 'Hard to tell on a first meeting, but he seems a thoroughly nice bloke. The age thing's a bit of a facer for us, but it obviously means nothing to them. And even if we loathed him on sight there'd be sod all we could do. They're way beyond needing our approval, let alone our consent.'

'I don't understand,' I sobbed. 'I can't make her out!'

'So what's new?' He gave me a little shake. 'Have we ever?

Hm? She's always been too many for us, Joss, that's what makes her such a study. I dare say she's too many for him, too, and that's part of her attraction. Anyway, if he loves her a bit more than she loves him, that's the way round I for one want it, yup?'

'But I want her to be happy!' I lurched away from him to take tissues out of my bedside drawer, and blew my nose loudly. 'Whatever they do tomorrow won't be how I pictured the wedding of our only daughter!'

I hauled myself up to sit against the bedhead and Nico did the same.

'I'm not sure I pictured Lizzie getting spliced at all, let alone the full white-satin-and-orange-blossom monty. It didn't do Hal any good, and this is Lizzie we're talking about here . . . I mean, come on.' He sent me a sideways, eyebrow-lifted glance. 'Be honest.'

Under this onslaught of cheerful realism I could only shake my head dumbly.

'Our daughter,' he continued, patiently, 'will get on with her own life in her own way as she always has done, and the biggest favour we can do her is to get on with ours. Unless she comes crying for help, in which highly unlikely event we'd pull out all the stops.'

'Of course we would.' I pressed my hands to my eyes. 'No question.'

'As to her being happy, we'll probably never know.'

'No.'

'And anyway you're up to your eyes in civic duties.' He nudged me. 'Plenty to divert you. Chin up.'

I smiled damply. 'I'll try.'

'No, face it, you are.' He picked up his bedside radio – digital. Last year's Christmas present from me. 'I must say I'm rather looking forward to having a son-in-law I can go to for fatherly advice . . . Spot of bedtime comedy?'

The last thing I heard him say as he tuned in was: 'Interesting . . .'

No matter what the day threw up, Nico always slept like a baby. Long before the sketch show had finished, his breathing grew heavy and guttural, whereas I was still fully wired and fretting for Britain, my eyes popping out of my head.

I got out of bed, switched off the lamp on my side and the

radio on his, and went downstairs to the kitchen to make tea. If I was going to fret I wanted the space to do it properly.

On the side near the kettle lay the envelope Elizabeth had given me. I'd been engaging in a perverted form of deferred gratification and hadn't mentioned it to Nico, whose lack of domestic curiosity was one of his defining characteristics.

I stared down at it – was there anything more secretive than a plain, sealed envelope? – and then carried it, with my mug, to the table and sat down. Confronted with this more immediate challenge, my tears dried up. So did my mouth. I took a couple of slurps of scalding tea, and opened the envelope.

Inside, face down as I lifted the flap, were two postcard-sized photographs. On the back of one Elizabeth had written: *Ed and me, Budapest*; and on the other: *Ed and co, Lakes*.

I picked up the first one and turned it over. There the two of them were, standing on a bridge – the famous Chain Bridge, I assumed – in snow, wearing thick winter clothes. His arm was round her, his gloved hand like a great protective paw encircling her shoulder; he was looking not at the camera but at her. She wore one of those hats with a broad, fur-edged brim, pulled down over her eyebrows. Between brim and scarf all I could see of her was the gleam of her eyes and her luminous smile.

She'd never mentioned Budapest.

Trembling, riven with confused emotions, I turned over the other photograph. Edward, this time in shirtsleeves, leaned back on a wall, arms folded, a pair of sunglasses hooked into his breast pocket. I suspected he'd been told to remove the sunglasses by whoever was taking the picture, his face was slightly scrunched up against the light.

And then there were his children.

Why hadn't I thought of children? There'd been something about the way he described his flat . . . But a widower once recovered would want a change, to start afresh; and the children, after all, would be grown up. A big flat in town would be ideal for all of them.

I took another gulp of tea, the mug clinking against my teeth, and made myself study the other faces in the photograph. Edward's daughter, standing behind the wall with her hands in her pockets, looked about Elizabeth's age – dear God, there were going to be issues there, surely! A likeable, open face beneath a cloud of curly hair, a man's shirt with the sleeves rolled up, hands in hip pockets, an air of casual competence. The son was a few years younger, not as tall as his father or sister but stocky and well built; black hair ruffled into points in the modern manner, the suggestion of maintained stubble; a level gaze. He sat on top of the wall, his elbow resting on Edward's shoulder, his fingers covering his own mouth so it was hard to tell if he was smiling. Not, was my guess. In fact no one was. There was something Victorian in the plain, steady expressions of the Chapman family group.

I laid the two photos side by side on the table. Three of these people were strangers, (and I was beginning to think the fourth might be, too), but in less than twenty-four hours they were going to be part of our lives.

By this time tomorrow I would be mother-in-law to a man older than my own husband; and step-grandmother to two adults who at this moment, in all probability, wished me and mine would fuck off and die.

I almost wished I could. But I was mayor of this town, and the role was like the floating spar to which I clung in the maelstrom. That was me; that was mine; and no one could touch it.

Pathetic.

I began to cry again and as I raised my hands to my face I knocked over the mug and its content spread over the photos, obliterating Ed and co beneath a pool of chimps' tea.

Three

Standing in the rain, on the pavement opposite the register office in North London, I asked myself: How many parents do this?

A no-brainer really: not many.

Nico may have been right to point out that we'd never expected white lace and stephanotis, but as mother of the bride I was surely entitled to a role more dignified than that of spy at our daughter's wedding. Though in fairness he had tried to save me from myself.

'Don't do it,' he said. 'You'll only upset yourself. The more space you give her, the more likely she is to come round.'

'Come round? What's she got to come round about? It's us who ought to need winning over.'

'Maybe, but that isn't how she sees it.'

'She won't know I'm there,' I promised. 'I just want a glimpse of her on her wedding day.'

'See?' He directed a finger at my face. 'See what you're doing?'

'No. What am I doing?'

'Making a drama.'

'If ever there was a situation that needs no dramatizing . . .' I began threateningly. He put up his hands.

'OK! Point taken. But don't go torturing yourself, Joss. Please – just don't.'

'I won't. I'm not.' With a supreme effort, I added: 'It will make me happy to see her.'

'Hmm.' He was unconvinced. 'And –' he pointed a warning finger at me – 'don't let her know.'

'What do you take me for? I shall be a face in the crowd. And anyway I've got to be back for a library opening.'

'I never thought I'd say this, but thank God for public office!'

He remained grumpily protective until I left the house. And now, sheltering from the drizzle in the doorway of a shop where the size of the clothes was in inverse ratio to their price, I recognized that I wasn't happy, I was torturing myself and I was starring in a tragic comedy of my own making. But I had to make some kind of emotional investment in this day, and if these were the only means at my disposal, then so be it.

London doesn't like a stationary person. Try it some time. Nothing aggravates the hurtling city-dweller more than someone just standing there, no matter how blamelessly. In fact the more self-effacing you are, the more they despise you. I was pressed against the shop window, hands in pockets, elbows tight to my sides, making myself small as a hunted animal, but to no avail. A girl with a clenched mouth wanted to look at the one exiguous lycra top that was directly behind me, and when out of consideration for her I stepped to one side, I blundered into a man locked in blank-eyed communion with his BlackBerry. He didn't stop talking, but raised his arm to ward me off as if I'd been a knife-wielding maniac. I was vouchsafed a sudden, vivid insight into how the indigent must feel. Simply by standing still I'd become first invisible, then an obstacle and finally a public nuisance.

Damn it! If I was going to be a bag lady I might as well be an assertive one. I threw back my shoulders and strode forward to the edge of the pavement. In a trice a cab screeched to a halt right next to me, sending up a shin-high fan of dirty water and disgorging a young woman in cleavage-friendly pinstripes who behaved quite literally as if I wasn't there, casually scraping my instep with her stiletto and narrowly missing my eye with the spokes of her DKNY umbrella. Two men converged on the cab and engaged in a mute locking of horns before one backed down and – I swear this is true – pretended his mobile had rung in order to save face.

Through all this I had managed not to move, but my sense of being right up there with several tons of discarded chewing gum and dog shit was increasing by the second.

Keep the faith, I told myself. Maintain the objective. Once you've seen them, you can go home.

One thing my years at City Hall had taught me – the happy

couple couldn't afford to be late. Not if they wanted to get hitched, get lunch, and get back to work. (Getting laid I discounted as no longer an issue.) Register office weddings ran like clockwork, a nuptial conveyor belt, in one side and out the other, like cremations. And also like cremations there was a real danger of supporters getting mixed up (especially in the case of ancient and emotionally exercised relatives) and proudly witnessing the union of the wrong couple.

The rain intensified, and I put my hood up, warily. It seemed only yesterday that the hooded raincoat was synonymous with unimpeachable respectability, wholesome young girls in school crocodiles or spectators by the water jump at cross-country events. There had followed the parka, anorak and kagoul, all garments designed to protect the wearer from moorland moisture or the gritty dampness that accompanied the collecting of engine numbers: wholesome outdoor kit redolent of fresh air with top notes of nerd. Today, in the interests of camouflage, I had looked out the blue Stormjammer I'd purchased during our family's brief and unsuccessful flirtation with camping. For practical purposes the hood, when up, shielded the face and had a button-through visor fastening. Here and now this blameless garment, combined with my supermarket combats and too-new trainers (not yet even christened on the jogging circuit), simply screamed ASBO. Any passing community law enforcer would be forgiven for thinking my faux Mulberry shoulder bag was nicked.

Two minutes to twelve, and suddenly there she was. Or there they were, but with a parent's sensitized eye I noticed Elizabeth a second before her soon-to-be-husband. She looked handsome and businesslike, chin up and shoulders back in a well-cut grey business suit. Edward was just behind her, not so much deferential as a man who declined to be hurried. That was good. The ability to march to the beat of his own drum would stand him in good stead if he were to share the road of life with my daughter.

Just as Elizabeth was about to go up the steps to the town hall, he caught her arm and turned her to face him. Like me, they were instantly changed from participants into obstacles, even from here I perceived the pettish, irritable way that other people manoeuvred round them; but unlike me they weren't bothered by the looks and the tongue-clicking. They were islands in the stream.

Edward said something to Elizabeth, and even from here I sensed the softening in her. He drew her against him and they kissed. His head bent down, hers tipped back; her hand rested on the side of his face in a gesture of the utmost tenderness. Like the iconic Cartier-Bresson couple, they were oblivious to everyone but each other. When a particularly impatient passer-by ricocheted off them they drew apart, laughing, and Elizabeth ran smartly up the steps, with Edward following at his own pace.

I didn't wait to see them come out again, hitched; I didn't need to. That kiss was enough to give me the reassurance I'd travelled all this way in the hope of finding. It had taken less than five seconds for me to know that our daughter truly loved the man she was in there marrying. If there was a tiny imbalance – and I was no longer so sure – well, as Nico said, at least it was in her favour, and no harm in that.

In the ticket hall of the tube station I untied my hood, pushed it back, and fished my mobile out of my handbag. Interestingly, standing still, or even wandering aimlessly, while talking on a mobile, seemed to confer greater credibility, but I still moved to one side, with my back to the wall between the self-service ticket machines and the snack vendor, to make my call.

He picked up at once. 'Hey, yer worship, how are things in the world of undercover surveillance?'

'I saw them.'

'Well done. They made it to the whatsit on time, then?'

'With two minutes to spare.'

'Anything to report?'

'Only that they seemed happy.'

'I'd have expected nothing less.'

'Well – you never know. But they really did. You can't fake that sort of thing, and anyway why would they, they didn't know I was there.'

'No . . .' I could hear his curiosity. 'So you were what, just so I can picture the scene, sort of skulking in a doorway?'

'To begin with. Then I was standing on the edge of the pavement getting extremely wet.'

'Poor darling, the stuff you put yourself through . . . Look, I have to go, I'll see you tonight and you can fill me in on the details. Safe journey. Chuff, chuff.'

He hung up before I could remind him that by the time he got home I'd have had to turn myself round and get out again to my library opening in the boondocks, so the debrief would have to wait.

Suddenly, I was absolutely shattered and chilled to the bone. On the return train it wasn't too hard to feign a cold to disguise my emotional state.

Scarcely a day went by at the moment when I didn't render up fervent thanks for the clean, comfortable mayoral Merc and its unflappable driver, Reg, who would pick me up at my front door, deposit me at my destination, and return me safe and sound afterwards. This invaluable facility meant that this evening all (did I say all?) I had to do was turn myself from bag lady into Madam Mayor in half an hour flat.

Elizabeth rang as I was in mid-change. On the train I'd considered this contingency and mentally rehearsed for it, in order to get the tone of my response right.

'Darling! You're a married woman?'

'I am, and I'm sitting next to my very own married man.'

'Many, many congratulations to you both.' I slipped a skirt off its hanger. 'And a big welcome to Edward, we hope to see him again soon.'

'You and Dad must come down here. Don't worry . . .' There was a pause, during which I thought I detected her sardonic, downturned smile. 'Edward's an accomplished cook.'

'We'd love to.'

'Sorry about – you know – if all this seemed a bit hole-in-the-corner. That's not what we intended.'

'Listen,' I said, pulling up my skirt with one hand, 'it's your day.'

'Correct,' she said crisply and then added, as if agreeing to let me pay the bill: 'Well, OK. Thanks.'

'Any plans for this evening?' I asked brightly, surreptitiously pressing the hands-free button and laying the handset on the bed while I did up the skirt and reached for the tinted moisturizer.

'Supper and an early bed.'

'Best thing,' I agreed. 'I forgot to ask – where are you?'

'At home.'

'Your flat?'

'That's right. Ours now, remember?'

'Yes, of course.'

'Oh, and I forgot to say, the reason I rang was to say thank you very much for your card. And what was inside.' We had sent a handsome cheque, and the promise of my mother's diamond earrings which I had not wanted to commit to the post.

'That's all right,' I said and couldn't resist adding: 'The very least we could do.'

'And Granny's earrings. I've always admired them as you know. It was very generous.'

'Our pleasure. The earrings were going to be yours anyway. As for the dosh – save it, blue it, burn it – no strings.'

She didn't respond to this waffle, but said stiffly: 'You didn't have to.'

She was a rotten thanker, but I wasn't playing that game. 'As a matter of fact, darling, we did. You'll just have to indulge us. It's only money after all.' I wiped my hands on a tissue and picked up the eyeliner just as Edward came on the line.

'Jocelyn – Joss? I'm henceforth committed, body and soul, to your daughter, but she's a lousy receiver of gifts.'

I removed my hand from my eyelid and laughed silently; realized he couldn't hear me and said: 'You forget, I know that. And it doesn't matter.'

'I'd like to add my thanks to hers.'

I was suddenly embarrassed. We'd wanted to give something to Elizabeth, but now that our cheque had been perceived as a joint wedding present I could see how inappropriate it might seem to a man who was at least a couple of years our senior. I started to mumble something, but he continued charmingly.

'It was extraordinarily generous of you and Nico. We'll put it in a box under the bed till we've decided what to do with it and believe me we shall extract every ounce of value.'

'We just thought . . . something extra, that you might not otherwise . . .'

'And we'll be writing.'

'There's really no need.' I realized with a shock that I sounded just like Elizabeth, and he responded as I had a moment ago.

'There most certainly is. I'm old-fashioned that way.'

'Look,' I said, 'Edward, it's infuriating, but I have to dash . . .'

'And we're holding you up. Go, at once – we'll see you soon.'

'Give her a motherly kiss from me.'

'It would be my pleasure, though motherly may be beyond me – bye.'

'Bye, Edward.'

When I put the phone down, I found, once again, that my eyes were leaking, and I had to wipe off and redo my make-up.

As we hummed quietly out of the city, Reg glanced briefly at me in the rear-view mirror.

'Nice quiet day today, ma'am? Bit of a catch-up?'

'Reg – don't ask.'

'Oh dear. Never mind, nothing like a new library to cheer a person up.' He glanced over his shoulder as we turned on to the bypass and then said, this time without looking at me, 'Spot of music, ma'am?'

'That's a very good idea.'

'Let's see what we got . . .'

What we had was Classic FM – Vaughan Williams. As the suburbs gave way to wet green farmland and rounded, spinney-topped hills, the lark ascended on its spiralling thread of music, a descant to my melancholy.

At the library I was fine – Doctor Theatre came to my aid and ensured that I turned in a reasonably dignified perform-ance, managing to remember people's names and not to spill tea down my front. But in the car on the way home I wilted again. Reg, ever the diplomat, offered neither comment nor enquiry, and allowed *Great Film Themes* to speed us home. But as he held the door for me, he said, 'Goodnight, ma'am. You take care now.'

Nothing like a kind word to open the floodgates. By the time I plumped down next to Nico on the sofa I was once more a pretty soggy spectacle. He was in his pyjamas and an Aran sweater and smelled pleasantly of whisky. Following a swift, practised assessment of my condition he extinguished 007 and made a show of giving me his undivided attention.

'So, worshipful, how'd it go?'

I'd stopped pointing out the wrong form of address, because it afforded him so much innocent amusement.

'I need petting like a little woman, not treating like a civic dignitary.'

'Then you came to the right place.' He leaned down and took off my shoes. 'Bloody hell, your feet are cold.'

'They haven't warmed up since this morning.'

'I don't want those in bed with me. Swing 'em up.'

I turned sideways and he plonked my stockinged feet on his lap and enfolded them in his large, warm hands. 'Soon have you right.'

I leaned my head back on the arm of the sofa. More tears oozed from my eyes and crawled down into the hair at my temples. The tears were silent, but Nico's long-wedded ears heard them anyway. Without looking up from his massaging, he remarked:

'Been a bit of a day.'

'I'm afraid so.' I sniffed and wiped the tears with my fingers. 'Oh God, panda eyes.'

'Hardly. Anyway, I've always rather cared for those. Reminiscent of the sainted Dusty in her heyday.'

'She called when I was getting ready to go out.'

'Really? From the other side?'

'Elizabeth.'

'Feeble joke.'

'They were at her flat. They weren't going anywhere.'

'Damn right. Even in this day and age newly weds have other fish to fry. How did she sound?'

'Fine. She said thanks for the cheque and sorry if – if—'

I foundered, and Nico supplied: 'And you said not at all, we perfectly understood, their day, etcetera.'

I nodded.

'All sounds highly satisfactory. What about the blushing groom, speak to him?'

'Yes.'

'Over the moon, was he?'

'He was concerned that Elizabeth hadn't sounded grateful enough.'

'Ha!' Nico threw his head back. 'He still has much to learn.'

'But it was nice of him. He said they were going to put the

money aside and indulge themselves in some way, they hadn't yet decided how.'

'Excellent. There you are.' Nico handed my feet back. 'Go and put some socks on.'

I pulled my knees up to my chin and sat with my feet clasped in my own hands. Nico kept his smile trained on me.

'Better?' he asked. His voice was tenderly solicitous but his thumb was once more hovering over the remote. Who could blame him? James Bond had last been seen suspended by dental floss over a fathomless fissure in the Andes.

'Better,' I said.

'Mind if I . . .?'

'Go ahead.'

'Boy's stuff, but none the worse for that.' He clicked.

I envied him his ability to be so easily diverted. Still, I couldn't prevent my own eyes flicking automatically to the screen's bright, moving colours. Back on the Andean peak, Bond was abseiling down vertical scree while a giant raptor made murderous passes at him. He had somehow managed to remove his jacket and was brandishing it one-handed like a matador's cape to fend off the bird's marauding talons.

'Anyway,' I said, 'I was very heartened by what I saw.'

'Good . . .' Nico tilted his head slightly towards me, but his eyes still on the screen. 'Struth, that's no way to treat bespoke tailoring . . .'

'Are you listening?'

'Yes, I am.' He glanced at me. 'Only you did say I could watch.'

'I did, but I didn't mean it – do you mind?'

'Not in the least. Actually, what am I saying? You're absolutely right, our daughter got married today and I'm slumped in front of the telly.' He switched off again and folded his arms as if to prevent further dalliance with the remote. 'I fear I've been infected by Lizzie's attitude. She makes out it's nothing – that's how I behave. And it's so not nothing.'

'No.'

He took my hand. 'You were saying . . . In spite of earlier misgivings, you were heartened, in spite of appearances.'

'I was. Elizabeth was radiant.'

'Radiant, you say? Crikey.'

'She was in work clothes, but her face, the body language, everything – she loves him, Nico.'

'I'm delighted to hear it.' My hand was squeezed and returned to me. 'Though I have to say that in my lazy way I'd regarded love as pretty much a given in these circum-stances. It's so much easier to take things at their face value.'

I forbore to point out that on their last visit Elizabeth had been so undemonstrative towards her fiancé that had we taken things at their face value we'd have been forgiven for thinking she didn't give a stuff.

'I was glad I went.'

'Good. I'm glad you did, too. It's put your mind at rest.'

I was just thinking that I wouldn't quite go that far, but he read my thoughts and asked chirpily: 'How was the new library?'

A little while later I left him and Bond to get on with it and went upstairs. I ran a bath and undressed. Then I stood before the full-length bedroom mirror and subjected my reflection to an unflinching scrutiny.

There comes a point, and I'd reached it, when a woman looks better either fully clothed, or lying down. Standing bolt upright, barefaced, butt-naked and top-lit is a young woman's game; every dimple, dent and nodule is thrown into sharp and unflattering relief.

That said, for someone of my age I wasn't in bad shape. Thanks to running twelve miles a week I was the same weight I'd been at thirty, and weekly sessions at the gym ensured that what my body lacked in bounce it made up for in defi-nition. In the right clothes, the right circumstances and (crucially) the right frame of mind, I could do several years younger. Oh, and in the right footwear. These days barely a week went by but that I acknowledged the truth of my mother's saying that a woman wears her shoes on her face. The mayor's secretary, Hilary, had delivered a stern warning of her own on the subject.

'If you must do glamour,' she said, in the tone of one who had seen more lady mayors than I'd had hot breakfasts, 'do it from the ankles up. You wouldn't believe the feet I've seen. And it's your feet that are the tools of your trade. That and your head,' she added pointedly.

Back then, at the beginning of my term, I was still a bit scared of Hilary, so I'd gone straight out to one of those slightly dull shoe shops that specialize in quality and comfort, and bought, at considerable expense, three pairs of all-purpose medium-height court shoes in brown, black and navy, plus (a purchase which I had mentioned to no one) some light support tights, which I rustled into the house under cover of darkness and removed at once from the packaging. I had never regretted it, nor ceased feeling grateful to Hilary.

This, though, was the real, unsupported me, at which I stared with neither vanity nor shame, but in a spirit of dispassionate enquiry. What I observed was that while you could pump up the infrastructure, there was very little short of the hypodermic or the surgeon's knife that you could do about the outer carapace. The skin on the inside of my upper arms and my neck was distinctly crepey, and my flesh had the appearance of a thin quilt thrown over a folded deckchair. I placed my thumbs in my armpits and my fore-fingers above my breasts and hitched everything up an inch. My nipples bobbed up obligingly to the more central, forward-looking position they'd occupied a couple of decades ago.

Dream on.

I let go and they quietly resumed the status quo and their more familiar elliptical shape. I placed my fingers and thumbs on my temples and did the same with my face. Here, a tweak of only half an inch – less, a centimetre – re-created an earlier me. The grooves between my nose and mouth evaporated, my jawline appeared, my cheeks became smooth and fresh. As I let go I tried smiling to soften the blow but the effect was macabre, like the death rictus of some primeval corpse from a peat bog.

'Your bath'll get cold.'

Nico was on the landing, his specs dangling from one hand.

'I'm just going to get in.'

'So what exactly are you doing . . .?' His tone became amorous, he advanced, smiling wolfishly. It was flattering, but self-esteem is vital to sex, and prolonged self-examination had done nothing to enhance mine. I reached behind the door for my dressing gown.

'Reflecting,' I said.

'It's what mirrors are for,' he agreed. He folded his specs and slipped them into his shirt pocket. 'Fancy a lie-down before your bath?'

'If I say no—'

'You mean it.' He put his arms round me. 'I know. I listen to Jenny Murray. I shall be devastated, naturally, but I shall accept your decision as final.'

Enfolded by him, feeling his familiar, thick, sturdy erection against my stomach and his hands all over my back, I had time for another two seconds' reflection – this time on how fortunate I was to have a short-sighted husband – before we both toppled over on to the bed. As we did so his specs slithered out of his breast pocket and I instinctively swept them off the duvet and on to the floor before they were crushed. Which was selfless of me, because it left me unable to protect myself.

'Ouch!'

'I beg your pardon . . .'

'I've got nothing on . . .'

'I noticed that.'

'And you're wearing a belt . . .'

'You know you love it – quick, give us a hand before I go off the idea.'

'I was the one who said no, remember?'

'I didn't believe you then, and I don't believe you now . . .'

'Hang on – socks?'

'Bugger . . .'

I watched him hop about.

'Satisfied?'

'Let's hope so.'

'Ha bloody ha.'

Eleven minutes later we were both lying in our preferred post-coital attitude – on our backs, with our arms above our heads, wrists crossed, like victims of some ancient ritual killing. More echoes of the peat bog.

'So, what were you doing?' he asked.

'Nothing.'

'Thinking gloomy thoughts?'

'A bit.'

'In that case,' he gave a fruity laugh, 'I'm glad to have been of some small service.'

When I didn't respond to this shameless fishing, he changed tack.

'Would you like me to freshen your bath?'

'Now you're talking.'

'No sooner thingy than whatsit.'

He swung his feet out of bed and hauled himself upright. His still-engorged cock hung out at an angle of forty-five degrees and had a drip on the end of its nose.

'What are you looking at?'

'You,' I replied.

'Well, don't. It's right up there with watching someone parking.'

'I was ogling. You do it all the time.'

'Excuse me – no. Ogling happens before. After, it's just plain staring, and it makes a chap uncomfortable.'

He disappeared into the bathroom. A moment later I heard, beneath the flushing of the loo, the old bath gurgle away, followed by the cheerful roar of the new one filling up. Nico's voice floated through from the landing.

'. . . bubbles?'

'Sorry?'

He appeared in the doorway, a bottle in each hand. 'You want to be soothed, or invigorated?'

'Soothed.'

'Of course. I just did the invigorating . . .'

'Don't flatter yourself!' I called after him. But he was right. I was smiling again, and the body which had so dismayed me a little while ago felt warm and smooth and polished; it was aglow with the lustre of love.

Four

People talk of the 'empty nest' as if our children only fly away once, when they are fully grown. Whereas in fact we lose our children at regular intervals along the way. That is, we lose the current child, the one we've become used to, in order to get the next one. The child herself slips away in a trice: sleek, swift and free as a snake sloughing its skin. The danger for us lies in hanging on to the old skin, in the hope that by sheer force of will we can fill it again with the child that used to be.

Nico and I were never possessive or controlling parents – too lazy probably – so we handled this shape-shifting better than most. In the case of Hal anyway, who grew and filled out and yodelled down the vocal register in the approved manner as the hormones kicked in and his social life blossomed exponentially. What you got with Hal was an expanded version of what you'd had before. Like looking through the optician's lenses, the focus changed but the view remained essentially the same. Apart from his need to present a moving target (hardly unique among modern young men, but which I attributed to the experience surrounding his sister's arrival) he was his father's laid-back, personable son. His metamorphosis from boy to youth and from youth to man were traceable; we could keep up.

But when it came to Elizabeth, neither upbringing nor gene pool were as powerful as her own startling singularity. Every now and then she'd show us flashes of ourselves, and our hearts leapt – yes, yes, there we are! we'd cry. We recognize that! We understand! But the flashes always turned out to be fool's gold and we were left where we'd started – in the dark.

And that's where I was now, lying wide awake on Elizabeth's wedding night, picturing her in the arms of her new husband. Without any warning, another skin had been shed.

*   *   *

Sleepless, I riffled through memories, as you do. One early epiphany had taken place when she was only ten, and we were on holiday in France, our first without Hal, who had opted for the greater social opportunities of surfing in Cornwall with the family of a school friend.

We'd taken a house in the Lot, five miles from the nearest town. The house was two hundred years old, with a loft full of bats and a broken-backed tobacco barn leaning drunkenly against the southern wall. On all sides around the roughly mown garden, with its token swimming pool and bosky corners, stretched the endless silent countryside: the deciduous forest where the wild boars, the *sangliers*, lived their secret lives; the waist-high meadows of long grass and wild flowers over which buzzards circled slowly in the blue, watching the minute life that teemed beneath our sun-heavy feet; the lily ponds and turreted hamlets that always seemed deserted. The shimmering daytime was rich with the smell of lavender, thyme and wild garlic and buzzing with crickets. Deer lay so low you could pass within a yard of them and never see unless they started up. Wild strawberries ripened in hours. Lizards throbbed and darted over the white gravel of the drive and the scorching paving stones by the pool. The evenings were clamorous with frogs and late at night we sometimes heard other creatures, bigger beasts that moved softly near the house, with sure, stealthy footsteps and grunting breath.

Half a mile up the lane was a scruffy smallholding. The couple who lived there kept a dozen lanky hunting dogs in a run at the side of the house. At one end of the enclosure was a ramshackle platform, and whenever anyone went past, the dogs would race up on to the platform and stand in a row, baying amiably and shaking their long ears with a sound like carpets being beaten. At first we were self-conscious about this noisy salute, thinking it would disturb the owners, but after a few days 'saying hello to the hounds' became a daily pastime.

Almost opposite our house, set back from the road and screened by trees, was an ancient miniature chateau in a poor state of repair. The woman in the *boulangerie* told us that it was owned by Parisians who only visited from time to time, for *le chasse*; certainly we never saw them. It was hard to imagine anyone, let alone smart, prosperous metropolitans of the *bon-chic-bon-gens* type living at the chateau. The building was largely unmodernized, the windows ill-fitting and cracked, the doors misshapen, and the garden long since allowed to go native in the swarming embrace of the surrounding brush. Pigeons flew in and out of the chateau's lichen-scabbed conical tower, and the stone walls were dank with moss to a height of two feet above the ground. What one could see of the ground floor was spooky and unwelcoming. Once, when we were walking round it, we heard the urgent, startled scrabbling of animal's feet from inside. Or what we hoped were animal's feet.

'That'll be the werewolves,' said Nico. He pulled a face at Elizabeth to show he was joking, but we all knew he needn't have bothered. If she'd been scared to death she wouldn't have let on, especially to us.

'Can we go in?' she asked.

We exchanged an amused, admiring glance over her head.

'No,' I said.

'Why not? There's no one there.'

'Because we'd be trespassing.'

'Like the werewolves.' This was a challenge to Nico, but he played it with a straight bat.

'Precisely.'

That evening when Nico was in the bath I heard him intone, in the voice of a horror-film trailer, the opening lines of Walter de la Mare's 'The Listeners'.

'"Is there anybody there? said the traveller; Knocking on the moonlit door . . ."'

'Yes,' I said, putting my head in. 'Me. That'll do . . .'

'I only said.'

'Well, don't.'

The following day the temperature ratcheted up a few more degrees. By the afternoon the heat seemed to have bleached the colour from everything. We'd embraced the local habit of taking it easy for a couple of hours after lunch, but today there would have been no option. The house, the garden, the surrounding fields and woods and their occupants all seemed petrified, held in stasis by the sun's implacable glare.

Nico dragged a lounger into the slab of shadow between the back wall and the tobacco barn and fell instantly asleep. I stretched out on the sofa in the living room, with an award-winning novel for company. Elizabeth went for a swim and then lay curled on a mattress beneath the oak tree on the front lawn, plugged into her Walkman. There was something trusting and companionable about our separate ways and places of resting, and both Nico and I were proud of our daughter's grown-up ability to be quiet and alone, without whining in the heat.

I woke at four, quickly and cleanly, as if someone had called my name. But there was no one in the room and the silence was thick and heavy. Needle-sharp strips of white light showed between the slats of the shutters – the afternoon sun was still high. The prize-winning paperback lay face down on the floor next to the sofa where it had slithered nearly two hours ago. My bookmark, a postcard of a late Rembrandt self-portrait, lay next to it. The painter's beady, sagacious eyes stared up at me from his world-weary potato-face. I reached for the book, found my page – I'd been in the twenties for two days – and replaced the postcard. My cheek felt creased and sticky where it had pressed down on the rumpled cushions.

Stretching and sighing I got up, slipped into my flip-flops, and shuffled through to the kitchen. I took a bottle of Evian water out of the fridge and held it against my forehead, and then against my chest and the inside of my forearms, before pouring myself a glassful.

The others must still have been asleep; there was no sound from anywhere. I gulped down the water and poured myself another glass before replacing the bottle in the fridge. In the hall, the front door was ajar, and a wedge of dazzling sunlight fell across the worn tiles. I tried to anticipate the heat so as to be prepared for it, but as I stepped out, its dragon breath scorched my face and arms as if I'd opened an oven.

Half-blinded, I walked over the grass to the oasis of shade under the tree. It had moved round a little, and Elizabeth must have moved with it, because I couldn't see her. When I stepped into the shade I realized she wasn't there. Her Walkman lay on the mattress, its wires and earphones trailing off on to the grass and snaking away between the dry stems.

Turning on the spot, I scanned the garden, but there was no sign of her. She wasn't in the pool, and the blue and white crocodile lilo was propped in its place against the wall. I walked round the corner of the barn, but Nico was still dead to the world on his lounger and I didn't disturb him.

A little more quickly, I returned to the house and went into each room, becoming increasingly agitated as one by one I found them empty. My search, begun in a spirit of casual enquiry became suddenly urgent, my heartbeat quickened and I was sweating.

'Elizabeth?'

I hadn't spoken loudly, but I could hear the fear in my own voice.

'Elizabeth . . .? Lizzie – are you there?'

Framing my words as a question was pure self-delusion – pretending that she was hiding, just round a corner, in the bathroom . . . when I knew, somehow, that she wasn't.

The silence was like a blanket thrown over me. Nico's poem mocked me – had anyone been listening? At that moment, our sunny, slumbrous isolation seemed sinister. We were, after all, outsiders, *les Anglais,* those English people in the rented house. Strangers, to be watched and observed. Could anyone be watching now, hunched in the woods among the *sangliers,* or with the deer, deep in the long grass?

My flesh crept.

Upstairs, I pushed open the shutters in our bedroom and called with my hands cupped around my mouth:

'Elizabeth . . .?' And then again: 'Eliza-beth!' That was the first time it wasn't a question.

As I stood there, waiting, listening, hoping, Nico appeared on the lawn, barefoot and yawning, raking the back of his head with his fingers. I ran downstairs, and he turned as I burst out of the house.

'What's up?'

'I can't find Elizabeth!'

'Don't worry – she'll have pottered off somewhere.'

'Nico – she's ten! And she doesn't potter off, as you put it. Why would she do that, when she never has before?'

'Her gadget's here.' He picked up the Walkman.

'So why hasn't she taken it with her?'

'Search me, but since it's normally surgically attached she should be back soon.'

'Nico – she isn't anywhere – I'm scared.'

'Now, come on . . .' He put an arm round me. 'Silly question, but have you tried the loo?'

'I've tried everywhere.'

Suddenly he left my side and walked fast to the side of the pool. He looked up and down, leaned forward and peered; turned back, rubbing his face fiercely.

'Phew, you've got me going now . . . Just checking.'

'She's a good swimmer.'

'I know, but you read these things.'

'Oh God!' Because I'd succeeded in making Nico anxious I was panicking properly now. 'Where is she?'

'Right under our noses probably. She could be asleep and not heard you yelling.'

'But she got up, she was there, she left the Walkman—'

'Somewhere else, come in out of the heat.'

'I've been all over the house!'

'Joss —' he laid his hands gently my shoulders – 'calm down and shut up for a moment, OK? I'll do another sweep indoors. You do a circuit round the edge of the garden. Don't go mad and wander off into the woods or I'll wind up searching for both of you, and I promise there'll be no heroics if either of us bumps into a wild boar. Outside the garden, we go together, yup? But,' he added more gently, seeing my expression of stark terror, 'I'm sure that won't be necessary.'

Five minutes later we'd done our respective circuits and were no further forward; my legs were trembling and my stomach had turned to water. My imagination in overdrive ran its horribly plausible film before my mind's eye. Predatory paedophile cruises country lanes in search of prey. Pretty prepubescent English girl is stretched out, alone and unsupervised, on grass near road. Sweetly plausible, paedophile pulls over and asks girl some token question. 'Is there a farm down here? Really? You want to jump in and show me?' My sick, cold dread allowed of no sensible questions concerning language problems, or the likelihood of our sensible, London-reared daughter accepting a lift from a stranger in a foreign land. Cleverer, older girls than Elizabeth had been abducted and . . .

'Nico – I think we should call the police!'

'Steady on. Brave and calm. We haven't exhausted all the possibilities yet.'

'But while we're doing that, anything could be happening – I think we should call them now!'

'Look.' The syllable was heavy with tried patience, but Nico's face, normally so fresh-complexioned, was pale, and his eye sockets grey. 'Call them by all means if it will make you feel better. I very much doubt they'll spring into action right away, all police know that nine times out of ten these things are a false alarm. But you ring, and I'll take the car and do a swing up and down the lane for a mile or so.'

'OK.' I wanted to say, 'You do it,' but he was already walking into the hall, and emerged now with the car keys, clicking the unlock button, crunching over the white-hot gravel, sitting with the door open as he turned the ignition. Some stupid, stupid man thing, like not asking for directions, was preventing him from making the call to the police. He wanted to find his daughter himself, even though precious minutes were draining away while he assuaged his idiotic pride.

But I was no better. As the car pulled out into the lane I realized I didn't know where to begin to make a call to the local police – not the number, not where they were, nothing. I rehearsed what I had to say in French.

Excusez-moi, mais notre fille est . . .

What was 'missing'?

. . . notre fille est allée. Elle est perdue. Elle a seulement dix ans. Nous sommes en vacances à . . .

What was our full address?

Prêt de . . .

My mind was a white-out. What was the name of the nearest village?

Paralysed by my inadequacy, I began to cry. I was no longer hot, now, but cold – shivering

But I had to do something! Sobbing, I ran down the drive and out of the gate. In the lane I stopped – Nico would be covering all this – and then crossed over and went in the direction of the chateau. It was always further than I thought – the fact that we could see the top of the tower from our house was deceptive – and the woods seemed to close behind me, tree on tree, cutting me off from the road. My laboured breathing was loud in my ears and with each heavy, uneven footstep I felt the threat of stress incontinence. People did wet themselves with fear – you saw it in films, and it was about to happen to me.

'Elizabeth!'

And then, at the very moment I called her name, I saw her, as if my shout had been one not of desperation, but of recognition. She was inside the house, at one of the first-storey windows but – and this was the odd thing – she was sitting on the sill with her back turned, looking away from me, into the house.

'Elizabeth!' I shrieked, shrill with relief. 'Get out of there! Come here! What on earth are you doing?'

Now she turned, slipped off the sill and raised a hand. 'Coming.'

A moment later she appeared, quite calmly, coming from the back of the chateau. Neither of us had ever smacked her, but I had to fold my arms to prevent myself hitting her then.

'Where have you been?'

'You saw.' She nodded at the window. 'Up there.'

'But why? How did you get in? Didn't you hear us calling? Dad and I have been sick with worry. He's gone driving up and down the road to find you!'

'It's all right, I'm back.' Nico walked past me and put his arms round Elizabeth. 'Thank heavens for that. Hello, sweetheart.'

Cruelly, I detected that a tiny part of his relief was for himself, for having been proved right, for not having made a fuss.

Elizabeth hesitated for a moment before returning the embrace. Her eyes met mine over his shoulder.

'Sorry.'

Nico's spontaneously loving reaction to our daughter's reappearance had the effect of making mine even less appropriate.

'Didn't you hear us? We were yelling our heads off – we were about to call the police!'

'Let's leave it there, shall we?' said Nico, steering Elizabeth back towards the house with his hand on the nape of her neck. 'Panic over.'

'I answered,' said Elizabeth, testily. 'I said, "Here."'

'Not nearly loud enough. And anyway, you shouldn't have been in there, it's someone else's house. How could you?'

'The back door was unlocked. I was only taking a look. Like the werewolves,' she added, deadpan, without looking at her father, who obligingly roared with laughter.

'How were the blighters?'

'They were fine.'

Sulking slightly, unable to snap out of it, I followed them back over the lane to the house. I felt ganged-up on. And conflicted, because though I'd been right to be scared, and angry, I shouldn't have let that spoil the moment of relief.

In the interests of 'letting it go', and because we knew we wouldn't be coming back here, we didn't ask her what the inside of the chateau had been like. In my case there was a slight sense of not giving her the satisfaction. Childish, but there it was.

We never asked, and she never told us.

But I was unable, ever, to erase the image of my daughter sitting calmly and quietly in the window of that creepy house, her back turned to the outside world, and to us; quite unperturbed as her parents went berserk, crazed with anxiety in the broiling afternoon sun.

I half-wanted to wake Nico, now, and ask him whether he still remembered this as vividly as I did, and if so, what he made of it. But we had always steered clear of discussing the incident, sensing it (I tried not to think 'she') had the power to hurt us.

I continued to toss and turn, alone, badgered by the past. There had been another incident; less mysterious, potentially more damaging. It was the Easter holidays. Hal was in his last year at Bristol and had elected to remain there in the slum property he shared with two lads and two girls. Elizabeth was coming up to A levels and had spent the three weeks off from boarding school having driving lessons (she was a natural), conducting a strictly off-the-premises relationship with a drummer named Eldridge and intermittently revising.

What with one thing and another we'd hardly seen her, so it was a surprise when one evening she wandered into the drawing room as I was watching the six o'clock news, and sat down, swinging a foot and staring uninterestedly at the screen. Her very presence sucked away my concentration.

'Hi.' I clicked mute. 'How's it going?' I'd perfected the art of the casual, all-embracing, non-intrusive enquiry that allowed of any of a wide variety of interpretations.

'I'm all right. What about you?'

It was most unlike her to bat the question back, and that, with the slight emphasis on the first and last words, made my antennae stand to attention.

'Busy at work – you know.' At this time I had a conveniently flexible job as manager of the gift shop at the local National Trust property, Studdingham Hall.

'M-hm,' she said, as if she didn't believe a word of it. 'Is the house open for the summer yet?'

This enquiry indicated an astonishing and unprecedented level of interest. I was used to the idea that our lives were peripheral and secondary to hers and would never have expected her to notice the pressure I'd been under for the past few days. It was remarkable enough that she had registered the season and its implications at all.

'Next weekend,' I said. 'So there's the usual sense of panic getting ready.'

'Right.' There was a pause. I remember it so well – not an open-ended silence, but a hesitation, heralding more to come.

'Mum . . .'

'Yes?' I kept my eyes on the prime minister, pressing the flesh in Brussels.

'Where's Dad?'

She was looking at me now. I glanced at my watch. 'Back any minute I should think.'

'In other words, you don't know.'

'No,' I said, 'in other words, nothing. He's on his way home from work.'

'You know jackshit about what he gets up to,' said my daughter.

I zapped the PM. 'I beg your pardon?'

'You're too trusting.'

'There's no such thing,' I said piously, but I was trembling. 'Trust isn't quantifiable, it's just there.'

'Listen to yourself!'

Unfortunately I had been, and I'd heard what she could hear. 'What brought this on?' I asked, knowing the answer.

'Mum . . .' She groaned under the weight of her exasperation. 'Get real.'

'What do you mean?'

'He's playing away.'

'What?'

'Dad. Having an affair?' She tilted her head at me, eyebrows raised, did I really not get it?

'I beg your pardon?' Every word – every syllable – was now just a means of deferring the inevitable.

'Read my lips: he's shagging that fat bitch who was at your cocktail party.'

'I'm sorry?'

'That woman who always comes. You always invite her. The one who's always so nicey-nicey with you. Her husband's a *friend* –' she made quotation marks with her fingers – 'of Dad's.'

'Alex?' This time it wasn't really a question; I knew she was right.

'Probably. Who cares? I saw them at the theatre the other day, it was written all over them. You're worth six of her, Mum.' She got up and stood looking down at, and on, me. 'But that's no reason to kid yourself it's not happening. Get in there and see her off. Put a stop to Dad's sad little fantasy before he convinces himself it's the *real thing*.' More quotation marks, made right in front of my face.

With that she left the room, and the house, and went off for her evening with Eldridge, leaving me shell-shocked.

I told myself I didn't have to take the word of a stroppy seventeen-year-old. After all, what had she actually seen? Nothing. She had seen her father with Alex (who was, I agreed, on the fat side) and was giving me the benefit of her adolescent intuition. But the seed was sown.

I didn't mean to trap Nico, just to put him in a situation where I could study his reaction. But I couldn't bear to wait, either. When he got in that night I adopted a tone of polite enquiry and came straight to the point.

'Elizabeth thinks you're having an affair with Alex.'

'Lizzie?' He pulled a kind of mad, frowning smile. 'How would she know?'

That was it then.

'So you are.'

He sat down on the edge of the bed and put his hands over his eyes. 'I don't know what to say,' he mumbled.

'Nor me.'

'Of course she'd know.'

'It wasn't magic! It wasn't some sixth sense! She's not telepathic, she saw you, Nico! Written all over you, was how she put it, actually.'

'Shit.'

'Yes, wasn't it? What rotten luck.' That was a low blow because I knew the 'shit' wasn't for being rumbled but for by whom.

I was jealous, wretched and humiliated; Nico was guilty and remorseful. I decided to believe him, more or less, when he said it was nothing – the fat woman had made a determined play, and he had always been easily flattered. But as the whole sorry business played out and we returned, bruised, to one another it was the unspoken aftershocks that rattled our marriage. We had no idea that Elizabeth paid us so much attention, and the knowledge that she did, and what was more that she held opinions, was almost more disturbing than the breach of trust itself.

She must have heard our voices and my tears, sensed the stifled turmoil in the house, but she herself never mentioned it again. When I tried to broach it with her she cut me off. 'OK, Mum – deal with it, yeah?' A week later she went back to school – and what would prove to be starry A levels – and left us to it. She never, as far as we knew, told her brother. What I most recalled now was her certainty that she was right, and her fearsome candour in asserting it. It was hard to avoid the impression that she had overtaken us, that she cast a worldly eye over our failings and wanted to protect us from ourselves.

On the other hand . . . As a mother I was in the habit of gleaning what comfort I could, and out of all the mess and unhappiness I squirrelled away a few precious words:

You're worth six of her, Mum.

I was?

Given her opinion of Alex that probably didn't amount to much but still. In my daughter's comparative assessment, I'd come out ahead. You might say, 'but she would say that, wouldn't she?' I say: 'no.' Our daughter was niggardly with expressions of affection. The mere idea that she had a sense of my value, that she had compared me with another woman and found in my favour, was revelatory, and if she thought I was going to forget it she was very much mistaken.

Eighteen months later, when she was at Leeds and we were over it, Nico revealed what had passed between him and her at the time. We were returning from a lunch party and I was the designated driver, so he was slightly pissed and disposed to unburden himself.

'I cornered her and said my piece,' he declared.

'Did you?' I said frostily. He'd get no encouragement from me on this one – I preferred not to go there.

'I didn't feel I could very well not. The thought of her going back to school with that on her mind . . .'

'Or with it on yours, I imagine.'

'Sure, absolutely . . . Anyway, I broached the subject. She was scarily composed, it was like being up before the beak.'

'I'd have expected that.'

'Yes, I agree, I didn't anticipate tears or anything, but I confess I was bracing myself for a smart whack in the solar plexus.'

'Instead of which she let you off lightly.' I felt I was entitled to my soupçon of sarcasm. 'Shall we leave it at that?'

'Believe it or not that's exactly what Lizzie said!' Nico was clearly pleased with this coincidence. 'Said it was our business and she wasn't interested.'

'She was interested enough to tell me about it,' I pointed out.

'True. But that was as far—'

'And to suggest I get my ass in gear before you went any further with something we were both going to regret.'

'OK.' He looked out of the window for a moment, then to the front again. 'Yup, OK. I'm sorry, Joss.'

But when I didn't reply, he couldn't resist adding: 'I didn't mention it to pick old scabs, but because I find her so remarkable.'

'Well,' said my friend Denise, 'face it, she is. She's an extremely impressive young woman.'

Denise was entitled to her view. She was still married then, wife of a card-carrying philanderer and mother of an indigent surf bum and a bereavement counsellor who had presented her with two grandchildren born out of wedlock.

'I wish we were closer,' I sighed.

'I hate to say this, but get over it, girl. You want closer? She saved your marriage, you can't get closer than that.'

'She didn't save it. She put the skids under it.'

'Correction, Nico put the skids under it – or nearly. She cared enough to intervene. Be grateful, Joss. Really.'

It seemed inappropriate to take the conversation any further with all that Denise was going through at the time. But the whole business left me holding another of Elizabeth's discarded skins.

However distant she appeared, she was keeping an eye on us.

Five

I impressed on Hilary the absolute necessity of keeping clear one of the three dates Elizabeth had offered for dinner with her and Edward.

'We weren't at her wedding, so we have to, we must,' I explained. 'This is a three-line whip, Hilary.'

'I understand perfectly,' she said. 'Let's go for the last one then, shall we, and keep our fingers crossed.'

I knew that soothing, businesslike tone, and I wasn't having it.

'I've got a better idea,' I said. 'Let's go for the last one, and if something comes up we'll get Peter Carroll to stand in for me.'

Peter was the deputy mayor, of whom Hilary's opinion was only medium.

'Yes. Yes, we could do that,' she said, in the tone of a mountaineer who acknowledges that there is, of course, always the option of cutting the rope.

'You know I wouldn't ask unless it was important.'

'Of course not,' she conceded.

'So perhaps you could call Peter today some time and book him for that evening, just in case. It won't be a problem for him; we both know he'll be tickled pink.'

'Right you are.'

'Thank you, Hilary,' I said. 'I appreciate it.'

You might think that I was being unnecessarily placatory. Hilary was, after all, my secretary. But that didn't mean that I was her boss. Neither of us was under any illusion that she was the Sir Humphrey to my Jim Hacker. As, to be fair, she had been with every mayor over a fifteen year period.

The initial chemistry between us had not been good. There had been only one other lady mayor during Hilary's tenure, and it had not gone well (I was told this on the quiet by other people; Hilary's discretion was watertight). Though ten years younger than me, her long experience and cast-iron competence made me feel even more of a novice than I was. As well as doing an exemplary job at City Hall – some said practically running the place – she was a walking tribute to Per Una at M&S and was happily married, with three grown-up children all doing well in their chosen walks of life, and four grandchildren; we had clocked up only two, courtesy of Hal and Cathryn so even on that front she was ahead of me.

To begin with I combated this with a show of feisty independence. My first mayoral initiative was to do away with a top table at the inaugural dinner following mayor-making. Hilary never said, 'I told you so.' She didn't have to. I could scarcely be seen, let alone heard. There were other bones of contention in those first few weeks – the senior citizens' tea party, the long mirror in the mayor's parlour to name but two – but I shan't go into them. We didn't exactly cross swords, Hilary was far too polite for that, but we did our fair share of sabre-rattling.

The turning point in our relationship came with the great thank-you-letter debate. I've always been a believer in the efficacy of the prompt and courteous written thank-you. After each engagement I would sit in the back of the car and scribble down one or two observations of the 'stunning hat', 'do hope your son gets through' variety, and draft a thank-you note around them. These notes, sometimes as many as three a day, then went into the in-tray for Hilary to process on the Samsung.

After one particularly busy week, Hilary's creamy cheeks showed the merest hint of pink.

'Madam Mayor—'

'Joss.'

'About these letters.'

'Yes, Hilary.'

'I just wanted to say that you do realize you're setting a challenging precedent.'

'What my successors do is up to them.'

'I don't mean them. I mean for yourself. You are going to be attending literally hundreds of functions in the next twelve months. To write a note after every single one really isn't necessary, and you'll be making a lot of additional work.'

I affected an air of apology. 'And for you, too, Hilary. I'm sorry, I hadn't looked at it in that light.'

It was a mischievous shaft which found its mark. The cheeks went a touch pinker.

'Oh, I imagine I shall be able to cope. A little extra work never bothered me. I simply wanted to warn you against making a rod for your own back. The workload is quite intense. And relentless,' she added, switching on her computer to indicate that the conversation was at an end, and I could put this disobliging analysis in my pipe and smoke it.

But the conversation left us both with food for thought and marked the beginning of a sea change in our relationship. I continued to draft the thank-you notes, which, along with my idiosyncratic hats, became my mayoral signature, and Hilary continued to type them up, henceforward without a word of complaint. She was soon so proficient in my style that three simple bullet points on the back of a menu would result in a perfect letter.

Six weeks in, without any discernible alteration in our dealings with one another, we had become the firmest of friends and allies, bonded by mutual respect and a real, though never articulated, fondness. I continued to call her Hilary and she to call me Madam Mayor (in the presence of others) or nothing at all (when we were on our own).

On the day in question, before I left for the city parks annual staff awards, she said almost casually: 'I spoke to Councillor Carroll. Something has come up. He'll be happy to stand in for you on that date.'

'Marvellous. Thank you, Hilary.'

I seemed to detect a glint in her eye as she added: 'It's a finger buffet with the Scouts at the leisure centre.'

'Splendid,' I said. 'He'll be perfect for that.'

The drive to Camden took two hours. Elizabeth had invited us to spend the night, but we'd declined, and were due to arrive, and dine, relatively early so as to get back not too late. Our reasons for not staying were various. Though it was a Friday, Nico had to be at the theatre at eight the next day and I had two mayoral engagements to attend. More importantly I didn't feel ready to spend the night with the newly-weds in their marital home. I was barely used to the idea of our daughter's marriage, let alone the full bed, bathroom and bumps-in-the-night monty. Children may be appalled and disgusted by the evidence that their parents Do It, but the converse is no less uncomfortable.

Nico drove the second half of the journey into London because he was calmer in city traffic. As we proceeded by fits and starts down the Finchley Road he stole a glance at my set profile.

'Cheer up, Joss, it's going to be great.'

'I do hope so.'

'Look at it this way – what could be nicer? We're going to dinner with our daughter and son in law. This is the beginning of a whole new chapter. I'm really looking forward to it.'

'I wish I was. I worry that—'

'Don't, Joss.' He put out a hand and squeezed my knee. 'The first duty of guests is to enjoy themselves. They're entertaining us. Let's sit back and allow ourselves to be entertained, yup?'

'You're right,' I said. 'I know you are. I'll do my best.'

He gave my knee a brief pat as if to say that's the spirit, but I was still uneasy.

This did change somewhat when we arrived. The flat, in a rare purpose-built apartment block overlooking the Regent Canal, had never looked nicer or more welcoming. They'd done something with the lighting, there were fresh flowers on a side table, and a delicious smell in the air. Champagne flutes stood ready on a tray. Baroque strings twiddled in the background. Elizabeth was sleekly handsome in cream suede trousers and a white wrap-around shirt – her Katherine Hepburn look. Edward wore cords and a black polo. Glancing at Nico, in his granddad tunic, drawstring bags and espadrilles, I wondered what he made of this other man's style. Nico's clothes were a go-hang statement, at least partly dictated by his waistline; Edward's embodied the insouciant natural chic of a man with a fortunate metabolism.

When we all had a glass in our hands, Edward raised his.

'We're going to have to kick this champagne habit – but not just yet. Welcome, Nico and Jocelyn, and here's to many more such occasions . . .' He put his hand on Elizabeth's neck, beneath her hair. 'To the four of us – the family!'

'To us!'

'The family!'

We quaffed, and were refilled. Because of the sense of celebration we all remained standing, as if this were a cocktail
party. I could feel myself relaxing. Elizabeth looked fabulous;
both she and Edward radiated happiness; the ambience couldn't
have been more hospitable. There was a dawning possibility
that I was going to enjoy myself.

Conversation remained general over the drinks – their
planned holiday in Kerala, general reflections on housing, a
discussion of the upcoming season at Nico's theatre, my light-
hearted account of a couple of recent mayoral engagements.
But when Edward excused himself and disappeared into the
kitchen I was aware of a minute breach in our social defences
into which, thankfully, Nico stepped.

'This is great, Lizzie. I can't tell you how we've been looking
forward to it.'

'Really?' she pulled her slightly sardonic smile.

'Of course, really. And you know, this flat –' he gestured
expansively with his glass – 'seeing it this evening I'm not
sure how you could do better.'

'Yes, we do love it,' she agreed. 'But we need more space.
Another couple of bedrooms, one we can use as a study and
one so we can have people to stay, comfortably. Edward's
kids for a start.'

Oh God, yes, I thought, I'd forgotten about them; but once
more Nico moved cheerfully forward without breaking stride.

'I can see that. But don't rush into anything. Wherever it
is it'll need to be perfect to top this.'

'I'm not sentimental,' said Elizabeth, a remark that quali-
fied as understatement of the year. 'It's only bricks and mortar.
And,' she added, holding her glass up before her face and
staring at the bubbles, 'I think we could be happy anywhere.'

'Darling girl.' Nico beamed at her, but put his arm around
me; he knew me so well. 'That is music to our ears. Ah, the
chef – we're summoned.'

The table looked so pretty, dressed in a plain white cloth
and napkins, with polished silver and pink tea lights in art
deco holders. There was a centrepiece – I remember this so
clearly – of creamy petals floating in a shallow glass dish.
Beneath the petals, at the bottom of the dish, lay smooth grey
pebbles, overlapping like fish's scales. I was struck by the

simple beauty of the concept; and moved by the thought of our brusque daughter first imagining, then creating it. I wondered if the petals were real, and if they were, if she had gone out and chosen flowers specially. And the stones – storm-cloud coloured, but so calm, somehow, and so perfectly matched – where had she found those . . .? I hoped no one would notice my too-bright eyes.

'This looks absolutely lovely,' I said, in a voice that was also a shade too bright.

'Don't look at me,' said Edward. 'We have the lady of the house to thank for the decor.'

'Quick and easy once you have the material to hand,' said Elizabeth. 'And so much less fiddly than sagging tulips.' She waved a hand. 'Do sit anywhere.'

Fine, I thought, be as gruff as you like, you can't fool me this time.

Over dinner I spared a not very sympathetic thought for Peter Carroll at the Scouts' finger buffet. Here, we were served pear, Roquefort and endive salad, lamb tajine and amaretto syllabub. The starter and pudding had been put together by Elizabeth, the main course cooked by Edward, a sensible division of labour, since she had neither aptitude nor inclination for cooking, whereas he clearly liked nothing better.

'Bloody hell, Edward,' said Nico. 'Is this standard fare in your house?'

'No, I'm out to impress the in-laws.'

'Mission accomplished. This is historic.' He pointed his fork at me. 'Don't go getting any ideas, woman.'

'It's absolutely delicious,' I agreed. 'All of it – good team-work.'

'Oh, yes,' said Elizabeth. She shot a smile at her husband. 'Teamwork, we got it.'

Nico turned to her and began reminiscing about tajines of long ago in the great Djemaa-al-Fna square of Marrakesh. Reflexively, I turned the other way and bit the bullet.

'How are your family, Edward?'

'They're well, thank you for asking. Not that I would necessarily be the first to know if they weren't.'

'Well, quite.'

We exchanged a discreetly collusive smile, our eyes not quite meeting. We were both feeling our way, trying to strike an exquisitely delicate balance between the common ground of parenthood and the less even one of being in-laws.

'It must be tricky for them,' I suggested, 'you marrying again, and to someone so much younger . . . No one could blame them if they were a bit slow to come round.'

'As a mater of fact,' he said, 'that hasn't been a problem. Beth's played a blinder – you know, kept her distance, maintained a low profile, not pushed for more intimacy than what's on offer. The old horse-whisperer's trick.'

'Horse whisperer . . .?'

'Keep still and let them come to you.'

I believed him, if only because no one knew better than I that the aloofness which he took for emotional discretion was my daughter's default mode.

'Anyway, Rob's not a problem and Bryony's in New York at the moment.'

'Really? So is our son.'

'Good heavens.' We contemplated this pleasing coincidence for a second, and he added: 'I shan't lose too much sleep over it. They are adults after all, and in this day and age families come in a wide variety of flavours.'

'What flavour are we, do you think – us, here this evening?'

'Oh . . .' He glanced around. 'Sweet and sour?'

This, I reflected, could have described most families, but I took his answer to be diplomatic rather than evasive. Could there be a more socially intricate and complex group than ours? The invisible threads that link individuals – threads of gender, of age, of consanguinity, of parental and romantic love, of common interest – criss-crossed between us in a positive cat's cradle of connections, all of which had to be borne in mind at all times if we were not to become hopelessly entangled.

'. . . must meet them,' Edward was saying. 'In due course.'

'We'd like that very much.'

'Tell me,' he said, signalling by his tone a change of subject. 'Did you have to forego a mayoral function to be here this evening?'

I told him about Peter Carroll and the Scouts, with a few embellishments which made him laugh.

'Is it strange,' he asked, 'being a public figure?'

'A little,' I conceded. 'But interesting – and rewarding.'

He leaned forward. 'You're off the record here, you know. Be frank.'

'I am being. Let's see, downsides . . . Hard on the feet, hands and social life. A test of stamina quite often.'

'And patience?'

'Sometimes.'

'I bet.'

'It's an honour,' I explained. 'An honour and a reward. The very least I can do is carry out my not very onerous duties with a good grace.'

'I'm sure they're delighted with you.'

'They are!' This was Nico. 'Sorry to earwig, but they are. They can't believe their luck.'

Elizabeth got up and began clearing away the main course plates. 'After this, anyone mind if I have an intercourse cigarette?'

Edward put his hand on her arm. 'You know what I think.'

'They don't mind.' She nodded in our direction. 'Do you?'

The question had been rhetorical, but Nico and I shook our heads vigorously.

Edward said: 'You know perfectly well what I mean.'

'I'm cutting down, aren't I?'

'That's what you tell me.'

She pulled an exasperated face, and took the plates out. The three of us avoided one another's eyes. Those threads again – too complicated.

When Elizabeth came back she was carrying a packet of Dunhills and her lighter. In what I interpreted as a gesture of defiance the lighter was not one of those cheap disposable ones, but the full electroplated monty. She took out a cigarette and lit it with a flourish and a swift, sharp exhalation of smoke like a dragon revving up. Edward directed a rueful smile at her and she blew the next mouthful at him. I was so, so glad that he nagged her about her smoking, and that while she may or may not have been altering her behaviour – yet – she was treating the nagging as the evidence of love it so obviously was.

Edward turned to me.

'Do you have to make speeches all the time?'

'Quite often.'

'She likes it,' said Nico. 'She's good on her feet. Give her a row of expectant upturned faces and a rousing introduction and she delivers every time.'

'That must be where you get it from,' said Edward to Elizabeth. 'The performance gene.'

Elizabeth tapped her cigarette into the lid of the Dunhills box. 'Maybe. Though I think what we each do is very different.'

'Oh for sure, no question,' he agreed. He pointed at her, while addressing himself to us: 'You should come along and hear her at the open mic some time.'

'Open mic?' Nico's eyebrows shot up. 'You mean stand-up?'

'Lizzie, you never said.'

'He's being ridiculous,' said Elizabeth, 'I only ever did it once when we went somewhere with Rob. It was a kind of dare, and I was pissed enough to have a go but not too pissed to think.'

'She was really bloody good,' said Edward.

'I survived,' said Elizabeth, but she did look quietly pleased with herself. She liked to surprise us. 'I shan't be making a habit of it.'

'So what sort of material did you do?' asked Nico, now positively crackling with curiosity, both parental and profes-sional. 'Who were you most like?'

'I've no idea.'

'Edward?'

'Let's see . . . Ben Elton?' Even I could see that this was a dangerously dated example. Elizabeth closed her eyes and thrust her hands into her hair, cigarette still between her fingers, in serious danger of self-immolation either from the smoul-dering tip or sheer exasperation.

'Gimme a break, I wasn't that drunk.'

'We used to like him, didn't we?' I said emolliently. 'Surely he's given it up now . . . Doesn't he collaborate with Andrew Lloyd Webber?'

'Yes,' said Elizabeth. 'I rest my case.'

'I was just trying to give the flavour,' said Edward. 'Not to be ageist, but someone your parents and I would know. I'm not au fait with all the new people myself.'

'Who cares, you gave it a go!' Nico was plainly enchanted, shaking his head and gazing at her with unashamed admira-tion. 'Good for you, Lizzie!'

'Right up there with getting married, huh?' she said.

'Anyone who can stand up in front of an audience and attempt to make them laugh is deserving of total respect.'

'Less of the "attempt", Dad,' said Elizabeth. 'I succeeded. They laughed.'

'But let's face it, darling,' said Edward, 'the Talking Shop isn't exactly the Glasgow Empire.'

'Cheers. Enough already. I'm going to get the afters.'

I would have been prepared to let it go there, but Nico was like a dog with two tails and a juicy new bone.

'I must say I'm gobsmacked.'

'I can't think why,' she said, exiting.

'Come on,' Nico called after her, 'This is us we're talking about – your aged progenitors. We didn't even know you two were getting hitched. Didn't even know you and this chap were an item, for fuck's sake!'

'We didn't know you,' I said, pointing at Edward.

'Point taken.' He chuckled; he was a hard man to faze. 'Anyway, she more than held her own.'

'Did she do us?' Nico asked Edward.

'Not that I remember.'

'You're being polite. I bet she did.'

'You mean you hope she did,' I said.

'Sorry to disappoint you, Dad.' Elizabeth entered with frosted dessert glasses on a tray, 'You didn't feature.'

'Why not?' asked Nico. 'I thought stand-up was all about getting stuff off your chest.'

'Possibly,' said Elizabeth crisply, 'but you two were never on it. Pudding, anyone?'

In spite of her father's goading she declined to discuss it any further. We moved on to the much safer topic of American foreign policy. For a gnat's crotchet Nico and I caught each other's eye, sharing the realization that we had glimpsed another side of our daughter we had known nothing about.

I wouldn't normally have drunk coffee after dinner because it keeps me awake, but on this occasion I accepted a second cup because of the drive home. I remember we were talking about London – how we both loved and hated it and how it never got anything right but managed to stay fabulous – when there was a sound in the hall and Edward turned his face to the door with an expression that I instantly recognized as parental – pleased but wary.

'Ah . . .! Now who can this be?'

'Rob, of course,' said Elizabeth, and rose to take the cafetière into the kitchen. The three of us gazed expectantly at the doorway where, seconds later, a young man appeared. A dark-haired, brown-eyed young man in jeans and a black T-shirt, instantly recognizable from his photograph.

'Hi – oh, hi.'

'Hi!' we all cried. Edward stretched out an arm in the direction of the new arrival in a way that was part welcome, part embrace, part introduction.

'This is my son, Rob. Rob, meet Nico and Jocelyn, Elizabeth's parents.'

'Great. Hello. I'm so sorry,' he said charmingly and unapologetically as he shook my hand, then Nico's. 'Am I interrupting something?'

'No, no,' we chorused, as Edward pulled up another chair to the table. 'Interrupting? Far from it!'

And that was the first of my lies.

Just before he sat down, he leaned over the table and tapped the surface of Elizabeth's beautiful centrepiece, so that the flower petals bobbed and spun and a few droplets of water spilled on to the cloth.

'What's this you've been having?' he asked. 'Rose petal soup?'

Six

Nico and I had every reason to believe in our staying power. Why wouldn't we? A marriage could ride out the spike of a minor infidelity, it was attrition that wore it down.

In our case, that meant my low patches. The blues, which in spite of my GP's authoritative diagnosis and the clear efficacy of the right medication I could not bring myself to dignify with the title clinical depression.

The reason I couldn't was not embarrassment, nor even the feeling that to do so would be a social solecism, a burden on one's friends like complaining of poverty (though that is what I felt). Like all right-minded, broadsheet-reading, Radio Four listeners, I recognized that depression was nothing to be ashamed of. What stopped me was the sense that mine was small beer. There were people out there with real, grown-up depression, the sort that cut them off from the rest of the world, and brought them to the brink of suicide – and beyond.

These sufferers put me in my place. There was a grim and terrible grandeur to their condition which I did not perceive in mine. What ailed me was the common cold to their full-blown malaria. Hideous to admit, but I almost envied them their superior suffering. My problem was that I could function, after a fashion. I could do my job, sit on committees, attend social occasions and appear to all intents and purposes my usual self. Until the adrenalin drained away – with the blues for company I had driven back from countless gatherings with tears pouring down my face. True depression, surely, showed itself in a stone-faced, dull-eyed, hopeless inertia, whereas I was caught between my almost unnatural ability to put on a good face, and the fathomless pit that threatened to engulf me the moment I stopped. There was always a point in every day when the final diversion was gone, when the very last person has fallen away, and myself was all I had.

Nico, of course, was that last person.

At my worst I had sat in theatres and in restaurants with Nico, weeping, lost to myself and to him, not caring if other people saw me, unable either to leave or to control myself. I never wanted to die – I wasn't brave enough for that, thank God – but I had often wanted simply not to be, to be erased, set aside, until things were better. Or to be someone else. Because after all, who was I? At these times I scarcely knew Jocelyn Carbury, and the little I glimpsed of her I both despised and feared.

Fortunately for me, Nico did know who I was, or said he did and, incredibly, amazingly, loved the person he knew. Can you wonder I forgave him Alex? Phrases to describe his role, phrases like 'believed in me', 'there for me', 'helped me through' and so on, are inadequate because they are too precise. They imply action, whereas nothing is harder, nor more essential, in such situations than solid, calm passivity – the capacity not to be proactive, nor to offer solutions but to be part of whatever solution presents itself. And Nico, God help us, was inherently the least passive person I knew; a force of nature – eager, energetic, sanguine, buoyant, inspired by the expectation of happiness and success.

No one but Nico and a succession of ever-younger GPs knew about my blues. Our 'charmed' life had this one closed room. Much – no, most – of the time I was who I seemed to be; when I wasn't, the sharing of that wretched, breathless, confined space must have been almost intolerable for Nico. But if it was he never said so.

How could I not love him? I owed him so much.

So, yes, we had staying power. But it was not a quality we'd handed on to Hal. He knew how to fall in love, and how to make people fall in love with him – that was the trouble, he did it all the time. When he'd married Cathryn twelve years ago it had been the happiest, shiniest wedding anyone could remember, and Elizabeth had been the most striking brides-maid, chic in a turquoise cocktail dress, with her hair up. But I'd had forebodings, and been proved correct. After Jed was born, Hal's business star was in the ascendant and he was away more and more. Cathryn worked, they became a family only in name. By the time Chloe was seven, and Jed four, their father was hardly ever there. His absence became insti-tutionalized; we almost managed to convince ourselves that this was a perfectly normal way of life in the modern world. Well, it may have been, but nature abhors a vacuum, and the next thing was Sian from the Frankfurt office and a slow, painfully civilized divorce. I was terrified we wouldn't see the children, but we should have known Cathryn wouldn't take it out on us. We continued to be friends, and to be close to Chloe and Jed. Hal was now based full-time in a New York apartment, not with Sian, but with Lili from Seoul. I still sometimes woke in the night and cried for the sadness of it – for our handsome, fallible son, and our generous daughter-in-law, and our delightful grandchildren, getting used, as most modern children must, to emotional make-do.

I mention all this because you would think, with all that useful life experience, that I would have learned something about human nature, its properties and management. All I can say is that experience is one thing, self-knowledge another, and neither is a blind bit of use when fate tosses you a wobbler.

'Charming boy of Edward's,' Nico said on the way home after dinner.

'He seemed nice enough,' I replied. 'I just hope he and Elizabeth are OK.'

Nico reached out and gave my knee a little shake. 'They're fine. You heard what Edward said.'

'Yes,' I said. 'But it's early days.'

It was gone 1 a.m. when we got home, and we went straight to bed, but it was our habit to read for a while no matter how late we were. We assumed our usual positions; me sitting with my knees bent up like a lectern, supporting my novel; he on his side, leaning on his elbow, with his head resting on his hand. My eyes travelled down the print without taking in a word; every so often I turned a page for form's sake, consigning to oblivion the author's tight plotting and carefully crafted prose. I wanted to be last awake so that I could be alone with my thoughts.

Nico had professed himself 'completely buggered' and it wasn't long before he closed his book – the voluminous auto-biography of a celebrated theatre director – with a decided 'clunk' and switched off the lamp. But instead of feeling for my hand and aiming a drowsy kiss at it he rolled towards me,

extended an arm over my lap, and nuzzled his face into the
side of my breast, near my armpit. I unfairly suspected this
small-hours ardour of having something to do with the celebrated director's notoriously gamey private life.

'Remind me what you're reading . . .?' he enquired absently,
his hand finding my other breast.

I turned the page. 'Still the same.'

'Not exactly racing through it, are you?'

I glanced down at him over my reading specs. 'It's quite
absorbing.'

'If you say so.' His fingers played with my nipple with the
delicate, watch-winding motion that – usually – never fails to
get me going.

'She's a good writer,' I remarked, returning pointedly to the
text.

'Bitch,' murmured Nico amiably, and now it was not only his
voice that was thickening with lust. 'Mind if I butt in . . .?'

'Actually, darling – I don't think I'm up for it tonight.'

'Eh?' He pulled his head back to look up at me. 'Are you
OK?'

It was a joke between us that I never had a headache. Even
with the blues, my body would usually respond to Nico, even
if afterwards I wept on his chest because the void was still
there. I let down the whole of womankind with my tendency
to say no and mean, oh, all right then. Nico could have been
forgiven for not taking this rejection seriously, but it all goes
to show how the body can send out its own clear, undeniable
signals: no dice.

'I'm sorry,' I said.

'No worries.' He withdrew his arm. 'I and my brutish
appetites shall retire forthwith. And, hey –' he leaned up on
his elbow and kissed my cheek – 'there's always a next time.'

'Yes.'

'Night, Joss.'

'Night.' I made a kissing face back, but he was already
turning away and pillowing his head on his bent right arm,
ready for sleep.

Relief outweighed the small shock I felt at his ready acceptance and prevented me from fully realizing that with that
acceptance we had crossed a boundary, and were now in
uncharted territory.

For form's sake I stared at my book for another ten minutes or so, until Nico's breathing became gently stertorous. Over the years the stertorousness had increased, to a point just this side of snoring, and I generally found its gravelly rhythms quite soothing. Tonight, it was the signal that I had what remained of the night to myself. I closed my book and placed it carefully on the bedside table before switching off the lamp. As I slithered down under the duvet, Nico murmured reflexively, 'G'night, sweetie . . .' and I froze.

'Night,' I whispered, 'sleep well.'

I lay completely motionless until I was certain he'd dropped off. Then and only then did I lie back and pick over my impressions of the evening. I was like Anna Gantry.

'*In the pantry, chewing on a mutton bone; How she gnawed it, how she clawed it, when she thought she was alone . . .*'

I couldn't exactly gnaw and claw, but I could gorge my imagination on the evening just gone.

Rob had pulled up a chair between me and his father, but his attention was focused on me. That could, of course, have been simple politeness; he was his father's son.

'It's riveting to meet you,' he said.

'Really?' This was Nico, who in any gathering of less than a dozen assumed all conversation to be general. 'As a matter of fact it must be.'

'As you see, they're surprisingly normal,' said Elizabeth dryly.

Rob leaned back, smiling. 'But you're still unexpected.'

'Would you like a coffee?' she asked.

'No, thanks, but I could go a beer.'

She got up. 'There's some in the fridge.'

'I'll get it—'

'Stay where you are, I'm closer.'

'Cheers.'

I glanced at Nico's face as we watched our daughter go into the kitchen to fetch the beer. She could only be a few years older than her stepson, closer to his age than his father's. If I found it hard to think of Elizabeth and Edward in bed together, it was still more uncomfortable seeing her through Rob's eyes. She had what the model agencies call a good back – long and straight, the fitted shirt emphasizing her slim waist and the

insouciant racehorse-swing of her hips beneath the blond suede.
Her strong-jawed face was framed and softened by a sleek brown
bob. She was handsome, elegant, a little forbidding . . . I told
myself to hold that thought; forbidding was good.

She came back and passed an open bottle over the table to
Rob. 'There you go.'

'Thanks.'

I caught Nico's eye, and with it his infinitesimally raised
eyebrow. Marital body-shorthand for: 'Yup.'

'So good to see you.' Edward was addressing his son. 'What
have you been up to?'

'You mean generally, or right now?'

'Both.' Edward looked round at us all, smiling; it was
obvious that now the moment of introduction was over he was
enjoying his son being there. 'Either!'

'Moving the sick from A to B and dreaming of fame.'

This answer was clearly intended to provoke questions from
the uninitiated and Nico duly obliged.

'Now, come on, you're going to have to enlarge on that.'

'I'm a hospital porter at St Mary's.'

'Good for you.' This time I'd got in first. 'And isn't that a
sufficient claim to fame?'

'What a nice thing to say.' He gave me a frowning smile.
There was an almost camp sweetness about him that he must
have known was utterly charming. 'And you're absolutely
right, it ought to be.'

'But your sights are set on greatness,' declared Nico.

'Well, I wouldn't go that far, but a tiny shaft of limelight
would be jolly.'

Jolly? This time I didn't look at Nico. Elizabeth was gazing
impassively at Rob over her coffee cup. She presumably had
a handle on all this, but she wasn't about to share.

'Upon what stage,' asked Nico, 'is this limelight likely to
be found?'

It struck me that his verbal manner and Rob's were
surprisingly similar.

'Performance poetry,' said Rob. He gave a nod of acknowledgement: 'Eh, Liz.'

So that's what he called her. Not the lover's Beth, nor the
fond paternal Lizzie, but sensible, grown-up Liz. Matey Liz.
Sexy Liz? I put it from my mind.

'This is all so fab!' Nico was rapidly closing on cloud nine. 'A whole family full of performers!'

'What?' Rob looked around the room and came back to me. 'Joss – don't tell me you're a sword-swallower.'

'No.' I laughed and shook my head.

'But she struts and frets in the public arena,' said Nico excitedly. 'She's a mayor, for God's sake!'

'You're not are you?'

'Yes.'

'Wow,' said Rob. 'I shall have to revise my view of mayors.'

'You see, they're not all stout aldermen with high complexions and soup-stained ties,' said Edward.

Rob raised his beer to his lips but kept his eyes on me round the tilted bottle.

'I'll say.'

His throat moved slightly as he swallowed. He wiped his mouth with the heel of his hand.

'Anyway –' I signalled time out – 'this isn't about me. So, have you been slamming tonight?'

'I wish. I've been on the A and E rat run since six.'

'RTA?' asked Edward, with a knowledgeable air.

Rob took another swig. 'Coach and a container lorry on the West Way. Not as bad as it sounds, not much more than a shunt really, but the coach was full of OAPs on their way to *Mary Poppins*. Lots of shock and cuts and bruises, and traffic chaos, of course – hope your route doesn't take you back that way.'

We assured him that it didn't, and Nico couldn't resist adding, 'I hate to say this, but your day job must provide first-class copy.'

'Inspiration, Dad.' Elizabeth had been pretty quiet till now. 'Not copy.'

'Whatever.'

'I suppose,' said Rob. 'But I'm not really a chronicler of events.'

'No, no, but your own reactions to them, presumably? Your feelings?' persisted Nico. He could be incorrigible sometimes, but because he meant no harm people perceived none. Whereas I, who walked a tightrope of tact could put one foot wrong and suffer a catastrophic fall from grace.

'Fair point,' said Rob.

'Have you eaten?' asked Elizabeth. 'Because if you haven't, you'd be doing us a favour.'

'No, you're all right.' It was one of those inside-out modern usages which might have annoyed me, but didn't.

'We'll be having it for breakfast, else.'

'If you put it like that . . . How about a doggy bag?'

'Coming up.'

She went out once more into the kitchen. No one made the smallest objection and I sensed a general acceptance that she was happier with something to do. There was a tiny hiatus, punctuated by clinking plates and rustling tinfoil.

To fill it, I glanced at my watch and said: 'Well, Nico, perhaps we should think about hitting the road . . .'

'But you can't,' said Rob. 'I only just got here.'

'You did,' I agreed, 'but we've been here for hours.'

'Steady on, Joss, you make it sound like some hideous trial!' This was Nico. Everyone seemed determined to either interrupt or traduce me.

'And,' I persisted, 'it's been absolutely lovely, but we have a long drive and things to do in the morning.'

I pushed my chair back as I said this, and stood up. Nico was an appallingly bad leaver and it wasn't unknown for me to be standing by the car, minus the key, while he hadn't made it past the hall and was still in there, enthusiastically enquiring about the provenance of the hosts' Victorian watercolours.

Elizabeth returned with a package which she put in front of Rob. Edward stood up slowly, with a show of reluctance. Nico also pushed his chair back, but both he and Rob remained seated, looking up at me.

'That is a beautiful necklace,' said Rob.

'Thanks.' I touched it, and left my hand there.

'It's absolutely great on you.'

'Nico gave it to me.'

'Did I?' said Nico. 'Remind me.'

'In Siena.'

'Oh, yes . . .' He peered. 'It is nice, isn't it? Good for me.'

This got a laugh and I was able to say 'Come on,' with a teasing grumpiness, and proceed into the hall. Everyone else followed, Rob last, leaning in the doorway, a little pocket of watchful silence with his bottle of beer, while we said our thank-yous and goodbyes.

Edward opened the front door and I raised a hand and waved over the heads of the others.

'Bye, Rob – lovely to meet you.'

He lifted the bottle and dipped his head briefly, saying something I couldn't hear, but which looked like: 'See you.'

Going down the stairs I'd been momentarily swept by a wave of confused emotion, sweet and sad – the warm, premonitory breath of things to come.

Nico moved suddenly, rubbing his face and smacking his lips in his sleep, and my skin prickled with a thrill of shame and shock. I laid a tentative hand on his shoulder, testing; I wasn't sure what for, but the results were anyway inconclusive. My husband was miles away.

My friend Georgia, Lady Clarebourne, came as my escort to the opening of the exhibition of local artists. Nico was unavailable for daytime events and didn't much care for exhibitions, whereas Georgia was a devotee of the visual arts and for some reason considered it an honour and a privilege to assist me with my mayoral duties.

She looked, if anything, more mayoral than me, being fabulously posh, tall and soignée, with a cut-glass bone structure and impeccable manners. Had she chosen to go into politics instead of marrying one of the richest men in the county and bearing handsome sons who were on Christian-name terms with minor royals, she would have been God's gift to the Tories. But she was coolly disdainful of all politicians, considering them seedy and self-serving. Odd, then, that she regarded my appointment with such awe and admiration, as if I had never wheeled and dealed in the corridors of power, nor dirtied my hands with compromise in order to gain my objective. I tried to disabuse her, but nothing would shake her loyal partiality.

'You're an independent, Joss – a free spirit.'

'Yes, but that doesn't mean I don't have an agenda. That I don't want to get things done.'

'Naturally. And you're the woman I want to do them!'

When accompanying me, she always asked in advance what I was going to wear, in order, as she put it, 'not to clash'. That she invariably looked stunning wasn't her fault – she simply was not one of nature's second fiddles. For the local artists she was perfect, in a green long-skirted linen suit, green wedge-heeled sandals and a white scarf draped loosely, Arab-style, round her neck. Vintage Clarebourne: classic, with a bohemian twist.

After a late and largely sleepless night I had managed only a basic level of unimaginative smartness. One thing about my mayoral wardrobe, I could always lay my hands on three or four unexceptionable default items with my eyes shut.

'Thanks so much for this,' she said as we sat behind Reg en route to the city art gallery. 'I am such a lucky girl.'

'Not at all,' I said. 'And with a following wind we can have lunch afterwards. Hilary assures me I don't have to leave for the Lions draw till five.'

'The Lions . . .' Georgia assumed a wistful expression. 'That sounds fun. I don't suppose you need a right-hand woman for that, do you?'

I could have sworn I saw Reg's neck pink up; he loved Georgia. But I had to disappoint him.

'It really is just a case of standing on a platform at the rugby club for twenty minutes and taking six tickets out of a hat. I'd be telling a lie if I pretended I needed someone else there.'

'Of course, of course! Oh, well, it was worth a try, eh, Reg?'

'Definitely, m'lady.'

Like a furtive child passing notes in class I opened my bag and under the pretence of consulting my diary wrote a short note on one of the 'Next Year Planner' pages at the back:

But lunch is NON-NEGOTIABLE, I wrote. *I need to talk!*

In answer, without so much as looking at me, she laid her hand on mine.

'So, how was it, ma'am?' asked Reg. 'Good exhibition?'

'It was hugely enjoyable,' said Georgia. 'There's a great deal of undiscovered talent in this town.'

'Lady Clarebourne is being polite as usual,' I said. 'There were an awful lot of pet portraits and lifeless still lifes.'

Reg pulled a face in the mirror. 'Oh dear.'

'That's most unfair.' Georgia laughed in spite of herself. 'Neither you nor I could have done half as well. I don't know about Reg.'

He shook his head. 'Useless at art. Couldn't draw a house even now.'

'Anyway,' I said, 'none of us is pretending to be an artist.'

'True,' said Georgia, adding gently, for form's sake: 'And a good thing too.'

We returned to the town hall and I got out of my regalia and assured Hilary I'd be back in time for tea and nose-powdering by four.

'She's such a treasure,' said Georgia, as we headed for the Sumatra Spice. 'The way she looks after you. Like the wife every woman could do with.'

We ordered chicken satay, vegetables with lemon grass and coconut milk, and Singapore noodles to accompany our white wine. Georgia and I were not among those women who regarded food as the enemy, rather as a well-loved but overenthusiastic friend whose company we enjoyed in moderation. The Sumatra Spice was a favourite of hours and we didn't allow my need to talk to stop us eating heartily.

All the same, Georgia spoke very little for the first three-quarters of an hour and was sitting back behind her empty plate while I was still twiddling noodles.

When she eventually spoke it wasn't wholly encouraging. 'It's hard to know what to say.'

From anyone else, this would have been the preamble to an exhaustive, and very probably exhausting, analysis of the situation to hand. But Georgia was nothing if not straight.

'Please try,' I said, adding cravenly: 'This is my treat by the way.'

She raised an eyebrow. 'Joss – you're surely not trying to buy my good opinion?'

'Of course not.'

'On the other hand,' she mused, keeping her eyes on me while tapping the rim of her glass against her chin, 'what is it you want me to say?'

'Something comforting?'

'Have you mentioned any of this to Nico?'

'Of course not,' I muttered.

'Mind you, I say "any of this", but it's not really anything, is it? All you're saying is that you've experienced a coup de foudre . . .'

'All?'

'It can happen to anyone, at any time. And it's all in your head at the moment. You have nothing to be ashamed of.'

Oddly, this wasn't what I wanted to hear. 'No?'

'Listen, Joss.' She leaned forward, managing to look both sympathetic and commanding, and simultaneously motion to the waiter. 'Don't wilfully misunderstand me. You know what I meant. "There's nothing half so bad as wanting makes it' – did I get that right? Something along those lines . . . All I'm saying is that in the eyes of the world, or more to the point of those who were there, nothing happened. So you don't need to put on a hair shirt quite yet.'

I shook my head.

We declined coffee and took delivery of more wine. Georgia didn't touch hers. Half-heartedly I reminded myself of the Lions' draw and the consequent imperative to be upright and fully-functioning at 5 p.m., but at that precise moment the rugby club seemed as remote and inaccessible as the dark side of the moon.

Georgia stared off to one side, presenting me with her perfectly chiselled, patrician profile.

'How old again?'

'Twenty-three? Maybe twenty-four?'

'Twenty-three . . . Giles is twenty-eight. Simon's twenty-five.'

'Yes, yes, I know, I know!'

'Joss, that absolutely was not a dig. I was simply trying to put things in context.'

'Context? My God, Georgia, my daughter is his stepmother!'

'So that makes you his step-grandmother.'

'Don't.' I dropped my head in my hands. 'Don't!'

'I'm just rehearsing the facts as known.'

'What on earth am I going to do?'

'Nothing, of course.' She sounded quite shocked. 'However uncomfortable it is now, it will burn itself out, you know that. Give it time. Distance and time.'

I couldn't meet her eye. After all she was only saying what we had all said to our offspring when their hearts had been given a mauling, and for which we'd received precious little thanks and occasional abuse. Though I would never have dreamed of abusing Georgia, she could tell that her advice provoked much the same scornfully incredulous response.

'I realize,' she said, 'that's not what you want to hear, but that's because it's true.'

It was, but now I realized why the young were so scornful. For one thing, I wasn't looking for a cure; and for another, I had an awful feeling that distance and time would only exacerbate my symptoms.

Before we parted company outside City Hall, she said: 'I'll tell you one thing, though. Most women – most people – go through their whole lives without experiencing this intensity of feeling.'

'I don't know . . .' I felt a sharp, unwelcome scrape of disloyalty. 'I did, I'm sure I did, with Nico.'

'Really?' There was a note of genuine curiosity in her voice. 'Did you not, with Julian?'

'I must have done, mustn't I? Anyway –' she put her cheek to mine, one side, then the other – 'it is something to be treasured.'

As she walked away I entertained a picture of our respective husbands: Julian, Lord Clarebourne, doubtless sitting, bored witless, on some magistrate's bench at this moment or chain-smoking his way over the Clarebourne acres in his four-by-four; and Nico in his chaotic office at the theatre, surrounded by Dickensian piles of paper and books, in the middle of which the screen saver of 'team Carbury' (his inapposite name for me and the children) beamed brightly from the PC . . . Good men, both of them, loyal, loving and true; and in Nico's case so much more than that – the man who had always been able to save me from myself, but who in these circumstances would not – could not – be given the opportunity.

And whatever I thought, or told myself, about Nico, he seemed distant, insubstantial; almost (whisper it, and oh, how I hated myself!) a distraction that I pushed aside, so that my mind's eye could feast on that bright, focused, young face, the brown eyes that seemed to take note of – and appreciate – everything about me, the voice with its modern, estuarine edge that was directed right into my ear and mine alone . . . Over and over I ran the tape, again and again I told myself I had not imagined it. More and more I became convinced that something had happened, and not only to me.

* * *

Or had it? Was I the archetypal sad elderly party entertaining ridiculous fantasies? I didn't even have recourse to the catch-all excuse 'menopausal'; I was long past that. My doctor – who for some reason did not, with hindsight, seem quite so appallingly youthful – had taken me off HRT a couple of years ago because, in his words, 'it's done all the good it's going to'.

So that was that, then; it was official. The hormones had had their last hurrah and the oestrogen was officially coasting downhill towards oblivion. Any fun Nico and I were still enjoying was down to our own inventiveness and some residual afterglow, the ghostly psychosomatic activity of an amputated organ.

But no matter how often I told myself that we were getting old, I didn't quite believe it. In my mind 'the old' were a race apart, as strange and distant as the Iceni. We and our contemporaries were vibrant, happening adults in our prime, subject from time to time to the inconvenient effects of ageing. There were, of course, the official communications from Planet Old – the pension, the railcard, the winter fuel allowance, the free prescriptions – practical reminders that we had indeed reached some kind of milestone, but we still felt, like Nico with airport security, that the rest of the world must be as amused and incredulous as we were. Why wouldn't we? It was in our interests to keep the ranks closed and maintain the communal denial. We could sit round and discuss arthritis and memory black holes, but only because it was all so droll, as if our generation, and we in particular, were the first to have ex-perienced them.

Out there, though, it was different. Every so often, like an unwelcome reflection in a shop window, I saw myself as others saw me and realized that nothing changes. Or everything does.

It happened once in a shoe shop, one of those with an improbable name like 'Pink' or 'Echelon' . . . a place where you'd look a long time before you found a comfy brogue. Hilary would have had a fit, but these were my pre-mayor days. I was looking for something to wear to Denise's birthday party. The invitation stipulated *Dress: Drop Dead!* and in the shoes I was trying on, I very probably would. I said as much to the nice girl who was serving me, as I teetered before the tilted half-mirror in a pair of exiguous diamanté tart's heels.

'But it'll be worth it, don't you think?' I enquired semi-rhetorically, posing this way and that, with my Gap cords hoisted up round my knees like some misguided Blackpool paddler. 'I mean, if she says Drop Dead, she means go for it, right?'

'Absolutely,' said the girl.

'She is one of those people,' I went on, 'who was born to party. I know for a fact that she'll look simply amazing, so I need to keep my end up . . . The dress I'm wearing is a plain silver shift. I've had it for ages, but I haven't been able to get into it for a couple of years. Now I can, so what the hell? But it does need wicked shoes . . . which these most certainly are. I wonder about dancing . . . Do you have those special pads to stick inside?'

She shook her head. 'You can get those in Boots.'

'In Boots, right.' I chuckled at the weak pun and she gave me a faint, baffled smile.

'It's so hard to tell in these,' I said, yanking at the cords. 'Why is one never wearing the right clothes on these occasions?' She didn't answer, but I needed no encouragement. Buoyant on a retail-roll of Big Sur proportions, I crashed on: 'Go on, you twisted my arm, I'll take them, and if I break a leg on the dance floor you'll be hearing from my lawyer.'

'Oh, no . . .'

I sat down, and bent to undo the minuscule sparkly buckle on my right ankle, and it was then that I caught the look that passed between the girl and her colleague at the till; the merest, fleeting, wordless exchange, but it spoke volumes.

'Jesus, another wrinkly telling us the story of her life, what does she think this is, a shoe shop or a counselling service?'

At that moment, like a rookie surfer, I lost my balance, fell off the wave, and plunged into a welter of private embarrassment. My face was on fire and I couldn't look at the girl as I passed her the shoes and slipped on my Hush Puppies. Fool! Idiot! Stupid, stupid cow! How many times had I stood behind women – they were invariably women, and of a certain age – in queues, who insisted on using a simple commercial exchange as a chatfest; who told the checkout girl the story of their lives; who explained to the butcher that they needed an extra-big joint because their son, daughter-in-law and two grandchildren were staying the weekend, but on the other hand she was a vegetarian, so maybe a bit smaller than that would probably do; who believed, in the face of all the evidence, that the shop assistant would appreciate an exhaustive account of the events leading up to this purchase; who thought the act of paying for goods could be some sort of micro-friendship.

'Bye for now,' said the girl, in her practised, ding-dong, customer-relations voice. 'Enjoy the party.'

I paid and fled. 'For now'? Was she insane? If I ever entered her shop again it would be too soon. The giant, shiny carrier that would normally have given me such a glow of pleasure was like the mark of Cain, it might as well have had 'Sad Old Bag' scrawled in day-glow capitals across its glossy flank.

And where was it written that most women en route to second childhood turn into their mothers? I had adored my mother – now gone to a better place where she understood the principles behind the central-heating thermostat, where the waiters were as decorously flirtatious as those she remembered from between the wars, and people really knew how to enjoy themselves – but there was something unsettling about her genetic inheritance. The face I made when I looked in the mirror, my abstracted little gestures with cutlery when I first sat down at the table, my hatred of windy weather, the way my eyebrows grew, my instant, sentimental response to music in the street, my preternatural ability to retain the lyrics of show tunes – a hundred verbal mannerisms and behavioural tics over which I had no control were hard-wired in my DNA as they had been in hers. Struggle as we might for autonomy and freedom it seemed Mother Nature had the female line in a grip of steel.

The turning-into-one's-parent syndrome did not as far as I could see present in men to anything like the same extent. When I raised the topic with Nico, he said: 'What, Dad? God forbid.'

'Would it be so terrible?' I asked. 'You loved Gerry.'

'Oh, devoted. He was wonderful in his crusty, bigoted, philistine way.'

'Steady on. What about the charm, the wit – the looks?'

'True.' He beamed. 'I inherited all those.'

Late that evening when I was back from the Lions, and in my dressing gown, Georgia rang.

'I thought I'd see how you were doing.'

'Hang on . . .'

In response to Nico's enquiring look I put my hand over the phone and mouthed her name, adopting the slightly martyred air of someone who was going to have do some serious listening. He was watching one of the nation's favourite DBEs casting her bedroom eyes over a murder victim, and fluttered his fingers as I left the room. In the kitchen I pushed the door to and sat down at the table.

'OK.'

'It's an awful time to ring, have I disturbed something?'

'We were watching telly. Or Nico was.'

'Yes, Julian's glued to that, too. I swear if there was an election he'd vote for her even if she was standing for, I don't know, breastfeeding in pubs or something.'

'They all would.'

'But you are genuinely all right, are you, Joss?'

'Yes.'

'I hope I wasn't too stern.'

'You were saying what had to be said. I know that.'

'I'd be a poor sort of friend if I didn't remind you of one or two salient factors in all this.'

I couldn't speak. Suddenly and unexpectedly, I welled up. My heart went into spasm, and the tears sprang to my eyes.

'Joss?'

'Mm . . .' I croaked, brokenly.

'Oh God, Joss – I do wish I was there!'

'I feel such a fool . . .' The effort of sobbing quietly made my nose run more freely than usual and I availed myself of a piece of kitchen towel. 'Hang on . . .'

Georgia waited patiently while I blew, sniffed and mopped, and then said: 'You really are on the rack, aren't you?'

'Yup. I really, really am.'

'I'm so sorry. I feel so helpless.'

'And the more painful it is, the sillier I feel.'

'There's nothing silly about it.'

'Georgia.' The sudden silence from the drawing room alerted me. 'I've got to go.'

'Go. See you soon.'

'Bye.'

When Nico came in he found me loading the dishwasher.

'Who did it?' I asked, clattering busily with my back to him.

'No idea, the whole of the Manchester sex industry is either a potential suspect or a potential victim and there are two more episodes to go, of which I shall miss the second anyway, so it was all a bit pointless. But there's nothing like a dame, and la Waring was as compelling as ever.'

'Good.' I rummaged under the sink for dishwasher tablets, but I could feel him watching me. Or more specifically my bottom.

'Right then,' he said. 'Think I'll hit the hay.'

'Yes, you do that.' I picked cack-handedly at the tablet wrapper. 'I just want to sort out a couple of things for tomorrow and I'll be up.'

'Fine.' I closed the machine and he came and put his arms round me, resting his chin on my shoulder. 'Don't be too long.'

He made a yawning motion, digging his chin into my shoulder; this usually tickled, but not tonight. 'What's in the diary for tomorrow, yer worship?'

'The Literary Lunch.'

'Good, you enjoy those . . .'

We stood there in silence for a moment, me wrapped in Nico's arms, my finger on the 'start' button. His cheek was against mine and he must have felt something, because he kissed me and said: 'What's up?'

'Nothing.'

'"Nothing shall come of nothing". Come on, tell me.'

I could have. I should have. If I'd spat it out then and there it would have become smaller, I'd have been aligning myself with him instead of with what currently filled my head and heart. I could have cried properly, been understood, comforted . . . we might even have come to laugh about it in time. But information hates company. I wanted to keep it all to myself, to suffer in secret, to let my feelings flourish in a private hothouse.

I said: 'I suppose I'm still thinking about Elizabeth.'

Nico, relieved, released me and ran himself a glass of water. 'There's nothing to worry about. She's in clover. You saw.'

I pressed the button. 'I never said it was rational.'

He leaned on the sink, holding the glass against his chest. 'Perhaps you miss her.'

'But she wasn't here before.'

'No, but she's moved on.'

He was offering me a way out and I took it. 'You're probably right.'

'It's all good,' declared Nico, adding, as he headed for the door: 'And if the lad's anything to go by the grown-up children aren't going to give her any grief.'

I went to the spare bedroom to select and put out clothes for the Literary Lunch, a process that had long since lost its power to charm. It was mostly a case of remembering who had seen you wear what on a previous occasion, and there was always a delicate line to tread between being a well-turned-out mayor and one who used her position as a shopping opportunity. It took me less than two minutes to settle on a pink and grey suit with a peplum jacket and a Jackie-Kennedy pink straw pillbox. I completed the ensemble with tried and trusted navy courts which tonight I found utterly dispiriting. I glared at them with pure hatred for their sensible, inoffensive comfiness. In a thoroughly unwelcome out-of-body experience I compared my last night's persona – the real me, I told myself, to whom Rob had so charmingly responded – with the one I'd be obliged to assume tomorrow. Then, I'd been casual and European in a terracotta linen skirt and a black cotton shirt; Nico's necklace, beaded sandals, relaxed and unfussy. Tomorrow's smart ensemble, especially those bloody awful shoes, was nothing more than a uniform.

Nico was reading when I went into the bedroom. As I moved to my underwear drawer and opened it, he said, without looking up: 'Along with everything else, this bloke was a spanker.'

'Really?' I took out clean, matching undies, and Lite-Legs for the next day.

'And a spankee. His main spanking companion was Francesca Jameson, remember her?'

I laid them on the chair. 'Actually no.'

'Yes, you do. She wrote that tome about Lady Jane Grey. Hang on, there's a picture . . .' He riffled back a few pages and held up the book facing me.

'Oh,' I said, glancing abstractedly. 'Maybe.'

Nico tapped the photograph. 'She was the uber-totty of the time. Posh, fanciable but glacial was how she came across

– a bit of a challenge. Not so, according to this. Couldn't
wait to be put across his knee and given a good seeing-to
with the Mason Pearson.'

He chuckled happily. Normally, I would have too; we'd
have looked at more pictures, he'd have read out selected salacious passages and events would have taken their course;
tonight his cheerful relish filled me with dread.

'I'll be back in a tick,' I said. I heard him say 'Where –?'
but I was gone.

Down in the kitchen I found Elizabeth's envelope and took
out the photographs. The one of her and Edward, I replaced.
The other one, still bearing, like tear-stains, the marks of spilt
tea, I held in both hands, and gazed at until my eyes were
sore.

When I returned to the bedroom Nico had fallen asleep on
his book, his glasses skewed and his mouth open. Not wanting
to wake him, I turned off the lamp, undressed in the dark,
and scarcely disturbed the duvet as I slipped into bed.

The next morning I got up early and went for an hour's
run over my most punishing circuit, the one that took in
several steep gradients and the path across the centre of
Sebastopol Gardens, the most exposed area in the city. Over
recent months I'd not been such a regular runner, but the
Well Woman 10K Challenge loomed, and my pride wasn't
going to let me disgrace myself. This morning I was also
calling on the psychological benefits of the exercise. The
steady thump of my feet on the tarmac, the slow pump of
my heart and lungs as they adjusted to the pace, the swing
of my arms, the fresh air on my face – all helped to ease
tension and restore perspective. I had begun running twenty
years ago as an antidote to the blues, and it was still my
most reliable short-term fix.

Sebastopol Gardens may have been bleak, but it afforded
an unrivalled view of the city. On the far side, before the
descent, I allowed myself a short breather. The patterns of
streets, crescents, parades and terraces were like the whorls
on a seashell, and in spite of new development – some of it
horrible, some very fine – the cathedral held its own, its massive
cruciform shape and gothic spire a tribute to past faith.

Having restored the bigger picture, I set out on the homeward stretch and was reminded, as always, that running downhill was a lot harder on the legs than going up.

At eleven I was standing in the kitchen having a coffee while waiting for Reg to arrive, when the doorbell rang. Walking through to the hall, my calves complained.

'Mrs Carbury?'

'That's me . . . oh!'

I took the flowers, and the woman smiled at me.

'Nice surprise on a grey morning.'

'Yes.'

'Enjoy. Bye now.'

'Bye.'

I closed the door and stood there in the hall, looking down at the white and pink bouquet nestling in its cellophane frill. There was a card stuck in the middle on one of those little plastic forks. In the kitchen I removed the card and put it on the table before snipping off the cellophane and tangle of decorative paper ribbon and pushing them into the bin. The half dozen blooms and their attendant stiff, greyish greenery I stood in water in the sink. Then I sat down at the table and took the card out of its envelope.

Nice to meet you. Rob x

A heart can leap – I can testify to that.

Nice to meet you. Rob x

I peered again. It wasn't his writing, I reminded myself, in fact it was probably that of the woman who'd just come to the door – but it was his thought, his impulse, and his hard-earned money rashly laid out to give me this moment of over-whelming, shocked, blushing delight.

Nice to meet you. Rob x

Something *had* happened.

'Flowers!' said Nico. 'A secret admirer?'

'One of them,' I said, airily.

'He's a bit of a skinflint.'

'The library staff aren't made of money.'

'In that case,' said Nico, 'it was very decent of them. And you deserve it.'

Seven

If Georgia's was the voice of conscience, then Denise's was that of license. There's none more evangelical than the born-again, and Denise was a born-again sensualist. Throughout her marriage to the increasingly wayward and goatish Larry she had retained an air of banked-up fires, and the retired DI had applied the bellows with a vengeance.

Because life had become so hectic and because, unlike Georgia, she was not escort material, I had seen very little of Denise since becoming mayor, but now I desperately wanted to talk to her.

The best that we could shoehorn into my schedule was tea in a city centre hotel that provided a wincingly genteel background for Denise's plunging T-shirt and ankle bracelet. She cast a wry look around the place.

'Boy . . . Slaves to pleasure, us.'

'I'm sorry.'

'Go on then, babe.' She spooned sugar into her tea. 'Make it worth my while.'

Ten minutes later she pushed her cold tea aside and ordered a glass of wine.

'So – forgive me – but what exactly is the problem?'

'It's not exactly a problem . . .'

'Too right it's not.'

'But – for one thing we're sort of related . . .'

'That provides useful camouflage.'

'For what?' I asked, alarmed.

'For his passionate admiration, stupid.' She shook her head. 'Honestly.'

'And for another I feel guilty.'

'You're not guilty of anything!' Denise's voice rose, then dropped again. 'What are you guilty of?'

'Liking it?'

'That's allowed.'

'And then there's Nico.'

'Ah, yes.' Denise sighed. 'The lovely Nico. Does he know?'

It was no coincidence that both she and Georgia had asked this same question though from diametrically different perspectives.

'No.'

'Quite right. What he doesn't know won't hurt him, and the secrecy's half the fun. I assume.' She looked at me for confirmation.

'I don't know if I'd call it fun.'

'Pleasure? Thrill?'

'Denise – I'm not going to do anything.'

She shrugged. 'Even if you are, you're not answerable to me.'

'But I'm not. Honestly.'

'All the more reason to lap it up, then. Am I allowed to smoke?'

'No!'

She closed her bag. 'Joss, why did you tell me about this?'

'I wanted your opinion.'

'Did you? Did you really?'

'Yes!'

'Well, I've given it to you for what it's worth. Take it or leave it. But don't argue with me, I've got no beef. Any argument you've got is with yourself.'

'You're right,' I said. 'And anyway, I know it's trivial.'

'You don't think that, you just think you should. And anyway, if you do want it to be trivial, you know what to do.'

'What?'

'Tell Nico.' She picked up her glass. 'Cheers!'

The days went by. The flowers drooped and died. And I didn't tell him.

One mayoral undertaking for which it was impossible to enlist an escort was the Well Woman Run. Denise was quite simply out of the question; there was only room for one fitness fanatic in her house and the position was filled by the DI. Even if Nico's gender hadn't rendered him ineligible he regarded running on anything but a need-to basis as dangerous lunacy.

As for Georgia, it was against everything she held dear to exercise in public.

'I'm sorry, Joss, but I'd rather die,' she said the year before, when I'd enlisted as a civilian. 'I think it's absolutely heroic of you all, but count me out.'

Easy for Georgia to say, who was one of nature's thoroughbreds, tall and leggy. For me, jogging was what enabled me to keep in shape while cooking and eating the sort of meals that Nico and I liked.

On this as on most issues the council chamber was divided, but not necessarily along party lines. One half considered it was quite enough to have a lady mayor who was an independent without her making an exhibition of herself in shorts over 10Ks; the other half took the view that it was thoroughly sporting, in both senses of the word, and showed the sort of energy and enterprise that could only be beneficial to the public perception of City Hall.

My participation in the run meant that Peter Carroll had to take my place on the official starter's dais and say a few brief and appropriate words about – on this occasion – proposed improvements to the county's breast-cancer screening programme. The firing of the starting gun traditionally fell to whichever relatively clean-living and coherent celebrity the organizers had been able to get hold of. This year's was considered something of a coup – the children's TV presenter Donna Delaney, she of the amusing hair, exposed navel and figure guaranteed to engender early-onset puberty in her younger male viewers and ensure that *Wicked!* was a firm favourite with fathers throughout the land.

Needless to say, Peter was only too delighted to be doing the honours.

'Should I mention that you're taking part?' he asked earnestly, keen to give an impression of seriousness.

'Absolutely not,' I replied.

'Well – whatever you say. Just so long as you know we all consider it a bloody good effort.'

Hilary took a strictly practical line. 'I hope you've got the right shoes.'

'Hilary – I run three times a week.'

'That's not an answer.'

'Yes, I have the right shoes. I paid the GNP of a small

third-world country for them in SportZone, they've got moulded soles, gel inserts and go-faster lines, in fact they do just about everything but run the race for you.'

'I'm very glad to hear it,' said Hilary, like an adult talking to an overexcited child, 'because you've got the flower show on Monday.'

'Yes,' I said, having forgotten. 'I hadn't forgotten.'

Various people called on the Saturday night to wish me well. The first was our daughter-in-law Cathryn, who announced herself and then put the children on the line in turn.

'Good luck, Gran,' said Chloe. 'Did you get our card?'

'I expect it'll arrive on Monday.'

There were muffled cries of 'She didn't . . .!' and 'You said . . .!' before Chloe returned. 'It's well funny, we spent ages choosing it.'

'I'll look forward to that.'

Jed was, as usual, more laconic. 'Don't get too excited, it's not that hilarious.'

'I shall like it anyway.'

'Gran being tactful as usual.'

'Gran being honest.'

'Hope it goes OK.'

'It will. It's not very far.'

'Bye.'

Cathryn came on again, saying in a lowered voice and through gritted teeth: 'Chloe wants my head on a plate for not sending that card in time.'

'I told them not to worry.'

'You know what she is, your granddaughter . . .' The voice dropped to a whisper. 'Anal's not in it.'

'She'll be prime minister.'

'Hm. Look, we were originally intending to come up, bring a picnic, cheer from the sidelines, but I'm afraid we've been lured elsewhere.'

'Good,' I said. 'It would have been lovely to see you all, but I can't believe watching a thousand women panting round the streets is the kids' idea of a good time.'

'We wouldn't have been watching a thousand, just you,' said Cathryn loyally. She was a sweetie; whenever I spoke to her the scab that had formed over the wound of Hal's

departure cracked, and bled a bit. Also, though she was punc-
tilious about never bad-mouthing our son to us, or never in
our hearing anyway, it was impossible not to feel some guilt
by association. Was there something in his upbringing we
could have done, or not done, that might have altered his
behaviour? But Cathryn had the grace and sense to recognize how much we loved him (as, to be fair, she had done)
and there was never the slightest taint of accusation.

'Anyway,' she went on, 'let's meet up soon on a day when
you're not going for gold and we can all relax and catch up.
The children were only just saying they haven't seen you and
Oompa for ages.'

'We must,' I said. 'This year is ridiculous, but we must
make time.'

There was a little pause, then she said: 'Very good news
about Elizabeth.'

'Isn't it? A bit of a surprise, but he's so nice.'

'We look forward to meeting him.'

I sensed a minute froideur. 'You will. We'll organize something.'

'Give her our love. I have to go. Enjoy the run!'

'I'll do my best.'

'That,' she said, 'goes without saying.'

Next on was Elizabeth.

'You haven't asked us for sponsorship,' she said in her blunt
way.

'No, well, it's not fair on one's family to be endlessly—'

'But Edward's only just joined and he's a great believer in
Well Women. Aren't you?'

'I am!' called Edward in the background.

'So,' Elizabeth went on, 'we'll give you a hundred.'

'Darling, that's so generous.'

'If you finish.'

'If?' I protested. 'If?'

'Calm down, I know you will.'

'Thank you.'

'You and Dad OK?'

'Yes, yes, we're fine. And you? How is everyone?' Given
this opportunity I crashed on. 'It was so nice to meet Rob.'

'He's not bad, is he?' I heard her turn slightly away. 'We're
discussing your son.'

'Unfocused!' called Edward. 'Underachieving!'

'Hear that?'

I could, though there was a ringing in my ears. 'At least if he's underachieving he's doing it with something worthwhile,' I said.

'You should meet his sister,' said Elizabeth. I couldn't quite get the weight of this cryptic comment, and so stuck to face value.

'We'd like that.'

I heard Edward say something, this time intended for Elizabeth's ears only.

'Oh, yes,' she turned from him to me. 'And by the way, I'm being reminded to tell you that you made quite an impression.'

'Sorry?' My skin prickled as the goose bumps rose across its surface in a kind of Mexican wave.

'On Rob. He thought you were rather good news.'

'Goodness . . .' I gave what I hoped was a warm, sophisticated, grown-up chuckle. 'In what way?'

But that was as much as I was going to get from Elizabeth. 'Take it from me,' she said. 'A parent knows. We'll write the cheque now. Good luck, have fun.'

Until the last couple of minutes I'd been thoroughly uncomfortable with this conversation, predicated as it was on my age and position in the family. Now, I was floating, soaring – I was not deluding myself! And now I had this precious nugget – 'good news' (I dispensed with the 'rather') – to squirrel away and examine at my leisure, like a miser with his gold.

'How was she?' enquired Nico, soporific from sharing my pre-run carbo-load of lasagne.

'She sounded very chipper,' I said. 'They're pledging a hundred.'

'Good lord, does Edward know?'

'He suggested it.'

'Splendid, I like him more and more.'

Nico stretched his arms above his head luxuriously. On impulse, one I didn't care to analyse, I leaned over and kissed him.

'Hey –' he tried ineffectually to grab me – 'that was nice.'

'Don't get your hopes up,' I said. 'I need my beauty sleep.'

'Good God, yes,' he agreed, swinging his legs down and yawning. 'Far be it from me to waste the energies of a finely honed athlete the night before a race. You carry on, I'll finish up down here.'

The last thing I heard before falling asleep was my husband declaiming 'Lepanto' as he plumped up the cushions downstairs.

The run took place on Sunday morning – bearing out the theory that sport, along with shopping and going to the dump, had replaced organized religion in the nation's life – and Nico had booked a late lunch at the Mason's Arms for us and the Clarebournes.

'Do you think,' he mused, 'that when we walk in it'll be like Sardi's in New York and everyone will rise to their feet and applaud wildly as you walk to your table?'

'No,' I said. 'And you can forget making an entrance. I shall probably be wearing bedroom slippers and leaning heavily on your arm.'

'What, no killer heels?'

We were carrying on as if everything was all right, but it wasn't. Alone, I was on a furtive, feverish high; in public, somewhat resentfully distracted; with Nico I was ragged with guilt and a kind of raging impatience which he didn't deserve.

As if to rebuke me, conditions for the run were not good. The sky over the cathedral was the colour of tarmac and a brisk, chilly rain blew into our faces as we foregathered. 'Climate change? What climate change?' we groused through chattering teeth.

The start and finish of the run was in Doubleday Park, named after the city's benefactor, the founder of Nico's theatre. The park was a notoriously exposed spot and I was glad to have made it into the fast-for-one's-age band, which meant beginning slightly nearer the front. Even so I kept my fleece on until the last minute. As one of the few regular runners on the council I'd been on the committee that had instigated the run ten years before and had been instrumental in the provision of plenty of portaloos and a team of tidiers to collect discarded clothing and return it to numbered tents for collection later. On the dais Peter and Donna were in animated conversation beneath a gold umbrella, he in a pristine Barbour, she, despite the rain, in the Kids TV uniform of pre-shrunk T-shirt, and jeans that just skimmed her well-waxed pubis.

'How to look good in the rain . . .' The woman next to me sighed. 'But only if you're that age and size.'

'I hope he doesn't bang on interminably,' said another, 'or we'll all seize up before we start.'

Fortunately – probably because he'd taken pity on poor underdressed Donna and wished to escort her gallantly to the coffee tent – Peter kept it short. Donna shouted 'Go, guys!' and flinched girlishly as she fired her pistol. We were off.

At least it stopped raining halfway round. I did creditably, but not as well as in previous years. Several members of the Townswomen's Guild, dressed as Orks, lumbered past me at the midway point, and only Nico's stentorian of 'Come on, yer worship!' from the doorway of the Cock and Bull put sufficient fire in my belly for me to regain my lead over them by the finish.

We had evolved a system; Nico would hurry back to the car park, collect the car and hover like a getaway driver, engine running and hazard lights on, near the entrance to the park. Today it was our intention to carry out the pick-up even more speedily than usual, so I'd be home in plenty of time to shower and change before lunch with the Clarebournes. But as I emerged from the property tent with my fleece there were Peter, Donna, and Cyril Dick, the photographer from the local paper, standing in a row with big silly grins on their faces.

'You're the proper mayor!' cried Donna, on being introduced. 'I can't believe that!'

'Can I get a picture?' asked Cyril. 'Deputy mayor, in the middle if you would.'

Even I could see that this configuration was a touch sexist, but Peter needed no second bidding and Donna and I obediently took up our positions on either side of him. Though I couldn't actually see Donna in her slightly damp T-shirt and her freshly applied make-up, simply knowing she was there, just the other side of Peter's perky paunch, was demoralizing. Heroine of the hour I might be, with two thousand pounds worth of sponsorship and a more than respectable time for my years, but I was not looking my best. My hair was lank and sweaty, my face bare and red and apart from the shoes my running kit had seen better days.

'Happy people, please,' instructed Cyril, 'say "sex"!' A few of the less jaded runners and their supporters had gathered behind him, mainly to admire Donna, so there was no chance he was going to take a snap and a spare and let us go. This was a big moment for him. Reminding myself that it took more muscles to frown than to smile, I grinned.

'Let's try something else,' he suggested. 'Madam Mayor, could you come into the middle now, and show the others your medal?'

About time too, I thought as we changed places and I tried to banish the picture of Nico drumming his fingers in the getaway car. Centre stage, I lifted the medal off my clammy midriff, assuming an expression of modest pride. But as I looked towards the camera I saw Rob, standing in the crowd, a few metres behind Cyril's left shoulder. He raised a hand and mouthed: 'Hi!'

'Attention, now, Madam Mayor. Lots of admiration, you two. Donna, lean forward a bit. Lovely.'

To my right, there appeared the deepening cleft of Donna's cleavage. To my left, not wanting to miss out on anything, Peter leaned forward too. I had rarely felt so uncomfortable.

'Fan-tastic.' Cyril clicked, and held up the camera for inspection. 'Want to see yourselves?'

'No, thank-you,' I said, but the other two took a look, laughing merrily, and Donna assured me that I looked 'amazing' and it was 'a really fun shot'.

'I'm so sorry, but I do have to go,' I said. 'Thank you so much, Donna, for giving up your time – it was lovely to meet you.'

'No, no, really – well done, you. And everyone – it was awesome.'

She was actually a very nice girl. Another reason why I wanted clear blue water between her and me as soon as possible.

'Bye then,' I said.

'Sure, sure, Jocelyn,' said Peter generously, 'you run along – a hot bath and a stiff drink, eh? Donna, you've been fabulous, can I offer you a spot of lunch courtesy of the City Fathers? There's a very nice little Italian in the square . . .'

Rob was approaching. Oh, fuckity-fuck, the unfairness of it! All I could do was adopt an I-have-given-my-all-to-my-public air of weary nobility, but that required greater and more subtle acting skills than I had at my disposal. At least he didn't give Donna a second glance, but came directly to my side, put a hand on my arm and deposited a soft, light kiss on my blotchy cheek.

'Hey – well done!'

'Hello, Rob . . .!' I allowed laughter and pardonable bafflement to account for my blushes. 'What on earth are you doing here?'

'Liz said this is where I'd find you.'

Why hadn't she warned me? Lots of people ran in full make-up. In normal circumstances I'd have spat upon such vanity, but this was different.

'But why . . .?' I babbled. 'What brought you up here in the first place?'

'Poetry gig at the Yard – know the Yard?'

'Indeed I do. Elizabeth used to go there.'

'That's right. She told me all about it so I thought I'd look you up.'

'Well . . .'

'Did you like the flowers?'

'They were absolutely – you shouldn't . . .'

'I've never sent flowers before. Grown-up or what.'

His eyes rested on me. I pulled my fleece over my head, but when my head popped through he was still looking at me.

'So what do you do now?' he asked. 'Celebrate?'

'Sort of . . .'

I was so flustered, so caught on the cusp of delight and panic, enchantment and despair, that I didn't notice Nico until he was more or less upon us.

'What's going on?'

'Oh – hi, darling.' Never could relief and disappointment have been so closely aligned.

'The rozzers will be thinking I'm a kerb-crawler . . .' A smile of recognition dawned. 'Hello – is it? Can it be . . .?'

Rob acknowledged that it was, adding rhetorically: 'How's it going?'

'My dear fellow!'

They shook hands and slapped arms in a manly way.

'Don't talk to her for too long.' Nico jerked a thumb in my direction. 'She only wants you for your money.'

'I was coming to that.' Rob took a handful of change from his pocket and held out two pounds. 'A bit sad, but every little helps.'

'Don't be silly,' I began, but Nico took the coins and slipped them into the bag round his neck.

'Who's being silly? His money's as good as the next man's. Appreciated.'

'Pleasure.'

'I have to whisk her away – we're going to have lunch . . .' I saw his eyes brighten and knew immediately what he was going to say. 'Hang on, how's this for an idea, why don't you join us?'

'Nico, for goodness' sake, Rob doesn't want . . .' I started to say, on a note of warm, humorous sophistication, which was completely wasted on both of them.

'Why ever not? He's got to eat.'

'Yes, but with us lot?'

'Actually,' said Rob, 'that'd be great. As long as you're quite sure I won't be intruding.'

'How could you do that?' cried Nico. 'You're family now.'

'No rush,' he said, when we got home. 'Table's not till one.'

No rush? It was twelve twenty, and the drive would take fifteen minutes, which meant I had just under half an hour to assemble a fresh, fragrant look, casual enough for a pub lunch with friends but sufficiently arresting to ensure I retained my 'good news' title.

While they had a beer in the kitchen, upstairs I did a fair impersonation of a headless chicken on acid. I must have tried on half a dozen different permutations of tops, trousers, skirts and belts before settling on a less-is-more ensemble of well-washed jeans and a white shirt. There still remained several thorny questions to be addressed. Tuck in or tie at the waist? Collar up or down? Sleeves rolled up, cuffs turned back, or buttoned? I opted for tied at the waist, collar up and cuffs turned back, added gold studs and white loafers, and flew downstairs, being sure to take the last few steps at an insouciant if slightly breathless stroll.

Rob favoured me with an admiring glance. 'You look great.'

'Doesn't she?' Nico put a proprietary arm round me. 'But then she usually does.'

'I'm beginning to see that.'

'Let's go,' I said, 'they'll be waiting.'

The Clarebournes, thank heavens, have perfect manners; 'gracious' would imply a touch of *de haut en bas*, a hint of patronage – but certainly graceful. They were sitting in the saloon bar with his-and-hers bits of the Sunday paper.

'Don't worry,' sang out Georgia, removing her reading specs as we approached. 'We told them we might be late, and why, and they're only too happy to hold the table. Mm . . .' She pressed her cheek to mine. 'How was it?'

'Fine.'

Nico claimed his own kiss. 'She's too modest. She was splendid, came storming in, in one and three-quarters.'

'Many, many congratulations!' said Julian, in whose hand a bottle of champagne had magically appeared. 'You are drinking, I take it?'

'Lovely, thank you.'

'And who's this . . .?' Georgia peered enquiringly at Rob, as if she hadn't guessed the moment we walked in.

'I'm so sorry, how rude of us, this is Rob – Edward's son – Elizabeth's stepson? Rob, these are our very old friends Lord and Lady Clarebourne. Georgia and Julian.'

I had to assume that Julian had been fully briefed, but I needn't have worried; a bloodline stretching back to William the Conqueror was more than up to the occasion.

'Excellent, how do you do? Were you there to witness this triumph?' asked Julian, shaking, then pouring. As they did so Georgia caught the waiter's eye and made a minuscule gesture in Rob's direction to ensure another place was set, before turning back.

'What a nice surprise.' She covered his hand briefly with her own, smiling brilliantly. The whole warm, sophisticated older-woman shtick came quite naturally to her, and she was looking the part too, in a bouclé tweed pencil skirt and fine grey cashmere cardigan with the Clarebourne pearls. 'Welcome, Rob.'

'I hope you don't mind,' he said. 'Nico was very insistent.'

'Of course he was! And of course we don't mind, far from it. Sit, sit, everyone, and, Joss, tell us properly how it went.'

'There's really not much to tell,' I said.

'A personal best?' asked Julian.

'I wish. A whisker slower than last year.'

'Nevertheless, you look delicious, if I may say so. Not a bit like a woman who's just run ten miles.'

'Ten kilometres,' I corrected him.

'OK, never mind, still a hell of a lot more than the rest of us could have managed.'

'Except possibly Rob,' pointed out Georgia. I wished I'd said that.

He held up his hands. 'You're joking. I couldn't run all that way. Isn't it horribly boring?'

'Certainly not,' I said, 'because you go on to autopilot, think your thoughts, and dream your dreams.'

The men exchanged a glance. 'She makes it sound positively enticing,' said Nico.

'And then there's the audience,' I said, turning to Rob. 'The roar of the crowd – something you could relate to.'

'That would be my main problem, though,' said Georgia. 'Being watched by all those people.'

I was conscious of a see-saw moment, of which Rob was the conversational axis. To my intense relief and gratification he came down on my side.

'No, I'm with Joss. I can just imagine coming round that final bend, or the home straight or whatever – that must be wicked.'

'There speaks a natural exhibitionist,' said Nico.

Julian raised an eyebrow. 'Something you'd know nothing about, of course.'

'*Moi?* I'm wounded.'

'But tell me, Rob,' said Georgia, 'what is this relationship you have with audiences?'

At lunch I sat between Rob and Julian, but they had moved us to a round table that would have seated six comfortably, so we weren't too close. I knew that in spite of appearances – she was the most socially adept person I knew – Georgia was watching and assessing us.

Rob was utterly charming. In response to questions about himself he struck the right note of self-deprecation and youthful passion, but he was also a brilliant listener, paying the compliment of his full attention to whoever was speaking, and managing to be present, and interested, even when silent for quite long periods; 'active listening', I'd read about it. I'd been a little worried about the impression Julian would make; not, I'm afraid, because I cared about Julian, who was well able to look after himself, but for how it might reflect on me. Nico's and my liberal credentials were impeccable, but Julian was a card-carrying, cheque-writing Tory, who affected a style of dress referred to by Nico as 'country cad'. Today this comprised a shirt of broad blue and white stripes teamed with an MCC tie, mustard-coloured trousers and brown brogues with elaborate punching and tasselled laces like something out of a P.G. Wodehouse golf game. The whole thing screamed Posh and Proud. Julian was snobby enough to have loathed Mrs Thatcher, which was something in his favour, but this was not a fact that was likely to emerge over lunch. He was ruddy-faced, his bristly-hair sported a parting straight and true as a Roman road, and his weight, in consequence of a fearsomely active lifestyle, had remained the same for over thirty years. In almost every way he was the polar opposite of Nico, which was probably why they got on, though their friendship was secondary to that of mine with Georgia.

We had once been on holiday to Scotland with the Clarebournes, but it was not a mistake we were likely to repeat. Georgia and I had similar biorhythms and body clocks and hit our combined stride immediately, but the same could not be said of our respective husbands. On holiday Nico liked nothing better than to rise late, lunch simply and well, snooze, read and dine at length and vivaciously. These were the prerequisites, over and above which little was required but a soupçon of history, a smattering of culture and a modest amount of walking (for the purpose of working up an appetite). Julian, unfortunately, did not know the meaning of relaxation and was a stranger to culture. In spite of living in a house with more books, antiques and art treasures than most people saw in a lifetime, his reading was confined to the organs of various country sports and the fat stock reports, and his interest in the arts restricted to the insurance value of what was contained in the Clarebourne estate. He had once been to see the opening night of a play at Nico's theatre and had fallen asleep well before the much-trumpeted nudity at the end of the first half. His favourite film was *Gigi* and he retained an affection for Dickens whom he had read at school, and the songs of José

Feliciano, notably 'Baby, come on light my fire' which he claimed to have played a part in his seduction of Georgia. Curiously, as well as being a crack shot and a wizard with dogs he was a committed conservationist who had created a wild-flower meadow on the estate.

When the subject of Rob's poetry came up I feared some Prince Philip-like outburst along 'Bah – sissy!' lines, but it was not forthcoming. Instead, he nodded and listened civilly and confessed that he was not much of a poetry man, but had a sneaking regard for John Betjeman who at least took the trouble to rhyme.

'He's a bit of a hero of mine,' said Rob.

'An old Marlburian like myself,' said Julian, with an air of modest pride.

Rob nodded. '"Summoned by Bells", right.'

'You surprise me,' said Nico. 'I mean he's a national treasure and all that, but isn't he a bit old hat?'

'I wouldn't know. I just think he's great.'

Nico spread a large hand, conceding the floor. 'Good for you.'

'So tell us,' said Georgia, 'about your own work? Are you the new Betjeman?'

'I wish.'

I felt a fierce, proprietary pride in his fielding of their questions. But I was having the greatest difficulty in eating my duck breast with blackberry sauce, spinach and pommes mousseline, and my glass of red wine had gone straight to my head. When the conversation moved on to mutual friends, Rob turned to me.

'How's that? It looks nice.'

'Perfect, but I'm not hungry.'

'Must be all that exercise. It suppresses the appetite.'

'That's true, actually.'

'I know.'

I put my knife and fork together. 'What time's your performance?'

'Six, but don't worry – I'll go straight there after this.'

'That's a lot of time to kill.'

'I'll practise.' He lifted his glass of beer. 'And maybe have another of these, or two.'

'Do you get nervous?'

'Oh, yeah.'

All the time we were talking he kept his eyes on my face as though the conversation was just a pretext for looking at me. This was flattering, but it also meant that I couldn't study him as I would have liked – the level of intensity would have been unbearable – so I kept glancing up and down and this way and that like a demented puppet.

'By the way,' he said, 'I love what you're wearing.'

'Tried and tested.' I touched the collar of my shirt. 'A default option.'

'Don't you mean a classic?'

'Nicely put.'

'Rob,' said Georgia in a soft but commanding voice, 'it's very rude of us to discuss people you don't know.'

'That's all right, I hadn't noticed.'

'Was the beef a good choice?'

'Terrific, thanks.'

'Now,' said Julian. 'Anyone for pudding?'

'Cheese for me,' said Nico.

'And me. Ladies?' We declined. 'Rob?'

'No thanks. Would you excuse me a moment?'

While Julian ordered cheese, I spotted Rob outside. He was talking animatedly on his mobile, and something about this image made me utterly desolate.

'Joss.' Nico nudged me across Rob's empty seat. 'Coffee?'

'Sorry.'

'I think you should, you're in danger of dozing off.'

'Leave her alone,' said Georgia, 'she's entitled.'

After lunch Rob refused all offers of a lift, thanked us profusely and set off to walk to the Yard. As Georgia and I stood before the mirror in the ladies, she said: 'I do see what you mean.'

'Do you?' I was ambivalent. I wanted her understanding, but also her acknowledgement of something unique and particular.

'He's a sweet young man.'

'You reckon?' I said, picking up my handbag. 'I wouldn't go that far.'

She glanced at me. 'He coped so well with all of us.'

'Why wouldn't he?' I asked snappily. 'He was getting a free lunch.'

The words 'nose' and 'face' flitted across our combined consciousness, but Georgia was far too tactful to utter them.

'All right, Joss.' She looked at me in the mirror. 'I'll shut up.'

When we got in, Nico exhorted me to take a nap, but although I got into my dressing gown and lay on the bed, sleep, as they say, eluded me and I went back downstairs to find Nico spark out in front of *Kramer vs. Kramer*. The TV guide lay open and face down on his stomach, the rest of the paper was strewn carelessly across the floor. The rain, which had eased off during the middle of the day, was once again hammering down; in the garden the leaves shuddered, and the patio tiles seemed to flinch and leap beneath the onslaught, but in here the TV flickered, and Meryl and Dustin emoted, competing gently with Nico's crackling purr . . . It was the kind of snug domestic scenario that would till recently have gladdened my heart on a Sunday afternoon, especially these days when down time was at a premium. I would have sunk into it as into a warm duvet, joining Nico on the sofa and entering a pleasant twilight world somewhere between dozing, reading and following the film's old, familiar narrative. This afternoon I struck a jarring note. I picked up the remote, muffled the Kramers and stood there, jumpy and restless, feet together and arms tightly folded, as unrelaxed as it was possible to be.

The change in volume caused Nico to open an eye.

'Hiya . . . not sleeping?'

'No.'

'Endorphin overload . . . Poor darling . . .' He stretched a somnolent arm in my direction, but I ignored it, and he let it fall back heavily. 'Mind if I . . .?'

'You carry on.'

'I'm such a lazy bastard . . .'

I didn't disagree, but then I wasn't supposed to. No one had more energy and enthusiasm than Nico for the things he enjoyed, or a greater capacity to chill out when the opportunity presented itself.

He rolled on to his side, dislodging the TV guide which slid to the floor. I went over to the window and stared out at the rain, my reflection haggard in the unseasonably darkened glass – the pathetic fallacy made flesh. Who, I wondered, had Rob been talking to on the phone? A friend? A fellow poet?

A colleague from the hospital? Or a girlfriend, some lovely, weirdly dressed young thing who spoke his language and didn't give a stuff? I pictured him at the Yard, sitting alone in its austere, echoey café, reading through his work. Or perhaps – I made myself confront the possibility – he wasn't alone; perhaps that phone call had been to arrange to meet someone there. My mental picture altered to include another figure, laughter, intimacy, the *lingua franca* of a different generation. I winced and caught my breath at the self-inflicted pain. For a brief moment I actually considered going to the Yard that evening. I could turn up at the last moment, enter discreetly as a shadow and sit quietly and attentively in the back row, so that he would have a tantalizing glimpse of me but not be quite sure, so that he'd look for me afterwards, but not find me because I'd be gone . . . These images had the fantastic charm of a fairy tale, but even I could see they were no more realistic nor appropriate to my situation. What, after all, would I tell Nico? Who, as if to remind me, snuffled and snorted as he shifted position on the sofa.

I had to get a grip. This luxuriating in pure feeling was a lazy, self-indulgent, ridiculous waste of energy. More than anything, it was delusional. 'Reality check' Elizabeth would have said; but then anything she would have said simply didn't bear thinking about.

Lethargically I picked up the more lightweight of the two colour supplements and sank into my preferred armchair, the one with the long, deep, slightly sagging seat and the high, threadbare arms and back. I wrapped my dressing gown tightly round me and drew up my knees to my chin.

There was all the usual stuff: agonizing modern social dilemmas, what the beautiful people would be wearing on the beach (crucially, masses of bling with their bathers), the confessional columns of hearty, funny women and skinny, cynical ones; and ah, yes, the obligatory article that served as a pretext for 'something for the boys', this time headed 'Fifty and Firing on All Cylinders'. There had never been a better time, the writer opined, to be an older woman. Free, feisty, financially secure and fabulous, the woman of a certain age was not just sexy and desirable but, apparently, the 'squeeze of choice' for many a younger man. All the usual suspects were photographed in their mature glory – Rampling, Lumley, Mirren, Sarandon,

Deneuve, – as if that was supposed to make the rest of us feel any better. Idly, I tried to work out which one I was most like, whose mould I might be thought to be in. Roughly (very roughly) speaking I had Rampling's physique without her feline beauty, and people had occasionally commented that my voice was like Lumley's. I cudgelled my brains and – no, that was about it. To honest even that was pushing it. On the other hand comparisons were odious, and for a woman to be attractive, especially in her later years, it was essential for her to be *heureuse dans la peau*. And all those photographed, apart from their natural advantages, had a solid commercial investment in their looks and the income to manage it.

In the course of the article various younger men expressed their enthusiasm for older women. Jake, 34, a systems analyst, apparently adored our 'sophistication and sense of humour', whereas Daniel, 30, a shoe designer opined – somewhat rashly in my view – that we 'became more beautiful with age' and Sean, a professional rugby player said he hadn't known sex could be that good until he 'took up with an older lady'. All encouraging news, except that none of them was under thirty. When it came to age-gaps there was a kind of tacitly acknow-ledged cut-off point beyond which lay the murky territory of the borderline perv.

The sound of the phone made me jump. Nico rolled over and opened an eye as I answered it.

'Hello?'

'I'm sorry to disturb you on a Sunday evening,' said Hilary, 'but I did wonder how it had gone.'

'How nice of you. Very well, thanks, I was pleased.'

'Only the weather was so dreadful.'

'It didn't come down that much during the race. And anything's better than heat.'

'Did you meet Donna Delaney?'

'Peter was in charge of her, but we did all have to submit to being snapped by the man from *The Crier*.'

'What was she like? She seems nice on the telly. Please don't tell me she was the bitch from hell.'

I wondered what Hilary was doing watching Kids TV until I remembered her grandchildren lived close by.

'She's charming. Just as pretty in real life and a good sport to boot.'

'What a relief. You watch these things with the children and pray the people they like so much aren't all on drugs and doing it with everything in their path.'

'No.' I laughed, it was a surprise to hear these worries, voiced in this way, from Hilary of all people. 'Or if she is, it doesn't show.'

'Right,' she said, 'I'll leave you to your well-earned rest. Don't forget Reg'll be with you at ten thirty for the show-ground.'

'I'll be ready.'

I put the phone down; eyes closed, teeth gritted. Horticultural show – Hobbs printed dress, Wedgwood blue linen jacket, white straw cartwheel hat, blue shoes.

Nico was now fully awake and sitting up, his hands clasped behind his head, a libidinous grin on his face.

'Woman in a dressing-gown . . .' he intoned. 'How shaggable is that?'

Eight

Perhaps it was as well that at present Nico was at least as busy as me, preparing for the theatre's six-week summer season of family entertainment. It was not a period he looked forward to with unalloyed pleasure, lacking as it did even the traditional fun and frolics of pantomime, but the solid funds that it injected were indispensable, so he put his best foot forward. Still, many an evening was spent musing over what passed between desperate actors and their equally desperate agents when discussing the offer of touring as a luminous animal with an outsize head.

After the Well Woman Run I'd let a week go by before phoning Elizabeth, and it was Edward who answered the phone.

'Joss, how are you? The cheque's in the post.'

'Oh, for goodness' sake, I didn't ring about that.'

'You'd have been quite entitled. Well done by the way.'

'Thank you.'

'Rob was in total awe.'

'Your son is very polite.' I made myself say that: 'your son'.

'Incidentally it was extremely kind of you to treat him to lunch. I hope he wasn't sponging too shamelessly.'

'He wasn't sponging at all. Nico wouldn't take no for an answer.'

'I don't suppose he wrote, or rang, to say thank you, anything old-fashioned like that?'

I shared his disappointment, but managed an insouciant laugh. 'There really was no need. He couldn't have been more appreciative, it was a pleasure to have him there.'

'Hmm . . . Anyway, I expect you'd like Elizabeth.'

'If she's there.'

'She is, she's just logging off . . .' His voice faded before returning momentarily. 'Bye. Regards to Nico.'

'Hi,' said Elizabeth. 'How's it going?'

I was never quite sure what the 'it' in this question stood for. The mayorship? The garden? My health? Our marriage?

'Fine.'

'I hope you didn't mind Rob showing up.'

'Quite the opposite. I was just saying to Edward, he was a delight.'

'It was pure coincidence that he was going to be at the Yard. He asked after you guys and I'm afraid I put him on your trail.'

'Well,' I tried something out, 'he owes you, because he got an eyeful of the lovely Donna Delaney.'

'Really. He never mentioned that. Is there nothing these C-listers won't do for the money?'

Ecstatic though I was that Rob hadn't mentioned Donna, decency dictated that I put my daughter right on this one.

'She didn't get paid. It was for charity, folks.'

'Profile then. Photo opportunity. Call it what you like, it's all publicity and they'd sell their grannies to get it.'

I still thought she was being hard on Donna, but let it go. What did it matter when Rob had not only asked after me (I edited the plural) and failed to comment on, or even notice the nubile Donna?

' . . . all worthwhile,' Elizabeth was saying. 'The old home town was good to our boy. They want him back.'

'What?' I said stupidly. 'Rob?'

'I think that's who we were talking about.'

'I'm sorry, I was being slow.'

'He's got a whole gig to himself next month. We're going to come up for it.'

'Wonderful! Don't forget to give us the date so we can get tickets.' I realized I was gushing, and reigned myself in. 'Subject to the tyranny of the diary, that is. And you must all come and stay.'

'I do know it's a Sunday . . .'

Organized as ever, she was able to give me the date and I reciprocated with that of our weekend in London.

'We hope you'll be able to make dinner on one of the nights.'

'Shouldn't be surprised,' she said briskly. 'I'll email you.'

'OK.'

'You do pick up your home emails, don't you?' Her tone was suspicious.

'One of us always does.'

'Thank God for that.'

The exchange had been positively matey by our standards, but that was a mixed blessing under the circumstances. The feelings I was harbouring at the moment made any increase of intimacy with my daughter a downright liability. When I put the phone down my heart was racing as if I'd just had a near miss on the motorway, and tears, as they so often did these days, sprang to my eyes.

With the emotional water table so high, I had become particularly susceptible to music. Every sentimental song of yearning and loss, of hopeless, helpless attraction, of belief in love against all the odds, every anthemic ballad and country sob story, just about anything by Elgar, Tchaikovsky or Rachmaninov, set me off.

Even Reg had cottoned on to this sensitivity. Just for once I was grateful for my age and the excuses it presented.

'Mozart OK, ma'am?' he'd ask, looking over at me in the mirror. 'Or would the Monkees be better?' And I'd be faced with the agonizing decision between the pure romantic beauty of the one, and the cheap, instant fix of the other. A harder choice than you might think in my frame of mind. To narrow the field I went through our own CDs and selected as anti-sentimental a handful as I could muster, which in effect meant spoken comedy (even Tom Lehrer had too winning a way with a tune). But though in every other respect a paragon, Reg didn't share my sense of humour and the oddness of sharing a confined space with Rambling Sid Rumpo and my driver's politely baffled smile was simply too stressful. We resumed the status quo, with two differences: a large box of aloe vera impregnated tissues appeared on the back seat of the Merc, and Reg began to talk more.

He had two pet topics: his daughter, Lisa, and his hobby, which was metal-detecting. Lisa was a theatre school alumna who could have given Donna a run for her money in the cuteness stakes, and who had recently landed a part in *Chicago*. To describe Reg as a proud father was like calling Hannibal an enterprising chap. He was over the moon, chuffed to monkey's, in his glory – could, in fact, have died happy except that would have meant missing Lisa when (as would undoubtedly happen) she starred in *Phantom* a few years hence.

But while there was only so much I could say about Lisa – nothing, really, except acknowledge Reg's completely justifiable pride and admire photos of her in the evermore turbocharged micro-costumes required by her role – the metal detecting was rather fascinating.

'See this, ma'am?' he said, fishing something out of his pocket one morning as we stood by the open car door. 'Roman silver.'

'Reg . . . amazing . . .'

'I was the first person to handle that in nearly two thousand years.'

The coin had the head of an emperor on one side, surrounded by script too worn to read, and on the other a seated figure holding a trident in the manner of Britannia.

'I cleaned it,' said Reg. 'You're not supposed to, but I wanted to take a good look.'

'I'm so glad you did.'

'You ought to come some time, ma'am,' he suggested. 'You and Mr Carbury. You'd be most welcome.'

These days, whenever someone spoke of Nico in that casual, friendly way – especially someone as transparently nice as Reg – I was awash with shame.

'You never know,' I said, getting into the car. 'We might. Mayor finds greatest ever Anglo-Saxon hoard, how does that sound?'

Reg bridled slightly, the expert humouring the amateur. 'There'll be a few twentieth-century manhole covers first.'

'I can imagine.'

'But if you do stumble on anything, the reward goes to charity.' He closed the door and got behind the wheel. Perhaps he thought he'd chatted enough for one morning, because he added: 'Feel like a bit of music today?'

'Why not?'

'Spot of Elgar?'

'I leave it to you, Reg.'

As we drew away the first swelling notes of 'Nimrod' threaded the air. I picked up my briefing notes, but only in order to be alone with my thoughts. I knew when I started that I'd regret – the return to reality would be eye-wateringly harsh – but like an addict, furtive and driven I indulged myself. Where was he now? What was he doing? Who with?

And did he ever think of me?

I suppose we are all programmed to obsess about what we cannot have, and to take what we do have for granted. Isn't that what they say about money, and sex? I had fallen head over heels in love with Nico, and he had been head over heels in love with me. We had been each other's to command and to revel in, magnetized by our love and by passion. Conversation, sex, emotional support, baby talk, the whole panoply of mutual adoration, was on tap. That easy, ready communication was unavailable to me now. Not since I'd been a schoolgirl with a crush on Naomi, the games captain, had I suffered such agonies, and this was incalculably, incomparably worse. Like nail-biting, scab-picking, the awful secret damage that's known as self-harming, I waited to be alone and then opened a wound, because it was all I had.

Rob. Plain name, ordinary young chap. That was the trouble, I could see that. It was my heart I'd lost dominion over, not my head. He was not a godlike being, no Jude Law. Nor dazzlingly witty, Eddie Izzard need have no sleepless nights. As to the poetry, I didn't yet know, but how would I be able to tell? He could be the new Auden or another McGonegal, my critical faculty was on hold. And in the unlikely event of my recognizing dross, I would lie, and my lies would stand for the kisses I couldn't have. I had simply fallen for him. To fall; a verb with many roles. Falling in love . . . falling in line . . . falling for it . . . falling pregnant . . . falling foul . . . before the fall . . . A fallen woman. But could there be said to be chemistry if only one person fell? If chemistry was the collision of disparate elements, then surely for me to experience this turmoil there had to be something coming the other way?

Obsessively, I picked over my tiny stash of memories. His very first appearance in the doorway at Elizabeth's flat, carrying the cool London night in with him, literally a breath of fresh air. And then his sudden closeness, sitting down next to me, favouring me with his bright-eyed attention. Yes, that was a great part of it: attention; the voice in my ear, combined with the casualness of the young, which, I told myself, could not dissemble. He was never less than civil, but programmed politeness, the sort that constituted a cast-iron social front, wasn't in his generation's make-up.

'Ma'am?' Reg was looking at me in the mirror.

'I'm sorry Reg, I missed that.'

'You were miles away, ma'am.' He switched off the music. 'Just entering Parsloe Place.'

We were on our way to the area WI's golden jubilee. I peered out of the window. 'Already?'

'Light traffic this morning. Two minutes to party time.'

I had to laugh, or I might have cried.

The Yard was a converted steam-engine shed only a hundred yards from the new mainline station on the far side of town. On the night of Rob's gig, the plan was for Elizabeth and Edward to come up by train and meet us there.

They'd smartened it up a bit since the days when one or other of us used to come and collect Elizabeth from discos and concerts. Then, it still had the appearance of a shed, and poor soundproofing meant that the thud and howl of the music made the ranks of family saloons shudder in the bleak car park. Sitting there waiting to the accompaniment of 'Yesterday in Parliament', I used to long for the windows to lighten and the scream of guitars to give way to the echoing voice of the compère. These were the signals for keys to turn in a hundred ignitions. A minute later the double doors would open and a flood of teenagers would surge out into the night. Lucky the parent who spotted his or her offspring early on, and flashed the prearranged headlight-code to advertise their whereabouts.

Now, the car park was lit, and there were more lights around the walls of the Yard, which had in turn been rendered and painted, and carried billboards advertising the website and upcoming attractions. Beyond the new, partially glazed doors was a large foyer. As a councillor I knew about these developments and had attended the opening of the new and improved Yard, but Nico was duly impressed.

'Well, I never,' he said as we walked across the car park. 'A community centre already.'

'Much more than that. They do plays here, you know – new work and so on. You lot should look to your laurels.'

'Are you implying that we're complacent?'

'Not exactly.'

'We do new work. All the time.'

'You do, when it's been tried out somewhere else first.'

He looked aggrieved. 'We haven't trousered any handouts, we can't afford to take enormous risks.'

'I know.'

He held the door for me. 'I have my trustees to please. And my audience.'

'It's all right,' I said. We were in the building, and my heart was beginning to beat faster. I no longer had any stomach for the fight, small as it was. 'I wasn't getting at you.'

'There they are!'

Elizabeth and Edward were standing at a pedestal table, holding plastic beakers of red wine. A half-full bottle and two more beakers stood on the table. We greeted each other and Edward said: 'We thought we might as well have a bottle, then we can top up and take it in with us.'

'Good thinking.' Nico raised his beaker. 'Here's to the poet.'

We joined in the toast. 'Where is he?' I asked Elizabeth.

'Preparing. He came up on an earlier train.'

'This may be a silly question, but have you heard him before?'

'Yes. They have an open mic poetry night at our local pub.'

Unbelievably, it appeared she was going to leave it at that. 'So what should we expect?'

'Wait and see.' She was deadpan as only she could be. 'I wouldn't want to spoil it for you.'

The Yard had three 'performance venues'. In descending order of size, these were the Shed (established bands, discos and dance); The Platform (seating for seventy-five); and The Cab (small space for more intimate events). Rob was booked for The Platform, which looked, as we took our seats, as if it would be just over half full. Neither Nico nor I had any idea whether this was good.

'What do you reckon?' he whispered. 'Triumph or tragedy?'

Before I even had time to shrug, Edward supplied the answer, saying happily: 'He'll be pleased. This is more than respectable.'

'Excellent. Mind you –' Nico gave another glance round – 'I haven't felt this conspicuous since we had to lead off the dancing at the Caledonian Ball – we must raise the average age by about twenty years.'

'Speak for yourself, Dad,' said Elizabeth.

'I do.'

Without looking at his wife, Edward picked up her hand, kissed it, and returned it to her. His, I realized, was the equable nature she'd been waiting for all her life.

At any kind of live performance, I suffer from feeling part of the show. Just as nervous fliers have to concentrate to keep the plane in the air, I have to focus, smile, frown, and otherwise keep faith with those on the stage or some mysterious bond will be broken and everything collapse in a dismaying welter of disillusionment. Circumstances this evening conspired to exacerbate this. We were only four rows from the front and right in the centre, so would surely be visible from the stage. The moment the lights dimmed I began hyperventilating and it took a supreme effort of will not to shift to the edge of my seat.

There was no announcement. He just came on, carrying a chair in one hand and a bottle of beer in the other; black jeans, red T-shirt, black and white trainers; designer stubble; a watch buckled through his belt-loop at the front, so that the face was tilted towards him. The applause of his small audience was light and friendly; we were well disposed and eager to be proved right. Only Nico let out a *whoop* which, though regrettable, had the effect of locating our position. Rob lifted his chin slightly in our direction, and began.

Whatever my expectations, he confounded them. I had dreaded failure, in any one of a variety of flavours: naffness, youthful pomposity, clunky use of language, shambling presentation. There were none of these. The boy was composed, clever and accomplished. His comic poems made witty use of rhyme and metre and made their point with enviable economy of effort, like verbal cartoons. His more serious ones – mostly responses to places and events – were thoughtful and intense. There was no obvious straining after effect. He was a real performer who instinctively knew how to work us, and the space. The material was well selected and the pace just right. He only sat on the chair for a couple of poems, the rest of the time he used it as a prop, a table for his beer, or he leaned on the back, put a foot on the bar . . . He was at ease up there.

Which was more than could be said for me, down here. The adrenalin was pumping round my system like a Jacuzzi. At his best moments – the perfect pause, the finessed timing, the heart-stopping word – I experienced a great *thump!* of something that was not exclusively love, longing, sadness or pride, but a complicated mixture of all four, almost too powerful to contain.

Like a true pro, he saved the best till last. I knew the show was only an hour, and at around the fifty-minute mark, it came: the sign. The coded message that only I would be able to decipher, bedded in the centre of a poem called 'Angel Cake':

> '*And feed our faces on flowers,*
> *And drink lager and love,*
> *And finger-lick crystals of sugar,*
> *From dishes sprinkled with petals of cream . . .*'

There! I knew where he'd found that image, and when, and to hear it used to such effect brought the tears bubbling up again like a hot spring, so that I was glad there was still five minutes remaining in which to compose myself before the lights went up.

When they did, Nico gave another *whoop*, and we all clapped high above our heads, part of a general applause which this time round was warmly enthusiastic.

'Bloody good show!' said Nico, slapping Edward on the shoulder when Rob had left the stage. 'The guy's a star.'

'Not bad, was he?' Edward agreed, glowing with modest pride. 'Joss, what did you think? Not too embarrassing, I hope?'

'He was wonderful,' I said, adding, God help me: 'He could go all the way.'

'Whatever that means in the world of performance poetry.'

Such was my ignorance I could think of no one but Pam Ayres to provide a yardstick and she, though splendid in every respect, was just (oh, hell!) too old to compare.

'Are we going to be able to buy our hero a drink?' enquired Nico loudly as we filed out. 'Or will he be too busy signing autographs?'

'Don't worry, Dad,' Elizabeth threw over her shoulder. 'The buying of drinks is obligatory.'

In the event Nico's autograph-signing scenario wasn't that wide of the mark. When we got to the bar Rob was already there, a bottle in his hand, the centre of an admiring group of contemporaries. Bleakly, I recognized our part in the mix – the slightly out-of-place family supporters. But the moment he saw us he raised the bottle and called, 'With you in a minute!'

Nico bought a round and we waited at the far end of the bar. And waited.

'Do you think he knows all those people?' I asked.

'He does now,' said Elizabeth.

'Ah,' said Nico, 'the freemasonry of youth.'

Some fifteen minutes later Rob extricated himself and joined us. Edward and Elizabeth congratulated him with the air of people who would have expected nothing less, but Nico exercised no such restraint, enfolding him in a bear hug and declaring that 'the whole place was in love with you!'

'Glad you liked it.' Rob laughed and was released, then it was my turn.

'Extremely well done,' I said, holding my glass firmly with two hands so no embrace was possible. 'That was a memorable evening.'

In my effort to be serious, had I sounded stuffy? Pompous, even? 'What impressed me the most,' I crashed on, 'was the variety – the way you slipped from one mood into another without losing us.'

'Thanks, Joss.' He favoured me with his attentive look, as though this was the opinion he'd been waiting for. 'I appreciate that.'

Edward tapped his arm with a finger. 'Particularly liked "Angel Cake",' he said. 'Not heard that one before.'

'Yes,' said Elizabeth. 'Glad to know my humble petals were of use.'

Everybody laughed, and Nico went, 'Aaah!' and pointed a finger at Rob, as if they'd caught him out. I tried, and failed, to join in the laughter. With a light touch, and all unwittingly, my daughter had stolen something from me and I stood there empty-handed.

They didn't stay the night, for the eminently sensible reason that the station was right there and everyone had to work the

next day. Having established that they could catch a train back
to town at ten, and given that it was now only eight forty-five
we found a table and Elizabeth went to order baguettes at the
bar while Edward retreated to the Gents. Rob fiddled dexter-
ously with a roll-up and I tried not to think what he was doing
to himself.

'It must be odd,' I said, 'going from this to your job.'

'How do you mean?'

'You know, the excitement, the buzz, the spotlight . . . And
then the grim monotony of the wards.'

'There's no monotony. That's life and death you're talking
about.'

'True.' I smarted under the implied reproof and perhaps he
understood, because he went on:

'Anyway, I'm not on the wards, I'm a bird of passage. Up
and down in the lifts, back and forth along the corridors, here
and there, this and that. Never a dull moment.' There was a
rhythm to these observations, he made them sound like a
poem.

'Yes,' I said, 'I can see that.'

'Bit like your job, really.'

He smiled, and I felt forgiven. Edward returned and sat
down between us.

'Beth tells me you're coming down to town.'

'That's right. We'd like to take you out to dinner – anyone
who wants to come,' I added, as casually as I could manage,
wafting a hand to include not just Rob, but the whole world.
'Your daughter, too, if she's around.'

'What a kind thought,' Edward said pleasantly, 'but Bryony's
still in the States at the moment.'

Had I noticed a split-second cold spot? Rob's eyes were
lowered as he stubbed out his cigarette. The baguettes arrived
and the moment passed.

What is it about railway stations? I suppose *Brief Encounter*
and a hundred other films where lovers are sundered by the
smoke and shriek of the mighty steam engine have made them
into Proustian places, freighted with associations. Even in an
electric age you only had to look up to leave behind Café
Nero, Smiths and Sock Shop, and see the Victorians' exquisite wrought-iron footbridges, and the ethereal iron and glass

fan-vaulting that soared above. I imagined that all the voices of all the farewells, meetings and reunions over more than a hundred and fifty years were captured up there beneath the echoey arches.

I fell in with Rob as we walked with them to their platform.

'You must let us know your future programme.'

'Sure. I can email it to you.'

He seemed preoccupied. Whatever he said it must have been hard returning to his other world. There was a great burst of laughter from the others, generated by some remark of Nico's. I caught a reflexive smile on Rob's face, and wished it had been me who put it there.

'Nico's great,' he said.

'He has his moments,' I said, jealously.

'Does he have a picture in the attic? He seems not to have a care in the world.'

'He has a very fortunate disposition,' I agreed.

'I just hope that when I . . .' We both knew what he was going to say, but he managed the change of tack quite gracefully. 'If I achieve all he has I'll be half as good value.'

We were on the platform, and it was time to go. Edward kissed my cheek.

'So what does Monday morning hold for you?'

'Sherry in the mayor's parlour at midday for the cathedral volunteers. Primary school concert in the afternoon. Evening – sorry, can't remember.'

'How does she do it?' Edward asked Nico.

'Search me.'

'We'll see you in London, then,' said Elizabeth. 'Don't wait, the train'll be here any minute.'

We made our farewells which in Rob's case constituted no more than a wave. I told myself it wasn't personal, he was feeling flat. But I still couldn't shake off the impression that he – that we, if there was a 'we' – had taken a step backwards.

'I must say,' said Nico on the way home, 'everything seems to be working out awfully well.' He glanced at me. 'Happy now?'

The black void opened and howled between us, but it was only me who could see it.

'Yes.'

'What a nice evening. I didn't know what to expect, but he strikes me as a serious talent.'

'Me too.'

He chuckled. 'Better book him while I still can.'

Georgia was one of those attending the next day's sherry party. She'd rung me in delight when the invitation arrived at the cathedral office.

'But that includes me! Can I come?'

'Naturally.'

'It doesn't matter that we're chums?'

'Why should it?'

'It might look as if you were using the mayoral facilities for a bit of personal socializing.'

'Georgia. Think of your colleagues. Think of me.'

'No.' There was a brief pause as she did so. 'No, you're right. I shall jolly well be there to leaven the mix.'

That had been a while ago. Now, when Georgia was self-appointed monitor of my state of mind and emotional well-being, nothing short of a blue-chip natural disaster would have kept her away.

The majority of the volunteers and their spouses or partners arrived in a coach or on foot. Georgia, ever the good sport, had given a lift to a very frail old lady in her burgundy Audi Allroad, and parked bang outside City Hall's main entrance, courtesy of the old lady's disabled badge ('the reward of the virtuous' as she put it).

'Hallo, Mrs Hammond,' said Hilary, who often helped out on these occasions. 'Good to see you. How are you?'

'All the better for seeing you, dear,' replied Mrs Hammond gamely, taking possession of her glass of M&S amontillado. In terms of the slight but discernible animus between Hilary and Georgia, this was a definite point to Hilary, but Georgia, never knowingly discombobulated, swept it effortlessly aside.

'Hilary! I didn't realize you'd be pressed into service.'

'Morning, your Ladyship, yes, I never miss these little parties,' was Hilary's robust response. 'They're for the people who just quietly get on with it.'

Too late, she realized that she'd given the point straight back, but Georgia was far too much of a lady to remind anyone that she herself was a guest and therefore precisely such a person.

'Absolutely. No, no sherry, thank you, I'm a chauffeuse today, but Hilary – if you had a fizzy water . . .?'

From a short distance away I watched this little vignette being played out, and as Hilary was effectively sent to fetch water, Georgia caught my eye and gave the suggestion of a wink.

The next hour or so passed in discussion of those non-spiritual aspects of cathedral life in which the volunteers were involved: the WI tapestry, the shop, the café, the interactive virtual tour, the outreach corner and the flowers. Perfectly pleasant though it all was I had never been more conscious of the essential emptiness of my role. I was a representative of the council, of the dignity of my office, a figurehead – but no more. They knew, and I knew, that this time next year someone else would be dispensing the sherry and civic benevolence. I conducted whole conversations on autopilot, my mind elsewhere. God knows what it must have been like to be a career politician or, worse, a minor royal. Glancing at Georgia, I considered that she did indeed have to do this much of the time. She was a JP, patron of this and that, doer of good works, member of innumerable fund-raising committees, chatelaine of one of the county's loveliest houses . . . and she was in it for the duration. My admiration knew no bounds.

At one o'clock as the volunteers began to disperse, she came over to me.

'Time to scoop up my passenger. Thank you for a very agreeable interlude.'

'My pleasure.'

'And what about life beyond the parlour?' She gave me a coolly quizzical look. 'Everything all right?'

'The same.'

'Well . . . You know where I am, Joss.'

'Yes, I do. And don't worry,' I added in answer to her unspoken offer. 'I will.'

'Just so long as you do.' She gave me a speaking look, and touched my arm. 'Bye for now.'

'Bye, George.'

'By George, I've done it!' Nico slapped the letter down on the kitchen table. 'Feast your eyes on that, Joss.'

I began reading, but excitement overcame him and he snatched it back.

'She's coming!' he exclaimed, smacking the letter with the back of his hand. 'She's bloody well coming – talk about a coup!'

'Who's coming? Where?'

'Esther Waring – the dame that there is nothing like! I wrote to see if she'd come to the first night of *After Illyria* because in that biography I was reading the old goat said she began her career as the chambermaid – anyway, she's said yes! I wrote to her agent, but she wrote back herself. Here it is, in her own hand: "I'd be delighted to come, it's not a play that's revived often, and I'm so in favour of local theatre. Feel free to call, but regard the date as booked." How bloody nice is that?'

'Very nice,' I said. 'Well done.' I went over and gave him a kiss, but it was a lost gesture, both of us absent for different reasons.

'The bollocks . . .' murmured Nico. 'She is the absolute bollocks . . .'

I tried to share his excitement. 'When is that?'

'Third Friday in July – you will be able to come, won't you?'

'I don't know. Of course I'd like to. Send an official invitation quick as you can, and if there's nothing in the diary then, of course.'

'Only this is one not to be missed,' he went on, almost as if I hadn't spoken. 'I'm genuinely gobsmacked. I was chancing my arm approaching her . . . I expected a polite but friendly brush-off from some hired Rottweiler, but what d'you know? This!' He brandished the letter again.

I felt myself shrinking. How long, I wondered, could he maintain this level of euphoria? But I knew the answer – indefinitely.

He had every right, I told myself as I sat behind Reg en route to a fund-raiser at the soccer club (third division on the up, and looking to build a new stand). There was scarcely a red-blooded male in the country, of any age, who wouldn't have popped his cork at the prospect of meeting Dame Esther. Her early period (you couldn't call it her heyday, because she had never been out of favour), dressed in a man's suit in

TV's *Dirty Work* had been instrumental in many a bloke's sexual awakening, and since then she had turned in a series of equally magnetic performances as everything from Hedda Gabler to DI Stratton, angel of the Met. She was Up There – sex symbol, consummate actress, national treasure, one of the boys. Universally adored. Inappropriate and childish as it was, I felt a tiny, twisting worm of jealousy. Nico was permitted his boyish effusions – a loyal wife, God help us, was even expected to join in – but my own equally quixotic passion had to remain secret. Worse than that, I had positively to deny it. I felt resentful, and cheated, and hated myself for both.

Reg sent me a glance. 'Five minutes, ma'am.'

'Thanks, Reg.'

He smiled to himself. 'Only lady present tonight, I should think.'

'So I believe.'

'Don't you worry, ma'am,' said Reg. 'They'll be drinking out of your shoe.'

This may have been an exaggeration, but it did help me get my head up, as they say in the football world. There were very few occasions when I capitalized on my lady-mayor status, but tonight I felt justified in doing so. As a compliment to my hosts I was dressed in the City colours, a sharp shift dress in red with a black fascinator and black shoes. Pretty damn smart, though I said so myself. I adjusted my chain of office, checked my face, and prepared to strut my stuff.

Reg must have picked up on my change of mood. As I got out of the car, he said: 'Go get 'em, ma'am.'

The chief executive of City came forward, hand outstretched, beaming from ear to ear.

'Madam Mayor, this is a great pleasure. And what a splendid outfit, we'll take that as a compliment.'

The event was a roaring success, and I was – well, let's just say that Hilary would not have approved. I had two – or was it three? – drinks without recourse to the Thai Bites buffet, flirted shamelessly with board, staff and players and made a short and amusing speech. Or at least I think it was amusing, there was plenty of warm laughter and applause, but whether for what I said or my slightly un-mayoral vivacity I couldn't be sure. But even here, there was no hiding place. Word had got already got round about Esther Waring's visit to the theatre – two tickets for the first night of *After Illyria* were the star lot in the auction, and fetched a staggering eight hundred pounds, with the successful bidder the butt of a good deal of genial lewdness.

I left at nine o'clock, and the chairman declared me an honorary life member and kissed my hand before seeing me to the car.

'So, ma'am,' said Reg. 'A good evening, I take it.'

'Yes,' I said, unclipping the fascinator and placing it across my lap, where it sat like some exotic fancy pet.

'They're doing well, City,' he said. 'But I'm more of a rugby man myself.'

'Oh, Reg!' I exclaimed. 'You are such a darling!'

'Thank you, ma'am.'

The next morning my headache was exacerbated by the uneasy feeling (familiar to all who have enjoyed themselves a little too much the night before) that my all-woman performance in the City hospitality suite may not have appeared quite as sparkling to others as it had to me. Mercifully, I had only one engagement, a comfortably low-key and undemanding afternoon tea party with the young mothers' group on an edge-of-town estate.

I rang Hilary, and said that I would be in at two thirty.

'No problem,' she said. 'How did it go last night?'

I affected insouciance. 'Bit of a boys' night in, you know, but perfectly jolly.'

'So I understand,' said Hilary, in a bristly tone. 'You've had two emails already.'

'How do you mean?'

'The chairman and someone called Petrarchus Ionides, who I suppose is a player. Brian says they're all foreigners at City now.'

'Quite a few are, certainly,' I murmured weakly. 'I think Ionides is their new midfield signing.'

'I wouldn't know. But they're all very appreciative of your visit. You were obviously a big success,' she added, as if I had just been caught flashing my smalls on the front page of a red-top.

I was glad she couldn't see my agonized grimace. 'Jolly good.'

There was a challenging pause. 'Reg said the same thing.'

'Reg?'

'That you enjoyed yourself.'

'Well, yes – I mean, I did. It was a very convivial occasion.'

'Good,' said Hilary. 'See you at two thirty then.'

I put the phone down very gently and made my self a cup of chimps' tea with industrial quantities of sugar. Had I behaved like an idiot? Had I, as the young – as Rob – would say, embarrassed myself?

Any appeal I had for Rob must consist in my acting my age: dignity, humour, elegance, composure – these must be my watchwords. Being the snazzily dressed but slightly tipsy toast of City FC was so much the opposite of the person I wanted to be in his eyes that I dropped my head in my hands and moaned.

The trouble was I was no longer quite sure who I was. And every time I caught a glimpse, I didn't care for it.

Though I didn't think so at the time, the young mums of the Rosemount Estate were exactly what I needed. An hour in their company was like a brisk rub-down with a rough towel: bracing and therapeutic. They treated me with bluff, kindly tolerance, acknowledging that it was my job to be there and theirs to let me do it.

The community centre was a square, low-rise seventies building, and the room we were in had windows that overlooked a scrubby children's play area and a block of flats named Brontë House. Set out along one wall was a row of Formica-topped tables where stood the refreshments and a toy tombola. I bought a pounds-worth of tickets and won a small doll in the Donna Delaney mould, with puce hair and a bare midriff, which I gave to the little girl queuing next to me. In the far corner was a toddlers' corner, marked by a bright green plastic mat, with more toys and a Wendy house. I lowered myself gingerly on to a beanbag, praying I'd be able to get up again unaided, and was immediately laid siege to by Jay (only a year old his proud mother assured me, though he could have passed for twice that), who pulled himself up on my trouser legs and stood there, weaving slightly and staring into my face with large, limpid, thickly fringed dark eyes. From time to time a sticky hand reached out to grab my chain of office. I smiled a lot, he not at all; anyone conversant with telly-anthropology would have been in no doubt whatever who had the upper hand.

'You've made a hit there,' said his ravishing mother, who had introduced herself as Danielle.

'He's beautiful,' I enthused. 'He's going to break a few hearts when he's older.'

'Yeah,' said Danielle, deadpan, retrieving her offspring. 'I expect she will.'

For tea, we perched on child-sized wooden chairs at equally low tables; a situation that was a great leveller but made me awfully glad I had worn the trouser suit. The group I joined consisted of Katie with her sons (I checked) Arran, four and Paul, seven months, and Mila with her daughter Crystal, two. Next to me was Katie with Paul sitting sideways on her knee, brandishing a moist chocolate finger biscuit. His brother was leaning on the table next to me so that it was particularly difficult to avoid the questing biscuit which, as Katie grew animated in conversation, drew ever closer.

'He wants you to have that,' opined Arran.

'Does he?'

'Go on.' Arran pointed across me 'He wants you to have it.'

'But I'm not going to take it, it's his.'

'He doesn't want it. He'll drop it in a minute. Then he'll yell.'

'Oh dear.' I tried to distract Arran. 'Have you had some cake?'

'No, the cake's well crap.'

'Arran!' With commendable promptness Katie swung round, causing the chocolate finger to describe a long smear across my sleeve before it flew across the room. 'Don't use that word!'

'Why not?' said Arran in a reasonable tone. 'You do.'

'Don't get gobby with me – sorry.' She pulled an apologetic face, and then saw the smear. 'Oh, sh— Oh, I'm really, really sorry, did Paul do that?'

'It wasn't his fault. And don't worry, it's washable.'

But nothing would console her; she passed the deafeningly outraged Paul over the table to Mila and began scrubbing at my sleeve with a paper napkin. I had to stop her before the chocolate was irretrievably absorbed into the weave.

'Tell you what!' I shouted, 'I'll pop out and give it a dab with some water!'

'I'm really, really sorry,' she said again, mouthing wildly against the din. 'Are you sure?'

'Absolutely. He's lovely!' I bellowed, tickling Paul's crimson cheek with my finger. 'But I think he needs another biscuit!'

I went to the cloakroom pretty sure that poor Arran was going to get it in the neck. While I was mopping my sleeve with a wet hankie, Danielle came in. I caught her eye in the mirror and she pulled a sardonic half-smile.

'Poor you.'

'Oh, I'm fine. But I owe you an apology.'

'No,' she waved a perfect manicure, 'you're all right.'

'It's so hard to tell at that age.'

'I know.' She went into one of the cubicles but continued to talk over the rustling and trickling. 'Have you got a family?'

'A son and a daughter. Both grown up.'

'Any grandchildren?'

'Two.'

'My mum's got five.' There was a rush of water and Danielle emerged and passed her hands under the tap. 'She's the business. I don't know what I'd do without her.'

We threw our paper towels into the bin and stood looking at ourselves and each other in the mirror. I felt separated from something, and just for once it wasn't Rob. Because I was never likely to see Danielle again I turned to her and said: 'You should be very proud.'

'Cheers,' she said. 'I am.'

I hadn't said of what, but we understood one another.

The invitation from the theatre management looked formal enough, but I detected Nico's mischievous hand in 'Madam Mayor and escort'.

Hilary was impressed. 'Didn't Mr Carbury do well?' she said. 'Netting such a big fish? And there's nothing in the book for that evening. But it'll mean a quick turn round after the Young Farmers, so you'll have to bring your stuff here in the morning.'

I was awfully glad she didn't take the opportunity for a major excursus on Dame Esther's all-round fabulousness. She probably felt, like me, that we'd all had enough of it to last a lifetime. But loyal as ever she must have had my image in mind, because she asked: 'What were you thinking of wearing?'

'Gosh,' I said, who had thought of little else, 'I haven't got a clue. It's much too far away.'

'Not that far, ma'am.' She bridled slightly. 'I think you should treat yourself to something special.'

Nine

O ur weekend in London followed a particularly hectic few days, so that when we boarded the train at five o'clock on Friday afternoon I had the warmly satisfied feeling of having earned a break and, as we rattled south, rising excitement at the possibilities afforded by the next forty-eight hours.

A trolley came round and we ordered drinks – whisky for Nico, G and T for me. Nico raised his.

'To fun!' he announced. 'And all who seek it!'

We tapped tumblers and began to talk about Hal, who had emailed, to say he was coming over for a few days on business, accompanied this time by Lili. Until very recently the prospect of meeting our son's new partner had been a source of some anxiety and foreboding, but having absorbed the shock of Elizabeth's marriage we felt ready for anything. I still had one or two concerns, though.

'Do you think I should call Cathryn?'

'About what? I imagine she knows he's coming. At least part of the exercise is presumably for him to see his children, and for them to meet Lili.'

'I don't know . . . Solidarity?'

Nico frowned. 'Between whom?'

'Women. Mothers. I don't know.'

'Honestly, darling, that's a generous impulse, but I can't help feeling it's misplaced. They're all adults, finding a way forward – fairly successfully as far as I can see. Just stand back and let them get on with it.'

'I haven't seen the children for ages . . .'

'You're very busy this year.'

'Yes, but . . .' I glanced down at my gin. 'Not right now.'

'Joss.' Nico leaned forward, removed the gin and took my hand, firmly. 'You're with me. Husbands have rights too, especially adoring ones, and I claim my forty-eight hours of freedom.'

It was well said, but I was uncomfortable with the turn the conversation had taken, and returned to Hal.

'Do you think we should ask them to stay?'

'I'm sure they'll ask if that's what they want to do. But you know Hal – there'll be a tight schedule, and he knows you're under a lot of pressure just now. A flying visit is my guess.'

'I don't want to seem inhospitable the first time Lili comes.'

'You won't. For crying out loud, darling, you'll be doing her a favour. She's bound to be a bit apprehensive, she'll just want to tick the box and move right along. If it's serious, there'll be plenty of other occasions, if it's not it won't matter.'

I couldn't quite bring myself to let it go, perhaps because here was a topic over which it was perfectly justifiable – even honourable – to fret, and it was a while since I'd had one of those.

'I just hope it will go all right – with the children.'

'I'm sure it will. Children are programmed to get the best out of situations. It's a survival mechanism. The selfish gene, yup?'

'And poor Cathryn.'

'She is not poor. She is a very smart, very sensible woman who wants the best for her family and who has managed, pretty astoundingly I admit, not to bear a grudge. We're very fortunate.'

'Yes – yes, we are.'

'So let's let them get on with it.' He posed, giving me a sidelong look. 'Because we're worth it.'

I smiled, and he said: 'That's nice. I want to lighten your heart, Joss.'

On a good day with the light behind it, Bonman's could be said to be in Lancaster Gate; in less forgiving conditions, Paddington. Once inside any distinction ceased to matter because it possessed, in spades, the prerequisite of any good club, of being its own world, of whom members were the sole and privileged inhabitants. The outside of the building had a blue plaque advertising that the 'thinker and essayist' Claud Bonman had lived there for ten years at the turn of the last century; I had only ever met one or two non-members who had heard of Claud, and no one, members included, who had read any of his *pensees,* though there were a few dour, narrow volumes in the library. His portrait in the smoking room showed a thin, whiskery man with bulging eyes and an air of distracted intensity. Claud aside, the place had the snug, sequestered charm of a boutique hotel, with the crucial difference that in such a hotel we would have felt discreetly obliged to live up to our surroundings, whereas here we blended into them as if they were our natural habitat. It was an environment expressly designed to put members at their ease; the moment we entered the receptionist greeted us by name.

Our room looked out over the green, high summer tree canopy of Sussex Gardens below which the unheard traffic swam back and forth like trout in a stream. We'd always found the anonymous comfort and seclusion of hotel rooms sexy, and as I gazed out of the window Nico came up behind me and clasped my breasts.

'Fancy testing the facilities in the time-honoured manner?'

I removed his hands and turned round so that I was facing him with a big smile and a ready excuse.

'There isn't time.'

He glanced at his watch. 'Hate to say it, but it won't take long.'

'I want to shower and change – and eat, I'm starving.'

'Fair enough.' He tapped my shoulders. 'Go on then, get yourself in a fit state to accompany me on the town.'

Our choice of play had been governed by convenience and availability, so we had eschewed the latest hot ticket at the National in favour of a new political comedy in Shaftesbury Avenue. Before leaving I rang Elizabeth to touch base.

'We saw that the other night,' she said. 'It'll make you laugh.'

I wasn't quite sure whether this meant she herself had laughed, or that our tastes were so wildly divergent that what left her cold would have us rolling in the aisles.

She added laconically: 'We had a call from Hal.'

'Yes,' I said, 'he's coming over, don't know yet what his plans are, but—'

'Our chance to meet the bold Lili.'

'Yes.'

'Another shock for you and Dad.'

'Not at all! We're looking forward to it, it's high time—'

'Mum – joke. Settle down.'

We both knew she hadn't been joking, but I left it there anyway.

'Are you still on for tomorrow?' I asked. 'We booked the Pomadoro for eight.'

'We'll be there,' she assured me. 'We did mention it to Rob, but you won't be surprised to hear he's got other fish to fry.'

'Fine,' I said, as my heart hurtled and crashed. 'That's as it should be.'

'He's coming round on Sunday,' she added, 'to use the Internet. Feel free to drop in. He's mysteriously fond of you both so I'm sure he'd like to see you.'

The 'mysteriously' was just Elizabeth, and I edited out the 'both'. At the foot of the cliff my heart stirred back into life.

The play was fast and funny with a high profanity factor and a well-known sitcom star in the lead role. We agreed that the piece could have been written as a vehicle for him, containing as it did several wonderfully inventive splenetic rants of the kind associated with his TV persona. We enjoyed it, but indulged in a few rants of our own at the expense of West End theatres – the extortionate prices, the discomfort, the uselessness of the programme, the impossibility (due to insufficient barmen and loos) of having a drink and a pee in the time allowed at the interval . . .

'Listen to us,' I said, as we sat in the Good Fortune Chinese restaurant afterwards. 'We used not to be like this.'

'One of the pleasures of advancing years,' said Nico, 'the freedom and vocabulary to spew bile. It's why we laughed at the play – identification.'

'But I don't want to be bilious.'

An aromatic procession of dishes began to arrive, and Nico raised his hands in a gesture of happy surrender. 'My darling – you may have come to the wrong place.'

The next day stands out in my memory as one of shiny near-perfection. Perhaps I hadn't given myself sufficient credit for the sheer attrition of the mayoral schedule. Most of the engagements ranged from interesting to amusing, but their sheer number, and the pressure they exerted to perform, was relentless. The sense of being off the leash was a heady one and

London with its happy memories (and enchanting possibilities) was an earthly paradise.

Walking was what we liked. It was what we'd done when we were young with no money, and now we'd come back to it, with the advantage that if we got footsore we could hop in a taxi whenever we chose. The weather was lovely, and we set off at nine, fuelled by Bonman's historic breakfast, took a bus to Camden Lock, and headed south along the Regent's Canal, stopping for cinnamon cappuccinos by the houseboats at Maida Vale, and continuing all the way to the City. It was our intention to look round St Paul's, but we were put off by the flocks of queuing tourists and continued towards the river, via Postman's Park. As usual there was no one else there and we had the walls with their hundreds of stories to ourselves. I was reading about a ten year old boy drowned while saving Jess, his dog when Nico came and put his arms round me.

'It's so nice to be just us.'

I nodded against his shoulder.

'And you look absolutely lovely today. I'm a lucky man.'

I shook my head so slightly I didn't expect him to notice, but he pushed me back and peered into my face. 'Joss? What's the matter?'

'Nothing.'

'Too much honest sentiment for a Saturday lunchtime?'

'Probably,' I sniffed and dug out a tissue. 'Damn, you can't take me anywhere.'

'Ah, but I can, and speaking of lunch . . .'

We found a pub with a view of the river and sat outside on a wooden balcony. We had a parasol but the sun was hot on our arms and the Thames glinted and gleamed between cruising river traffic. With the club breakfast a recent memory, and the Pomadoro's Italian feast in prospect, we chose salads, which Nico sabotaged with a large bowl of chips.

'To share,' he explained, popping one in.

'Don't expect me to salve your conscience.'

'You can't come to a riverside pub in London and not have chips. It's sissy.'

'They do look good . . .'

'Don't worry –' he pulled the bowl towards him – 'I'll save you from yourself.'

It was three by the time we left the pub. Nico, enervated

by exercise, two pints of best and the lion's share of the chips, headed back by tube to Bonman's for a snooze, while I hit the shops.

It was a long time since I'd gone out looking at clothes without a mayoral agenda. Under no circumstances could I be said to have needed anything – my wardrobe had never been fuller – but it was awfully nice simply to browse, with an open mind, a paid-up credit card and Hilary's advice still ringing in my ears.

I justified Bond Street on the grounds that it would be less crowded than Covent Garden and the shops would be cooler, in every sense. Also, unlike Georgia, I was not someone who never made mistakes, and in these more rarefied retail zones there was less chance of making a serious error of judgement. Seeking ideas I prowled, cast about and snuffed the breeze like a lioness downwind of migrating wildebeest.

When I saw the cream silk shirt dress in the window of an American designer boutique, the expression 'good enough to eat' became real: saliva actually rushed into my mouth. I could already feel the sleek slither of its perfect cut, the light-reflecting, face-framing elegance of the turned-up collar, the casual caress of the rolled-back cuffs. It was almost the only item in the window. Next to it was a simple wooden chair with a long rope of pearls looped over the back, and a pair of brown, woven-leather court shoes with four-inch heels lying beneath, one upright, one on its side. The stylist who had devised this simple, devastatingly seductive scenario deserved a medal. Someone in there had seen me coming and placed nirvana in my path . . .

Twenty minutes and the best part of a thousand pounds later I floated out of the shop, relishing the heft of the thick, expensive carrier bag with its black rope handles and inside, the soft whisper of cream silk swathed in a delicate meringue of tissue. By the time I reached the tube station I was already beginning to descend from the high brought on by retail excess and entering that uncomfortable intermediate zone where the twin voices of common sense and conscience made themselves heard. I could buy something almost identical for half the price in Cavanagh's in the market square at home . . . a grand would recarpet the landing . . . it was not too late to take it back . . . But the train arrived, and the die was cast.

*   *   *

'Yes,' said Nico, 'it's nice. Very elegant. I'd need to see it on of course.'

He sounded distinctly underwhelmed, but then he had only just woken up.

'I could wear it tonight,' I suggested.

'Whoa, risky. All that tomato sauce?'

'If I start worrying about spillages I'll never wear it at all.'

'Good point.'

Still, I didn't wear it that evening. The reason I gave Nico was that I hadn't got the right shoes with me, and he seemed unaccountably relieved, confessing that it 'might have been a bit OTT for family dinner at the Pomadoro' and approving my safe choice of black trousers and a pink top with a kiss and 'I've always liked you in that.'

But the truth was I wanted to save up the new dress. I wanted to wear it new, to see off the Dame.

We were at our table ten minutes ahead of time, but it was another twenty-five before Elizabeth arrived, on her own and tight-lipped.

Nico, never one to sidestep an issue, asked at once: 'What have you done with Edward?'

'He's at Heathrow, collecting Bryony.'

'She's coming back from New York?'

Elizabeth glanced at her watch. 'In baggage reclaim as we speak. I sincerely hope. Dad, mine's a large vodka and tonic.'

'Darling girl, no sooner said than done.'

'So,' I began gingerly, 'will they be joining us?'

'I damn well hope so. Edward, anyway. Who knows what her Ladyship will decide to do?'

It was clear we were skating on the thinnest possible ice. Now was plainly not the moment to ask why Edward, with a legitimate prior engagement, had to drive all the way to Heathrow to collect his grown-up daughter from the airport on a Saturday evening. To do so would be to throw petrol on Elizabeth's already smouldering ill humour.

Her drink arrived, and I waited till she'd taken a hefty slug before asking: 'How are you, anyway? How's work?'

'Oh,' she said acidly, 'work. That old thing.'

'Yes,' I said. 'Anything good coming up that we should know about?'

She took another swig, with the air of someone self-medicating. 'Nothing out of the ordinary. This Wednesday it's 'The Secret of Staying Happily Married'.

'Steady on,' said Nico, 'and you didn't talk to us?'

She shook her head. 'You get a mention in the intro.'

'We do? Fantastic. Hear that, Joss?'

'Don't get too excited,' said Elizabeth, 'you don't know what I say about you yet.'

'What?' Nico put his arm round me and pressed his cheek to mine. 'Get away. Look at us – me and the old Dutch – we're happy, aren't we?'

Elizabeth glanced away from us, over her shoulder at the door. 'Yup.'

'They could easily get snarled up in traffic on the way back,' I said. 'I suggest we wait for, say, another twenty minutes? And then give our orders and carry on.'

'Mum – Edward will ring when they're inside city limits.'

Nico nudged me. 'Yeah, Joss. No one's ever out of touch these days. Except us, perhaps.'

'Fine, I just thought if we had a plan . . .'

'Excuse me a moment.' Elizabeth got up and disappeared in the direction of the ladies.

'Hey-ho.' Nico popped an olive in his mouth. 'Here's a pretty kettle of fish.'

Even half a kettle of fish would have done me. The Anchor's smoked chicken and avocado salad was a long time ago, and I'd covered miles since then.

'Just our luck,' I groaned, 'I'm absolutely rattling.'

'Let's have some garlic bread.'

'That'll ruin our appetites.'

'No, it won't, it'll go some way to satisfying our hunger, which is the general idea. If we wind up spending less on Luigi's veal chops, that's all to the good.'

The garlic bread coincided with Elizabeth's return. She said, 'Thank God!', picked up a slice and demolished a third of it in one mouthful, while we chewed busily on ours like a couple of hamsters, giving her time.

'I'm sorry,' she said, wiping her hands and mouth on a paper napkin and claiming another slice.

'Darling,' we chorused, 'Lizzie, for goodness sake, it's not your fault!'

'I know it's not, but it's a bloody nuisance just the same, when this has been fixed for weeks. The moment I realized it was Bryony on the phone I knew there was every likelihood he'd go haring off. She's got him right –' she made a downward motion with her thumb – 'there.'

'It's the prerogative of attractive daughters.' Nico stroked her hair as he said this, and it was like watching a liontamer with a particularly fractious subject. But to my astonishment she put up her hand and held his for a moment before returning it.

'If you say so, Dad.'

'And here they are!' cried Nico, rising to his feet. 'So all's well that ends well!'

I looked towards Edward and his daughter, but not before I'd noticed Elizabeth close her eyes for a split second, in silent prayer.

The first few minutes were lost in a welter of greeting, introductions and apology, the laying of another place and the delivery of menus.

'Let there be wine,' said Nico, 'and then let's order, so we can talk.'

While all this happened I observed Bryony and tried to match this young woman with the competent tomboy in the photograph. It had to be said that on first acquaintance she seemed neither spoiled brat nor hoyden, but an absolute sweetie. She was a little taller than her brother and had the same likeable looks. Her hair, worn shoulder-length, was enviably thick, and she had the sort of lashes that would never need mascara. A short, provocatively curved upper lip lent her round face a Bardot-esque sexiness. Though in her late twenties she presented like a teenager, with slouchy frayed jeans that brushed the floor and a washed-out grey T-shirt. From the moment she arrived waiters were magnetized to our table and Nico was the happiest of bunnies, indulging in a little avuncular flirting and quizzing her about her life.

'So what's New York got that London hasn't?' he wanted to know; adding with his usual chauvinistic flair: 'Some handsome fellow with exemplary teeth?'

Not having met Nico before, things could have gone either way, but fortunately Bryony seemed to find this droll.

'Oh, yes, plenty of those! But no, I've been on a buying trip.'

'More, more – what did you buy?'

'Spring ranges for the store I work for.'

'So you're in fashion?' Nico breathed.

She beamed, flattered. 'Only the retail end.'

'Only? Only? Hear that, Joss? What other end is there?'

I left them to it. Elizabeth, face in neutral, appeared to be checking her text messages. To draw attention away from her rudeness, I turned to Edward.

'We're so glad you made it, both of you.'

'There was never any question that we would. Failing acts of God, there was tons of time.' As he said this he glanced at Elizabeth, and his tone made it clear that even if there had been a problem, however minor, he was not going to admit to it. 'How about you?' he went on. 'Off duty and at large – what have you been up to?'

I described the show, and our day, and he listened in his quietly attentive way (that must be where Rob got it from) and endorsed my view of Postman's Park as one of London's undiscovered treasures. We moved on to a sharing of other well-kept secrets, including markets, galleries, a Greek barber in Camden High Road and a Polish restaurant in Acton where the most food and fun was to be had, he said, for the least money. And all the time I could feel Elizabeth, a cold spot at the table, resisting any attempt to be drawn into conversation by me, or by Nico, whose charm offensive on Bryony was the most obvious irritant. How childish, I thought, why couldn't she just shape up for a couple of hours in the interests of family harmony and a pleasant social occasion? Accustomed as I was to her moods and manner, right now I was ashamed and embarrassed. However awkward it was for her having these grown-up stepchildren, surely she could stop herself behaving as though she were in competition with them? Especially this girl who, whatever her faults, was coping with a delicate situation a great deal more gracefully than our daughter.

As usual, Nico seemed oblivious to these tensions, and proposed grappa with the coffee. Thankfully, Bryony saved us from ourselves by saying she was shattered and really ought to hit the sack, and that was the signal for the party to break up. She went to the ladies, and Elizabeth and I stood out on the pavement while the men wrangled amiably about the bill. I was still cross enough with her to let it show.

'What on earth's the matter?' I asked.

'I'm astonished you have to ask.' She took out a cigarette and lit it, inhaling fast and hard as if it were some necessary drug.

'I am anyway.'

She looked away, eyes narrowed. 'I could try "none of your business", you know.'

She was right. She was a grown woman. I felt the wind leave my sails.

'It's that bloody girl,' she said.

'I've got to say, she seemed—'

'Nice? Why wouldn't she be nice, with Dad all over her like a cheap suit? She hates me, Mum!'

'I think you're being—'

'No I'm not.'

'Surely—'

'She didn't address a single word to me all evening. Not even hello. She knows what she's doing. I know it. Edward knows it. Classic – and here she comes, my cute little nemesis . . .'

The other three emerged, Nico holding the door open for Bryony, Edward carrying her rucksack. Elizabeth dropped and trod out her cigarette.

'Not. One. Word. She wants me vaporized.'

I would have demurred again, but it was too late.

We made our farewells. I got a friendly embrace from Bryony, the merest cheek-brush from Elizabeth, and the three of them headed off to where Edward's car was parked. I wondered if Bryony was staying at their flat, or if she had somewhere of her own to go to. Was she as uncomfortable as Elizabeth with the situation? If she was, she didn't show it; she was, as they say, dealing with it. They walked three abreast, but when the crowded pavement dictated otherwise it was Elizabeth who shortened her stride and fell behind. That was my epiphany, the moment I knew that my daughter had been speaking the truth and was vulnerable. I yearned to run after her, and put my arms round her and crack that stupid, adamantine carapace with the strength of my embrace. The last words she'd said, as she touched her cheek to mine, were, 'See you.'

'Well,' said Nico, linking his arm through mine, 'that was all very jolly, in the end.'

I murmured something, and glanced over my shoulder, but Elizabeth and the others had gone.

I said nothing about Bryony except to agree how charming she was. But the next morning over coffee in the atrium of the Wallace Collection, I reminded Nico of the open invitation to drop in at Edward and Elizabeth's flat. Unusually, he was lukewarm on the subject.

'What do you think . . .? I mean, we've sort of done that, haven't we? It's nice to be on our own.'

'I wouldn't mind, though – Elizabeth was a bit down last night.'

'Was she? No, she was OK, surely. A bit stressed, a tad piano perhaps, but nothing out of the ordinary.'

'Still, I'd like to. To set my mind at rest. Indulge me.'

'If you put it like that . . .' He put his hand over mine, and it was warm as toast. 'Don't I always?'

'Yes,' I said, 'you do. And I appreciate it.'

'To Camden we shall go.'

I squeezed his hand. 'Thank you.'

I was grateful on more than one count. Last night I had 'come clean' with Nico; that is to say I'd told the truth (but not the whole truth) about not being up for it at the moment. I was very tired, I explained, my mood was a bit low, but he mustn't think it was personal, nor the full-on blues.

'Darling Joss,' he'd said. 'Contrary to appearances, I am not a beast. In fact I'm easily pleased. As long as we understand each other, I'm happy.'

The following afternoon we took the bus to Elizabeth's. At Nico's insistence we carted our bags to the top deck, and he was almost childishly delighted to find free seats at the front. His hand lay on my knee as he took in the view and pointed things out. He was quite right about mutual understanding, but for it to happen both parties had to want to be understood.

I wasn't expecting Rob to open the door to us, and it was left to Nico to express surprise and delight.

'Rob – my dear fellow – here for Sunday lunch in the manner of dutiful sons?'

'I did have something, but I'm really only here for the broadband.' He smiled at me. 'Hi, Joss.'

For a moment I thought he wasn't going to kiss me, but he stepped forward in stockinged feet, and I felt his mouth on my cheek; a glancing touch, but singular.

'Hello, Rob.'

We put down our bags. Elizabeth came into the hall. She looked drawn and was wearing glasses which she now pushed on to the top of her head.

'Oh, there you are,' she said. She might or might not have been expecting us; her dispassionate tone gave nothing away. She glanced at her watch. 'Time for a little something – tea?'

We declined and joined them in the living room, which was a pleasant welter of Sunday papers with a soundtrack by Jacques Brel. Rob padded in behind us, giving a good impersonation of a young man with other things to do, but who had been brought up not to ignore visitors. Edward got to his feet, with the pink cheek and rumpled hair of a man only recently asleep.

'Joss, Nico, splendid . . .' He scrubbed at the top of his head. 'I'm afraid you catch us in the traditional postprandial slump.'

'Looks good to me,' said Nico. I could tell he was a little uncomfortable at having disturbed the family's hard-earned repose, and that just for once it was down to me to make the running. But not before he'd satisfied my curiosity on one point by asking: 'Your lovely daughter here?'

'No, she's back in Hackney where she belongs.'

There was a microscopically awkward moment. Elizabeth turned the music off and began shuffling papers together. 'Come on, sit down.'

'We're not staying,' I assured her. 'We've got time in hand for the train, and you were only another couple of stops on the bus.'

'Good idea,' she said. 'Sit anyway, if it's only for ten minutes.'

We had been put on notice. As we sat down, I reminded myself that it was she who'd extended the invitation in the first place, but had clearly not mentioned it to her husband and was not taking responsibility for it now.

I was on the sofa. Rob sat on the floor with his back against the arm. There was something intimate in our relative positions; I could have placed my hand on his head. I noticed a tiny patch of white hair, like a splash of paint, behind his right ear.

'By the centre,' Nico chuckled. 'You must be glad we live where we do.'

Edward frowned. 'Why's that?'

'In-laws who drop in – a traditional nightmare.'

'Oh, please.'

It was a shade too close to the truth and our smiles felt forced. Rob came to our rescue by saying: 'But this is a weird one, isn't it?'

We obliged by asking, what was?

'In-laws and so on. If this was in some American sitcom you'd criticize it for being contrived.'

'If this was in a sitcom,' said Elizabeth, 'that'd be the least of its problems.'

'They can make anything work over there,' said Nico, trying to ease things off at a tangent. 'They have about a hundred writers working on one show.'

'Obviously,' went on Rob, undeflated, 'it doesn't affect me, but do you guys ever look at each other and think – what?'

All of us laughed, a touch nervously, except Elizabeth who said: 'I can't say I do.'

Nico tilted his head and made a you-me gesture at Edward. 'I think he means us.'

'I think you're right.'

Elizabeth got up. 'Well, I for one could use a cup of tea so if you'll excuse me.'

I followed her. 'Don't get me wrong,' I heard Rob say to the others, 'but you've got to admit it's unusual.'

Nico said something sotto voce and there was a burst of laughter as I entered the kitchen. Elizabeth had switched on the kettle and was standing next to it, leaning on the worktop with the lower part of her face sunk in her hands.

'All right, darling?' I asked. She nodded without removing her hands.

'I hope you don't mind us showing up like this. You did say it would be all right.'

She nodded again and said, in a muffled voice, 'Yup.'

The rattling purr of the kettle got louder and then ceased.

A trickle of smoke rose like a thought bubble next to Elizabeth's head.

I picked up the jar marked tea. 'How many – I'd better ask.'

'Don't bother. Just me and you.'

I poured water on to tea bags. As I took milk from the fridge, Elizabeth said: 'Thanks for coming. It's nice to see you, Mum.'

'Oh, darling . . .' With a superhuman effort I reined in the emotion that threatened to overwhelm me. 'I'm so sorry about Bryony. But it will pass.'

'If you say so.'

'I do. And anyway you don't have to take my word for it. It just will.'

There was another burst of laughter from the other room. She said, ruefully: 'They're happy.'

I took the chance to use his name: 'Rob's keeping them amused.'

She gave a brief, bloodless smile. 'He does that.'

'Maybe,' I said, 'Rob will win her round. I mean, if he's perfectly comfortable with the situation she may kind of – catch on.'

'Hasn't worked so far. In fact I strongly suspect I'm the bone of contention.'

'You don't know that.'

'Hmm.' She picked up her tea. 'Tell me something.'

'If I can.' I reached for the sugar jar; something told me I might need it.

'Do I seem depressed to you?'

'Depressed?'

'Clinically depressed.'

'No.' With no time to think, it was a knee-jerk answer, and now she looked up at me with the familiar, challenging, don't-mess-with-me directness.

'Only I know you've suffered from time to time, and these things can be genetic.'

'The curse of the Carburys, I don't think so.'

She shrugged. 'It happens.'

'No,' I said, sounding a lot firmer than I felt. 'You've had a lot of life-changing stuff going on, and you're justifiably worried about some of it, Bryony and so on, but that's different.

If you think it's more than that, you should go and see a doctor.' I put my hand on her arm. 'You must, darling.'

'Mmm,' she said. 'Perhaps I will.'

'But I don't think you are.'

'Good.' She was deadpan. 'So that's all right then. Shall we join the gents?'

Back in the living room there was only Nico and Edward, Rob having retreated to the computer. The music was back on, but Jacques Brel had been replaced by Bob Dylan's *Nashville Skyline*.

'He may have gone soft,' Nico was saying, 'but he's still a legend.'

'Legend.' Elizabeth made a face. 'Dad, that is such a cop out.'

Fifteen minutes later, we left. I absented myself to use the bathroom, and when I came out the door of the study was open.

'Bye, Rob,' I said. 'We're off.'

'Hey.' He pushed his chair back. 'Sorry to be antisocial.'

'You weren't.'

'I've got another gig at the Yard, will you come?'

'If the mayoral schedule permits.'

'Look on their website, yeah?'

'I will.'

'We could have a drink.'

'That'd be nice.'

Another kiss. His Sunday-afternoon cheek was slightly scratchy against mine, but his lips were warm and soft.

'Cheers, Joss.'

'Bye.'

I was trembling as the others emerged from the living room. Trembling with excitement, with anxiety, with a terrible sense of my own treachery. I put my arms round Elizabeth who submitted a little stiffly to my embrace.

'Look after yourself,' I said quietly. 'I'll ring during the week.'

'Do that.'

'And talk to Rob.'

'About that?' She shook her head. 'You're joking. Not my place.'

* * *

Nico tried to pretend that the train ride home was part of the holiday, but gin and dry roasted peanuts couldn't prevent an anticlimactic mood settling over us. One advantage of this change of gear was that I felt more able to say: 'You know Elizabeth's having a tough time with Bryony.'

'What, that nice girl? Surely not.'

'She said so, and I believe her.'

'You're right,' reflected Nico. 'One thing you can say for our daughter, she's almost suicidally truthful.'

'I feel so, so sorry for her, Nico. No wonder she was in poor form last night, it must be appallingly difficult.'

'Classic stepmother stuff, I suppose. Tough, I agree. On the other hand I think we can assume that it's a phase, and will wear off.'

'Nico, Bryony's not a teenager. She's an independent woman with a mind of her own.'

'Which Lizzie feels is set against her.'

'Yes.'

'What a bugger . . .' I could tell that Nico, though mainly sympathetic to Elizabeth, was perturbed at the idea of the lovely Bryony (a) having a bitchy streak and (b) venting it on a member of our family.

'I do have one idea,' I said cautiously.

'Lay it on me.'

'If Rob could be got on side . . .'

'Rob?'

'He obviously has no issues, so if one of us were to—'

'Joss.' Nico had put down his drink and was staring at me with a furrowed brow. 'Stop right there.'

'You haven't even heard what I was about to suggest.'

'Don't even think it. Don't go there. Any intervention from us, of whatever kind at whatever time or place, would be wholly and disastrously inappropriate.' He picked up his drink, adding: 'And I am unanimous in that!'

'I see.'

He must have heard how crestfallen I was because he continued in a more emollient tone: 'No, honestly, I'm all for your being a tigress in defence of your young, but what young Rob said earlier is true – the whole situation is a bit weird, and extremely delicately balanced. In all probability it will right itself, but there is absolutely nothing that we could or should do.'

Gutted and foolish, I looked out of the window through a sparkle of tears. I could feel Nico still looking at me.

'Joss?' he said gently. 'You do agree, really, don't you?'

I nodded.

'Cheer up,' he said, much more like his old self. 'She's just jealous.'

It was a reflection on my current mindset that several seconds elapsed before I realized he meant Bryony, and not Elizabeth.

Ten

Whenever I read one of Elizabeth's articles I was brought up short by the unexpectedness of her subject matter. While appreciating that house style and the demands of the tabloid market placed certain conditions and restraints, I could still not reconcile what I read with the daughter I knew.

The introductory paragraph – the 'sell' as it was called – would pose a question and announce (in the third person, though I knew that often Elizabeth wrote these herself) that Elizabeth Carbury had spoken to a number of individuals, in this case couples, in a quest for answers. The small photo at the top of the page showed a recognizable but untypical Elizabeth, taken at a slight angle and wearing a gently enquiring smile. The reference to us was simply that we had been married for forty years, which 'In the age of Bridget Jones' had got the columnist thinking. Not gobsmacked with admiration, I noticed, just thinking.

Interviews followed. There was very little opinion, other than the underlying one of the paper and its readers: that the solid values of Anglican middle England were the best. At the beginning of each interview the subjects were introduced with a few pertinent facts – age, jobs, family, location and number of years married. They then proceeded to speak as it were for themselves, to give their testament without apparent prompting from the interviewer.

Except, I reminded myself, that Elizabeth was there. Not just there, but in charge – steering, encouraging, probing, soothing, making these people feel sufficiently relaxed to confide in her and several million readers. It was so hard to imagine; to reconcile this sensitive emotional midwife with the abrasive young woman I thought I knew better than anyone.

I read the article intently, twice, once on the way to City Hall and again in the evening after the grammar school speech day. The interviewees were a mixed bunch, selected for their diverse takes on marriage, but what they all had in common (though this might have been down to Elizabeth's writing and editing skills) was an unruffled self-belief that stopped just short of smugness. When they spoke of marital ups and downs, of fallings-off and driftings apart, there was never any doubt they had the right stuff to pull them through. Of course this could have been a retrospective judgement on my part, since the headline trumpeted, pre-emptively: 'Forty not out – the secrets of a happy marriage'. The reader could be in no doubt how it ended. But I wondered, if Nico and I had been subjected to insistent questioning, whether we would have emerged with our confidence so shiningly intact.

I was struck by one comment, which stayed in my mind long after the paper was thrown away. Amid all the relentless fidelity, forgiveness and indomitable fortitude, one woman (Joan, sixty-nine, a retired headmistress, married to Colin, sixty-seven, a barrister) showed a sharp flash of candour.

'I'm not daft,' she said. 'I've always known I'd never find anyone who loved me as much as Colin does.'

I had no idea whether the paper's editorial policy allowed for the vetting of content by interviewees, so I couldn't know if Colin had approved the inclusion of this remark. At any rate I saw it as providing an insight not only into the mind of the wise, pragmatic Joan, but into Elizabeth's, too. If judicious editing could assist in promulgating the paper's ethos, it could also allow the opinion of the interviewer to show through. I remembered what Nico had said about the see-saw being a bit heavier on Edward's side, and that being no bad thing. Perhaps that was the case, and she knew it, and this woman was saying it for her.

She rang that night as I was putting out my clothes for the county show (green suit with black trim, black courts and jaunty black bowler). It had been a fine day and even at ten it was still not quite dark. Nico was out working in the garden and I called down to him: 'I've got it!' He was listening to Diane Krall through the French window, and lifted a relaxed hand in acknowledgement.

'Coincidence,' I said down the phone. 'I was just reading your article.'

'And were you uplifted?'

'Actually, yes.'

'They were nice people,' she conceded. 'There's usually at least one total prat, but not on this occasion.

'You did a good job, though. You brought out the best in them.'

'Thanks.'

'And how are you?' I asked.

'How am I . . .?' I wondered if she was going to pretend, as was maddeningly possible, that there had never been any problem and our exchange had never taken place, but she said: 'Well, I went to see the doctor.'

Opting at this stage for a statement rather than a question I said, evenly: 'Good.'

'And he didn't think it was clinical.'

'Right.'

'Like you, he pointed out all the life-changing events, which can place a strain on a person. And I can't argue with that.'

'No, indeed,' I agreed, but couldn't resist adding: 'Most of them good.'

'Most, yes.'

Now I could hardly fail to pick up the cue. 'Have you heard from Bryony?'

'Mum, I don't hear from Bryony.' Her voice was steely, but I detected a warning note. 'I am a non-person as far as she's concerned.'

'It'll pass,' I said, adding rashly, 'she seems like a nice, intelligent girl, she can't keep it up for ever.'

'Don't bet on it.'

'And anyway there's Edward, they're obviously close and this must be awful for him, the two women he loves most in—'

'Please don't lump me together with her.'

'I'm not, you couldn't be more different, but you do have Edward in common.'

There was a pause, during which I detected the small sounds of a cigarette being lit.

'I tell you what,' she said. 'I'm looking forward to Hal's visit.'

'Yes,' I said, 'we are too.'

She exhaled. 'It'll give me a troublemaker of my own to trot out.'

* * *

The county show meant an early start. I was due to take brunch (all local produce) with local farmers and manufacturers in the hospitality marquee adjoining the Sawston's Feed tent, at 10 a.m., followed by a tour of selected stands and exhibitions and a couple of hours at the main arena. Hilary's briefing included the usual list of key names – 'Don Marshall, Chief Exec. Hanley Tractors', 'Godfrey Challoner, Challoner and Michael Land Agents', 'Beatrice Stone, Bee Natural Honey', 'Jenny Rayner, Tory prospective parliamentary candidate' and so on – and a note to the effect that I might want to 'bone up on heavy horses' because I'd be seeing a lot of them. I hadn't boned up, but I did know that that there were only so many times you could use the phrase 'gentle giants' and that I'd do better to keep quiet and assume an expression of serious interest and enquiry.

The showground was a good forty minutes out of town and I'd been rather looking forward to a quiet interlude with Reg and his soothing DJ skills, so I was disappointed to find that it was City Hall's other driver, Vic, who was on duty.

Vic was younger than Reg, and his manner was both more formal and more insinuating. Reg's solid, gentlemanly discretion created a sense of perfect security. With Vic, I always felt watched, and not in a good way. I was sure he talked about me to everyone he knew. Now he stood holding the car door, his head very slightly tilted as he greeted me. Something in this attitude conveyed the idea that the age gap between us was greater than was actually the case.

'Good morning, ma'am!'

'Good morning, Vic.'

'And how are you today?'

'Well, thank you.'

'Been running this morning?'

'I have as a matter of fact.'

'Saw your picture after the Well Woman thing – with Donna Delaney.'

'Yes,' I said discouragingly. I didn't want Vic's views on either my performance or that of Donna.

'So now it's off to the agricultural show.' It was not a question, and anyway he had closed the door, so I didn't answer. He got in behind the wheel. He was wearing gloves. It was no good.

'What a glorious day for it,' he opined as we pulled away.
'Isn't it.'
'Still, I see you brought your umbrella, ma'am, just in case.'
'I did.'

I would have liked some music but didn't trust Vic's taste and didn't know him well enough to suggest anything. I concentrated on Hilary's notes, but his gaze kept flicking on to me in the rear-view mirror, making it hard to concentrate.

'Escort not with you today, then, ma'am?'

This was pretty typical – Vic knew perfectly well that Nico was too busy to accompany me on all but the rarest occasions, so why was he asking? And anyway he wasn't really asking, since Nico plainly wasn't there; he was making an observation, one rendered curiously snide by the addition of the little word 'then'.

'He's at work,' I said. 'He's particularly busy at the moment; the summer season starts soon.'

'Ah, yes!' Vic lifted one leather-clad finger from the steering wheel. 'Esther Waring.'

'That's right.'

'My partner and I are hoping to come on that night.' He glanced at me in the mirror. 'We're big fans.'

'Oh dear,' I said, 'I think it may be invitation only.'

'The reception, yes, naturally, ma'am, we wouldn't expect that – but we've put in for tickets to the play. Hope to catch a glimpse of Esther while we're at it.'

'Why not?' I said.

Vic made a giddy-up noise and twitched his head. 'She's one of a kind, isn't she, ma'am? Fabulous actress, fabulous. And what age is she?'

'I've no idea.'

'Older than she looks, by my calculation.' Another twitch of the head. I thought that if I didn't get out of this conversation soon I might very well crack Vic's skull open with the heel of my shoe.

'Better take a look at this,' I murmured, and bent assiduously over the briefing notes. In this way I managed to keep my eyes down, while not actually reading, for the next three-quarters of an hour.

Rob, I thought, would not be able to credit someone like Vic . . . Then I remembered that Rob was a hospital porter and so was exposed to a far greater and more various swathe of humanity than me. He probably pushed Vics galore around in his wheelchair and had to listen to their insufferable views all the time, aggravated by illness. My heart contracted in a now familiar pulse of sweet, melancholy yearning.

I smuggled the photograph Elizabeth had given me out of my wallet and laid it on top of the briefing notes, studying it now through a different lens. Now Rob's guarded look seemed gently thoughtful, whereas Bryony's confident, open stance appeared truculent.

'All right there, ma'am?' Vic was peering at me. 'Five minutes.'

I shuffled the notes together and replaced them in their folder. 'Thank you.'

'Homework all done, then?'

There it was again, the weasel 'then', that so subtly implied senescence. I pretended not to hear, slipped the folder into the pouch on the back of the driver's seat and gazed out of the window.

'Not up for a laugh, our madam mayor,' I imagined him saying to his partner later. 'A bit snotty. Not one of my favourites, to be honest.'

One of the ongoing problems associated with my year's tenure was how to manage the seemingly endless flow of food and drink. I was reminded of one of those pot-luck suppers where everyone brings a course – no one wants to appear mean and the result is far too much of everything. Whatever event was scheduled, the organizing committee in question was desperate to appear as hospitable as the one before, so there was always something to be ingested. As well as the constant flow of full-on, knees-under lunches and dinners (of which there were plenty), there were a myriad of other oddly-timed indeterminate functions serving anything from coffee and biscuits to tea and cake with every permutation of wine-and-nibble in-between. To eat even a token amount of what was on offer on every occasion would have been to court chronic indigestion and exponential weight gain. Alcohol was contraindicated for a variety of reasons (several of which I had demonstrated at the City fund-raiser), but soft drinks were both calorific and bulky, and my bladder lacked the elasticity of youth. Reg and I had evolved a mental map of filling stations with toilets at every point on the City ring road, where I could take a pre-emptive stop before our destination, and it was then down to me to regulate the intake. But I was not on sufficiently easy terms with Vic, and the large mug of heavily sugared chimps' brew I'd taken before setting out was already weighing heavy as we turned in at the main gate.

As we proceeded at the prescribed five miles an hour between interminable stands, it started to cloud over. Vic sucked his teeth sympathetically. 'Looks like you may have been right to bring the brolly, ma'am.'

At brunch in the Sawston's Feed's tent, I sat between the Sawston's CEO and a prospective parliamentary candidate; the latter was a wired, thirty-something lady lawyer who having achieved great things in one field had fixed her sights on doing the same in another and had done her homework. In front of her on the table was a tall glass of iced mineral water and a BlackBerry.

'I notice you were on the planning committee,' she said. 'I wonder if you could tell me anything about the proposed new Princes Way shopping mall?'

On my tour of the show, I bumped into Georgia. I might have known she would be there; Julian was a big beast in landowning circles and she had several entries on display in the floral art tent. She hadn't actually won anything except a Highly Commended in the seasonal medley section – a deceptively informal but ravishing tumble of tea roses in a Victorian cider jug – but when I ventured the honest opinion that she'd been robbed, she waved my indignation aside.

'I still like yours best.'

'So do I. I win hands down in the "would we want it in the drawing room?" stakes, but that's just the thing – mine's décor, not art.'

During this personal exchange, the CEO, who as my guide was anxious to have me safely in my seat in the main arena by twelve fifteen, had withdrawn to a discreet distance. He was gazing with a polite, uncomprehending smile at a towering structure of driftwood and arum lilies, but I couldn't fail to notice the tweak of the cuff and lowering of the lids that meant he was glancing at his watch, and Georgia noticed me noticing.

'I mustn't keep you chatting all day. Duty calls.'

'Sorry, George.'

'Don't be, your turning up was like a ray of sunshine.'

I was rather more surprised to run into Denise, filling in for a friend behind a stall selling home-made jewellery.

'I get the picture,' she said. 'I'd love to chat, but I'm tied up at the moment.'

'So I see.'

She leaned forward, glancing to right and left. 'Could you squeeze me in for a sharpener and a debrief some time?'

'Yes.'

'Call me.' She straightened up and beamed at the CEO, who stopped looking tense and beamed back – they all did.

I did see Julian, though only at a distance. He was one of a group standing by a pen in the rare-breeds section. The county show was one of the few places outside the services where most men wore hats. Julian's was one of two brown fedoras, and I counted three tweed caps, a bowler and a rather fetching Indiana Jones number with a plaited headband (though I suspected that in Julian's book the latter would be designated irredeemably nouveau). Nico quite often affected hats of an ancient and unstructured nature, but they were not, as here, part of a uniform, but an indication of nonconformity – his bohemian credentials.

The CEO handed me over to my next minder, Robin Clover of Clover's Keg, 'brewers of fine local beer since 1875', and his wife Jo; local royalty, commercially speaking.

The hours passed so much more pleasantly than I'd expected that I was quite surprised when three o'clock came and the hospitable Clovers walked me back to the VIP car park.

The driver's door of the mayoral Merc was open, and Vic was sitting half in and half out, reading Elizabeth's newspaper. At our approach he dropped the folded paper in the foot well, jumped up and came round to open the door for me, ostentatiously shooting his cuffs.

'Good afternoon, ma'am.'

'Hello, Vic.'

I turned away from him to say my goodbyes, but Vic was not, like Reg, a man sensitive to boundaries, and spoke as I did so.

'Enjoy your day, ma'am?'

'Yes, thank you.'

'Sun came out for you after all.'

'Yes.'

'It's been really good fun,' said Jo, stepping forward to shake my hand in such a way, God bless her, that she cut the sight line between Vic and me. 'Will you be coming to the Beerfest in August?'

'I'd love to, but I don't know if it's scheduled.'

'Let me know if it's not,' said Robin, 'and I'll get Kim to bang out an invitation asap.'

'And,' chimed in Jo, 'you can wear another hat!'

'It's a date. And speaking of schedules . . .'

Knowing that Vic was waiting, impatiently, at the door of the car, I deliberately dawdled over departure.

I was due at a reception on the science park at six, for which there was no need to change, so we drove back to City Hall. Vic, perhaps miffed at being cut out of the conversation with the Clovers, was mercifully quiet. But an unlooked-for opportunity for a small revenge came his way on arrival. Having deposited me at the mayor's entrance, he called as I was halfway up the steps.

'Ma'am!'

I turned to see him waggling the folder containing the briefing notes.

'Forgotten something?'

'Oh – thanks.'

As I took the folder from him, Elizabeth's photo slipped out and flopped to the ground. Like a flash, he picked it up and returned it to me, giving it a glance as he did so.

'Family picture, don't want to lose that.'

I didn't need to say anything. However cursory the glance he'd given the photo he would have seen that none of the people was Nico, or Elizabeth. But I suppose I was flustered.

'No, no – just some people I know – must have got mixed up – thanks. Bye.'

I was glad he couldn't see my burning face. His: 'See you in an hour and a half, ma'am,' followed me up the steps as I fled.

* * *

The lady lawyer's interrogation at brunch had reminded me how far I'd fallen behind on matters such as the proposed Princes Way shopping mall, so I took the opportunity to catch up on some paperwork. Common sense dictated that with another imbibing session just round the corner a cup of tea was the last thing I needed, but when Hilary produced one my resistance crumbled.

'Two sugars,' she said. 'And a biscuit. You need the energy.'

'Thank you.'

We presented an oddly domestic scene – me at my desk in my M&S foot-gloves; my high heels standing neatly by the coat rack; above them, my suit jacket on its hanger and my hat on a hook; Hilary, a somewhat unlikely angel of the hearth, administering tea and chocolate digestives. Perhaps it was this *faux* cosiness that prompted me to ask where Reg was.

'Off duty this week. He and Maureen have gone down to London to see his daughter in her show.'

'I'd forgotten about that.' I heard the grumpy note in my voice, and added: 'He's so proud of her.'

Hilary had also caught the grumpiness, and interpreted it correctly. 'Vic's not so bad.'

'You think.'

'It's just his manner.'

'I'll take your word for it.'

I wondered why people said that – that some disobliging form of behaviour was 'just' someone's manner. Like Vic's 'then' it was a small syllable with big implications. In this case it was offered as an excuse, when it was no excuse at all. How else was one to judge a person if not by his or her manner? I did not (thank God) know Vic well enough to perceive the excellent qualities he kept hidden, and I was not telepathic. The man I'd been obliged to share a confined space with for the best part of two hours was a smug, insinuating creep. The mere thought of him studying my precious photograph made my palms sweat, and prompted me to retrieve it from the folder.

'Thanks, Hilary,' I said. 'Invaluable as ever.'

'Did you enjoy the horses?'

'I did. I was ignorant, but the Clovers were good company. They're going to invite me to the Beerfest in September, by the way.'

'They'll need to be smartish, your autumn diary's pretty full.'

'I told them that.'

I handed her the notes, and she took them, but still held them out. 'Don't you want to keep these?'

'Sorry?'

'For the thank-you letter.'

'You're right, what am I thinking of.' I took the folder back and Hilary left the room, but not before I'd felt the brush of her sagacious, speculative glance.

I was able to leave the reception at seven and was home by half past. My jaw felt tight from the effort of being polite to Vic – 'Champagne all the way today, then!' – and I couldn't relax immediately, even though Nico was in the kitchen assembling the ingredients for his signature spaghetti carbonara.

'Hope you're up for this.'

'I shall be, certainly.'

'Well earned g and t?' he asked, raising his own to tempt me.

'No, thanks, not at the moment. I'll go up and get changed.'

'Good idea. I shall defer the final stage until you're ready.'

As I made to leave, he said, 'You've got a couple of emails you might want to pick up.'

'Thanks.'

'One's from Elizabeth.'

'Did you read it?'

'No.' He cracked an egg with a flourish. 'It was FAO you.'

I'm at the Yard on Wednesday 15th, Rob had written from Elizabeth's laptop. *Great to see you if you can make it, and don't forget to come to the bar afterwards. R x*

I must have read the message a dozen times in the next minute, scanning it for possible ambiguities, but there seemed to be none. The 'you' might have been open to interpretation had it not been for the 'FAO Joss'.

It was an invitation. A personal invitation to me from him. 'Joss!'

And not just an invitation to see him perform, but to have a drink, to be two people who wanted to be in one another's company . . .

'Joss . . .!' Nico's voice drew closer as he came to the foot of the stairs. 'How are you doing? Only I've reached the critical egg moment and I'm starving.'

'Coming!' Adrenalin surged through me like strong drink. I pressed 'delete', and 'quit' in quick succession and jumped up from the desk. 'Carry on, I'll be there in two ticks!'

When I came into the kitchen in cotton trousers, T-shirt and flip-flops, Nico was folding the beaten egg into the spaghetti.

'That looks good.' Happily, I put my arms round him and heard the exclamation of delight that showed how rare the gesture had become.

'Hey.' He pushed the pan to one side and turned to face me. 'You do, too.'

'Do I?' I looked down at myself. 'In my sliggins and sloggins?'

'I like them. Always have.'

I kissed him briefly and gave him a gentle push. 'Get back to the stove, man, you're not the only one starving around here.'

On the table stood an open bottle of red wine and two of our prettiest wine glasses, the ones with the twirly stems and the grape pattern. I sat down at the table and he put a plateful in front of me. Nico had always been a good cook, spontaneous and imaginative, and his carbonara looked and smelt delicious.

'Pepper, signora?' He brandished the grinder above my plate.

'*Si, per favore.*'

'Parmaggiano?'

'*Si.*'

He picked up the grater and the last couple of ounces of Parmesan and rubbed a pile of shavings on to the spaghetti.

'*Grazie.*'

'*Prego, signora.*' He added cheese to his own plate, tossed the grater into the sink and sat down opposite me, rubbing his hands. 'Good, excellent! Sometimes I think I missed my vocation.'

He poured wine, and we clinked, each of us happy.

'So what did Elizabeth want, or shouldn't I ask?'

'Oh . . .' I waved a hand. 'It was just a doctor-type query.'

'Women's work,' he agreed. 'Tuck in.'

Eleven

Hal called us at seven o'clock on their second morning in London and asked if they could come up for the day on either Saturday or Sunday. We were still in bed, but I sat up and riffled through the mental filing system for the section marked 'diary'. I had a retirement home tea to attend at four on the Sunday, but we were able to offer lunch, and I suggested they come out as early as they could. It turned out they'd met up with Elizabeth and Edward the night before.

'I've got to say he's a top bloke,' said Hal. 'After a couple of minutes I forgot all about his age.'

'We like him,' I agreed. 'And Elizabeth seems very happy.'

'I've never seen her so loved up, but I thought she looked a bit stressed.'

'There's a slight problem with the stepdaughter.'

He said breezily, 'That's part of the job description, surely.'

I thought it was all very well for him to say, who had put clear blue water between himself and his responsibilities.

'How's Lili coping with all these relations?'

'Sailing through. After all, she's only met one so far, and she's got dozens.'

'Have you seen the children yet?'

'Saturday.'

'Is Lili going?'

'Of course!' Hal was the most easy-going man in the world, but the words carried an edge of irritation. 'She's invited. Cathryn invited her.'

I sometimes wondered if he realized the exceptional qualities of the woman he had left.

'Oh, good. I do hope that goes well, darling.'

'It will, we'll make sure it does,' he said, closing the subject. 'Look, Lili wants to say hello. I'll pass you over.'

'Oh, Hal . . .' I wasn't ready to speak to Lili, especially as

I realized she'd been nearby, listening to his end of the conversation.

I heard him say: 'There you go,' and the phone was passed over.

'Mrs Carbury? This is Lili here.'

Her voice was light and tripping, the voice of a young girl though I knew she was Hal's age. The accent was East Coast American with a just discernible oriental twang.

'Hello, Lili.'

'We're so looking forward to seeing you at the weekend.' She put the accent on 'week' in the American way. 'It's so kind of you, I know how busy you are.'

'Not at all, you're . . .' I was about to say 'family' but I wasn't quite ready for that, and substituted, 'You're most welcome,' which sounded stiff and formal, like a maître d'.

'Is there anything I can bring along?' she asked.

I pictured them in their smart London hotel and wondered what she'd have done if I'd said yes.

'Definitely not – don't worry, I'll keep it very simple, I want to talk to you and Hal not be stuck in the kitchen.'

'Good thinking.'

'Is there anything you can't eat?'

'If there is I haven't come across it yet.'

'Splendid. Well . . . See you then, Lili.'

'Can't wait.'

Nico, still flat on his back, had been watching and listening throughout this exchange and now held out his hand with a grabbing motion. I fended him off as Hal came back on the line.

'She means it – ever been in a Korean market? Everything but the hooves.'

'That's great.' I had the distinct feeling that while this was something they could joke about between themselves, I shouldn't be included. 'Hal, Dad wants to speak to you, I'll let him sign off.'

'Sure. Cheers, Ma.'

I passed the phone to Nico, and the two of them spent a couple of minutes male-bonding over sport, airline security and the hire car (a Nissan Altima).

When he'd rung off, he said, 'I'm looking forward to that – it'll be a real step forward.'

I knew he was right. And I had missed Hal a lot, in a fraught, conflicted way: his big, easy personality, his boy-in-a-man's-body charm, his expectation (all too often and undeservedly borne out) that everything would be just fine . . . The trouble was that currently this meeting, like almost everything else in my real, day-to-day life, was an obstacle impeding my way, blocking my view, diverting my energy from where it wanted to be – with the result that if I wasn't careful there would be little pleasure to be had from either. I was like a secret addict, living my life on two levels; and like an addict I was neither proud of myself, nor sufficiently ashamed to do anything about it.

As the weekend approached I realized that while yet again I'd committed myself to no fuss, it wasn't quite as simple as that. For notwithstanding Hal's 'omnivore' comment, and Lili's politeness, I suspected that family meals chez Wang were lovingly prepared set pieces of course after course of hot and delicious food. Lili herself might be a typical New Yorker with nothing but vodka and fresh lemon in the fridge, but she almost certainly came from a culinary tradition which for freshness, flavour and abundance put ours in the shade. If I was going the simplicity route, it had better be high-end.

I bought in a side of wild salmon, jersey royals, garden peas and a pound of raspberries.

'A veritable feast,' said Nico as I swathed the salmon and herbs in tinfoil.

'The taste of an English summer, I hope.'

We had that, in spades. It didn't just rain, it poured, with a dark, roaring insistence that under normal circumstances would have had us putting a line through the day and hunkering down with the papers. Instead of which, having abandoned any idea of a relaxed lunch in the garden, we had to make a quick decision between the dining room and the kitchen. The kitchen won, on the grounds that while Lili might not pick up on the nuances, Hal was family, and would be uncomfortable with any implied formality.

But using the kitchen meant further scooting round to create an atmosphere which spoke of easy, unashamed creativity without the attendant mess. By eleven we were in our 'relaxed' clothes and the salmon in its silver shroud was ready and waiting as the rain hammered on the windows. Nico sighed heavily at the thought of the cava and peach schnapps in the fridge.

'It's scarcely Bellini weather. If I'd known I'd have laid in a litre of Bristol Cream.'

We'd moved our car so they could park immediately outside, and at twelve o'clock the metallic blue Altima swung into the space.

'They're here!' I called. 'Open up quick, or they'll get soaked!'

I ran round to join Nico at the front door. He said, over his shoulder: 'They've got the children with them.'

'What?'

'Hello!' he cried. 'Welcome one, welcome all, leave your flippers at the door.'

Several times over the next three hours I found myself hoping that one of these days I'd have earned a family gathering that didn't require the diplomacy skills of HM's ambassador to Beijing.

Lili was a Korean Kylie, perhaps an inch taller than Chloe and half a stone lighter, wearing an emerald green micro-dress and gold sandals, and tiny hexagonal gold glasses which must single-handedly have rehabilitated spectacle-wearing in my granddaughter's eyes. Cathryn had a terrible cold, so had accepted Hal's offer to take the children out for the day. Both Chloe and Jed seemed robustly at ease under this dispensation, which though a lot better than the alternative, was nonetheless disconcerting. Hal was almost overwhelmingly expansive and genial, using bonhomie as a kind of screen to deflect too much intimacy. He was taking everything, all of us, in one gigantic stride.

As for me, I threw in another pound of new potatoes, defrosted some French bread and served ice cream with the raspberries. Lili greeted everything with tinkling delight, like slightly discordant wind chimes.

'This is for dying – you really have a way with ingredients, Joss. Did you make this mayonnaise yourself?'

'As a matter of fact on this occasion I did.'

'You mean to tell me you don't always?' said Nico, and he was rewarded with Lili's silvery laugh.

'I thought Lili deserved it.'

'Can I leave the skin?' asked Jed.

'Sorry, did you get some?'

'Only I really, really don't like it.'

'Well you don't have to eat it.'

'It makes me gag.'

'Jed . . .' Hal leaned over and removed the skin with his finger and thumb, dropping it on the edge of his own plate. 'Don't go on about it or everyone'll want some.'

'Wimp,' said Chloe. 'He's such a wuss about food.'

'Wait till I serve you my Korean feast, kids,' said Lili. 'Not for the faint-hearted!'

'Do you like to cook?' I asked.

'I do. But in Manhattan we don't that often. I cook some, and send out for the rest.'

'Sounds the perfect compromise,' said Nico.

'I cook,' said Hal. 'My shepherd's pie's famous throughout the lower west side.'

'You never used to, Dad,' said Jed. 'You weren't even a crap cook, you didn't do it at all.'

'Well, I've learnt.'

Lili turned to Nico. 'Do you cook, Nico?'

'I'm brilliant.'

She giggled and glanced at me. 'Is he kidding?'

'No, he's brilliant.'

'I have a limited repertoire of dishes I've perfected over the years,' said Nico. 'And from time to time I experiment.'

'Still the barbecue king?' asked Hal.

'I can safely say that given the right conditions I can cremate a burger with the best of them.'

'He can,' I said.

'Mum did a joint on the barbie the other day,' said Chloe. 'A whole leg of lamb. It was wicked.'

'She's a very clever lady, your Mom,' said Lili. 'I should learn how to cook a roast. Hal misses them.'

'Place in oven and apply heat,' said Nico.

'But then there's all that other stuff – gravy and roast potatoes and relishes and vegetables, and getting it all on the table at the same time . . .'

She and Nico discussed roasts. The children asked if they could get down until pudding.

'No,' said Hal, 'you're quite old enough to stay here and join in.'

'Dad's quite right,' I said, 'but on this occasion I'll exercise grandmother's prerogative and say yes.'

'Cheers, Gran.'

They were gone. I looked at Hal. 'I wasn't undermining, was I? I didn't mean to.'

'That's OK. I just don't want to turn into one of these soggy Santa fathers who never say no and send the kids home to give a hard time to their mother.'

'No,' I agreed. 'Poor Cathryn – how is she?'

'Streaming.'

I thought she must have loved that; a stinking cold in front of tiny, sparkling Lili.

Hal went on: 'But this is all with her total blessing.'

'I never doubted it.'

I saw him glance in Lili's direction. She and Nico were keeping each other amused.

'She's lovely,' I said.

'Isn't she? And don't be fooled – incredibly smart. She practically runs Greening Comstock.'

'I bet.'

I remembered now, some reference to Lili working for a bank. The contrast with Cathryn, doggedly negotiating the labyrinth of social services on behalf of her poor, unhappy clients, was stark. Hal must have seen it on my face.

'Cathryn is fine, you know.'

'I do hope so.'

'She is. She's looking great, she's getting out . . .'

'"Getting out"!'

'I mean she has a life, a social life. You have to stop seeing her in terms of me. She's her own woman now.'

'I don't,' I said. But he was right, I did.

After lunch I told the children they could go on the computer while we sat over coffee. Nico and I swapped ends, so to speak, and I asked Lili about her work.

'It's very challenging, very demanding – I love it to death. But I don't want to talk about that.'

She said all of this in exactly the same chirpy, charming tone of voice so it took me a second to appreciate that she was changing the subject.

'No?'

'No. I want to thank you, Joss, for extending me such a warm welcome, when it must have been hard for you.'

'No, no, I wouldn't say that.'

'I would, though. You love Cathryn, and you must have been sad when she and Hal split. You must have worried about the kids.'

'Yes,' I admitted, 'I did.'

'They're fabulous,' she said. 'Cathryn's doing such a great job.'

'Yes.'

'They've been fantastic with me, and they didn't have to do that. I didn't expect them to. I don't know what I expected.' She laughed, but I was starting to hear, and see the real Lili, the one behind the glitter and tinkle.

'You know,' she went on, 'Hal misses them so much, but he felt kind of guilty about seeing them, too. You know, absent-dad guilt, how to play it, all that. I told him he had to make the effort, be as good a dad as he can be. I'm so glad I came on this trip . . . I can see how they just adore him.'

'They do, yes.'

'And we have Cathryn to thank for that, too,' she said. 'I really respect her for how she's handled all this.'

One false intonation or ill-chosen word, the merest glimmer of smugness, and I'd have wanted to smack her face. But there was none of those things, and I warmed to Lili.

At three o'clock, mindful of my need to change before the senior citizens tea party, they left. The rain had eased off leaving an afternoon of queasily shining sunlight, and they were going to walk in the park before taking the children home.

'Can I lend you anything?' I asked Lili. 'Will you be all right for a walk?'

'I have a special see-through umbrella,' said Lili. 'And galoshes. Don't believe me?' She opened the boot. 'Ta-da!'

'By Jove she has, too,' said Nico, picking one up and letting it swing from his finger and thumb. 'I haven't seen one of these for years. Where did you get them?'

'Harrods. I figured I was in England, I should have galoshes.'

'They'll make your feet look jellied,' said Jed.

'Jellied but dry,' said Hal. 'You'll be laughing on the other side of your face when those trainers are sodden. Hop in.'

He closed the car door and put his arms round me – so tall, and rangy and lean, so utterly different from Nico.

'Come over and see us soon, yeah? When you've stopped being mayor.'

'We will.'

Nico and he exchanged a manly hug; and Nico cuffed his cheek. 'Bye, old boy. Thanks for bringing them, it was a delight.'

'Bye, Dad.'

Suddenly they were going, we were waving as they pulled away, and I experienced a small rush of panic that the occasion had not been given its due – something important should have been said, in acknowledgement of what was on any account a new chapter in our son's life.

Later I found my nicest card – one of three women at a box in the theatre, listening to a wartime concert – and sent it to Cathryn.

Do hope you're feeling better I wrote. *We missed you, but it was lovely to have the children, who did you proud and were a delight as always. Thank you for letting them come, and we hope to see all of you again very soon. Take care, lots of love, Joss and Nico.*

It was after I'd put this card in the post that I remembered: the important thing I worried about had been said, with neither fuss nor fanfare – by Lili.

'She sounds brilliant,' said Denise. 'Do you think they'll get married?'

'I don't know. I hope not.'

We'd managed to squeeze in our drink together in the café-bar next to the City Crafts Gallery where Denise worked part time. Though she'd never, as far as I knew, had any especially artistic bent, she gave off a creative vibe and had always enjoyed jobs on the edge of the arts world.

'Why?'

'Because that would mean the end.'

'You talk as if he's a Class A womanizer – remember I know something about those.'

'No, but he doesn't like fences – and this would be cross-cultural, with God knows what implications.'

'I think you're being old-fashioned there, Joss – people do it all the time these days. Anyway –' she got out her cigarettes, watching me as she did so – 'we didn't come here to discuss Hal.'

I closed my eyes for a moment. 'I'm seeing him in a few weeks.'

'Hang on!' Denise blew smoke over her shoulder. 'Hang on – you mean seeing him as in *en famille* or seeing him as in seeing him?'

'As in seeing him.'

'Joss – I've got to hand it to you, that's bold. Not to say rash.'

'I know,' I said.

'So, what form will this – date, take?'

'It's not a date. I'm going to see him perform his work at the Yard, and have a drink with him afterwards.'

'Is Nico going?'

'No.'

'Is he even invited?'

I hesitated. 'Not really.'

'Don't delude yourself, babe,' said Denise. 'That's a date.'

She was wasting her breath on the subject of self-delusion – it was my specialist subject. The answer to the question 'who did I think I was kidding?' was perfectly straightforward: myself. The proposed meeting with Rob would not, I reasoned, be a date because a date was between equals (I conveniently overlooked the other bit about being unattached). I would be indulging the boy, accepting his attention, graciously granting him a little of mine in return . . .

I was fooling most of the people most of the time, but myself, in the ugly modern parlance, twenty-four-seven.

Twelve

In the period between Esther Waring's acceptance and The Visit (the occasion had assumed quasi-regal overtones in my mind) she occupied a lot of Nico's attention, so I was able to think my thoughts and manage my moods without attracting comment. I did however have to field one awkward request.

'Joss, I was thinking – would you have any objection if I offered her a bed for the night? I'm sure she won't take us up on it, but I can't help feeling it would be a civil gesture.'

I agreed, though 'civil' was hardly the word to describe Nico's ferment. He was, as they say, gagging for it. From my perspective, the prospect of returning home at the end of what promised to be an extremely long day, and dancing further attendance on the Dame while Nico waxed ever more fulsome on Famous Grouse, was not enticing.

But he was her sponsor, and I was mayor. Protocol as well as common courtesy allowed me no way out.

Except that on D-Day minus three, Nico began to feel ill. Though far from being a hypochondriac he enjoyed such insultingly rude health that the slightest wobble presented like a near-death experience.

'Bugger!' he cried, in almost comical distress. 'I'm getting a buggering cold!'

Experience had taught me not to panic. I prescribed four-hourly paracetamol for the sore throat, plenty of hot drinks, and early nights preceded by baths as close to scalding as he could stand – the steam would help clear the congestion.

'I can't believe this!' He clapped his hand to his creased and (I noticed) perspiring brow. 'I never get colds! What was the point of all that Vitamin C? And the flu jab!' As if to illustrate his point he jabbed his own finger at me. 'What was all that about? Why did I spend an hour sitting in that palsied waiting room full of geriatrics waiting for that scary nurse to stick her fucking great needle in me if not to prevent this happening? Why?'

'The flu jab is for the flu, in the winter,' I pointed out. 'What you've got is a summer cold.'

'But I feel like shite!'

I was decorating a hat to wear to the St Mary's Mixed Infants Summer Fayre and had reached a tricky stage with an artificial flower. 'A really bad cold can do that.'

'A really bad – Christ! That's all I need, a full-on snotfest when I'm greeting Dame Esther. It was all going so well, and now all she'll see is a human Petri dish looming over her! She'll probably refuse to shake my hand in case I jeopardize her Goneril at Stratford or something! Jesus . . .' He rubbed his neck and grimaced. 'My throat's killing me.'

And the awful truth was, it very nearly did. Twenty-four hours later Nico was complaining, with some justification, that even his hair hurt. He was running a temperature of a hundred and three and his throat was so swollen and infected he could barely speak, let alone eat. In all the time we'd been together I'd never seen him so unwell. On one of the rare occasions I had ever used special pleading on age grounds, I secured a home visit from the doctor who stood at Nico's bedside and shook his head glumly in the time-honoured manner of family practitioners.

'I'm afraid this is full-blown tonsillitis.'

'I knew it . . .!' rasped Nico, from below. 'I fucking knew it . . .!'

'Look at it this way, Mr Carbury,' said the doctor. 'You'll never have a better excuse for a week in bed.'

It was fortunate that Nico's scarlet face was half-buried in the pillow, so the doctor couldn't hear his response. Instead he turned to me.

'You were right to call me. I can honestly say those tonsils are the worst I've seen in an adult, and the discomfort is far more acute in a grown man than a child. A hundred years ago your husband's condition would have been diagnosed as the quinzies.'

'What on earth are those?'

'A really savage throat infection – our ancestors regarded them as a sort of plague. There was a time when we'd have whipped the tonsils out, but that's almost unheard of now, and anyway it would be a massively invasive operation for an otherwise healthy man of your husband's age to undergo.'

I remembered, with a pang of remorse, my 'not the flu' shaft of yesterday. Nico lay with his eyes closed, looking frighteningly inflamed and wretched, his breathing shallow. I opened the bedroom door and moved out on to the landing, gesturing to the doctor to follow, and lowering my voice.

'He's got an incredibly busy schedule at the moment and a hugely important date coming up, is there any way he could just, sort of, be got on his feet – made to feel well enough to attend, and go back to bed afterwards? He's been looking forward to it for weeks.'

'When are we talking about?' He was already shaking his head.

I bit my lip and fixed him with a pleading look. 'Tomorrow evening.'

Another shake of the head. 'Out of the question, I'm afraid. And if it's any consolation he's not going to feel like it.'

On any grounds whatever there was no point in arguing. The doctor was adamant, but he didn't know Nico. After I'd seen him out I went back upstairs, and drew the curtains. The room sank and softened into a pink and sepia summer twilight. Nico lay very still, very hot, very unwell, his hair shucked up on the pillow, his mouth slightly open.

I stood by the bed for a full minute, brimming with an unnameable sadness. Then I went downstairs, feeling like an executioner, to make the calls that would spoil all Nico's fun.

The doctor was right. There was simply no question of Nico's going to meet Dame Esther, he was far too ill. As predicted, she'd declined our invitation to spend the night, so there was no accommodation problem to solve, but Nico had been going to give her a lift to and from the station. I was going to arrange a limo, but Nico was insistent that I should take her to the theatre, and attend the show in his place.

'Please, Joss . . . You can be my eyes and ears. Report back.'

'But what about you?'

'I shall lie here, dying by numbers, whether you're around or not.'

'Nico, I'm so, so sorry.'

'Not your fault. But do go. Please.' He felt for my hand, and his was dry, and hot. 'You'll provide the necessary home-side glamour.'

'Someone ought to be here. I'll ask Wendy.'

'If you must.' He closed his eyes. 'As long as she leaves me alone.'

'She will, she understands.'

'I want to feel sorry for myself in peace. I'll bang on the floor if I need anything.'

Before I left that evening I went to say *au revoir*, wearing the cream shirt dress I'd bought in London. Nico was lying on his side in the feverish semi-conscious state that had become the norm over the past three days.

I went and stood where he could see me. He opened an eye.

'Hey . . . You look great.'

'Thanks.'

'What about the . . . the . . .?' He waggled a hand feebly. 'Crown jewels.'

'Reg is taking me to City Hall first, before we go to the station.'

'Give her my – whatever's appropriate.'

I leaned over and kissed him. He smelt slightly acrid, his hair unwashed and his skin sweaty. 'I'll tell her you're a life-long fan and devastated to be missing her.'

'That'll do.'

He was already drifting into sleep as I left the room.

'Sounds like the quinzies,' said Wendy.

'You've heard of them?' I shouldn't have been surprised, but Wendy had babysat Elizabeth for us as a teenager and I'd never quite got used to her being grown-up.

'This area was famous for them. They got a mention in my local history class.'

'Good heavens.'

'Anyway, don't worry about Mr Carbury, I'll keep an eye on him.' She was sitting at the kitchen table with her jewellery-making box, and now she opened the box and began taking out the tiny wires, beads and forceps, laying them out on a cloth, like a theatre nurse. 'You look nice, by the way.'

'Thank you, Wendy.'

The phone gave two rings.

'Reg is here.'

'Off you go then.'

I hovered anxiously. 'He's taken his pills and he's got plenty of water by his bed. I think he was dropping off, but you might just take a peep—'

'We'll be fine.' Wendy gave me a bossy look. 'Go.'

Reg was sympathetic, but full of *Chicago*.

'It's a funny thing for a father seeing his daughter up there with half her costume missing.' He shook his head and sucked his teeth happily. 'Takes a bit of getting used to!'

'But you enjoyed the show?'

'Fabulous. Really fabulous. You know, near the knuckle, but really polished. And funny – we laughed. And the dancing – I don't know how they do it, night after night.'

'Years of training, I suppose.'

'That's it.' He glanced at me in the mirror. 'You said it. They make it look easy, but it's hard labour – those young people really earn their money.'

We had timed our drive to the station via City Hall so as to be there ten minutes ahead of time, the Merc parked in a prearranged priority bay, and us in position on the platform. It was a beautiful evening, but I'd brought a pashmina to cover the 'crown jewels' because even with Reg in attendance it felt a bit ostentatious.

I felt a thrill of nervousness as we stood there in what we had been advised was the first-class carriage zone. Whatever my private grumbles, Esther Waring was a big star. There were a hundred invited guests waiting to meet her at the theatre, and eight hundred more people in the auditorium itself, only a quarter of them members of the Friends, the rest just dying for a glimpse of their favourite actress in the nationally treasured flesh. I thought of Nico and found myself wanting to do him proud.

The last thing I expected was not to recognize her. Because she was a big star, I had expected her to be – well – big. Tall, anyway. And she was not tall, but tiny. It was almost as much of a shock as when I'd seen Marlon Brando in the flesh at a

film premiere, dancing with a duchess, his head on a level
with her brocaded bust. Could this, I'd wondered, be the
godlike being whose gleaming biceps had so thrilled me in
Streetcar? He was, as Nico put it, a short-arse.

Now, my gaze was directed several inches above where
Dame Esther's head actually was, when she said: 'Mrs
Carbury?'

Reg nudged me. 'Madam Mayor.'

'Yes?'

Finally I focused on her. She held out her hand, smiling.
'Esther Waring.'

'Esther – Dame Esther – hello!'

Caught on the hop, I was more than a bit flustered.

'We absolutely must dispense with the handles,' she said.
'I'm Esther, and you're Joss, surely.'

'Yes.'

'Nice to meet you, Joss, and . . .?'

'This is my driver, Reg.'

'Hello, Reg.'

'How do you do, ma'am?'

We headed for the car, with Reg, his neck extremely pink,
leading the way. Esther was wearing a close-fitting ice-blue
suit with a mandarin collar, and a knee-length skirt with the
suggestion of a fishtail at the back. Her hair was the colour
of jersey cream, the cut feathery and flattering; tiny diamond
earrings, kitten heels, a grey suede clutch bag with a faux
diamond clasp. I towered over her, but her lack of inches made
me if anything rather more in awe of her and I had to make
a conscious effort not to stoop obsequiously. As we crossed
the station forecourt we trailed a small Mexican wave of startled, then admiring, recognition.

Mindful of his passengers' unforgiving skirts, Reg opened
the near door of the car and then sprinted round to the other
side to open that one too. There was a split second's protocol
uncertainty before I nipped to the far side and Reg returned
to hold the door for Esther.

'This is fantastically good of you,' she said as we set off.
'I've never driven in an official car before. It's like being
royalty.'

'It is rather fun,' I agreed. 'I'm making the most of it.'

'And are you enjoying being mayor, generally?'

'Yes.' Since she seemed genuinely interested, I added: 'It's quite literally a once-in-a-lifetime experience.'

'I can imagine . . .' She smiled and nodded thoughtfully as though she were actually, at that moment, imagining it. Then she turned so that she was sitting slightly sideways on the seat, facing me. 'Joss, I'm desperately sorry about your poor husband.'

She had that agreeable knack which I generally associated with Americans and of which Lili had been the exemplar, of readily assumed and quickly established intimacy. I wanted to give Nico his due so that he could have some of that and be appreciated.

'He's done all the organization, the whole thing is down to him. He loves this theatre and your agreeing to come was a personal coup, he was thrilled to bits. I can't tell you how much he's been looking forward to this evening, and meeting you – well, I'm sure you can imagine.'

'I'm pretty devastated myself.' She pulled a funny, rueful face. 'You must know he wrote me the most irresistible letter.'

'Did he?'

She cocked her head and gave me an almost flirtatious, quizzical look. 'If he's half as charming in real life as he is on the page, I'm missing a treat.'

'Yes,' I said, and the knowledge that she was right sent a blade of remorse right through my heart, a blade all rough-edged with confusion. 'I'm afraid he is, and you are.'

She studied me for a moment and then said: 'Lucky things,' before turning away.

By the time we reached the theatre I was completely won over. That she was smaller and more fragile than I'd expected and had a hint of secret sadness about her was all part of it. I wanted to be her friend – anyone would have wanted that, and I knew without a shadow of doubt that Nico would have fallen in love with her.

All through the reception I saw her having the same effect on people. For men, the expected 'Phwoah!' gave way to the softer shine of the romantic crush within seconds; for the women, ready to be jealous or unimpressed, any tension was quickly diffused in smiles, then laughter – a real happiness that they were relieved of their bad feelings and gifted new, incomparably nicer ones. It was an effortless object lesson in how to win hearts and minds.

During the play that followed she sat in the front row of the dress circle, between me and the play's director, a quiet, clever man called Barry Shaw. Barry didn't do dressed up; he wore his customary unrelieved basic black. I was barely acquainted with him, but enough to know that he was prickling with the expectation of being patronized. He needn't have worried. Esther was all humility, asking searching, informed questions and expressing a pitch-perfect degree of peer-group admiration. Long before the curtain rose on *After Illyria* he was eating out of her hand.

The mezzanine level cloakrooms had been set aside for the use of special guests in the interval. Esther and I wound up standing next to one another in front of the harshly lit mirror. Abruptly she leaned forward and dragged her hair back with both hands. Her face, cruelly exposed, was narrow, intelligent, vivid – but there was no denying the many fine lines and the beginnings of a droop at the jawline. I was a little shocked, and she caught my eye and asked: 'Would you ever consider having a tweak?'

'No,' I said, 'I'm far too chicken.'

She let go of her hair and fluffed it back into place. 'I would.'

'Why?' I asked, adding truthfully: You look wonderful.'

'Thank you, Joss, but to misquote Dolly it takes a lot of time and money to look this natural. An hour or two under the knife would pay dividends in the long run . . .' Another woman came in, and she said: 'Caught in the act! We were discussing plastic surgery here.'

'Oh, were you? Goodness, in that case, don't let me . . .!' The new arrival beamed nervously and disappeared into a cubicle.

For the second act Barry and I made way for the lady chairman of the Friends and a representative of one of the season's major sponsors. Watching her work her magic on a new set of neighbours I was almost jealous. Though I knew she was an experienced hand, practised at putting people at their ease, I couldn't help but see myself as her confidante.

Afterwards, a dozen of us went for supper in the theatre's rooftop restaurant. At eleven o'clock, having made a small glass of Sauvignon and a Roquefort and endive salad go a long way, Esther had to leave for her train. Her smoothly expeditious farewells still managed to convey a charming show of reluctance, and we went down to where Reg was waiting in the square.

In the car, she opened her clutch bag and passed me a notelet in an unsealed envelope.

'Joss, would you give this to Nico for me?'

'Of course.'

'It's just one of those totally useless expressions of sympathy. And you never know – there may be some other occasion when I could make myself useful.'

'Be careful what you say!' I laughed at her diffidence. 'He'll bite your hand off!'

At the station we took her to her platform, and she put her hand out to Reg.

'Reg, thank you so much.'

'My pleasure, ma'am.'

'When I crack Hollywood the first thing I shall do is send for you.' She glanced at me. 'Assuming Madam Mayor will have moved on by then, I wouldn't want to deprive her.'

When the train came in, I thought she might offer a cheek, but she simply shook my hand, enclosing mine briefly in both hers, and said: 'Joss, thank you. That was a memorable evening. Please thank Nico for all his masterly organization.'

'I will.'

'His spirit pervaded everything. And tell him good luck with the season.'

She boarded the first-class carriage and sat down in her reserved window seat. I felt – not sorry for her, exactly, because she was not a sad person in the modern sense, but curious. What must it be like to feel the same despondency as any other elderly woman when looking in the mirror, but to know that so much more depended on it? I watched as she took a book from her rucksack and placed it on the table. Her face with downcast eyes was oddly neutral; but when she looked up and saw us still there, her smile was brilliant as she waved goodbye.

It was gone midnight by the time Reg dropped me off at home.

'Give my best to Mr Carbury, ma'am.'

'I will.'

'Pity he wasn't there to meet Dame Esther.' He hesitated. 'Nice lady.'

'I thought so too.'

'Good night then, ma'am. See you tomorrow at eleven.'

'Night, Reg.'

Wendy was watching one of the later *Rambo* films on Channel Five. Stallone – pecs gleaming, shoulders bulging, arms latticed with throbbing veins, blackened face streaked with manly tears – was fixing single-handedly to waste a heavily armed and highly trained enemy force. Wendy's eyes hovered lustfully on the screen and her first question sounded absent-minded.

'Did it go all right . . .?'

'Brilliantly. How's the invalid?'

'Oh . . .' She dragged her eyes away and switched off the television. 'He's been asleep mostly, on and off. Woke up about half an hour ago.' She frowned. 'He's really hot.'

This could have meant Stallone or my husband. I gave her the benefit of the doubt.

'I'll go up. Did you find your envelope? It was by the kettle.'

'It's in my bag.'

She packed up her jewellery kit, and I went with her to the door and waited on the step until she was safely behind the wheel of her Clio. Then I waved her off, set the latch and went upstairs.

The reading lamp on my side was on, angled towards the wall and away from Nico, who lay on his side, with his shoulders hunched under the duvet. As I came in he rolled on to his back, one arm wrapped round his head.

'Darling . . . hi.'

'Hi, yourself.' I leaned over and gave him a kiss – Wendy was right, he was burning up – and then sat down on the bed. 'How're you doing?'

'Bloody awful. Better for seeing you though.'

'Can I get you anything?'

He shook his head slowly, rolling his head from side to side, eyes closed. 'Tell me all about it.'

'Congratulations, it was a wonderful evening. Everyone said so. Most of all Esther.'

'Ah, Esther.' He managed a faint, bitter smile. 'Go on then, what was she like?'

I confess I experienced a brief urge to diss the dame, but almost immediately overcame it.

'She was lovely,' I said. 'Really. Just as gorgeous in the flesh and absolutely delightful. I hate to say it, but you missed a treat.'

'Did I . . .?' He coughed and felt for my hand. 'I know what I did miss.'

'What?'

He beat my hand weakly up and down on the duvet a couple of times. 'Being there with you, standing alongside my beautiful lady mayor . . .'

I had never been more glad that I'd said the right thing. Glad, and ashamed.

I handed him the note 'She sent you this.'

'Cheers.' He glanced at the envelope and dropped it, unopened between us. 'I say, Joss, am I due another pill of some sort?'

I did a quick retrospective calculation. 'I'll get them.'

When I came back in with the three tablets in my cupped hand, he dragged himself up against the bedhead and moaned querulously: 'When the fuck am I going to feel better?'

'Soon. A day or two.'

'I felt I'd reverted to childhood . . .' He swallowed the pills. 'Yeuch . . . Wendy came and peered at me from the doorway.'

'I told her to. She said you were asleep most of the time.'

'I was foxing.'

I said, 'She was watching *Rambo* when I got in, so she clearly wasn't that worried about you.'

'Bloody Rambo . . .' Nico slid down once more to the horizontal. 'I didn't know he was still out there.'

'On the wilder shores of Freeview he is.'

'Christ. He must be my age if he's a day.'

'You're conflating the actor with the role.'

'Don't get picky with me, Joss, I'm dying . . .' groaned Nico. His temperature might still be high, but his morale was definitely improving.

'Anyway,' I said more briskly, 'I'm going to get ready for bed.' I pointed at the envelope. 'Read your note, why don't you, that'll cheer you up?'

He picked it up and gazed at it lethargically. 'I will.' He put it down again. 'Probably.'

I undressed, hung the shirtwaister in the wardrobe and went into the bathroom. Glancing at Nico, I saw that his eyes were closed. As I cleansed, toned and moisturized, cleaned my teeth and brushed my hair, I thought of Esther Waring, who would probably only just be getting off the train. I realized that all evening I had been in that relation to her that other people so often occupied in relation to me – that of the eager-to-please host. Only she was a great deal more practised in the role of guest of honour than me, or even Georgia. All evening she had protected herself by drawing other people out. Unless she had been on professional autopilot and not listening to a word I said (which had certainly not seemed to be the case) she would have formed a very clear picture of me, of the absent Nico, our relationship to each other and the life we led – of which, in some mysterious way, she had become a part.

When I went back into the bedroom Nico's stertorous breathing advertised that he was out for the count. Esther Waring's note (which I saw now was a postcard), and the envelope that had held it, lay on the floor next to the bed. Telling myself that I was only tidying, and, going to put it on the table, I picked it up. Once it was in my hand there was no going back – I was bound to read it.

The picture was one of those Tate Britain pictures of the 1930s 'Percy and Jane having tea' by someone called Edward Gossard – it showed not just the couple, but their greyhound, curled up on the floor, and a young woman in a brown dress, reading. The tea tray, including a cut cake, stood on a low table in the centre of the picture, but no one was actually eating or drinking. The girl was immersed in her book. Jane was knitting and Percy, in spectacles, pencil in hand, was doing the crossword on the back of a folded newspaper. A French window stood open, a sunny garden lay beyond. The scene was to all intents and purposes peaceful and domestic, but conveyed a strong sense of each person's separateness, deep in their easy (or uneasy) chairs. Like so many English pictures of the period this one was both strongly narrative and evasive. There was a story – not necessarily even recognized by the participants – but it was for the onlooker to decipher and interpret. A well-chosen card, of the sort I might have sent myself.

I turned it over. Esther's handwriting was flowing and

cultivated but large, the blue ink flowing exuberantly over the
printed notes and filling every millimetre of space. There was
no date or introduction; she cut straight to the chase.

> *So sad to hear that you're laid low and that I shan't be*
> *meeting you tonight, after all our communications over*
> *recent months. I'll be in touch soon, and please don't*
> *hesitate to let me know if I can be of use again. We who*
> *support local theatre must keep the faith!*

Lack of space meant she'd had to sign her name vertically up
the side of the postcard. I subjected the whole thing to the same
scrutiny I'd applied to Rob's emails, diligently mining the handful
of dashed-off words for hidden meaning. But there was none that
I could find. The voice in the note was the same one she'd used
to me, to everyone – courteous, easy, charming, but economical.

I placed the card with its envelope on the bedside table
and looked down at Nico. I was struck as always by the
apparent innocence, the trusting quality, of those asleep and
felt ashamed of my knee-jerk jealousy. Nico's crush on Esther
Waring was declared, open, and shared by more than half the
male population. And even tonight, feeling terrible, he'd had
the sensitivity – and the sense – to make me feel top of the
heap, star of his show. And it had been his show, in every
sense; the disappointment must have been awful.

In the film, I'd have stooped and placed a pensive kiss on
my husband's forehead. In reality, I felt an urgent need to
distance myself from him and the reminder he represented of
my own faithlessness. I left the room.

Now, as I closed the door and sat down at the computer, I
made myself admit it: infidelity was in the mind. Until now
I'd have called the idea ridiculous. For heaven's sake, everyone's
eye wandered now and again, the spouse didn't exist who
hadn't strayed mentally from time to time. If thoughts and
feelings were what made you culpable, then none of us was
safe from censure. The deed was what made the difference –
the whole, crucial difference – between right and wrong.

I switched on, turning the sound down in case Nico should
be woken by the Avon-like chimes of the logging-on tone, an
unusual sound at this time of night. There could be no doubt
that I was engaging in treachery of a high order. My attempts

at self-absolution on the grounds that I had not actually 'done' anything, were worse than pathetic, they were mischievous – an excuse to continue doing exactly as I pleased.

It was good to know I had a conscience, but unfortunately it was like a neighbour's dog barking – distant and easy to ignore.

There were seven messages: three for Nico updating him on the theatre, three spams (Viagra, the wine club and walking tours), and – yes! – one for me from Rob.

> *Hi Joss, How you doing? Hope you're still on for Wednesday, one favour – any chance I could kip over at yours? No early shift next day! But I'd be in late, out early, no special requirements, sofa fine. If not, no problem, totally understand. Look forward anyway – plenty of new material to try out on you. Rob x*

This on the face of it brief and businesslike communication launched my heart on a queasy switchback. The easy informality of the opening might have been as between friends or the effect of an assumed intimacy . . . Instinctively, like a blind newborn finding the teat, I latched on to the latter. But the unequivocal banality of the next request cast me into despair. *Kip over at yours.* Even the most fevered imagination (and at present mine could go from normal to life-threatening in a heartbeat) would have been pushed to put a romantic spin on that. It was the affable, straightforward opportunistic freeloading of the young, predicated on the notion that we would both – Nico and I – be in residence and that we would most probably (nice couple that we were) say yes. No tension, no temptation, not a hint of inner turmoil. *Kip over at yours . . . in late, out early . . . sofa fine . . . no problem . . .*

But surely I was going to be 'in late', if not 'out early' too? We had a date, didn't we? I was trembling as I pressed 'reply' – devastated.

> *Hello, Rob – Yes, of course you can stay, in a proper bed even. Early start not a problem, I do a mean cooked breakfast.*
> *See you soon. Joss*

Meekly, cravenly, I'd adopted the tone that seemed expected

and invited by his – amusing, cheerful, hospitable – more Mrs Bridges than Mrs Robinson. What choice did I have? I asked myself as I pressed 'send'. The manifold anomalies of my position had me trussed up like a chicken. Everything I said or did vis-à-vis Rob was designed gently to nudge him into behaviour that would invite a different response from me. But that was as proactive as it got. If I had been Mrs Robinson, Benjamin's honour would have been perfectly safe. I was innocent without wanting to be.

The prospect of getting into bed next to my sick husband was even less inviting now, and I went downstairs to the kitchen. I considered and rejected tea and poured an amaretto over ice, telling myself as I did so that I was going to regret this late-night indulgence at the primary school tomorrow.

I opened the door and carried my glass out into the garden, turning the kitchen light off as I went so that outdoors seemed less dark. Above and beyond the soft glow of the city the stars were refracted into a sparkling haze by my luxurious tears.

When both the tears and the amaretto were finished I went back in, closed the door and made tea anyway. After the bleak let-down of Rob's message the question still remained: what exactly was it I wanted? I tried for the first time to imagine – to really imagine – what Denise would have considered the logical upshot: Rob and me in bed together.

It was impossible. Even when, with a considerable effort, I conjured up a picture of the two of us approaching that moment, kissing, embracing, fondling, sighing, the whole thing stalled when it came to the point where we undressed. It wasn't simply that the mere thought of taking my clothes off in front of anyone but Nico these days was too terrible to entertain, but that my image of Rob was not as an ardent lover, naked and rampantly aroused, but as a squire, a *chevalier*, something altogether more refined and complicated. When he looked at me and spoke to me – spoke only to me, or listened with that air of rapt, focused attention – I was in heaven, his to command. But it was more of that for which I yearned, and longed, and about which I fantasized so obsessively.

I suppose that in other words I wanted to extend, indefinitely, what is known by psychologists as the infantile stage. You might call it romantic. Georgia always maintained that the period leading up to the first kiss is the most enthralling – all is anticipation and imagination, and enchanting speculation. A thread of sexual tension, gossamer fine but strong as steel, keeps the two parties in thrall to one another. Given that mutual attraction is there, and the kiss does not end it, the second stage is then embarked on, one of (in my experience anyway) unbridled shagging. The test comes after that, when the shagging slows down and enchantment of a quieter kind has to be found in different ways. That's when being alone with each other ceases to be the be-all and end-all, and it's nice to be a couple out there, amongst other people who can provide a diversion, an audience, and a sounding board. Only after a long, long time – if such a period is granted – when one has reached the point of non-verbal communication and emotional shorthand does the desire to be alone together become once more an imperative. When I pictured Nico and me at these stages it was first facing one another, then side by side, then back to back.

But this analysis was no help to me in my consideration of Rob. Not only could I not see us in bed together, I couldn't even get beyond the present. I wanted to inspire in him the same romantic devotion, the same level of obsession and longing that I experienced. And then what?

The rest was silence.

About a week before Nico fell ill, on one of those rare evenings when we were both in, we'd watched an American made-for-TV film about a housewife in her thirties having an affair with her daughter's boyfriend. *So Not* it was called; as in 'so not a good idea'. The woman didn't look – in fact wasn't – much older than Elizabeth, and the boy was a sort of heavily sanitized skater, all blond streaks and frayed shorts. The relationship was initiated by the boy, Dane; the woman, Martha, put up only a token resistance. I watched, transfixed, as their two equally beautiful bodies heaved and undulated beneath the hand-threaded white linen in Martha's guest bedroom.

'This is laughably implausible, isn't it?' said Nico. 'The whole thing till now has been about what a good wife and mother she is, but this youth's got into her knickers within days of first asking.' He looked at me for confirmation. 'Am I right?'

'Ludicrous,' I agreed.

We watched for another half a minute, during which Dane and Martha reached a shuddering synchronized climax and fell back on their fluffy pillows in the cinematically approved recovery position, arms flung above their heads, chests heaving.

'So, that's all right then,' said Nico.

I laughed briefly. 'Her mascara hasn't smudged.'

'And –' he lifted a finger – 'no strap marks, did you notice?'

'They never have those.'

'But why not, I ask myself?'

'Perhaps she doesn't wear a bra.'

'Well, she should,' said Nico. 'I mean, for God's sake, she's stacked.'

I decided I was in no position to pass comment, humorous or otherwise. On screen, Dane leant over the side of the bed and took a cigarette packet from the pocket of his discarded jeans.

'Hey,' said Martha, 'you can't do that in here.'

Nico barked with laughter. 'Shagging a minor's fine, but a post-coital gasper's out. Only in America!'

'It'd give them away,' I muttered tensely.

'Because the whole place will reek of it and no one in this house smokes,' Martha explained obligingly.

'Of course,' said Nico. He beamed happily at me. 'Just as well I'm such an uxorious fellow, you'd catch me out in no time.'

'Just as well,' I agreed. We'd long since stopped mentioning the lapse with Alex.

'Whereas you're obviously a natural cheat, alive to all possible risks.'

'That's me.'

'Look, there they go!' Nico pointed excitedly at the screen. 'They're doing that thing with the sheets that no one in real life does!'

We generally derived a good deal of innocent amusement from the forms of behaviour exclusive to films and television: the assiduous swathing of sheets when getting out of bed; the looking quizzically at the phone after ringing off; the sliding slowly down walls, weeping, when distraught; the automatic pouring (not so common now) of two fingers of whisky as the drink of choice, the ability to swallow wine while chewing, and to have sex with one's trousers on (we'd once tried it and Nico was nearly emasculated by his zip); and so on . . . I wasn't laughing now. The whole Martha and Dane thing was much too close for comfort. It served to demonstrate in the most straightforward terms, the reasons why I should not only not take things any further but stop. Right now.

'Think that's enough, don't you?' said Nico, as he zapped the lovers' tense but tender farewell. 'It'll all end in tears anyway.'

I put my mug in the machine and went upstairs. Nico was in the same position, sleeping peacefully, and felt cooler. I slipped in next to him trying to disturb the duvet as little as possible, but he still murmured: 'Night, sweets.'

Thirteen

I got back from the St Mary's Primary School Summer Fayre at five, to find that Nico had been up. There was an egg-streaked plate and saucepan in the sink and a half-full carton of orange juice on the side. The television standby light was on, and the handset was absent from the charger. I found him spark out on the sofa with the telephone clasped to his midriff and the more left-leaning of our two newspapers on the floor beside him. As I went to retrieve the phone his eyes snapped open and for a split second he looked panic-stricken.

'Eh? Oh – Joss? What?'

'I'm back. I didn't mean to disturb you.'

'You didn't. I mean I shouldn't have been dozing.'

'Yes, you should.' I took the phone. 'What you shouldn't have been is out of bed.'

'I was bored witless. But by the time I'd made scramblers and dialled the office I was wiped out.'

'That'll teach you. Come on. Up.'

I helped him stagger heavily to his feet. As he did so his kimono flopped open to reveal an erection – half-mast but undeniably on its way up. We both stared. Nico pointed at it with a finger like a six-gun, as though giving a lecture on some species of small, dangerous animal.

'See that?'

'I could hardly fail to.'

'That's down to you, that is.'

'Up.'

'Well, quite. Down to you so far, up to you what happens next.'

'I mean,' I said severely, 'up – to bed.'

Nico leered. 'That's what I meant.'

'Don't be ridiculous, you're ill.'

'Could be just what I need.'

That was one thing about Nico, he was completely un-neurotic. He was so proud of his rampant priapism that it would never for a nanosecond have crossed his mind that I might not fancy a tumble with a man emerging from a period of illness – unwashed, unshaven and with breath like a car crash. But at least, I reflected guiltily, this gave me a valid reason to turn him down.

'You're joking,' I said. 'A man in your condition?'

'I'm definitely recovering.' He made a grab for me and nearly fell over. I caught his arm and steadied him.

'Nico, for heaven's sake.'

'All right, all right, you win.' He headed in the direction of the stairs, holding first the back of the sofa, then the door handle, then lunging for the newel post. He must have sensed me watching because he said, without turning round. 'I shall make it on my own . . . Don't worry.'

'I wasn't.'

I heard him mutter, 'Cruel, cruel . . .' as he dragged himself up the stairs. He hadn't bothered to tie his dressing gown, but there was no longer any sign of the erection.

Nico went back to work the following week – the Monday preceding Rob's gig at the Yard. If I'd been cast down by the implication that we were both invited, something happened on the Tuesday to give my increasingly susceptible emotions an upward tweak. Elizabeth called me at 11 p.m.

'Sorry about the hour, but it's the only time I can be sure of getting you these days.'

'That's all right, I was still reading.'

'How's Dad?'

'Asleep.'

'Not any more,' mumbled Nico.

'I'm going to take this downstairs,' I said.

'That's it, then you can talk about me . . .'

'Go back to sleep.'

I took the phone down to the drawing room. 'He is actually on the mend,' I said, 'but bad-tempered.'

'That's not like him.'

'He's tired. He was really ill. I was very worried about him.'

'Oh, you were?' She sounded quite put out. 'Should I have come up?'

Knowing her as I did, I was alive to the possibility of fallout. 'No, no, good grief!' I laughed nervously. 'It wasn't a family-gather-at-the-bedside thing. Just a thoroughly nasty infection. The awful truth is these things hit you harder as you get older.'

'Yes . . .' She sounded thoughtful, and I reminded myself that her husband was older than either of us. 'Anyway I'm glad he's better.'

'And what about you – feeling more cheerful?'

'I'm working on it.'

I thought, poor Edward, but instead asked how he was.

'He's fine.'

'What about the family? Seen much of them?' Even to me my tone sounded artificially nonchalant, but she seemed not to notice. This self-absorption, I was in a position to know, was one of the key characteristics of the depressed and one which played into my hands at present.

'Bryony came round to see Edward,' she said dryly. 'I was in charge of refreshments.'

'You really mustn't let it get to you. It'll wear off.'

'In how many years? During which I have to pretend not to exist?'

'You don't have to pretend anything. You're Edward's wife, he loves you more than any—'

'No, Mum, he doesn't.'

'You don't know what I was going to say.'

'You were going to say that he loves me more than anyone else, including his children.'

'Well,' I said, obligingly jumping into the hole I had just dug for myself. 'Something like that.'

There was a short pause – I pictured her drawing on her cigarette. 'That's where you're wrong, Mum. Don't judge other people by you and Dad. Edward's children come first and they always will.'

Smarting, and because I had no alternative that didn't involve the sort of raw exchange that I couldn't face, I let her injunction regarding me and Nico go.

'Has he said that?'

'He doesn't need to.'

I tried a different tack. 'It's not a competition.'

She gave a just audible snort of contempt. 'Ah, the endlessly accommodating cake of lurve.'

'Perhaps,' I said rashly, 'you should have one of your own.'

'What?' She sounded genuinely taken aback.

'You know, hoops of steel and all that.'

'Mum, Edward is sixty-four.'

'He won't be the one giving birth.'

'I thought you said it wasn't a competition?'

'I lied.'

Incredibly, I could hear the reluctant smile in her voice as she said: 'And this is a good reason to have a baby? To trump the stepchildren?'

Even though she couldn't see me, I shrugged. 'If you're going to be a wicked stepmother, you might as well go the whole hog.'

'That's outrageous, Mum!' I had really cheered her up. 'I never heard anything so downright immoral.'

'You haven't asked the right people,' I said, and she laughed. Laughed! I took advantage of the laughter to ask: 'Anyway, how's Rob?'

'All right, I think. We haven't seen him for a while.'

'He's no trouble, anyway.' There was a dangerous thrill in talking about him like this, so close to home.

'No,' she conceded. 'But he's not going to take sides.'

'Perfectly proper.'

'Yup.'

Shortly after that the call ended. I realized that I still had no clear idea of why she'd rung, and then I remembered her enquiry about Nico. It still seemed to me that that wasn't quite it. Maybe – just maybe – she had simply needed to talk; wanted the reassurance of speaking to me. Whether she'd received it or not I couldn't say and was never likely to know. But I was reassured on one important count: Elizabeth and Edward did not know that Rob was coming to the Yard or that he was seeing me. They did not know because it was none of their business. His visit was not a family thing, it was between us.

I had not turned the light on in the drawing room, and now I sat in the dark, digesting this. On the table next to me there gaped, open-mouthed, half a dozen huge stargazer lilies – part of a bouquet I'd been given by the St Mary's PTA. They were the most sensual of flowers – so big, and fleshy, pinkly freckled, the merest spider touch of their stamens leaving a fierce orange stain. And now, quite suddenly, they emitted a waft of overpowering scent. It was as if they understood my frailty and had made some collective decision to breathe their sickly essence on me.

Spooked, I went back upstairs and slipped into bed next to Nico.

On the day of Rob's gig, I went to lunch with Georgia at the manor. I'd been at a Chamber of Commerce meeting at City Hall in the morning, and I got Reg to drop me at home afterwards so I could change and drive out there on my own. Much as I loved the ease and comfort of the mayoral car it felt wonderfully free to be humming out of town and along the country roads in my trusty Mini, wearing jeans and a T-shirt.

The house was stern and grand, but the front door stood open, in a gesture that would have given Julian's expensive security firm a seizure. As I got out of the car, Georgia appeared.

'Hooray, you're here!'

'Just as well I'm not Fingers Finnigan.'

'Pish tush, it's broad daylight and I saw you from the window.'

We kissed, and she led the way through the house to the big kitchen-dining room at the back. Two plates and a salad bowl, all covered with cling film, stood on the table.

'I thought we could eat under the tree.'

'Lovely.'

'First things first.' She took a bottle of white wine from the sleek, retro Smeg fridge. 'Just the one?'

'Thanks. And then forget about me.'

'Whatever you say.'

She waved a hand at the food – 'We can fetch that in a minute' – and we went out of the door into the garden. She and Julian had sensibly kept a small area for themselves (I say small, but it was a third of an acre): a square of mossy terrace, a pleasantly lush, daisy-dotted lawn, and a mellow brick wall covered by a nectarine, now coming into fruit. The wooden table stood beneath the bent boughs of two wonderfully ancient apple trees; one end was laid for two, with a pale blue cloth and a breadbasket covered by a blue checked napkin; on the other lay Georgia's straw hat, book and glasses. She picked up the book and showed me the cover.

'I'm reading this. Do you know her?'

'No . . . But that doesn't mean a thing. I've been reading the same novel for weeks.'

'She's American, but awfully good,' said Georgia unself-consciously. 'And her medical stuff is frightfully impressive. Eye-watering. She must have done stupendous amounts of research.'

We sat down. For a long moment I simply breathed in the mellow, sequestered beauty of it all. Only in England, I thought . . . Only in England could you find this precise blend of grandeur and greenness, of openness and seclusion – the quiet sounds of midsummer, middle-day, sun-struck birds and humming insects . . . the scent of grass and old roses and lavender . . . and something else that filled the air around us: history. For one blissed-out second I wondered whether Nico and I should move to the country, or to one of the city's satel-lite villages. But wherever we went and however hard we tried we would not be able to recreate this; because this could not be created, it could only evolve.

'I know what you're thinking,' said Georgia.

'Go on then.'

'You're thinking how lucky I am.'

'In a way. Everything here is so magical . . . But maybe you're used to it.'

'It's home, but I hope I don't take anything for granted. And when I see it through other people's eyes I'm reminded how extraordinarily blessed I am.'

Something in her voice, an unguarded, almost wistful note, made me glance at her, but now her glass was raised and her face lit by her perfect, shining smile.

'*Santé!*'

'Cheers.'

'It's been ages, far too long, I want to know everything.'

She always said this, or a version of it, but she was discreet and never pressed me for what I didn't want to tell.

'Right,' I said. 'Nico's been ill, but he's better now. He had to miss the opening night with Esther Waring . . .'

'What a rotten shame, we did too – and he was so looking forward to that!'

'But she wrote him a charming letter and I'm sure she'll come again.'

Georgia rested her glass against her cheek. 'Was she nice?'

'Very. And Elizabeth's rather down, she has a wicked step-daughter.'

'Poor girl, how awful.'

'Or let me rephrase that, a stepdaughter who thinks Elizabeth's a wicked stepmother.'

'That must be perfectly hideous. And you?'

'Like a gnat in a paper bag.'

'Mayoral duties.'

'I'm not complaining.'

'I know you enjoy it,' she said. 'And I'd be able to tell anyway. You look fantastic.'

'Oh . . .' I glanced down at myself. 'Do I?'

'Hair, skin, eyes – ten years younger.'

'Thank you,' I said again. Georgia's gaze continued to rest on me for a few speculative seconds, but I didn't respond to the unspoken question.

She got up. 'Right, I'm going to get our lunch. No – you stay there. This is your chance not to be a gnat.'

I watched her walk away with her long, graceful stride. She was wearing a printed calf-length dress which on anyone else might have been frumpy, but which on her was softly elegant. But below the floaty hem, her delicate ankles looked thin, the shafts of the Achilles tendons like bean sticks. I thought: *We're old. We're two elderly ladies having a light lunch in the shade. Not as young as we were. Slowed down a bit. Three score years and then . . .*

This bleak thought led as night follows day to one about hair. Hair and the end of the world. If (as seemed far from unlikely these days) the world were to end before we did, microwaved by our collective vandalism, that meant we'd all be around to see things as they deteriorated; to endure a life of ever-dwindling resources. Frivolities like artificial hair colouring would be among the first to go. Suddenly, the world would be full of old ladies. The demographic mushroom would be made startlingly visible with all the rich and glamorous variety replaced by grey, white, and pepper and salt heads. No more 1661 – we'd all be rumbled.

Fortunately at this point Georgia re-emerged with our lunch on a tray.

'Here we are. Couldn't be much simpler I'm afraid.'

Our plates of prosciutto and salami, with almost-translucent shavings of Parmesan, looked perfect, and I said so. 'I'm always being confronted with more than I want these days.'

'What a nightmare,' she agreed. 'And you haven't put on an ounce.' She gave the salad a push. 'Practically zero calories, have plenty.'

We helped ourselves and began eating. In the general way of things you don't notice the feeding habits of the person opposite; an instinctive discretion prompts you to lower your eyes as that person's fork reaches their mouth, and they do the same for you. But on this occasion I couldn't help noticing, because there was something different about the way Georgia ate. She had fastidiously good manners as usual, but she was a good trencher woman, who straightforwardly cleared the plate, always complimenting another cook, and only holding back at her own table when FHB was the order of the day. Today I was conscious of a tension, a slight agitation in the quick, bird-like movements of her knife and fork, as though this lightest of meals was a challenge that had to be met, but to make the challenge too obvious would have been poor form. She seemed to be doing a lot of unnecessary cutting and moving about of the food on her plate, she took tiny mouthfuls, chewed intensively and her throat – in which the tendons, like those in her ankles, were plainly visible through the thin, white skin – moved effortfully with each swallow.

I had nearly finished before she was halfway through and slowed down to keep pace, but of course she noticed.

'Please,' she said, glancing at my plate, 'don't feel you have to wait for me. Have some more, do.'

'Perhaps I will,' I said, reaching for the salad. 'It's so good.'

'The dressing has walnut oil and green peppercorn mustard. And honey from here.'

'Delicious.'

I sighed with what I hoped was a kind of lazy, reflective relish, while Georgia pecked away on the other side of the table. To give her time and slow myself down I told her more about Esther Waring and she nodded and smiled and nibbled. But even so I only managed to outlast her because she put her knife and fork together and admitted defeat.

'It's no good, I'm beaten.'

'How are you doing,' I said, so casually that it was hardly a question.

'Not brilliantly.'

Understatement though it was, it cast a shadow over the table and placed a cold cat's paw of anxiety on my heart.

'I'm sorry to hear that. What's up?'

She shrugged, her glass against her mouth. I sensed she was fighting to master some awful, embarrassing emotion, and I made a business of pouring myself a glass of water.

After an interminable couple of seconds she took a sip from the glass and said: 'I don't know, Joss. I wish I did. Tests have been carried out.'

'You didn't say.'

'I haven't seen you much recently.'

'I know and I'm sorry.'

She waved a hand. 'We're both busy and long may that continue.' She pulled a face, not a funny one. 'Pray God it continues.'

I abandoned all pretence of detachment. 'Oh, George.'

'Sorry, I didn't mean to spread alarm and despondency. After all, I'm not despondent.'

'But you are worried.'

She pursed her lips. 'Mm. A bit.'

'When will you hear?'

'In about a week. It's a fortnight since they stuck things down me and up me, and at the time they indicated it would be about three weeks from then.'

'Why didn't you tell me?'

'You have a lot on your plate . . .'

'No! No, George, that won't do.'

'What could you have done?' At least in the face of my impatient anxiety she sounded more herself.

'I could have been in the loop.'

'There is no "loop".'

Something about the way she said this prompted me to ask: 'You have told Julian?'

She stretched the fingers of her left hand and turned the rings – I saw how easily.

'You haven't, have you?' I said.

'When there's something to tell he'll be the first to know.

But since at the moment there is nothing . . .' She waved a hand. 'What would be the point?'

'The point?' I was incredulous. 'For a start, he's going to go spare when you do tell him. And now I feel awful for making you confide in me, when he doesn't know.'

'I may turn out to be perfectly all right.'

'You may turn out to have nothing serious the matter, but you're not right. I mean for heaven's sake –' I struggled – 'hasn't he noticed anything?'

'Apparently not.' She stacked our plates together absently and put them at the far end of the table. 'You know what men are like.'

I thought about this and about Nico. But comparisons were odious, so I didn't go there, and instead I said: 'It took me less than half an hour.'

'There you are then.'

She was going to get up with the plates, but I put my hand on her arm. 'No you don't.'

'I'm capable of carrying two plates.'

'I dare say, but I want you to stay here and talk to me.'

She sank slowly back on to her chair. It was like an admission of defeat. I almost wished I had let her take the damn plates.

'I didn't mean to do this,' she said.

'Do what?'

'Go all Helen Burns on you.'

I had to laugh. Nodding at our surroundings, I said: 'Some Lowood!'

'And talking of Mr Rochester,' she said, 'which we were just about to, how's the smitten squire?'

It was unprecedented for this topic to seem like an escape route, but that was what happened now. I latched on to it like Leonardo DiCaprio with his piece of wreckage.

'Funny you should ask,' I said. 'I'm seeing him this evening. He's performing at the Yard and asked if I'd like to go along.'

'Just you? Or both of you?'

'Just me,' I lied, adding, as a conscience-saver, 'but he's staying the night with us afterwards.'

'And that would be . . . good, or bad?'

Mystery illness or no mystery illness, there were no flies on Georgia.

'Good,' I said brightly.

'If it weren't for –' I prayed she wouldn't say Nico – 'the domestic context.'

'I suppose.'

She gazed at me for a moment, then tapped the table briskly. 'Coffee?'

We took the things in together, she made the coffee and I carried the tray back to our table under the tree. I would have changed the subject, but there was no chance of that. She leaned forward with her cup held in impossibly thin linked fingers and fixed me with her most perspicacious look.

'What I can't make out, Joss, and what I really want to know, is – are you happy?'

This, as she very well knew, was a good question, and one to which my hesitation in all probability provided the answer, though she was too considerate to say so.

'I'm elated,' I said. 'Exhilarated.'

'On a high . . . I can see that. I'm not the only one who's dropped a dress size.'

'But,' I blundered on, 'obviously, you know, I would wish it otherwise.'

'Would you? Would you really?'

'I'm not proud of myself for feeling like this. In fact pride's gone right out of the window.'

She put down her cup. 'May I say something?'

'And if I say no?'

'Then I won't.'

'That's what I thought.'

She didn't smile. 'I think you should get that pride back.'

'Easier said than done, George. Like not worrying.'

'I appreciate that, but still. You are my wonderful, good-looking, impressive friend, star of the Council Chamber, mayor of this fine city. And who is he? Some nice boy who's been thrown in your path. No . . .' She put up her hand and closed her eyes. 'No, hear me out, Joss. I wasn't lying when I said I liked him. I thought he was personable and charming and all those things, but the main thing about him is he's young. And Elizabeth's stepson. Never underestimate the power of forbidden fruit, and he's just about the biggest no-no imaginable, which is why you hanker so desperately. You know you can't have him –' she peered at me – 'don't you?' I was silent.

'Well, don't you? Never mind, you do know. But if you want to keep his heart on a string, you have to be the person he first saw.'

I knew she was right, and I was touched that in spite of all her wise counsels and grave misgivings she understood what I wanted. The test of friendship – to know, to understand, to help you achieve your objectives with the least possible collateral damage to anyone, most of all yourself.

Not long after that I left. As we walked to the car, she said: 'Of course, I haven't asked you the most important thing.'

'Which is?'

'What on earth are you going to wear?'

'I don't know.' After what we'd just been discussing I felt like a child being indulged. 'I haven't decided. It doesn't matter.'

'Yes, it does.' She smiled at me, with a hint of sisterly exasperation.

'George . . .'

'It does. Pride, remember?'

I nodded. As so often these days I was on the verge of tears and I so desperately didn't want to cry in front of her.

'My advice,' she said, gently but firmly, 'is keep it simple. The simpler the better. Just be your splendid self.'

'Hmm,' I said. 'I'll try.'

I got in the car and she leaned down, arms folded. Her collarbones stuck out. When she grinned at me the effect was worryingly cadaverous.

'Remember,' she said, 'I'm on your side, Joss.'

'I know.'

'Good luck.'

Confronted with a real life or death situation my tears, paltry, self-absorbed things that they were, duly evaporated leaving me high and dry with the harsh reality of what Georgia had told me. That 'good luck' haunted me. If ever there was someone who needed luck . . . but there again, she was probably beyond its reach.

In her sure-footed way she had salvaged the what-to-wear issue from complete, humiliating triviality. In fact her earlier advice – about the need for pride and so on – had considerably added to its importance. I had to feign, even if I couldn't feel, self-confidence. I had to present as a self-possessed woman with many calls on her time, who was charmed to be invited and who had made space in her busy schedule to be there – someone, in other words, assured, who knew how to behave.

Alone in my bedroom that was not how I presented. I was so used to the rules, strictures and demands of my mayoral wardrobe, the semi-automatic clicking into place of the various interchangeable components – suit, hat, shoes, bag, bingo – for any given occasion, that I had practically lost the ability to make more subtle and complex choices on my own behalf. With plenty of time at my disposal I sat on my bed, surrounded by piles of clothes, and felt the first, familiar stirrings of panic. A bit of cognitive behavioural therapy came to my rescue; I made myself think – really think – about what Georgia had said and then acted on it.

I went and showered, using gallons of that shower gel that is supposed to leave your skin smooth and luminous as a Fabergé egg. I left nothing to chance; I also exfoliated and depilated, and used extra conditioner on my hair. When I was dry I applied body-part-specific moisturizers all over even though (I told myself) he would not come into contact with any of it bar a chastely proffered cheek. I put everything back in the wardrobe except black jeans and a blue shirt. Neither was new, both were faded and soft from many washings. But they made me feel clean and comfortable, ready for anything. I even considered wearing no make-up but rejected that as a show of confidence too far. Enhanced naturalness was what I was after. I compromised with a light covering of something called 'Mature Radiance' (so expensive that it had lain unused in my top drawer for months and I calculated that there was now about a tenner's worth on my face), a meticulously applied but near-invisible application of eyeliner and mascara, and the merest swipe of lipgloss. On the jewellery front I wore only my simplest silver ring earrings, rejecting even a chain on the grounds that earrings I was never without, while a chain was a consciously selected adornment.

I dried my hair upside down to achieve root-lift, and then tweaked and sprayed it into a style of carefully judged artlessness. I was changing handbags when the phone rang.

'Just off?' It was Nico.

'Hi – yes, any minute.'

'Enjoy. Give the boy an encore from me.'

'I will.'

'Really rang to say I may not see you later.'

'Oh?'

'I'm going down to London, if it runs over I'll have to stay.'

'OK.'

'Sorry about that.'

'No, that's fine. Thanks for telling me.'

He laughed. 'Well, mustn't keep you. Off you go. Bye, darling.'

'Bye.'

I put the phone down and left the house. I hurried, not because I was late, but because I wanted no time to think.

The Yard was about three-quarters full – more than respectable, considering that Rob, a relative unknown, was topping the bill. As I stood with my Diet Coke in the bar, the group of twenty-somethings next to me were talking about him.

'. . . blew us away at the Poetry Café.'

'Bit traditional for my taste – bit Paul McCartney. Crowd-pleaser.'

A shrug and a laugh in the voice. 'Excuse me? Who wrote the best tunes?'

'Bit populist?' persisted the critic. 'Bit – um – Blairy?'

This provoked a burst of laughter and some 'Ooohs'.

Someone else chipped in. 'Not everyone can be edgy.'

'Don't get me wrong, he can do it, but he's safe.'

'Maybe,' said the first speaker, a woman, 'this discussion is breaking down along gender lines.'

'He is cute,' agreed one of the blokes. 'Even I can see that.'

I carried my drink into the hall and sat about two-thirds of the way back, near the end of a row. It was a decision akin to the buying of a greetings card – one peripheral to the main event, but which had assumed a disproportionate importance. I wanted to have a reasonable view and to be visible, just myself, but I did not want to appear to have made too calculated a decision. This last was shot to pieces because the place was still two-thirds empty when someone sat down in the seat next to me, and I saw it was him.

'Hi, there,' he said. 'How's it going?'

'Good,' I replied – not a word I'd normally have used in this context, but then I knew the question to be rhetorical.

His eyes rested on me calmly, frankly; he was smiling. 'It's so great to see you here.'

'I wouldn't have missed it for anything.'

'I don't normally like it when there are people in that I know. But you're an exception.'

'Thank you.'

'Because you're here purely for its own sakc. No agenda.'

'Yes,' I said.

'Still on for a drink afterwards?'

'I look forward to it.'

'See you in the bar about nine thirty then.'

'Sure.' When had I last said 'sure'? Who did I think I was exactly?

He disappeared through the door on the left, non-public, side of the stage. From the corner of my eye I saw the people I'd been standing next to in the bar. In the same way you know when someone on television can see themselves in the monitor, I could tell that they'd spotted Rob, and it had reignited their earlier discussion; one of the young men was laughing, and I could hear them teasing him about saying Rob was 'cute'.

The place was filling up, both the seats, and the air with a warm, anticipatory hubbub. I imagined being Rob, backstage, hearing the crowd and knowing it was for him. I could imagine because this year scarcely a day went by when I didn't arrive somewhere and hear a similar sound, waiting for me. Except that in my case it was the office and its small significance that was awaited (that and in some cases a mild curiosity about my hat), and in his it was his own talent and presence – himself. And every one of those here – I glanced round – would have, and were entitled to have, an opinion. What Rob was about to do was the equivalent of parading naked in the market square. I could only suppose that the performance gene provided a measure of protection. Last time he had seemed so perfectly at home on stage, so perfectly himself . . . But even that, I supposed, was a trick – no, a skill. You centred yourself, developed a sense of who you were in relation to others, and then acted that self.

'Mrs Carbury? I didn't know you were a poetry fan!'

It was the head of English from the City North Community College – their prize-giving had been one of my earliest engagements. I tried, and failed, to remember his name.

'Hallo – yes. I came to one of these with some friends a little while ago and enjoyed it, so I thought I'd come back.'

He beamed down at me. *Macintyre? Mackintosh?*

'I've brought some Year Eleven English students.'

'What a good idea.'

'We have some really talented poets this year. I keep telling them poetry's the new rock and roll.'

'So I hear.'

'Well – see you later.'

'I expect so.'

Because, for whatever reason, I had not said: 'Oh, my daughter's stepson's on the bill', I felt I had created some sort of secret, and that it would be awkward if we bumped into Mackintosh/Macintyre afterwards.

He returned to his party, who were sitting nearer the front. When he'd sat down I picked up my bag and beaker and moved to a seat three rows further back and in the centre. I had to ease my way along past other people, but when I sat down I looked neither to right nor left, not wanting to know or be known.

Almost at once the lights dimmed and I was one of the crowd in the darkness.

Fourteen

He'd asked for a whisky. I poured one, and an amaretto for me, while he sat at the kitchen table. His khaki rucksack lay on the floor by his chair.

'Where's Nico?' he asked.

'In London,' I said. 'He may not get back tonight. He'll be sorry to miss you. Shall we take these upstairs?'

'Sure.' He took his glass, picked up the rucksack and followed me up to the drawing room.

'Such a lot of stairs,' I said.

'Yeah . . .'

'Here we are. Make yourself comfortable.'

He went in, glancing around, dropped the rucksack near the door and sat down on the sofa. He looked very much at home, one arm along the back, legs stretched out. He had made no comment about the house, he just seemed to accept, own and inhabit it, as he did the stage. I wondered whether to put on music. On my own, with Nico, or almost anyone else, I would have done, but in these circumstances would music appear loaded, to imply the creation of 'atmosphere'?

I sat down and raised my glass. 'To you,' I said. 'Congratulations on a terrific show.'

'Thanks. Cheers.' He took a swig. 'Joss, I hope you don't feel you have to keep me amused. You've probably got to do something official first thing tomorrow.'

'Schools swimming gala, ten o'clock.'

'You're taking part?'

I had to laugh. 'Good Lord, no! Opening, and watching – these are eleven- to thirteen-year-olds, keen as mustard.'

'It wasn't such a stupid question – you do all that running.'

'Not so much these days,' I said ruefully, 'and I should probably stop altogether.'

'Why?'

'Oh, you know, load bearing . . . attrition on the joints.'

'You look great on it.'

'Thanks, how nice of you to . . . well . . .' I fluffed and blushed.

What, I asked myself, would Mrs Robinson do in the face of a charming compliment from a man young enough to be her grandson? Or Esther Waring? Or Georgia, come to that? She, and they, all of them would remain calm, confident and composed. Take the compliment as their due and place it, as it were, in their buttonhole.

They would do that. I just experienced an urgent need to change the subject.

'You must stay up as long as you want,' I said and waved an expansive hand. 'Watch TV, listen to music . . . I imagine you're still on that famous high.'

'I always used to think that was luvvie bollocks – but it really does happen.'

'I bet.'

There was a pause, during which he gazed at me. 'This is mad.'

'What?'

'Sitting here with a mayor.'

'We only have the one head.'

'I don't know any other mayors.'

'I'm not intimate with many poets.'

As soon as the word 'intimate' was out of my mouth, I wished it back in, but if he registered it he didn't react. He had a sort of innate politeness that was beyond his years and an emotional sophistication that was very much of its time.

'Can't sit up all night even if I wanted to,' he said. 'Work tomorrow for me, too.'

'What time's your train?'

'There's one just after seven.'

'God, poor you.'

'I'll get an extra couple of hours once I'm on it.'

I could feel bedtime drawing on – the next stage, the next floor, the bathroom, all those things.

'Well—'

'I—'

We both spoke at once and were interrupted by the phone.

'Excuse me.' I picked it up.

'So, how was it? I thought you might be still out swigging champagne.'

'Nico . . .!' I sent Rob an inclusive smile. 'It was brilliant. We're just debriefing over a snifter.'

'I wish I was.'

'Oh dear, stuck?'

'Missed the last, so Cat and her husband are very kindly putting me up in Shepherd's Bush. I'll get an early one back tomorrow.'

'You and Rob will pass each other en route.'

'I'll look out for him. Give the bard my best.'

'I will.'

'See you tomorrow. Night, toots.'

'Night.'

I replaced the phone. 'As you've probably gathered, he won't be back.'

'I hope he doesn't mind me being here.'

'On the contrary, he said he wished he was with us. He sent his love.'

'He's so great,' said Rob, seriously. 'I suppose you know that already. You both are,' he added, his eyes on my face.

'Now tell me –' I swallowed the last mouthful of amaretto as Mrs Robinson crashed and burned – 'how's Bryony?'

He said, still looking at me, 'Stroppy as ever.'

'What? Stroppy? We thought she was lovely.'

'Come on, Joss, you know how she is. She can do lovely, she can do stroppy, big time. Don't tell me you haven't talked about it. She won't give Elizabeth the time of day.'

'It is an unusual situation,' I said carefully. 'You'd expect there to be tensions.'

'You certainly would if Bry's in the mix. She's a headbanger.'

This was music to my ears – absolving, as it did, my daughter from any responsibility in the stand-off.

'You'd never know.'

'Unless you're on the receiving end. She's a daddy's girl. A princess.'

I was about to say that was a pretty common phenomenon, but the relationship between Nico and Elizabeth didn't conform so I stopped myself.

'Things'll settle down in time.'

'I hope so,' he said, 'for your daughter's sake.'

Your daughter. That, whether intentionally or not, put me back in my box.

I stood up. 'Come on, I'll show you where you are.'

'Joss . . .'

'What?'

'Sit down.'

'Why?' I said, sitting again, slowly, on the edge of the chair.

'Because it's magic being here. Late, alone, together.'

'Yes.'

'And magic for me, just to sit here looking at you.'

The air between and around us seemed very still, holding us in place. But it hummed, too, with the intensity of the moment. For once, I didn't say anything fatuous, but waited.

'It meant a lot to me that you were there this evening,' he said. 'A hell of a lot. Everything.'

'I wanted to be there.'

'That's what I can't get my head round – what's so incredible.'

'I wouldn't have come out of politeness.'

'Wouldn't you?' He cocked his head slightly. 'You would.'

'Well, maybe.'

'But I believe you. I believe you, and I believe in you, Joss.'

'What does that mean?'

'That you are what you seem to be. Do what you want to do. That you really are the lovely woman I see, all through, like a stick of rock.'

'I'm . . .' I began to speak, to protest, but suddenly he was on his knees in front of me with his hands on my cheeks, holding my face.

'I adore you, you know that.' He peered into my eyes. 'Don't you?'

I've often wondered, were I ever to be mugged, whether I would be one of those women who failed to scream in case they got it wrong – who allowed themselves to be robbed at knifepoint because they were more scared of embarrassment. Now, although I had heard Rob perfectly clearly, I told myself that I couldn't be completely sure what he'd said, and that even if I had heard him right, I hadn't got the weight of it. I closed my eyes, which he must have taken as assent, because I felt his lips on my forehead. This is it, I told myself. Remember this – what it is to be idolized.

His hands left my face and I heard him move. The space where he'd been felt cool and empty. I opened my eyes, and he was standing in front of me, his rucksack over his shoulder.

'You'd better show me where I'm sleeping or I won't be held responsible.'

I got to my feet and he watched me as I walked ahead of him out of the room. Everything about me felt new, different, because I was seeing myself through his eyes.

I led the way up more stairs to the spare bedroom that wasn't full of the mayoral wardrobe, opening the door ahead of him.

'In here – and there's a shower room next door. All yours for tonight.'

Without looking in, he said: 'Luxury.'

'Anything else you need? I should have asked first, really, it's a long way down . . .'

'Joss.'

'What?'

We were standing on the landing. The low-energy bulb overhead threw a dim pool of light, like a street lamp.

'Thanks again for everything.'

'It's –' my voice was hoarse and I cleared my throat – 'it was a pleasure. You were fantastic.'

'*You're* fantastic.'

And so, for a held breath and for the second time, I simply waited.

Unlike before, he didn't move any closer, but seemed to allow his body to settle, as though this was not the middle of the night on some strange woman's top landing, but a crowded, dimly lit bar in which we had created (as couples do) our own space.

'Does he tell you that?' he asked. 'Nico?'

This time I heard perfectly clearly and equally clearly an answer was required.

I nodded. 'Yes.'

'I knew he would.' He dropped his eyes for a second and muttered: 'Gutted.'

'Sorry?'

He looked back at me. 'I said, that's a shame.'

'Why?'

'Because it means I'm not the one making a difference.'

Now the exchange felt like a dance, one of those slyly

flirtatious gavottes that you see in period dramas, a series of formal prescribed moves invested with erotic meaning by the participants. We were passing the words back and forth between us, moving hand over hand, conversationally speaking, closer to the point where something would be wholly admitted. Probably neither of us wanted to be the one to reach that point first. I remember it all so clearly, in such minute and exact detail, including thinking that our alternating words were like the soft uneven rhythms of one of his poems.

'You're wrong about that,' I said. 'You make all the difference.'

'Really?'

'Yes, really.'

'Not just saying . . .?'

'Not just saying.'

He studied me, his eyes moving over my face, drinking me in, reading me. And he read me pretty well, except that at that moment he couldn't have known there were two of me – one inside the other like Russian matryoshka dolls. The one he saw, and the one watching.

Our hand-over-hand progress, our dance, our poem, had brought us to some unsteady, vertiginous central point where I, at least, did not have the balance, or the nerve, to take another step; particularly so close to the bedroom, which lay with a neutral, interrogative air, beyond the open door.

'Goodnight,' I said.

He didn't reply, but as I went down the stairs I heard my name, following me, as if whispered in my ear.

I woke up to the sound of footsteps pattering briskly down the stairs and felt a prickle of shock because I had slept so soundly and he had stolen a march on me. I scrambled out of bed, pulled on my pyjama trousers and made myself look in the mirror. Reality check. The early morning after the late-night drinking. Never a happy scenario, and especially not these days when the soft tissues of the face sagged and parted company between midnight and six, and the wrinkles, 'the appearance' of which were smoothed out during sleep itself, reappeared with added depth and ferocity. In the distant lower recesses of the house I heard a tap running and the clink and rattle of the kettle being filled.

A couple of minutes later I'd splashed my face with cold water, cleaned my teeth, tweaked out a whisker that had grown overnight and flattened the mad stockade of hair on the crown of my head. I changed out of the pyjamas – nice but a bit personal – into my jogging kit, the experienced exerciser's outfit of bleached grey drawstring leggings and singlet, that was at once kind and concealing, and spoke of effort expended on personal maintenance. And which also showed off my arms, one of my better points, so far free from hammock-droop or bingo-wing.

I could not imagine how we would be with each other and decided to take my tone from him.

'Morning,' he said, right at home in our kitchen. 'Brew?'

'Yes, please.'

He opened the cupboard. 'Mug?'

'I'm not sure there's anything else.'

'You've got some cups, at the back there.' He pointed. 'You don't have anything fancy in the tea line, do you? Green, or whatever?'

'No. British brown.'

'Two mugs of builder's tea coming up.' He poured and added milk. 'That OK? Sugar?'

'Please.'

I could feel, now, what we were doing – we were sealing in the exchanges of last night, making safe our secret with a covering of easy, casual words and practicalities. I could do that.

'Where do you keep it?'

'Allow me.' I took the jar off the shelf. 'You?'

'No.' He watched me ladle in two spoonfuls. 'That surprises me.'

'I know. The sugar-taker – a pariah practically on a par with the smoker.'

He didn't smile. 'No, but with you being so fit.' He looked at me over his mug. It was decorated with popular quotations. '*Some of us are looking at the stars*' was the one I could see. My own mug was one the grandchildren had given me for Christmas: TURBO GRAN.

'It's like Air Miles,' I said. 'Or carbon trading. Every hundred yards I run is another teaspoonful of sugar I can have.'

'I hadn't thought of it like that.'

I glanced at my watch. 'We should go in about twenty minutes. Do you want some toast?'

'No, thanks. I'll save that for the train. You don't have to run me there, if I leave now I can walk it, easy.'

'All part of the service.'

'Then OK, thanks. Tell you what, do you mind if I go out in the garden for a smoke?'

My turn to say 'You don't have to—' but he cut me off.

'I'd prefer to.'

'Then I'll join you.'

I unlocked the back door. Outside, the air was fresh, damp and sweet, and the garden was beautiful. I couldn't remember the last time I'd been out here at this time of day. Rob perched on the low stone parapet with his mug next to him and applied himself to the makings. I sat on one of the wrought-iron chairs at the table. The seat was icy cold.

'"Morning has broken",' he said, 'or what.'

'Do you like him?'

'Cat Stevens? He did some good stuff.'

I remembered the Paul McCartney jibe from last night. 'I've got his "Best of".'

'We could play it on the way to the station.'

'I'll bring it.'

He lit the roll-up and looked around. 'Gorgeous.'

'We're very lucky. And Nico works hard.'

'I fancy a garden one day, but I haven't the first idea. Our parents were so not interested. We had a lawn with a wall round it, we played games and stuff, but it wasn't like this.'

'Neither was this when the children were younger. But it was never good for games. Unfortunately with a typical city garden the playing-field route wasn't an option.'

'It used to drive Mum crazy.'

It was the first time he'd mentioned his mother. The first time indeed that anyone in his family had mentioned her, and I was conscious of a delicate moment. I didn't especially want to be aligned, or to align myself, with her – fellow mothers. But not to pick up on the reference at all would have been insensitive.

'Do you take after her?' I asked.

'Yes, I do – you noticed I'm not like Dad.'

'That's Bryony.'

'Mum was small, dark and fiery. I'm small and dark, anyway.'

'Not fiery?'

'No!' He laughed. 'I'm the boring one.'

'Excuse me,' I said, 'you're a poet.'

He didn't answer but directed that calm, searching look of his at me.

'God, I love you.'

It was all true then. But I didn't answer in kind, and we smiled at one another.

'Was your mother artistic?' I asked.

'She was like you – a life-enhancer. A fabulous cook and a great party-giver. A bit of a handful.'

This represented more information than I could comfortably handle. So gentle, courtly Edward had had this firecracker of a brunette as his wife? This hard to handle party-giver? This was who my daughter was succeeding?

'You must miss her,' I said.

'Yup.' He took a last drag on his cigarette and pressed it into the damp grass before replacing the butt in the tin. 'Yes, I do. But Elizabeth's the best thing that could have happened to Dad. And completely different, which makes it easier.'

'I can see that.'

'Plus –' he got up and looked down at me – 'she brought us you.'

I glanced at my watch. 'We'd better go.'

On the way to the station we listened to Cat Stevens. The process of listening felt almost unbearably intimate. I wondered whether the forty years that divided us meant that we heard different things. During 'Father and Son' he must have sensed me glance at him, because I caught his eye just before I turned back to the road.

'Terrific song.'

'It is,' I agreed.

'Not that I was ever "ordered to listen" . . . but you know – generally pretty accurate.'

'Yes.'

When we arrived I pulled up in the short stay area and turned the music down. To switch it off completely would have broken the spell inside the car.

'If you don't mind,' I said, 'I shan't come and wave you off.' I gestured at my clothes. 'Not dressed for it.'

'You look sensational.'

'Bye, Rob. See you again soon.'

He gazed at me steadily. 'I hope so.'

'I'm sure.'

He gazed for another second and then, giving the distinct impression of tearing himself away got out of the car, leant back in to say: 'Regards to Nico.'

'I will.'

He closed the door and I watched him go into the station, his rucksack over one shoulder.

I drove to Doubleday Park and ran three circuits in a personal best.

'Utter shite,' said Nico over the phone. 'Late departure, signal failure – in fact signal failure to deliver a halfway decent service. Total shambles.'

'What a bugger,' I said. I had him on hands-free while I put on mascara in the magnifying mirror, and speaking with emphasis made my hand wobble. 'I am sorry.'

'No, no, it doesn't make any material difference. Here I am in the office, but I'd like to have come home first, and I'm out of sorts.'

'I can tell.'

'Sorry, babes.' He sounded more cheerful though not at all contrite. 'Where did you say you were off to again?'

'Swimming Gala at Elbrook Middle School.'

'No disrespect,' he chortled disrespectfully, 'but what earthly use will you be to them there?'

'I shall lend dignity to the occasion.'

'If you say so. Taking your cozzie?'

'Yellow polka dots and all.'

'That should do it. Look, better go – see you this evening, or will I?'

'I'm dispensing sherry in the parlour, but I should be back by eight thirty.'

'Can't wait.'

I completed the mascara just as Reg tooted briefly down in the road. Generally speaking nothing as vulgar as a toot took place, or was necessary – this was the discreetest possible reminder that time was getting tight. I picked up my hat and bag and flew down the stairs.

'Sorry, Reg!'

'No worries, ma'am. We're fine now.'

I handed him the CD. 'Could we have that on?'

'Certainly.' He looked down at it. 'I remember him. Didn't he change his name, like Cassius Clay?'

'That's right.'

Reg closed my door and got behind the wheel. He turned on the engine and slotted in the CD. 'Trip down memory lane.'

I had no engagements and no meetings between the swimming gala and the sherry party, so I asked Reg to take me home and pick me up again at four. There was a message from Georgia, asking me to ring. Once I'd changed out of my faintly chlorine-smelling clothes I called her back.

'I'm not proud of my vulgar curiosity,' she said, 'but how did it go?'

I realized then that something had changed. Because I found I did not want to talk to my oldest and dearest friend about any of it.

'Perfectly all right. Nothing to report.'

'I see.' Her voice was full of amused understanding. 'In other words, mind your own business.'

'George, you know that's not what I mean,' I said, though we both knew it was. 'It was a nice evening, he was very good – that's it, really.'

'You put him up for the night?'

'Yes. He caught the seven o'clock this morning.'

'I thought of you,' she said. 'Protective thoughts.'

I told her, God help me, that I didn't need protecting. When a few minutes later she rang off, I realized I had neither thanked her for lunch yesterday nor asked how she was. I called again to put that right.

'No change here,' she said, 'but I'll keep you posted.'

'Please, Georgia, do.'

'I shan't ask you to do the same,' she said. 'You know where I am, and I shan't be going anywhere.'

When I got home after sherry with the music festival committee, Nico was in the garden with a bottle of single malt and our friend Roger, one of those people in whose company it was impossible not to feel more cheerful; a mood-enhancing substance made flesh. He was busy outlining plans for his upcoming civil partnership ceremony, with Lewis whom he'd met on the Saga Nordic cruise.

'Studdingham Hall, do you know it? It's quite stunning, original Tudor ceilings, minstrels' gallery, knot garden, the lot. You will come?'

'Try and stop us,' I said.

'Only your best beloved says you're so taken up with mayoral duties there isn't a free minute.'

'That's a slight exaggeration,' I said. 'But it is busy, and when the free minute comes up I'm not up to much.'

'That true, Nico?' Roger raised a roguish eyebrow. 'Everything on hold till further notice?'

'Piss off, Rog,' said Nico. 'MYOB.'

Roger and I made *Ooooh!* faces at each other.

'Anyway,' said Roger, 'I shall be mortified if my oldest and dearest aren't there. I want Lewis to meet everyone.'

Nico topped up their glasses. 'Poor sod.'

'Careful who you call a sod.'

'Joss?' Nico gestured with the bottle. I shook my head.

'I might get myself a glass of wine, though. Will you stay for supper? Omelette or cheese on toast?'

'No, Joss, no, I shall leave you to your peaceful evening.'

But he made no move and they were still sitting there when I got back. Nico grinned drunkenly.

'That's better. I do like to see a woman with a glass in her hand at the end of the day. Joss, I was telling Roger about the boy poet.'

'He gave an excellent performance. Most of it we heard before, but there were a couple of new ones.'

'He's a very talented fellow,' Nico explained.

'You said. Now there's something we could do together.'

I found myself wondering, in what I recognized as a mildly homophobic way, whether Roger's motives were entirely cultural.

'Joss shall arrange it,' announced Nico grandly. 'In her capacity as patron of the arts. Did I tell you she entertained Esther Waring for me when I was felled by sickness?'

'Dame Esther – you never!'

'I did.'

'Nico, how hacked off were you?'

'Very, but she was very sweet about it, and she made a special effort to turn up last night – I forgot to tell you this Joss – and shake me by the hand, which she didn't have to do.'

He knew very well he hadn't told me and possibly wouldn't have if Roger hadn't been there to show off to.

'A great lady,' said Roger. 'So you met her at last.'

'I did. Meanwhile,' continued Nico affably, 'Joss was here providing shelter for the itinerant poet.'

He meant nothing by it, but I was reminded that when it came to infidelity of the heart, I didn't have a leg to stand on.

'Rog is such a gem,' Nico remarked later, after lights out. 'I could almost fancy him myself.'

'I wonder what Lewis is like.'

'I think he'll surprise us. Broad, bluff, blokey – that's my guess.'

We considered the guess for a moment. I could feel the urge to unburden myself of one of those gesture-statements, which are so curiously alluring and yet generally so unwise, stealing over me.

'I'm glad you saw Esther,' I said in a bright, upbeat voice.

'Are you?' There was a rustle as he turned his head towards me and then felt for my hand and grasped it. 'Are you really?'

'Yes. She was so nice and so disappointed not to meet you. Besides,' I went on, 'it shows she's genuine.'

'It does, doesn't it?' His enthusiasm and relief were almost childish, they made me feel like a witch, old in sophistication. 'She was at drama school with Cat and sees her from time to time and when they said I was coming down she—'

'Promised to drop in.'

'Exactly. I wasn't at all sure she would, but I hung on, and then of course she showed up and I could hardly bolt right away, and that was when I missed the train. A failure,' he added happily, 'for which I was soundly punished this morning, as you know.'

'There was nothing else you could do,' I said. 'When she'd made the effort.'

'That's what I thought. Oh, Joss –' he turned on his side

and put his arm across me, rolling me to face him in the dark
– 'I do love you.'

'I love you, too,' I said. It was true, but truth is never
simple.

Every so often the mayoral calendar threw up something so
bizarre I had to check with Hilary that I'd read it aright.

'National Association of Graveyards and Gardens of Rest?'

'That's right.' It was nothing new to Hilary, she'd seen it
all before, but with each new mayor she must have relished
this moment.

I referred back to the timetable. 'Awards Ceremony?'

'M-hm.'

'Awards? What for?'

'Graveyards and—'

'Gardens of Rest, yes – but what exactly? Best placing of
an urn? Most tasteful deployment of green gravel?'

'Pretty much.' Hilary was straight-faced. 'There's a copy
of their magazine in the folder.'

I sat down, took out the magazine and riffled through it.
*The new monumental masonry ... Pavilions of peace ...
Ellsworth's Elysian fields ... Landscaping at Nottage
described as 'sheer folly' ...*

'All you do,' said Hilary, 'is attend the lunch and afterwards
stand on the dais and hand over the prizes.'

I looked at her over NAGGR Quarterly. 'There's a lunch?'

'A very good one, I believe.' We were well into a double
act now. 'At the Moathouse on the ring road.'

'Handy for the crem.'

'Convenient for the delegates. It's a big catchment area,
they come from miles around.'

'How many?'

'Between a hundred and fifty and two hundred.'

It was extraordinary. There were two hundred graveyard
managers out there, in this area alone, and yet in several decades
of socializing and council activity I had never washed up next
to someone at a cocktail party and, in response to the usual
polite enquiry, been told: 'I'm a member of NAGGR.'

'What's the dress code?' I asked.

'Oh, it's dressy.'

'But presumably quite sombre? Muted?'

'The gents will be in lounge suits, but the ladies will be smart, and as colourful as they want to be. Think race meeting.'

'Right,' I said. 'Only I'd hate to get it wrong.'

'Quite,' said Hilary. 'It's a serious business, important to us all in a way, and they take it seriously.'

I'm ashamed to say I laughed like a hyena when telling Nico. He smiled, but introduced a note of caution.

'You're going to have to curb that hilarity, Joss.'

'Which is why I need to get it out of my system now.'

'I'll tell you for free who shouldn't be getting a statuette, that ruddy great bone orchard near the soccer stadium. It's a complete eyesore. Whoever is in charge of that needs naming and shaming. That sort of thing's an insult to the departed and an awful warning to the rest of us. Maybe you'll get the chance to mention it to someone.'

I decided to leave it there and was about to call Georgia and share the joke with her when something prevented me, and it stopped being a joke.

Despite Hilary's advice I was exercised over dress. I discounted black as too obvious, red as too bloodthirsty and white as too bridal. I never wore navy or grey and didn't have much in the other primary colours. That left pastels and neutral tones of cream, fawn and beige. I opted for the silk shirtwaister I'd worn for Esther Waring. Standing in front of the spare room mirror in my nightshirt I tried on a natural straw Breton hat. Too jaunty . . .?

Nico stuck his head in.

'Coming to bed, yer worship?'

'In a tick. I'm deciding what to wear for the NAGGRs.'

He came to stand behind me and whooshed his hands up under my nightshirt, so that the hem was under my armpits and he had a firm grip on my breasts. His chin rested on my shoulder as he gazed at my reflection in the mirror.

'That's a good look on you. Go like that.'

I'd had a letter from Rob. I'd put it in a winter hatbox – the only thing apart from birthday and Christmas presents that I'd ever hidden. When Nico had gone, crooning fruitily that I could leave my hat on, I took the letter out and perched

nervously on the edge of the cluttered spare bed to read it
again, poised for flight or concealment if I heard him coming
back.

Joss, he'd written – and somehow the simple use of my
name was far more personal and arresting than any endear-
ment – *Joss, thank you for a fantastic evening, for coming to
the gig and letting me stay. It was great having you there and
talking afterwards. Sorry to embarrass you, but I can't get
you out of my head. Is there any chance of seeing you again
some time soon? Or have I blown my chances already, by
writing this? Let me know. R x PS Do you text?*

Even in my heightened emotional state the PS provoked a
rueful smile. Texting had been a bone of contention between
Elizabeth and me and Nico for some time. The last label I
wanted was that of ageing technophobe, but texting I didn't
get. Especially predictive text that seemed to have been
expressly devised by some cool and cryptic sixteen-year-old
for the express purpose of making the rest of us say things
we didn't want. After all, I reasoned, if texting had come first
everyone would have hailed the telephone as a swift, direct
and simple way of making this awkward form of communication redundant for ever.

But suddenly I could see the value of texting – its quiet-
ness, privacy, informality and lack of intrusiveness, the
opportunity it provided for the informality and spontaneity
of conversation without the ever-present likelihood of putting
foot in mouth or blurting out ill-judged inanities or thought-
less indiscretions . . . I could also see that the continuance
of my relationship with Rob (I used the term 'relationship'
in the old, general sense, since I was by no means sure what
it constituted) might very well hinge on my lack of texting
ability.

I read the note again, swept by a luxurious tide of blurry
emotion as strong and cloudy as chimps' tea. I – we – had
Rob's mobile number in the book, but I could not call him
now. I'd ring – or perhaps send a postcard – tomorrow.

'Sorted?' asked Nico, as I got into bed.

'Sorted,' I replied.

The following morning I took my favourite postcard, the one
I'd been hoarding, from its perch on the bookcase, and

agonized at length over the few words I would dash off to
Rob. The postcard was a Jack Vettriano; a dark, leggy beauty
of the kind the artist favoured sat on a chair, gazing out of a
window into an empty street. The chair was covered by a dust
sheet. As always with Vettriano the picture suggested a narrative, but it was left to the onlooker to create their own story.
Was the woman abandoned or waiting? Was the house one
she had moved into or one she was preparing to leave? Was
her reverie one of dreamy contentment or bleak sadness? Hope
or despair? Was she lonely or simply solitary?

I knew that I was taking a risk with the postcard. Vettriano
was an artist (and not everyone would even have agreed with
the term) around whom, like Marmite, opinion polarized. Odd,
because he was the plumb centre of middlebrow. As I was –
Vettriano, Edward Hopper and Norman Rockwell were my
favourite artists, closely followed by the Dutch masters and
a variety of painters who crowded the walls at Tate Britain
but whose names were largely lost to memory. I liked a picture
with a story.

Nico didn't, by and large. 'They're brilliantly clever and
photographically exact,' he would say in affectionate defer-
ence to my taste, 'but they're telling me what to think and
feel. I want to make up my own mind and have some space
to do it in.'

What if Rob were of Nico's persuasion, took one look at
my postcard and thought: beyond naff. I was relying on his
Betjeman/McCartney streak to see things my way.

After much straining and several rough drafts I put my
boldest black pen to paper and wrote rapidly: *Yes, it was lovely.
Yes, we should. No, I don't, but I can learn. J*

I was pleased with this, its elliptical simplicity and its
suggestion of humour.

When I was ready I walked to the letter box up the road
and posted it. Reg drew up alongside as I returned.

'Morning, ma'am.'

'Reg! I thought you were a kerb crawler. I'll just get my
hat and bag, I won't be a second.'

'Plenty of time.'

In the car I read my briefing notes once more. As so often
there was very little required of me except to be pleasant and
go where I was put. I was one more administrative detail like

the table centres, the menu and the ladies' gifts. That suited me fine. Particularly as Hilary's notes showed that the chairman of the local branch of NAGGR was called Colin Stone, and the Nottage delegate was Victor Blessed. I dared not look any further down the list.

'They're a nice crowd, this lot,' said Reg as I closed the folder.

'Are they? You know them?'

'I've been doing this run, down the years, you come across people when you're waiting. Smokers, mostly.'

'I'm ashamed to say I didn't know anything about them.'

'They do good work. Someone has to care about this sort of thing.'

'I realize that,' I said, 'but – I think it's the idea of awards that seems odd.'

Reg chuckled. 'Bit of healthy competition's good for business, eh, ma'am.'

'Business?'

'Product, then.'

'Product?'

He raised a hand in submission. 'Call it what you like. We want our loved ones to rest somewhere nice, that's pleasant to go to, where they're not neglected.'

'Well said.'

We drove on in silence. For the second time I had been set right.

Ten minutes later we turned in to the Moathouse. Among the rows of parked cars were three coaches and a couple of minibuses.

Reg said: 'Here we are then, ma'am. Look, they're pouring in.'

Indeed they were, and Hilary had been right. The women, outnumbered by about three to one, were dressed as for a day at the races: frocks, hats or fascinators, impractical handbags and the sort of shoes Hilary warned against. I wondered if they were mostly spouses, or managers in their own right.

Ken affected the handover to Colin, who turned out to be a trim, dapper man in his early forties, with gelled hair and an engraved wedding ring.

'I don't know what your preconceptions were,' he said as he escorted me into the bar area, 'but we're a lively bunch.

It's like doctors and nurses, if you deal with death, you have to be.'

He was right. The decibel level rose exponentially over the next half hour until we went through. The dining room was set out with fourteen round tables, ours being nearest to the platform. The flowers, both on the tables and on the platform, were almost aggressively non-funereal, a riot of sunburst blooms in primary colours. At the back of the platform was a curious towering structure some six feet high and nearly as wide, covered with a white sheet which gave it the appearance of a stranded iceberg.

The main object of all those present, it seemed, was to do serious damage to the asparagus terrine, noisettes of lamb and peach Chantilly pavlova and get off their faces on a well-chosen array of wines.

At our table, as well as Colin and I, were Colin's wife Trisha, the lady secretary of the Awards Committee, two honoured guests from other branches (both men), an immensely distinguished-looking old gentleman who I took to be the longest-serving member, and our personable local bishop, Charles Pelham, whom I'd met several times before.

'Hallo, Joss,' he said. 'I thought I might see you here today.'

'Hallo, Charles.'

'You two know each other?' Colin was clearly impressed that we were on first-name terms.

'We bump into one another,' said Charles. 'It goes with the territory, as they say.'

I was placed between Charles and Colin, but before we sat down Charles said grace. I don't know if he'd made it up or whether it was the prescribed grace for the occasion, or even specially written for and by NAGGR, but he did very well, with a dryly amusing reference to enjoying our food now because we couldn't take it with us, and another to the value of hard work and good company, especially in the service of others. Just before we sat down he said: 'The departed are watching over us, but they are more than happy with their manna,'which got a good-natured laugh. He was a sufficiently sensible bishop to appreciate the need for introducing a note of informality early on to set people at their ease.

All I can say is it worked. By the time the pavlova was served the atmosphere in the room was positively febrile with excitement and conviviality. There was the usual 'naughty table' in the far corner, whose presence was marked with a lot of shrieking and bursts of raucous laughter accompanied by the impression that all the furniture might be about to fall over. The ladies at this table were discernibly younger, and from time to time one or other paraded across the room in the direction of the ladies' cloakroom, strutting her stuff, hips swinging, weaving slightly on steep stilettos, décolletages swooping over the heads of her appreciative fellow diners. I need not have worried about overdressing.

Rooting around for something to say to Colin that would show a lively interest, I asked him as delicately as possible about the large municipal cemetery Nico had mentioned.

'You mean on Dexter Road? Near the stadium.'

'That's the one. You do such good work, we wondered how that one came to be so neglected.'

'We're very conscious of Dexter Road,' said Colin, his brow so deeply furrowed that I felt almost guilty for bringing it up. 'It's an eyesore and quite frankly a disgrace. But unfortunately the new out-of-town superstore—'

'You don't mean they're going to build on it?' I was genuinely horrified.

'Not next week, or even next month, but unfortunately these people can buy up land whenever and wherever they want and just sit on it.'

'That's dreadful! What about the people – the people in the graves?'

'There are procedures . . . It's unbelievably complicated, not a topic for lunch, perhaps. Believe me, we're on the case, but I don't hold out a lot of hope.'

I filed this away to tell Nico and to bring up at the next planning meeting.

As the pudding plates were cleared, Charles leaned towards me. 'You haven't done this before, have you?'

'Absolutely not.'

'Have you studied the presentation list?'

'Not yet.'

'I should take a look if I were you.' He tapped his own and passed it to me. 'Best to be prepared.'

I could see what he meant. The list could have given Elizabeth's graduation ceremony a run for its money. There

were four densely packed sides of prizewinners, highly
commendeds, and special awards for things like long service
and contributions to the industry.

'Gosh,' I said.

'Gosh indeed. You'll be a long time stood, as they say.' He
nodded in the direction of my glass. 'That may seem like a
good idea now, but it won't after the first twenty minutes up
there.'

I took his point and took hold of my untouched tumbler of
water.

'I must circulate,' said Charles, pushing his chair back. 'And
I'm afraid I have a diocesan meeting so I shall be slipping
away, as they say. Good luck.'

'Bye, Charles.'

He left and the oldest member, Anthony Pettifer, moved up
to take his place.

'How do you do Madam Mayor.'

'Joss, please.'

'I hail from more formal times.'

'But may I call you Anthony?'

'You certainly may. And may I say how very elegant you
look?'

'Thank you. I wasn't sure – I didn't want to get it wrong.'

'Never in a million years. Soignée. Charming.'

I was warming to Anthony, old-school Lothario that he was.
I tapped the presentation list.

'There are a lot of awards.'

'Aren't there just? I might very well drop off, only I'm up
for one myself.'

'Congratulations.'

'I did nothing to deserve it, just lived an inordinately long
life and spent most of it in the same job.'

'You look simply splendid,' I said, almost coquettishly. I'd
unwisely had three glasses and was at the warmly vivacious
stage which, had there been anyone under forty at our table,
they would have found simply gross. 'What are you on?'

He gave me a look of Methuselah-like wisdom and tolerance and touched my arm.

'Nothing,' he said. 'But you are, my dear.'

'I beg your pardon?'

'On,' he said.

Colin was on his feet, smiling and holding out his arm in a shepherding gesture. I stood up and steadied myself under the pretext of replacing my chair.

'Good luck,' said Anthony. He was the second person to say that.

As I approached the platform in Colin's wake, I registered that something was missing and identified it as the mysterious iceberg. As I ascended the short flight of steps to take my place I realized that that was because the sheet had been removed to reveal an enormous tiered table covered with trophies. When I say trophies – there were brass angels, minute granite crosses, rough-hewn lumps of crystal, artistically mounted shards of flint, silver chalices, pewter caskets, urns, arches and mono-liths in every conceivable material, more cemetery-related goods than I could ever have imagined possible gathered together in one place . . . And then there were the certificates. Piles of them in parchment and artificial vellum, each with a red wax seal and a red ribbon tag, each destined for a perspiring left hand as the perspiring right rested in mine . . .

Colin held the back of my chair for me. As he embarked on his introduction I gazed out over the sea of flushed and happy faces and told myself to make the most of these few seated moments – they would be my last for some time.

It was gone four when I finally sank into the back seat of the Merc.

'How was it, ma'am?' asked Reg.

'Testing. I've been on my feet for nearly two hours. You wouldn't believe how many areas of expertise there are in graveyard maintenance.'

'There you go, ma'am. I've heard that.'

'Still, you were right. They were a sociable crowd. Before they began handing out prizes I had a really jolly time.'

'Nothing else in the diary for today, though,' Reg said comfortably. 'Time to get the weight off your feet.'

We swung out into the road. Behind us in the car park the members of NAGGR, many of them staggering beneath their trophies, others simply staggering, fanned out across the car park. No other motorist, I reflected, passing one of those coaches on the dual carriageway, would be able to guess the identity of the passengers.

As we picked up speed and the prospect of the free hours between now and bedtime began to seep through my system like morphine, I was seized by an idea.

'Reg – the football stadium isn't far out of our way, is it?'

'Not out of our way at all, ma'am. An alternative route. Would you like to go there?'

'Not actually there, but if it's possible do you think you could pull over at that big cemetery that's nearby? On Dexter Road?'

'Certainly, ma'am.' Reg overtook a queue of lorries as if they were standing still. 'In a bit of a state, isn't it . . .? Was that a topic of conversation?'

'Yes. I thought I might raise it at the next planning meeting, but I'd like to refresh my memory.'

'No problem, ma'am. Music?'

'Why not?'

He pressed the button and the sounds of Cat singing 'I love my dog' filled the car.

The cemetery must once have been an impressive, dignified, if gloomy place. It covered several square acres between the home of City and the industrial estate, but there was still an island of Victorian artisanal housing on the far side that gave a small hint of its original context. The church with which it had once been associated, if it still existed at all, would be miles away, its tower swamped by high-rises. This vast tract of graves was stranded and without honour.

Reg turned off the main road and into the parking area. The main gate that would have allowed funeral cortèges to drive in was padlocked, but buckled, as though people had tried to force it, but there was a smaller pedestrian gate with no latch at all.

'I shan't be long,' I said.

Reg looked at me in the mirror. 'Chain, ma'am.'

'Of course.'

I took the chain off and handed it to Reg who put it in the locked glove compartment.

'Take your time, ma'am.'

I felt a little self-conscious striking off down the cracked tarmac path between the graves, but when I glanced over my shoulder Reg was reading the paper. It was a bleak spot. After about twenty metres I came to a crossroads and turned right, up a long, gentle incline in the direction of the little houses. At once I felt cut off. The ground was so neglected that the tombs and monuments had the air of natural features; rock formations sprouting from the undergrowth or vast, elaborate termite mounds. I didn't imagine anyone had been buried here in the last fifty years, though here and there was evidence of more modest graves, their tops just visible above the long grass and prettily flowering weeds like the breeching backs of petrified fish. It was a hot, still afternoon with a lowering sky; the sounds of the city were stifled; my solitary footsteps made the merest desultory tap on the soft path.

I came to another junction and turned left. Ahead of me the great futuristic doughnut of the City stadium sat like an alien spacecraft. To the right were the rows of little houses, the occasional satellite dish clinging beneath the eaves like scouts from the mother-ship.

Looking down, I got a shock. A man lay in a sort of nest in the long grass; a young man in jeans, frayed baseball boots and a dirty shirt unbuttoned over his thin chest. He was lying in the foetal position, his eyes open but glazed. They seemed to move slightly to meet mine, but I could tell that he didn't actually see me. I was just one more blurred impression among many. In a frightened flash I took in the dark stain at the crotch of his jeans, his black-etched fingers and brown-rimmed nails, the lesions on his chalk-white forearms and the mess of newspaper, plastic, needles and soiled tissue that lay around him on the flattened grass.

I walked on and turned left at the next junction and left again, so fast that I could see the gate and the mayoral Merc before I felt the smallest stirring of conscience. I had walked by, literally, not even bothering to cross to the other side; just put as much distance between me and him as I could. I paused until my heartbeat and breathing slowed to something near normal before going on.

When I was almost at the gate I saw that there was another car parked there. A tall figure got out and came in through the rickety pedestrian gate. I recognized Anthony, my courtly friend from lunchtime. We were closing in on one another; there was no escape.

'Anthony, hallo.'

'Madam Mayor . . . great minds.'

'Colin told me there was a superstore application hanging over this place.'

'Really? I didn't know.' Though magnificently upright, the old man looked tired, and there was a sheen of sweat on his face. 'I come here sometimes.'

'Do you? Do you – visit someone buried here?'

'Yes.' He didn't elaborate. I thought of the feral junkie in his foxhole. Over Anthony's shoulder I saw Reg get out of the car and come round to open the passenger door.

'I hope they're not too far,' I said. 'It's dreadfully hot. Thundery, almost.'

'I shall take it very easy.'

'Good. Well . . . Goodbye, Anthony.'

'Goodbye, Madam Mayor, and thank you for your company at lunchtime.'

I returned to the car.

'That gentleman was at the do, wasn't he?' asked Reg. 'I saw him arrive.'

'A very nice man, he was on my table. He got a long service award.'

'Funny you should both drop in here.'

'He tells me he's a regular visitor. Reg . . .?'

'Ma'am?'

'There was a young man – a junkie – up there in amongst the graves. He looked in a bad way, but he gave me such a shock I simply fled. I think we should tell someone.'

'Dial 999. Would you like me to do it, ma'am, if you're a bit shaken?'

'Would you, Reg?'

'I'll turn off at the Texaco garage, do it right away.'

As we sat there at the side of the forecourt and Reg made the call on my mobile, the first large, threatening drops splattered on the car window, and there was a rattle of thunder. I thought of the people I'd just left – the living, the dead, and the dying – who would be caught in the storm.

Fifteen

'Superstore?' said Nico from the wardrobe. 'Do we need another? The words fish and bicycle spring to mind.'

'That's what I was told. But I have to say, at the moment it's so neglected, anything would be an improvement.'

'That's a counsel of despair, Joss . . . Jesus, I hate getting gussied up.'

We were in the bedroom preparing to go to the Sunflower Ball in aid of the local hospice, one of the rare events to which Nico accompanied me. On this hot August night it was black tie, but Nico's ancient DJ had been declared unwearably tight. He emerged from the wardrobe with a white Nehru suit (machine washable linen mix), he'd had made in Hong Kong a couple of years before.

'This'll be fine, won't it?'

'I suppose – no, I'm sure it will,' I said, though I was far from certain. The hospice fund-raising committee comprised as staunchly conservative a group as one could hope to meet.

'After all,' he said, picking up something in my tone, 'what can they do, throw me out? I'm your escort, for God's sake; it would be an insult to you.'

'What shoes will you wear?'

'Navy daps.'

'Nico . . .'

'Settle down, I shall wear my white maharaja slippers. Might as well go the whole nine yards.'

He kicked his pants in the air, caught them with one hand and threw them on the bed.

'Freedom!' He slapped his bare chest. The hair between his pectorals, unlike that on his head, was quite grey. 'I'm going to shower. Don't worry, I won't let you down.'

He left the room, and I lifted the magnifying mirror again.

He stuck his head back in: 'Except there's always a chance I might show you up.'

'For heaven's sake go and shower. Reg will be here soon.'

The process of getting ready to go out à deux meant, unfortunately, that I could think of nothing but Rob. Each stage of preparation, of prospective togetherness, seemed to separate me more from him, like a wall of white noise, and I longed for the privacy to keep the picture intact. I felt tense, chippy, dissatisfied with my appearance and irritated with Nico. How I was going to get through an evening of dancing to the Lew Halliday Sound and the Hit Machine Disco I couldn't begin to imagine. For once I found myself actually hoping that Nico would want to dip out early and I could graciously agree, pleading a heavy programme tomorrow.

The mascara brush grazed my right eyeball and my eye began to stream. As I plucked blindly for a tissue my nose started up in sympathy.

'Damn and blast!' I blew, dabbed, and took a deep breath. Putting on the full evening slap was no longer simple. A few years ago I'd had my eyes lasered, which had made a fantastic difference to my life, enabling me to drive, work and socialize without the need for endless changes of spectacles, but as the smoothly handsome South African surgeon had told me, what they couldn't do was reverse the ageing process and the long sight that went with it. Eye make-up in particular was a challenge, involving as it did the use of my supermarket reading specs, the magnifying mirror, a good light, and a constant readjustment of the focus to ensure I did not inadvertently go the Amy Winehouse eyeliner route – not a good look on a pensioner.

I reapplied liner and mascara carefully, bearing in mind that less (or the appearance of less) was more. I was overdue an appointment at Hair by Lynne, but I hadn't had time this week and had made do with my own efforts with the tongs. In all modesty the result wasn't bad. At least I hadn't run the risk of parting with that extra centimetre resulting in the *Cell Block H* effect . . .

'Gorgeous!'

Nico was back, pink and fragrant, from the bathroom, a towel clasped round his waist. He raised his arms.

'Look, no hands!'

Slowly, the towel slipped to the ground, proving that his libido as well as his self-esteem were undented by the recent quiet period.

'Honestly, darling, get a move on.'

'*Sois calme* – there'll be hours of standing around before anything happens.'

'I'll wait downstairs.'

He grabbed me as I went past. 'If I behave myself all evening, may I roger you rigid in just your chain of office after?'

'No.'

'Damn.'

As I went downstairs I heard him start to intone 'Dover Beach'. The 'Break, break, break . . .' very probably a comment on my hard-heartedness.

I had a text from Rob. These days I had advanced to the point where he sent me one a day and I responded in monosyllables.

Wn r u in town? I want 2 c u. Can it b soon?

He always ended, sweetly, with a yes or no question. I tapped in 'yes' and 'send'. Then I went into the drawing room and looked out of the window. Reg was outside. From his attitude, head tilted back and arms folded, I deduced he was listening to the radio.

I sat down in the chair near the window. I felt myself to be suspended between my three selves: Madam Mayor, represented by Reg in the mayoral Merc; Joss Carbury, as personified by Nico, bumping about and reciting in the bedroom above my head; and the one I scarcely knew, the fantasy woman, texting my youthful admirer, feeding off his admiration, pretending even to myself, that the weight of attention was mainly on his side, when the opposite was true . . .

'Right!' Nico came trotting down the stairs. 'Here I am. Let the atrocities commence!'

As I joined him in the hall, I couldn't help smiling.

'What's the matter?' He looked down at himself. 'Have I got toothpaste down my front?'

'You look nice.'

'Don't I?' He turned me so that we were both facing the mirror by the coat rack. 'Don't we both? A handsome couple.'

Reg liked it when Nico accompanied me.

'Good to have you aboard, Escort.'

'Thank you, Reg. Dancing till dawn – bring it on.'

'My wife and I love dancing. We've been taking salsa lessons.'

'Do you know,' said Nico, 'I've always liked the look of that? Where do you go?'

The city looked dusty and a little neglected; waiting for holidaymakers to return; for something to happen. The grass in the parks was dry and the roses – out far too early these days – almost over. Commentators – columnists, traders, broadcasters – always referred to August as 'summer' as though this were it, what we'd been waiting for, and the preceding months of May, June and July had been no more than a long, shiny overture. Whereas in reality August was sad; the season tipping from stasis into decline without, yet, the tingle of anticipation that accompanies the first of September . . .

But all this meant the mayoral calendar was relatively quiet.

I would be able to go to London.

Georgia and Julian had got up a party and were at a different table, but we saw them over drinks. Nico hadn't seen her for a few weeks, and I caught his appalled expression. Fortunately Julian covered the moment by expressing his shock over Nico's outfit.

'What on earth are you wearing, man?'

Nico jerked a thumb. 'I'm with her.'

'Madam Mayor, is that allowed?'

I shrugged. 'I'm allowing it.'

'He looks quite wonderful,' said Georgia, giving Nico a kiss. 'I insist on a dance.'

'I'll check my card,' said Nico, 'there's a waiting list.'

'Jesus,' he whispered, just before we walked in to the ballroom, 'she looks like absolute hell!'

'I told you.'

'I take it Julian knows, the poor bugger.'

'He does now.'

'God almighty . . .'

The seating plan separated us at dinner, and I was on the side of the table that gave me a view of Georgia. She had sensibly worn a dress with sleeves and a stole, but nothing could disguise the skeletal appearance of her neck, face and hands and her make-up, expertly applied, still lay over her pallor like a mask. Once, she felt me looking at her and caught my eye, giving me a little collusive jerk of the head, as much as to say, 'I know, I know, it's awful, but what can I do . . .?'

The minute the music started – a show medley to ease us into the evening – Nico took me on to the floor. We were no experts, but had retained just enough technique from the pre-rock group days to see us right on these occasions. Nico led with fearless elan, incorporating all sorts of unorthodox decorations of his own devising which provoked a ripple of amused applause.

'After this,' he said, as we sashayed up the side of the floor, 'I shall put myself about.'

'Good idea,' I panted.

'Starting with Georgia.'

'Do – but please remember she's not well.'

'Good point. Slow tempo only.'

At the end of the medley he returned me to my seat and struck off in search of Georgia. On our table, the hospice administrator Derek and his wife Anne (originally, like us, separated by the seating plan, but now reunited), beamed appreciatively. They had the air of professional wallflowers, or spectators; a couple who never danced and were quite happy not to.

'You were brilliant!' said Anne. 'Where did you learn to do that?'

I mopped my brow. 'We've been together a long time.'

Derek put his arm round his wife's shoulders. 'So have we, but it hasn't improved our dancing.'

'You have to enjoy it,' I said.

'Good point. It's not really our thing, is it, Annie?'

'No, but that doesn't mean we can't appreciate when it's being done well.'

'After all that, you could do with some refreshment, I bet.' Derek picked up first one bottle, then another. 'Two dead men. I'll go to the bar. What can I get you, ladies?'

The music had begun again and Anne and I watched the dance floor. The number was a quickstep to 'Let's Face the Music and Dance'. There were a lot of couples out there now and I couldn't immediately spot Nico, but then Julian was at my side.

'Madam Mayor – they're doing it, so why shouldn't I return the compliment, May I have the pleasure?'

'Excuse me,' I said to Anne.

She twinkled her fingers at me, and I submitted to Julian's firm ballroom hold. He was a more tutored dancer than Nico, but not such an instinctive one. I had long ago learned the prescribed moves that constituted Julian's repertoire, and we settled into them like the old friends we were.

'Did I say that you look especially splendid this evening?' said Julian, on a reverse turn.

'No – you reserved your comments for my escort.'

'He'd have sulked all night if somebody hadn't. It was my duty as a friend.'

'Perhaps you're right.'

'You know I am.'

I glanced round. 'Where are they? Can you see them?'

'In the centre, as you'd expect. But taking it sedately.'

Now I saw them. Nico had taken Georgia in a nightclub hold, his hands on her waist, hers on his shoulders as they swayed gently. Though easily as tall as him in her high heels, without the protective covering of her stole Georgia looked eerily insubstantial. Though I knew how much Julian disliked conversations that threatened intimacy of any sort, I felt I had to broach the topic.

'How is she?'

His face tightened. 'Far from well, but coping as you'd expect.'

'I can see that. Will she be having some treatment?'

'Yes. Starting next week.'

'Is that chemo?'

'Six weeks on, three weeks off.'

'At the Royal?'

'I believe so.'

That was his manner. His answer was not to imply any uncertainty but to close the subject.

'I'll call her tomorrow.'

'She'd like that. She's had to give up a few things, and she's bored.'

I left it at that. When the music ended Julian walked me back to my seat. Nico had somehow managed to parlay Anne on to the dance floor. Derek confessed himself gobsmacked.

'How did your husband do that?'

'By not taking no for an answer, I'm afraid. I hope Anne doesn't mind.'

'I'm sure she doesn't, but I hope he hasn't started something. We've always taken the view that dancing's something we don't do. If Anne gets a taste for it I'll have to get my act together.' He held the bottle over my glass and I nodded. 'You know I feel ashamed sometimes, being married to such an attractive elegant woman and not being able to dance.'

I was touched. 'But if she's not interested either . . .'

'I think she may simply be loyal. Till now, I mean –' he gestured – 'look.'

Under Nico's tutelage Anne was certainly getting into it; as we watched he subjected her to an exceptionally uninhibited cast off and return, catching her around the waist and sending her immediately into a reverse twirl. She may not have been a natural, but she was laughing and loving it.

'Don't worry,' I said. 'It won't last – it's just the Nico effect.'

Derek smiled wistfully. 'Someone should bottle that.'

An hour or so later, in the interval between band and disco, Julian came over.

'We're going now, chaps.'

Nico stood up and they clasped hands. 'So soon?'

'We've enjoyed it, but enough is enough.'

'Where's Georgia?' I asked.

'Powdering her nose.'

'Actually I need to do the same.'

Nico sat down again. 'In that case you've got time for another drink with Derek and me.'

I found Georgia sitting on a padded stool which she had moved at right angles to the row of mirrors and basins so that she could lean against the wall; it struck me that this was the first time I'd ever seen one of these cloakroom stools used, and also that the ladies was the place where so much that was

---

important took place – confidences exchanged, confessions made, hostilities opened and concluded, friendships initiated and confirmed.

'Are you all right?'

'Fine,' she said. 'Just taking five, as they say.'

'You're off now.'

'Shortly, yes.' She glanced at her watch. 'In fact I ought to get going. Julian will be jingling his keys.'

'He's not,' I said. 'He's having a last one with Nico.'

'Oh.' She leaned her head back and closed her eyes. Two other women came in, one of them someone I knew slightly, and disappeared into cubicles with a catch-you-in-just-a-moment air.

'Would you like some fresh air?' I asked.

'Sounds lovely. But I'm—'

'Here.' I held out an arm.

'Thank you.'

We went through the hotel lobby and out through the stone portico into the drive, so Julian would be able to see us as he came out. Each of the front pillars of the portico had a wide stone plinth, and I sat Georgia down on one of these.

'Thanks, Joss.'

'Not too cold?'

'No. Anyway, quite frankly piles would be a welcome distraction.'

I sat down on the opposite plinth, and we sat in silence for a moment.

'We're like a couple of heraldic lions,' said Georgia.

'Well, you'd know.'

She turned her head slowly, as if noting everything for future reference. 'Are you allowed to be out here with a chum? Shouldn't you be in there – being official in some way?'

'They'll manage.'

There was another pause. I think we both knew the real conversation was taking place in the silences.

'I enjoyed dancing with Nico.'

'I'm glad.'

'He's such a love.' She looked across at me. 'He really is, Joss.'

'I know.'

Another hiatus, during which we could hear the disco belting out Rod Stewart's 'Hot Legs'. Nico would be hard at it.

'Since getting this wretched diagnosis,' said Georgia, 'I've realized something interesting.'

That real conversation was beginning to surface now. 'What's that?'

'That being ill is like being old. It licences you to speak your mind.'

'Was there a time when you didn't?'

'I hope I've always been tactful.'

'But now . . .?'

'Now, why should I worry?'

'Georgia,' I said. 'I know what you're going to say . . . please don't.'

'You don't know. You can't.'

'I do. Anyway, you've said it already.'

'I'll say something else then.' She spread her long, thin hands on her lap, what there was of it, and studied them. 'As far as I'm concerned I shall always be your friend and whatever you do won't affect that.'

I waited, convinced there must be something she was going to add, that this had just been the prelude to something less agreeable. But no. Even in her debilitated state, Georgia was a savvy operator. She may have been, as she put it, licensed to speak her mind, but she had the good sense not to speak all of it; leaving me to fill in the blanks would be more effective in the long run.

Familiar voices made me glance over my shoulder. Julian and Nico were in the lobby.

'They're here.' I got up and held out my arm.

'Right.' She used it to help herself up and then stood tall and steady. 'Thanks.'

'Julian said you're starting chemo next week.'

'Unfortunately.'

'Let's hope it does the trick,' I said lamely. 'I'll come and see you.'

'I shan't be interested. As I understand it I shall be throwing up all the time.'

'You'll need someone to hold the bucket, then.'

The men arrived and we exchanged kisses and farewells. Some kind of tacit mixed-company agreement meant that we made no further mention of Georgia's illness. After they'd gone, Nico and I remained outside a moment longer.

'Back to the fray?' he asked gently. 'Or call it a day.'

'Fray, I think. I've been AWOL for the past half hour.'

He glanced at his watch. 'A couple more numbers and we'll be respectable.'

'I agree.'

'What about Reg?'

'I told him eleven.'

'Fine.'

With these small practicalities we wound down, stepping back from what was sad and frightening, for the moment. But as we walked back in and 'Satisfaction' reached out to envelope us, Nico put his arm round me and squeezed my shoulders.

'I know,' he said. 'I know.'

I couldn't answer, but not for the reason he thought.

Predictably we left later than planned because each successive number was one that we – or Nico, anyway – simply had to dance to, and while he kept various partners amused on the floor I worked the perimeter, making up for lost time.

It was near to half-past eleven when we emerged. Our car was one of the few given a special dispensation to use the gravel apron as opposed to the visitors' car park and was waiting discreetly in the shadows on the far side. The moment he saw us, Reg started up the engine and swung round to pick us up at the portico.

'I must say,' said Nico. 'I could get used to this chauffeur-driven thing.'

'I'm sorry we kept you waiting, Reg,' I said.

'No problem whatsoever, ma'am, it's what Classic FM was invented for.'

'Leave it on,' said Nico, 'we need a civilizing influence after what we've been through.'

Our journey home was taken in the company of Haydn. Nico held my hand the whole way.

At home we went straight up to bed. I was reading when Nico came through from the bathroom and sat down on his side of the bed with his back to me. His shoulders had an uncharacteristically disconsolate slump, which I pretended not to notice. I tried to keep my eyes on my book, but there is something peculiarly touching and vulnerable about a man's seated back-view, especially a well-rounded one. It's the bottom, I think.

He rubbed his face. I put the book down.

'Joss . . .'

'Mm?'

'Can I ask you something?'

'Do you need to ask?'

'Straight answer?'

I felt a cold little cat's paw of anxiety. 'No promises.'

'Am I a complete buffoon?'

With Nico, there was always the danger of assuming something was a joke, and what with my intense relief, that was exactly what I did now.

'Not a complete one, no.'

'Let me put it another way.' He still wasn't looking at me. 'Are you ever ashamed of me?'

This may have been less awkward than I feared, but it was still disturbing.

'Nico – no!'

'Just a little, perhaps? For being a bit of a buffoon?'

'I didn't mean that.' I closed the book. 'You know I didn't. I didn't think it was a serious question.'

'Understand –' he twisted round to face me – 'I don't want stroking. I don't need soothing. I really need to know.'

'Right,' I said, 'No.'

'Only it's very easy to fall into a kind of . . . you see other people do it all the time – to fall into a habit of fulfilling other people's expectations. Because it's easy. Or a lot easier than the alternative.'

The trouble was, I knew what he meant, and he read my hesitation correctly.

'You do understand,' he said, 'don't you?'

'Yes.'

'So am I? Do I?'

This was one of those starkly unprotected marital moments when there was none of the cushioning of mutual acceptance. No shorthand permitted, no allowances made. What troubled me was what might have precipitated it. If Nico felt exposed, and disposed to be ruthlessly honest, where did that leave me?

'We all have a social persona,' I began carefully. 'Everyone does, to some extent.'

'That's the received wisdom, certainty. It's that "some extent" I'm worried about.'

I lifted my hand in a gesture of helplessness. 'Yours is more successful than most.'

'Hm.' He banked the pillows on his side and sat next to me, legs stretched out, feet splayed, arms folded. 'I'm going to say something and I want you to approach it in a spirit of dispassionate enquiry.'

He sounded more himself, so I said: 'I'll try.'

'I think I feel the need to compete with you.'

'What?'

'Hold on. And because I do, and I can't, I opt for the no-contest angle. Hence the buffoon.'

'That's absurd,' I said. 'We're a team.'

'We always have been, that's true.'

I was afraid; that was the only word for it. 'Have been?'

'Not quite so much these days, admit it.'

'No – no, I won't.'

'Because you don't want to.'

'No, because it's not true.'

He sighed and pulled his hand over his face. 'Anyway, that's enough about us, let's talk about me.' There wasn't a hint of a smile in his voice. 'The point at issue is my behaviour. I am not an idiot, Joss.'

'Nobody, least of all me, said that you were.'

'But very often – a case in point was this evening – I behave like one.'

'Nico – you were the life and soul.'

'QED.' He rubbed his face. When he took his hand away his face in profile looked shockingly old and tired. Bleak. 'I take the point about us all having a public persona. But it's incredibly important to me that you still see me, and know me.'

'I do.'

'And love me.' He turned and stared at me, showing the bleak face full on and unprotected, as if baring a scar. 'And love me, Joss. Like you always have.'

I turned the lamp out before reassuring him.

*   *   *

I met Elizabeth for lunch near her office. I'd been attending a mayoral get-together which allowed for a night in town so I'd awarded myself the following day. The place she'd directed me to, Rizzo, was one of those sleek, spacious, bustling gastro-bars that have sprung up everywhere in the past ten years, with chrome furniture, agreeable young fusion staff, hexagonal plates and a high mixed-leaf count. I arrived first and a quick look round showed that we would not be the only mother/daughter combo in the restaurant. The rest of the clientele was made up of Friends-generation business people in black suits and tourists, who must have been delighted to happen upon one of those eateries which could have been in any city on any continent, and that wasn't a McDonalds.

I ordered fizzy water and got out the *Telegraph* crossword and my biro. I needed something to do; even now I still suffered from a vestigial unease about being a woman on my own in a restaurant. A few years ago on a holiday in Hong Kong (the one when he'd bought the Nehru suit) Nico and I had been hugely impressed to see, in a crowded second-floor restaurant where she and we were the only Europeans, a woman in her early forties, on her own, ordering an elaborate feast of several courses and tucking in unselfconsciously without the aid of book, newspaper or company. That, I'd considered, was true emancipation.

'Hi.'

Elizabeth directed a glancing kiss on my cheek before sitting down.

'Oh – hallo, darling.'

'Sorry I'm late.'

'Five minutes . . . unforgivable.'

'Shall we order and get it out of the way?' She picked up the menu, which was the size of a coffee table. 'One course and house white?'

'Fine.'

She looked elegant and striking in a crisply belted, fitted dark grey suit over a white T-shirt, and black high heels with a silver chain at the back. Her hair was swept back from her face, which looked bare of make-up except for a kind of expensive sheen that was not (as in my case) perspiration on this muggy day in the city. In spite of the heat I was quite hungry and ordered the calves' liver with celeriac mash and red onion gravy.

'Sounds nice,' she said, 'but we're out tonight. I'll have the carpaccio of roasted vegetables and some marinated olives.'

The wine arrived and was poured by our waitress, an enchantingly pretty girl with hair short as an otter's pelt. I said 'Thank you.' Elizabeth, the archetypal noughties consumer, didn't, but raised her glass.

'Cheers.'

'Good health. Speaking of which, how is the health? You look wonderful, I may say.'

'No, you're right, I feel fine.'

'Did you – I mean – any particular reason? Did you go to the doctor?'

'No pills if that's what you mean.'

'Excellent. I'm so pleased. What about –' I pulled a conspiratorial face – 'you know who?'

'Haven't seen her in ages. She's got a new boyfriend, so that's diverted attention away from us. From me.'

'With luck it'll sweeten her mood, too.'

'It would be nice to think so, Mum, but I'm not holding my breath.'

'And Rob?' I knew it was both silly and dangerous to discuss him with her, but saying his name gave me a sense of ownership and excitement.

'Getting on with it, as he does. Did we tell you he's taking his act up to the Edinburgh Festival?'

'No, you didn't.' The amount that I didn't know washed over me. 'What an opportunity for him. When's he going?'

'Um, what did he say . . .?' Elizabeth looked at her watch, which gave the date. 'I believe he could be there now, as we speak.'

I tried not to miss a beat, in an attempt to encourage my heart to do the same. 'Has he got a venue?'

'A friend of his has got a room over a pub, two nights only, open mic. But she has apparently told Rob to consider himself booked. He won't have to scramble for time. He is getting a reputation.'

Out of all this information, I heard only one word. She? I had naturally assumed that there would be a network of friends, fellow poets, people from the hospital, but in my silly ageing fantasist's way I had placed them to one side, different from us, not so important . . .

'Mum?

'Yes?'

'Did you hear me?'

'Yes.'

'I know that look. You were far away.'

'I'm sorry. But I did hear. Rob, the friend, the room, the reputation.'

Our food arrived, but suddenly I had no appetite.

'Oh dear,' I said, 'I made a mistake. It's too hot for this.'

'Change it,' said Elizabeth.

'I couldn't put them—'

'Or don't change it. It doesn't matter. They provide, we pay.'

I took her point and put in a mouthful. We ate for a moment in silence.

'Anyway,' she said, 'what are you doing for the rest of the day?'

I was ready for this one. 'I shall go to an exhibition.'

'Which one?'

'The Royal Academy. I know it's naff, but there's always something there I like.'

'Good idea. I'm just trying to think whether I could come with you . . .'

'That would be lovely,' I said, too brightly.

'Better not . . . I've got stuff to research.'

'Tell me.'

We moved on to her work. I ate all my lunch in the end, and she said: 'There you are, was that nice?' as if I was a child.

'Very,' I replied, though I'd hardly tasted a thing.

A little later, at two thirty, we got up to go. Out in the street she kissed me in a more considered way and even left her hands on my shoulders for a second. 'Mum . . . You all right?'

'Definitely.'

'If you say so . . .'

'I am.'

'It was really nice to see you. Thanks for coming in.'

'It's a holiday for me, darling. Honestly. And I'm so glad you're feeling better.'

She looked at me searchingly for another second and then gave my arms a brisk tap. 'Bye then.'

'Bye for now. Speak soon.'

Off she went with her long, purposeful stride, drawing the eye of several people, male and female. I went in the opposite direction until there was no chance we could see one another, and then I dialled Rob's mobile.

What I got was his now-familiar voice mail. I left a message.

'It's me at just after two thirty. I'll see you in Starbucks as arranged in about half an hour. If you're not in Edinburgh,' I added. Almost immediately I wished I hadn't, but I was too inept to stand there in the hot, busy street and change it.

The Starbucks in question was halfway between the hospital and the Italian gardens entrance to Hyde Park. All the tables on the pavement were taken by people making a regular latte last for the duration of a decent sunbathe and several mobile phone calls. Inside there was no air conditioning and it was stuffy and crepuscular, but there was a cluster of easy chairs near the back and I parked myself and my iced mocha in one of these. Having established I could see the door, I got out the *Telegraph* crossword again and stared at it.

How long would it be appropriate to wait?

What if he was in Edinburgh?

And what exactly was I doing here anyway?

'Hallo, Joss.'

This was why. This rush of glorious feeling, the sweet, soulful pleasure I derived from seeing this lovely young man sit down opposite me – me! – because he wanted to be there.

'You've got nothing to drink,' I said.

'I don't like what they sell.'

'Then why are we meeting here?'

'It's convenient to the park. I thought we could go to the park.'

Now, here's a thing. The park was a nice idea – romantic, even. The mocha was nothing to write home about, but since sitting down in the leather armchair I'd realized how nice it was to get the weight off my feet. I was tired. I'd worn pretty strappy sandals, flat, but one of the straps was beginning to give me a blister. The thought of going out into the dusty heat again and walking to the park – perhaps, who knows, continuing to walk after that – was a challenge, and one I was in no fit state to embrace.

'Do you mind if I finish this?'

'Please.'

He leaned his forearms on his knees and watched me. He looked city-tired – pale, unshaven, rather red-eyed.

'Just finished a shift?' I asked.

'A real bastard. Lorry turned over on the flyover.'

'How awful.'

He got out the makings. I pointed at the no smoking sign over his head.

'Fuck,' he said. I'd never heard him swear before. 'Another reason we should go to the park.'

We entered by the Italian garden and walked along the path by the statue of Peter Pan, where the usual gaggle of small children and their minders were feeding the ducks. Beyond them was a swarm of Japanese tourists taking photographs. I instinctively dodged out of the way of the massed lenses, not wanting to be the strange elderly Englishwoman spoiling the picture, but Rob had no such qualms and strode straight through the middle. I said I'd like to sit down, and we found a kindly spreading tree to lean against, a little further up the slope overlooking the Serpentine.

Rob got his makings out again. 'This is more like it.'

Like what? I wondered.

He looked at me. 'How are you doing?'

'I had lunch with Elizabeth, and she said you might be in Edinburgh.'

'Tomorrow.'

'I was a bit flustered. I wasn't sure if you'd be around.'

'What?' He touched my hand. 'Of course I'm around. We arranged to meet, didn't we? Oh, yeah . . .' He shifted to one side and flopped back full-length on the ground with one hand behind his head, his cigarette to his lips. 'This is my fantasy, you know? Or one of them.'

I felt neglected, sitting against the tree without him, but also curiously prim about lying down. This small tension made me sharp.

'Smoking in the park?'

'In the park, in the sunshine on a beautiful day with someone completely terrific.'

I was looking the other way, but I felt his finger running gently up and down my forearm.

'Joss . . .? What's the matter?'

'Nothing.'

'Now we've got that out of the way, what's the matter?'

'What are we doing?' I asked.

'I just gave you my analysis. So now it's your turn.'

'But that's not what I meant.'

'Ah –' his eyes were closed against the sun, but he smiled – 'you mean, as in, what do we think we're doing?'

He had put his finger with casual accuracy on precisely what I meant. I didn't answer. Below us, on the path by the water the party of tourists, many of them in white hats, began to move off. A veiled woman with an elaborate buggy and two young children pitched a camp on the grass and began opening plastic containers of drinks and snacks. A little way to our right a couple sunbathed neatly, she in a bikini and he in shorts, on brightly coloured towels. On the other side, further away, a gaggle of teenagers sat in a circle, smoking, drinking and laughing, an exclusive club of youth.

Where, I wondered, did we fit in?

'I bet,' mused Rob, saying it for me, 'that people wonder what the connection is.'

'The connection?'

'Between us.'

'I'm sure they do,' I said. 'And what is it?'

There was a silence. I felt as if I was watching a minute hairline crack crawl across a pane of glass, growing, spreading, sending out tendrils across the surface. Rob stubbed out his cigarette in the lid of his makings tin and sat up. His back and hair were covered in small bits of dry, brown grass.

'OK,' he said, and turned to face me. He sat cross-legged and straight-backed, something I could no longer do. 'Here goes. I think you're great, Joss. I like to think of myself you know –' he made a twirling gesture in the air, near his head – 'wearing your favour. Being your champion. Your squire. I want to be allowed to admire you, and to see you from time to time. I don't want to rock any boats or burn any bridges. I just need a place in your life. And –' he leaned forward – 'if possible, in your heart.'

'You have those,' I said. But there was a dryness, an emptiness, to the words. I had pushed him into making a declaration, and I should have known that it would never be enough. Or that it was too much, but finite. Yes, that was it. Too clear. Uncertainty, twilight, misty imaginings were the conditions needed to keep the luxury of romance alive. A famous playwright once said that creativity thrived on repression. Perhaps the same was true of romance.

I felt foolish, needy. And old.

'By the way,' he said, 'I've got something for you. Stay there.'

He reached back for his rucksack, unzipped the outer pocket and took out an envelope.

'There.' The envelope was an old one, torn open, the address scribbled out. 'Don't read it now, it's for later.'

'Thank you.' I took it and put it in my handbag.

He lay down again. I felt the dreaded prickle of tears.

'How's your friend?' he asked. 'The one with cancer?'

Georgia – oh God!

'She's having her first chemo session today.'

'Jesus, I feel sorry for her. It's not nice.'

'No.'

'She's going to need you.'

'I don't know . . .'

'Her friends, but especially you.'

Every word, every second, reminded me that I had not called her. I'd said I would, and I'd forgotten.

'Are you crying?' he asked.

'Not really.'

He rolled his head, and stretched out an arm towards me. 'Lie down by me.'

'I can't . . .' The tears were coming thick and fast now.

'You can. Nobody can see you when you're lying down, Joss. No one will wonder who we are. You can cry as much as you want, and I can put my arms round you and it will be a secret.'

Awkwardly I moved across and lowered myself on to my back. His arm was waiting to cushion my head and neck. Comforting, but uncomfortable, he didn't know my ageing body. Above me was an infinite dazzle of yellow and green leaves and blue sky. I felt the lines in my face fall away, as if washed away by the tears that trickled into my hair.

'Joss,' he said. 'My lovely lady. Don't worry.'

I shook my head dumbly, but I was sinking, flowing, blooming into relief.

'Don't worry.' He said again, and kissed me chastely on the temple. 'I want to be part of the solution, not the problem.'

On the train, on the way home, I rang and Julian answered.

'Absolute hell about covers it, I think. Thanks for asking.'

'Oh, Julian.'

'She's so sick, it's frightening.'

'I'm so sorry.'

'We were told what to expect. It's all part of the process.'

'Will you give her my love?' The form of words sounded limp and formulaic, and I added, daringly, because this was Julian I was speaking to: 'I mean really – my real love. Tell her I'm thinking of her.'

'I know,' he said. 'I will, Joss.'

Now, with a shameful thrill of deferred gratification I took out the envelope and removed the folded sheet of paper inside. I wanted it to be a poem, and it was; no title, but a proper poem, such as I'd learnt by heart at school, four four-line stanzas with an ABAB rhyming pattern. He'd selected a fancy copperplate font, such as you see on more pretentious menus. This made it a little hard to read, but that was fine, because I wanted to dwell on every word.

By the time I reached the last line I wished I hadn't. Dwelt, that is. For he'd anticipated my earlier question, and this was his answer; to himself, and to me. It was dry and droll and self-deprecating – very grown up. The last lines were these:

> *So let's stay sweet as we are*
> *Don't let a thing rearrange us*
> *Let's always meet in a bar*
> *And talk like passionate strangers.*

He was absolutely right of course. That was what we should do; what we could do, without hurting a soul. But I had wanted to be the first to say it.

Sixteen

Rob stayed in Edinburgh for two weeks. He was on a roll, other gigs had come up, and he handed in his notice at the hospital. Emotionally he may have been a status-quo man, but professionally he had torched everything in his wake. If he had been my son I'd have been frantic with irritation and anxiety. But he wasn't, and I didn't. Or not about that. Such practical considerations were for Edward (and by association Elizabeth) to worry about. All my energy went on trying not to imagine what his life must be like up there. Nico and I had been to Edinburgh a couple of times and I remembered only too well the sense that no matter how much you saw, listened to and took part in, no matter how many fringe events one attended or how much one drank or where, there was always a bigger, better party going on just round the corner, and that it would be gone before you got there.

That party, I told myself, was where Rob would be.

Elizabeth rang to say she and Edward were going up for a couple of nights.

'We intend to talk loudly about what a brilliant newcomer he is and hope the agents are listening.'

'Do poets have agents?'

'Search me – they do if they've got any sense, if they want to make a living out of it. And since the little toe-rag has left himself with nothing to go back to, he'd better shape up.'

She was talking, I realized, exactly like a parent.

'Is that what Edward thinks?'

'It's what I think, Mum. As far as I know Edward agrees, but I can't speak for him. One thing's for sure, we're not having Rob using us as a crash pad, let alone living with us long-term.'

It struck me that here was another area where Edward might or might not agree.

'I can quite see that,' I said.

'Why don't you and Dad bunk off and join us? You're not that busy at the moment, are you?'

'Busy enough, but anyway we can't,' I said, horribly conflicted. There was nothing I'd have liked more than to be in one of those dark, smoky audiences on my own – nothing I'd have liked less than having to play our complicated game of happy families. 'We've got a civil partnership ceremony to attend.'

'As you do.' Elizabeth gave a dry laugh. 'Have fun.'

We did have fun, in spite of ourselves, because the event put us on another planet, unrelated to any other preoccupations.

Only something so extreme – so gay in the old and new sense – would have worked, because the day before I'd been to visit Georgia. She went into hospital once a week for the chemo, and I could only hope the success of the cancer-nuking cocktail was in direct ratio to the severity of the side effects, because she looked – as Julian had indicated – like hell.

She lay on the sofa with her feet and head on cushions – more than one, she was so fragile and bony she needed the insulation – and since, as she said, even lifting her eyelids was an effort, she didn't.

'Excuse me, won't you . . .? It must be like talking to a corpse.'

The first time I'd gone – my guilt at not having called compounded by where I'd been at the time, she'd cottoned on right away.

'You picked the right moment, Joss,' she said in her flat, distant, minimum-energy voice. 'I haven't wanted to see a soul till now.'

I'd asked if there was anything I could do, if there was anything she wanted.

'Just you. Pull up a chair and keep me company. I don't promise to say anything.'

'That's fine.'

Then, we hadn't said much at all. I think I blurted out the odd piece of news, and she gave the occasional tiny nod or smile to show she was listening.

Today, though, she seemed microscopically more present. I had been briefed by Julian, when he met me in the hall, looking pretty rough himself.

'I'm going out, Joss. Nurse has been, and Mrs Pamenter's here if you need anything, she's been a complete brick.'

'Anything I should know?'

'She looks terrible. Simply frightening. But she's slightly better in herself this morning, because the chemo's well under way, and she's stood up to it pretty well. Fingers crossed the prognosis is fair.'

It always struck me as particularly cruel that severe illness and its accompanying weight loss stripped away the sufferer's individuality. After all it takes a trained eye to detect the differences in age, gender and appearance in a bunch of skeletons, and the very sick, like the very old, are turning back into skeletons before one's eyes. And as the all too solid flesh melts, along with its vibrant plasticity, so does particularity and beauty. Georgia on her sofa that morning was scarcely more than a collection of tissues; a rag, a bone and a hank of hair. There was no lustre, no light, and precious little substance.

But, as Julian had indicated, she was microscopically more herself.

'Look . . .' Eyes closed, she lifted a finger. 'My head.'

I got up and looked. Beneath top notes of Rêve, my friend gave off a faint, sour, unhealthy smell. I tried not to let anything show on my face.

'Well I never.' She had only lost a tiny amount of hair, but something curious had happened – where there was regrowth, the strands were dark, wiry corkscrew curls. 'Pubes on my head . . .' She breathed heavily. 'Like in . . . *The Fly.*'

'Yes,' I said. 'Have you tried walking on the ceiling?'

'Not yet . . . But I can . . .' Another enormous, embattled breath. 'Vomit . . . on food.'

Over the next three-quarters of an hour we conducted a conversation like monks in an order where only a few words per person, at prescribed intervals, were permitted. Spontaneity was virtually impossible, every utterance had to be fine-tuned to our glacial pace. I noticed the invitation to Roger's ceremony on the mantelpiece, and I told her we'd email photographs.

'You'll see Julian,' she said.

'He's going?' I confess I was a little shocked. 'Without you?'

'Under orders . . .'

'But you won't be on your own?'

'Of course not. Nurse is coming.' She opened her eyes for a split second, and their beam was like a laser. 'Don't worry . . . I'll hang on till he gets back.'

I'd never been so grateful for the Ladies Circle Charter Lunch, and the cast-iron excuse it presented to get away. Outside in the car I sat for a couple of minutes sobbing with shame and relief. When I'd got myself together and was on the road again, I reflected on the impossibility of getting such things right. If Georgia were to die in the night I would forever after feel remorse for my tongue-tied Britishness, my failure to say anything loving, philosophical, comforting – important. And yet to have done so would have been the equivalent of hoisting a flag with 'Last Rites' blazoned across it.

We hadn't mentioned Rob. Her last words had been, 'See you soon.'

So the partnership ceremony of Roger and Lewis was a happening in parenthesis. For its duration we were taken out of ourselves.

After my sad, difficult conversation with Nico, he had swiftly rallied and was back on form. Neither of us had forgotten what had been said, but he, having got his worries off his chest, had been able to move on; or at any rate to behave as if he had. Moreover he was like a dog with two tails to be going to a function where his style of dress would be not just acceptable but right on the money.

'I can wear the turquoise!' He was referring to a kaftan and trousers he'd picked up in Southall. 'I knew its hour would come.'

'You can.'

'And you'll be off the leash, too, toots. What will you give them?'

'Wait and see.'

'My favourite.'

With Nico going for the full wow-factor, severely understated elegance was my best – if not my only – option. I looked out my sleekest, plainest black shift, black slingbacks and my grandmother's seldom-worn diamond earrings and pendant. Hats were becoming less and less evident at today's

marathon weddings, but I decided the boys would appreciate
a hat and chose a sharp-brimmed matador, also in black. When
looking for a suitable bag – somewhere I knew I had a black
grosgrain clutch – I found some black transparent frou-frou
gloves that I'd bought to wear to one of Nico's music halls,
and added them to the ensemble.

'Not too black,' I asked, 'for a wedding?'

'By no means,' said Nico. 'Wicked widow chic is such a
good look on you, they'll love it. We're wasted on this town,
I tell you.'

The ceremony was at four, and Studdingham Hall, my old
stamping ground, was some way out. Spoiled by Reg, we'd
ordered a cab. When we arrived we soon realized that it was
one of those occasions comprising several phases, of which
the first, most serious phase was A-list only. Also – we had
to laugh – Roger and Lewis had clearly been so determined
not to conform to any Elton and David stereotype that they
had gone achingly tasteful and minimalist. Both were dressed
in immaculate dark suits with cream gardenia buttonholes. No
more than forty white and gold chairs stood in the simple
white silk Bedouin pavilion on the lawn, and a single flower
arrangement stood at the front, a languid fountain of orchids
and feathery green. A string quartet (albeit hand-picked for
slenderness and beauty, all in black) played sweetly. Aside
from the registrar who was a bouncy young woman in an
easy-care trouser suit and Birkenstocks, all was ineffable
elegance.

'Oops,' said Nico, sotto voce as we approached. 'Wrong
call.'

'Wait till later,' I said, as Roger and his intended turned to
greet us.

Fortunately for Nico my instincts were correct. The ceremony
was as simple, moving and dignified as any we'd been to. At
various stages the quartet played Albinoni and a lovely arrangement of 'Linden Lea', and a handsome young singer sang
'The sunshine of your smile', of which the words had been
printed on our order of service, so that we could join in the
chorus (a lapse into populism much appreciated by everyone).
Roger and Lewis spoke up clearly and firmly as they promised to support, cherish and be true to one another, and plain

white gold rings were exchanged. The best man was Lewis's fifteen-year-old godson; red-haired and freckle-faced, solemn as a judge throughout. The only hint of irony – and it was done so discreetly that there was only the merest ripple of amusement – was the music at the beginning and the end. The first was the theme from *Desert Island Discs*, the second 'Sailing By'.

After the ceremony, champagne and Kir Royal were served on the terrace. The other A-listers were mostly family, all of whom were delightful. Roger's mother buttonholed Nico and told him she was glad someone had got the idea, because she intended to let her hair down. Nico declared himself up for it. Lewis was a small, broad-shouldered man with greying dark hair and a Welsh lilt; he had played fly-half for Swansea for a while and had two Welsh caps, but was now a hospital administrator with a lucrative sideline on the sports-club after-dinner circuit. A man's man in the old sense, who nonetheless told us almost at once that Roger had changed his life, and we liked that.

Lunch was in the Great Hall, where the huge ogival wooden doors had been flung open to let in the summer sunshine, and the long tables arranged in a square to be sociable. We sat next to one another, with the best man's parents on one side, and Roger's sister on the other. She was a chip off the maternal block and raring to go, so Nico was happy. The best man's father turned out to be one of Lewis's erstwhile team-mates, a massive, jovial man with a nose broken so often (he explained) that the quacks had given up and just let it go squashy. His wife was a real looker, as sportsmen's women so often are, a true redhead with skin as pale as skimmed milk.

The food was absolutely delicious, perfectly chosen and executed – quail's eggs, gravadlax, a wonderful Thai seafood salad starring scallops and ginger, and tiny individual summer puddings with clotted cream. You could hear everyone cooing and purring with delight as each successive course arrived.

At the end of lunch, the only speech was that of Idrys, the best man, who managed to be both sweet and witty without appearing nauseatingly precocious and, crucially under the circumstances, without putting a foot wrong. When he'd finished and we'd toasted the happy couple, we congratulated his parents.

'I need hardly ask about his looks and charm,' said Nico, eyeing Felicity, 'but where does he get his oratorical gift?'

Ted jerked a thumb at his own chest. 'Where do you think? I taught him everything he knows.'

'Give over,' said Felicity, slapping him with the back of her hand. 'He's always been confident and he goes to a good school.'

'You must be very proud,' I said.

'Tell you what –' Ted leaned across – 'if he can manage this lot he can manage anything.'

Shortly after that the proceedings underwent a change of gear and abandoned all pretence of taste and restraint as Roger and Lewis, in lieu of a speech, sang 'You're the One That I Want' from Grease, with the rest of us providing the ooh-ooh-ooh's. It was by now nearly seven o'clock, they retired to slip into something more comfortable, and we were advised to take our drinks on to the lawn so that the band could set up in the hall.

While we were out there a second wave of guests arrived, including Julian, and Denise, with DI Douglas. They got caught up in a group near the champagne table, but Julian grabbed a glass and came straight over. He looked fierce and exhausted and was wearing a slightly strange double-breasted suit with turn-ups that looked more demob than bespoke.

'Hold it!' Nico took a photograph. Julian scowled.

'I'm only here on sufferance,' he said. 'I had orders to show up so that's what I'm doing, but it's an hour top whack.'

'We understand,' I told him.

'Glad to hear she's well enough to boss you about,' said Nico.

'Not my kind of thing, anyway . . .' Julian ran a finger round his collar. 'Roger's a nice enough fellow, but all this – quite frankly it goes against the grain.'

'You should meet Lewis,' I said. 'He's played for Wales.'

Julian grimaced. 'You think that's a commendation?' but I could tell he was amused by the idea. 'Where are our hosts, anyway?'

'Putting their rompers on,' said Nico. 'For when the band strikes up.'

'Dear God, I need to be gone by then!' Julian pinched the bridge of his nose. 'Anyway, I'd better circulate, or she'll want to know the reason why. Joss, do call round when you can, won't you? She gets a lot out of your visits.'

'I will.'

'Bye for now.'

'Bye, Julian.'

We watched him stalk off.

'Poor bugger,' said Nico. 'What must it be like?'

'Unimaginable.'

'What's he doing here? He ought to be at home.'

I felt suddenly impatient. 'For one thing Georgia wants him to be here, for however short a time, so he can report back – she told me so. And for another, the change will do him good.'

He looked at me. 'If it was you on your bed of pain, I'd find it hard.'

'Does Julian look as if he's having a ball?'

'Point taken.'

After this we went for a wander, to recalibrate. We went off piste and round to the stable block where the shop was where I used to work. It seemed a long time ago, but there was the usual selection of china, bath oils garden kneelers and tea towels in the window.

'They miss your touch,' said Nico, always the first to recover. We went on down to the ornamental lake, and he made me pose for a photograph.

'Look to the side . . . that is a killer titfer.'

'Dirt cheap,' I told him, 'from BHS.'

'Why pay more? Now, down . . . woman of mystery, that's nice . . . "Where did you get that hat? Where did you get that tile? Isn't it a lovely one and just the proper style?"'

As he sang this he capered and kicked his heels in the air, startling the ducks on the lake who sculled away at speed, leaving soft, spreading chevrons on the surface.

'Nico, stop, you're disturbing the wildlife.'

He did stop, and looked all round, then at me. 'At least they've gone. And there's no one else here but you.'

'Wrong!' cried Denise, emerging from the hydrangea walk with Douglas by the hand. 'Don't do anything disgusting!'

'Dirty Den!' Nico hastened to embrace her. 'And the luckiest man in town.' He wrung Douglas's hand. 'We were wondering when you'd stop ignoring us.'

'The second we saw you sneaking off for a snog,' said Denise. She came over. 'Hello, you.' Not only was she not wearing a hat, but she had also sprinkled glitter down her cleavage.

'You mustn't judge other people by your own standards,' said Nico. 'We were enjoying the grounds.'

'This is some place,' said Douglas. 'I've not been here before.'

He had been out of the force for five years, but you could still tell – there was a solidity of body and manner, an air of contained authority, and of being entirely at home in a suit . . . They were an odd couple, but it was easy to see the attraction.

The four of us took a turn by the lake for a few minutes until the sound of music drew us back in the direction of the house. As we walked back, the men fell in together and Denise and I brought up the rear.

'You look fan-dabby-dozie,' she said. 'Both of you.'

'Thanks.'

'Nothing will get Doug out of a suit. It's his comfort zone.'

'I can understand that.'

She linked her arm through mine. 'What about you? You feeling safe? Spinning all the plates successfully?'

'Sort of.'

'Another time perhaps . . .'

'Maybe.'

She asked: 'Was that Julian Clarebourne I saw earlier? I thought Georgia was ill?'

'She is, but she demanded representation, so he did as he was told.'

'He looks completely shot at.'

'You should see her.'

'Good point. Hey –' she cocked her head for a second, listening – 'they're playing our tune. Doug – dance with me!'

They went on ahead. Nico waited while I caught up. The tune, now we heard it, was Guy Mitchell's 'Singing the Blues'.

'God,' said Nico. 'Remember this? We had it on a seventy-eight.'

The Debonairs were no overstretched combo but a proper band, twelve of them in red jackets and gold ties, with gold-draped music stands and a conductor in tails. And it wasn't only their appearance that was splendid – it turned out they could play anything from Noel Coward to Oasis with consummate panache. There were two vocalists: the young man who had sung during the ceremony and a gorgeous black girl in a gold dress, both of whom were equally versatile. The principals reappeared, dressed for boating on the Thames circa 1920, and the joint began to jump.

'I didn't expect proper dancing, somehow,' confided Felicity, who was having a fag break on the terrace. 'I thought it would be more sort of club stuff.'

'I don't know what I'd expected.'

'Ted was a bit nervous, but it's such a lovely do, he's like a pig in shit,' went on Felicity happily. 'I think it's the most brilliant wedding we've been to.'

When I returned to the Great Hall I looked around for Julian, but he'd gone. Denise and Douglas were sitting round a table drinking with other people. Nico, a white rose between his teeth, was tangoing with Roger to the delight of onlookers.

I stood at the back, part of the crowd. Everyone was wildly, deliriously happy, the spotlight my husband was so enjoying reflected back on to their shining faces. How sad, I thought, that I had somehow been responsible for his feeling foolish and guilty for possessing what was by any measure a priceless gift.

Through the second half of August I heard nothing from Rob. Georgia finished her chemo and was a little better; Julian was going to take her away to Madeira for a few days which I was worried might be too much, but she swore she would just lie on the balcony and admire the view.

I had an official invitation to the opening day of the Clover's Keg Beerfest. Long ago Nico had nobly arranged to take Chloe and Jed to Center Parcs in Sherwood Forest for the weekend, so Denise came as my escort.

'He's done what?' she said in the car. 'The man's a saint.'

'We always take them away somewhere in the summer, but this was the best we could manage this year.'

'What about their father?'

'He's in the States.'

'I know he's in the bloody States, but doesn't he see them at all?'

'He was over recently,' I said. 'It's difficult.'

'Not that difficult.'

Denise's stroppiness, though well-meaning, was irritating, but I let it pass because for entirely understandable reasons she took a dim view of absentee fathers. There was no point in explaining that Hal's case was different, that he wasn't a bastard and was very far from being unfeeling; in her eyes he was just one more bloke playing away and shirking his responsibilities.

But she cheered up at Clovers Keg where as well as unlimited beer there was jazz, skittles, boules, darts and bowling for a pig, which she almost won.

'You nearly had a Wiltshire Old Spot in your passenger seat,' she told Reg on the way back.

'Is that so, madam?' Reg smiled indulgently. 'I've had worse. Music?'

The Pastoral swelled, and she settled back. 'Great day, Joss, thanks.'

'My pleasure.'

She fixed me with a speaking look. 'Anything to report?'

'No. He's away.'

'I didn't mean Nico.'

'Neither did I.'

So everyone's away?'

'Yes.'

'And does absence –' she lowered her voice – 'make the heart grow fonder?'

'I don't know about fonder . . .'

'Then—'

'Denise, I don't want to talk about this.'

'No.' She glanced at Reg. 'I can see it's not a good moment.'

'I mean, not at all.'

'Oh God,' she said. 'Oh my God. It's serious.'

That night I spent twenty minutes composing a text to Rob and another twenty sending it. *How r u doing? Success? Its bn 2 long. Joss x.* After which I was so rattled and miserable I was fit for nothing but bed and was practically catatonic when the kids rang from Rowdy's Rib Bar in Sherwood Forest.

Fortunately they were full of the amazing time they were having – the water chutes, the bungee-trampoline, the climbing wall, the chips and E-numbers with everything that they scarcely noticed. Nico came on last.

'Hi, darling, how was the Beerfest?'

'Fine.'

'Den enjoy it?'

'Too much. She was that close to winning a pig.'

'You sound absolutely shattered.'

'To be honest I am.'

'Look, you get some kip, and I'll see you tomorrow night.'

'Yes. Night, Nico.'

'Night, toots. We miss you.'

I missed them. If I'd been there I'd not only have been doing the right thing but distracted from thinking about the wrong one. Here on my own there was no hiding place.

And no answering text arrived either.

After the relative quiet of the holiday period the mayoral diary was packed for September, so when Elizabeth and Edward invited us down on the Sunday of bank holiday, we seized the opportunity.

We took the train again, and this time Edward picked us up.

'Did Lizzie tell you?' he asked in the car. 'We found a house.'

'I don't think we even knew you were looking.' I glanced at Nico, who lifted a 'search me' shoulder.

'We weren't in any particularly focused way, but the acquaintance of a friend . . . you know how it is . . . we heard on the grapevine that this house near Swiss Cottage was going and it was so nice we decided to take the plunge.'

'Isn't that funny?' said Nico, 'I had you two down as apartment dwellers from choice. You know, streamlined, clutter free, close the door and go.'

Edward laughed. 'We sort of are. But just when you think you know exactly what it is you want, something comes along and seduces you.'

When we'd arrived and were going up the stairs, Edward said: 'Bryony's joining us. I hope you don't mind.'

'Mind?' said Nico. 'What could be nicer?'

In the hall of the flat there was an appetizing garlicky smell. 'We're here!' called Edward. 'I've got them!'

In the living room Bryony, barefoot in jeans and T-shirt, was shaking cashew nuts out of a packet into a red pottery bowl.

'Caught in the act.' She waved the packet. 'Let me go and get rid of this and I'll say hello properly.'

'Hi.' Elizabeth appeared in the doorway we'd just come through. She was in jeans too but with a workmanlike edge – trainers, sweatshirt, glasses pushed up into her hair. 'Sorry, I was on the computer.'

'She works and works,' said Edward admiringly, as kisses were exchanged. 'I can't stop her.'

'Why would you want to?' said Nico. 'Hello, sweetheart.'

'You're having very simple fare,' said Edward, 'and you're letting the train take the strain, so everyone can relax and have a drink. Does Sauvignon suit you as an aperitif?'

We agreed that it did. From the kitchen, Bryony called: 'I'm bringing it.'

'Use the green glasses.'

'OK.'

We sat down. Nico slapped his knees and leaned back. 'In no particular order, we need to know about the house and your trip to Edinburgh.'

As Elizabeth began to describe the house, Bryony returned with the drinks and I found myself watching rather than listening. Elizabeth didn't say thank-you, but she did flash her step-daughter a quick glance of acknowledgement. Edward poured and passed glasses while Elizabeth continued with her description. Bryony sat on a chair near the kitchen door as if poised for fight or flight, but then I suppose she had heard it all before.

'A tiny garden but a wonderful deck on top of the ground floor extension,' Edward had taken up the tale. 'We can see ourselves having all our meals out there in the summer.'

'It sounds delightful,' I said. 'When will you move?'

'Our offer's only just been accepted, and we have to sell this – but by Christmas is the obvious target.'

'Tell them about the neighbour's dog.'

This was Bryony. I turned to look at her. 'Their neighbours have an amazing dog,' she explained. 'I couldn't quite believe it.'

'Go on then,' said Nico. 'Exactly how far can it go on the unicycle?'

Bryony smiled. *Smiled!*

Elizabeth said: 'No, it's absolutely enormous – a wolfhound. When it stands on its hind legs it can see over the fence, easily, which is disconcerting, as you can imagine.'

'We can only hope the owners haven't attached a hidden camera to its head,' said Edward.

'Yes, what are they like?' asked Nico. 'You can cope with the gigantic hound if you know it's in good hands and under control.'

'They seem charming . . .'

Conversation turned to the advisability or not of being too chummy with one's neighbours. I turned to Bryony.

'How are things with you?'

'They're – look –' she pointed over her shoulder – 'I'm in charge of the chicken, do you want to come and talk out there?'

'Why not?'

I followed her out, and watched as she opened the oven door, then tested and basted the chicken.

'Team effort today,' she explained.

'It smells delicious.'

'In answer to your question, everything's good, but I'm thinking of going back to the States.'

'Really?'

'I miss it. I felt very at home there, it suited me.' She leaned back on the work surface. 'I think I must have been a New Yorker in another life.'

'Driven?' I suggested. 'Workaholic?' I nearly added something about therapy but stopped myself just in time. 'Diet-mad?'

'Er, no. They – we – aren't all like that.'

'Well, I think it's great,' I said, and hoped I didn't sound too keen. 'How much organizing is there to do?'

'Not too much. My job's open for me, and I know now where to look for an apartment and so on. My bloke's coming too so I shan't be doing it alone like last time. I'll be going home in a way.'

She looked down at her bare feet, wiggling her toes. I found myself looking too. She had an immaculate pedicure with silver nail polish and wore a ring on her right big toe.

'Your father will miss you.'

'I'll miss him. But it's no distance these days, it'll give them an excuse to hop over the pond and have some fun.' I noticed the 'them'. 'They could do with a bit more of that.'

I took a calculated risk. 'They seem very happy.'

'They are. Dad's a new man. In fact –' she turned on the heat beneath a saucepan – 'now I know he's sorted, I can get on with my life.'

I relayed this conversation to Nico on the train.

'It's such a relief!'

'I can't say I've lost any sleep over it. It couldn't have gone on for ever.'

'Even this long was too much. Elizabeth was like a cat on hot bricks.'

'My money was always on her. No –' he put a hand up in surrender – 'no, too flippant. You're quite right, we should be proud of her. She's not one of nature's diplomats, but somehow she's contrived to hold steady and allow the situation to settle. Not easy if you're the stroppy, proactive sort.'

'Not easy at all,' I agreed.

But when in bed later I reflected on this conversation, I found myself taking issue with the word 'stroppy'. It or something like it was a term we were accustomed to use, perfectly affectionately, in connection with our daughter, but now I was vouchsafed a small revelation: it was no longer true. Looking back over the past few months I could see how the texture of our relationship had loosened a little, as she had, how it now breathed more freely. She would always be a formidable woman, but she had given and invited confidences and expressed affection, openly, in a way that would have been unthinkable even a year ago. Love for Edward had softened her and the demands of his family had eroded some of the sharp corners. It may even have been that with dealing with Bryony she had caught a glimpse of what it had been like for me, dealing with her. A little of the iron had leaked out and was still doing so.

Longing to share the revelation I turned to Nico and gave his shoulder a shake – and another. Nothing would wake him, but he rumbled and snuffled and rolled over heavily and snuggled into me with a kind of rooting, homing instinct. Just as instinctively my arms went round him and I kissed the top of his head.

That brought him closer to the surface more effectively than any shaking.

'Sweetheart . . . that's nice . . . What . . .?'

'Nothing,' I said. 'Go back to sleep.'

'No problem.'

The next day, Bank Holiday Monday, I called Elizabeth. Edward answered.

'She's in the bath.'

'For goodness' sake don't bother her then. I rang to say thank-you to you as well.'

'We loved seeing you both. It was a very happy occasion.'

'And Bryony. Going back to New York.'

'Yes, with her chap. I've got mixed feelings, Joss, as you can imagine, but it's her life. Hang on . . .' His voice was raised but more distant. 'Darling! It's Joss.'

'Pass her over.'

I heard the exchange take place.

'Hello, Mum.'

'Hi, darling. I only rang to say thank you – sorry to disturb your bath.'

'You are so not disturbing me. I'm lying here wallowing in Penhaligon's best with a cup of green tea and a book.'

'What are you reading?'

'It's called . . .' she checked. '*Frost in May*.'

'Antonia White. It's wonderful. But harrowing.'

'I like harrowing. It makes me feel I've had my money's worth.'

'In that case you're in for a treat, and I shall let you get on. That was a lovely lunch.'

'A team effort.'

'Yes,' I said, adding carefully: 'Bryony said that.'

'Did she? Glad to hear it. I shall say this very cautiously and only once, but the clouds appear to have blown over.'

'Well done, you.'

'Nothing to do with me. I just kept very still and waited.'

'I know, but that can be dreadfully hard.'

'Not,' she said, 'when you love someone like I love Edward.'

'Oh, darling.'

'One other thing while you're there.' Her tone became crisper. 'I didn't mention it when we were discussing Edinburgh.'

I sensed what was coming, like the touch of that first solitary raindrop on warm skin, and I said facetiously: 'Sounds ominous.'

'Just that Rob said he'd seen you.'

How I wished I could see her, to get the weight of this remark. There seemed no way to go but insouciance. 'Yes – yes, he did another show at the Yard. Dad couldn't come.'

'And since then, a couple of times.'

'Um . . .'

'The other day in London? Must have been after we had lunch. After that mayor's conference thing?'

'Oh – yes.'

I was all at sea; hopelessly adrift. What had he said? And why had he said anything at all, to her? My head swam.

'Mum . . .? Are you still there?'

'Yes.'

'It's OK. Why shouldn't you see him, he's family?'

'Quite.'

'Except . . .' She paused and when I didn't speak went on. 'You may think it's a secret, but he doesn't, you know?'

'I don't . . .' I tried to say I didn't know anything, but couldn't finish.

'He's a lovely, lovely boy, but this is something he does.'

'What?' I said faintly.

'Has pashes. Crushes. Finds a new muse.' Another pause. 'Mum?'

'I see.'

'You're the latest. He idolizes you; he thinks you're the dog's bollocks. Just don't – you know . . .'

'No.'

'Take it too seriously. And as I say for God's sake open the door and let the air in. Don't let it be a secret. Because I promise you that's not what it is around here.'

Had they all been discussing it, then? I was completely choked, unable to speak.

'I mean,' she went on, reading my mind, 'Edward's in the picture, he's used to it, but if Bryony knows she hasn't said anything, so don't worry. She's too taken up with her own life.'

'Fine.'

'I can tell it's not fine,' she said, more softly. 'But after you've put the phone down and had a good cry, it will be. Look at it this way, you'll have laid your burden down.'

'Yes.'

'I'm going to hang up now.'

Funny that we still say 'hang up' when it must be seventy years since anyone actually did so.

'Yes, yes – bye, darling.'

'Bye, Mum.'

I was glad of her practicality, that she didn't add 'chin up' or 'love you' or 'take care', or any of the small formulaic sweeteners that a different sort of daughter might have come out with at the last moment. She simply put the phone down and left me to get on with it.

And that was what I was going to have to do.

In a minute or two, I would.

Oddly, though the emotional water table had been abnormally high for months, I sat there dry-eyed and still as a statue. I was in the drawing room, and there was a light bank holiday drizzle falling outside the window, not enough to make a sound but enough to cause the more fragile brown-edged roses to tremble. Nico was down in the kitchen, I could hear him intermittently singing along with Classic FM as he performed a *Ready, Steady, Cook* miracle with the contents of the fridge.

'Joss . . .!'

He was at the foot of the stairs.

'Yes!' My voice sounded strong, normal.

'Do we have tomato purée?'

'New tube, in the box, cupboard over the microwave.'

'Got it . . . I'm making us a pizza!'

'Great!'

I had known all along that infatuation is foolish, and the risk I ran was being outed as a fool. But the last thing I had expected was for my *special* foolishness to be owned by other people. And for it not even to be unique! What had Elizabeth said?

'This is something he does.'

So I was the latest in a long line, one of a positive glee club of 'pashes'. And did that mean I'd got him all wrong, never known him? He had known me all right, got my number, big time. But I'd been so wrapped up in my fantasy – of him, or me, of what the two of us 'had', that I hadn't even been able to accept his perfect honesty. I'd wanted everything muzzy. If I'd set out to make a mess of things I couldn't have done a more complete job. And not just a mess, but a small, ridiculous, undignified mess. Anna Karenina I wasn't.

'Joss!'

'Here.'

'Basil?'

'No.'

'Bugger.'

'But there's pesto in the door of the fridge.'

'That'll have to do.'

As I recalled, Elizabeth hadn't once mentioned Nico. She'd warned me against having a secret, though, and since it appeared everyone else knew, then it followed that it was him she was thinking of.

What, exactly, would I say?

'I've been seeing our daughter's stepson.' *And?* 'I've been loving every moment. I've been able to think of nothing else, it's the most exciting thing that's happened to me in years.' *And?* There was no 'and'. That was it. The truth was so banal, so shamingly trivial, it hardly merited a confession. I was disappointed. No triumph, no tragedy. Nothing, really.

Nico came to the foot of the stairs again.

'Drink?'

'In a minute!'

'Shall I make us a Pimms?'

'Good idea.'

'Coming right up. "Full of the true, the blushful Hippocrene . . ."'

I was going to have to go down and be myself and act natural. I'd been doing that anyway, but now I'd have to do it without the aid of my secret, because there was no secret. I had to behave as though nothing had happened because, quite simply, it hadn't.

Seventeen

One Tuesday in early September Hilary discovered that due to an oversight on her part there was an anomaly in the diary resulting in an overlap between two early evening engagements. Rigid with mortification she arranged for Peter to stand in for me at the second, less important one, and I was free to take Georgia for a drive.

We went to the top of Hagelbury Hill, rumoured to be not a hill at all but a Bronze-Age burial site. It certainly had an artificial air, rising smooth, green and perfectly conical out of the surrounding arable countryside. One half expected a Teletubby to appear, waving its handbag.

Georgia was not bad, at the moment, but no one was counting any chickens. It was a day-to-day process. She'd put on a little weight and was going for weekly check-ups.

'This is delightful, Joss. But very good of you to give up an evening off.'

'Nico's got a planning meeting. I can't think of anything I'd rather do.'

'Except perhaps put your feet up.'

'Even that.'

There were a couple of other cars at the top, people exercising their dogs or just admiring the view. We got out and walked – very slowly – to one of the seats, where we sat down to watch the sunset.

'I don't want you to misunderstand me when I say this,' said Georgia, 'but I suppose I must become accustomed to this sort of thing.'

'What sort of thing?'

'Quieter pleasures. Watching rather than doing. Taking life at a gentler pace.'

'Maybe,' I said. 'We all have to slow down some time.'

'Not you, Joss. You're the human dynamo.'

I thought of my sore feet that day in London, my stiff neck when I lay down in the park, my knees that ached on the stairs . . .

'It's all done with mirrors. Anyway, chances are you'll be your old self, but you can't hurry it.'

'Old self . . .' She gave a grim little smile. 'There are two meanings to that phrase.'

'I was using the first one.'

We sat companionably, gazing. The sun hovered on a fluffy raft of unfeasibly gold-edged, salmon-pink cirrus clouds. The year was turning, but we'd brought jackets against the evening chill. A couple trudged up the spiral footpath with their dogs and said good evening before driving off.

'Peaceful,' said Georgia.

'I love this time of year,' I said, 'but I don't like the dark evenings any more.'

'No. Remember Bob Dylan?' She closed her eyes for a moment. '"It ain't dark yet, but it's getting there"?'

'Terrific song.'

'But bleak.'

'Realistic.'

She looked at me. 'You can still say that so fearlessly.'

'George, I'm not fearless at all. I just keep moving, engaging in displacement activities. I present a moving target.'

'For who? Who would be trying to hit you?'

'Any number of people might be.'

'Daft . . .' She tucked her hands into the sleeves of her jacket. 'What of the boy?'

'What of him?'

'Oh dear. Reality bites again?'

'I'm afraid so.'

'Poor Joss.' She laid her head on my shoulder. It was the tenderest gesture of friendship she could have made – not lording it over me but making a little obeisance, pretending I was strong.

Ha.

I heard her intake of breath as she sat up; even that was an effort.

'Terribly tough,' she said, 'because you can hardly avoid seeing him.'

'No.' I shook my head. 'I can, easily. He's close to his

father, but he's an adult, he doesn't exactly live in their pockets.'

'Just as well. I am so terribly sorry, Joss, I . . . Don't think for a moment—'

'George – I don't. To be honest you didn't have the slightest bearing on all this. I know you were on my side, and everything you said was right, but I'd be lying if I claimed to have gone out like a sensible grown-up person and acted on it. I didn't tell him to go, nothing like that. It was all more – random and a lot less admirable. The light got in and spoiled the developing process.'

I congratulated myself on the neat metaphor. One had to grab one's self-esteem where one could.

'Nicely put,' said Georgia.

We sat in silence again. The sun was beginning to immerse itself gradually in the horizon, like a stately swimmer taking to the waters. Soon it would be dark and too cold to be sitting out.

'Let's make a move,' I said, 'before we have to.'

When I'd taken Georgia home I took a slight detour and drove through the city centre. At the moment I still felt detached. The city was like a patient friend, waiting for me until I was ready to go back. For the first time in months I allowed myself to appreciate it; its graceful Georgian architecture and planning vagaries – some staggeringly imaginative and successful, others deplorable – its green spaces and narrow secretive side streets.

I drove round the square, past the theatre. The evening's performance was under way, but Nico and a small group of people stood on the pavement just outside the administrative office next door. I pulled into a parking space opposite. There was something fascinating in seeing him in a different context, unawares. He stood with one hand in his pocket, the other on the shoulder of one of the men. His head was tilted to one side; he was making a point. As I watched, he took out his free hand and made a decisive gesture with a closed fist. There was a kind of ripple of approval among the others. Sensing it, Nico turned and opened both hands as if to say – was I right or was I right?

The group dispersed, and he stood for a moment with one

arm raised, saying goodnight, and then went back in and closed
the door. It was like watching the sun go down for a second
time.

As well as the diary from hell, September threw up a certain
amount of regular council work. Just as well, because I was
still a highly unstable substance. It was understood that the
mayor could not be expected to attend every committee
meeting, but I was now over halfway through my year and
wanted to be keep my hand in. The planning committee was
of particular interest to me and I made an effort to be there
and raised my concerns under Any Other Business. It appeared
that Colin of NAGGR had been right – the supermarket giants
had simply opened their bottomless wallet and purchased the
old church, the ground next to it and its attendant graveyard.
There were no immediate plans to build, but it was generally
recognized that the sort of money required to fight back
rendered the option unavailable.

I asked what would happen to the people who were buried
there. No one seemed to have any idea. It was an unusual and
distressing situation, and unprecedented in the annals of the
committee.

Because Nico had been the one to draw the graveyard to
my attention, I reported back to him.

'Grim stuff,' he agreed. 'The dead presumably don't care
– they're either romping in the Elysian fields or completely
out of the picture – but how on earth would one reconcile,
let alone compensate, the living?'

I thought of Anthony. 'I've no idea.'

'I don't know which is worse, the prospect of the diggers
moving in next week, or the thought of it never happening,
not in our lifetime, and all those poor buggers just gradually
disappearing under long grass and litter.'

'The people at NAGGR would like to maintain it, but their
hands are tied. The supermarket owns the land.'

'Definition of a dog-in-the-manger attitude. But who are
we to feel smug? Either way it doesn't reflect well on any
of us.'

The conversation acted as a sort of lightning conductor; our
– my – other preoccupations were subsumed in contempla-
tion of this serious, grown-up issue and its ramifications. That

night we went about our bedtime rituals with the practised
dexterity and timing of the famous Morecambe and Wise
breakfast routine, passing and repassing each other in the hall,
on the stairs, on the landing, turning off various appliances,
drawing curtains, closing some windows and opening others,
dovetailing our respective use of the washing facilities so
perfectly that even allowing for my application of Miracle-
Lift-and-Total-Rejuvenate-Wrinkle-Banish cream we hit the
sack at the same time.

'Synchronicity,' said Nico. 'Like cooking Sunday lunch.'

'I beg your pardon.'

'Timing – takes years of practice.'

We read our books for half an hour. Mine was a novel set
in the farming community during the foot-and-mouth epidemic
– every bit as glum as it sounded, but full of arcane facts and
background information which forced me to concentrate. The
central relationship between the farmer and his son was well
done. Gradually, like a rock climber negotiating a tricky over-
hang. I was getting back to normal – but one tiny slip and I'd
be back at the bottom and in pretty poor shape.

Nico preferred non-fiction. He was in the early stages of
yet another scurrilous diary; this time politics. Every so often
he'd make a little sound that was an invitation to me to ask
him to read a passage aloud; I could take it or leave it, and
tonight I left it.

When I put the farming saga aside and turned my light off,
he did the same.

'Feel like *Book at Bedtime*? It's that nice Polish woman
tracing her grandfather.'

We liked the Polish woman, what we'd heard of her. You
could pick up the quest pretty much anywhere and not have
missed much – or not notice that you had – because her
journey was largely an excuse for a series of essays on her
homeland. Also, the incidental music was plangent and particularly haunting. We lay in the dark, listening. I lay on my back,
Nico on his side facing me. When the reader – an actress with
a richly resonant voice – reached a passage about her parents
and their love for each other, Nico touched my arm with his
finger.

At the end he let the music fade and then switched the radio
off.

'Nice.'

'Nearly finished – what's today?'

'Thursday, you're right. We'll miss her.'

'We will.'

'Shall we write in?'

'Email.'

'Email then?'

'Say how much we liked it. Get read out on *Feedback*.'

'They don't do likes on *Feedback*.'

'They do. Sometimes.'

'Go on then.'

'Maybe I will . . .'

We lay for a moment, facing one another. Then, again by some tacit mutual agreement our faces moved together.

'Night, darling,' he whispered.

'Night, Nico.'

But we didn't move apart again after the kiss. Our bodies began to react and behave as they were wont to do, as they knew how, to make their accustomed forays and connections, to slowly but surely turn on like a couple of old-fashioned televisions warming up.

Nico gave a gravelly sigh. 'Oh, Joss . . . how I've missed you . . .'

And then he kissed me again, so I didn't have to answer.

Reality, as Georgia said, may have bitten, but I wasn't out of the wood. For one thing, Rob was now back, texting and emailing. Rashly, he had sent me two more poems through the post. He wasn't cautious and neither was I. Part of me – a large part – wanted Nico to notice something and say 'What's that?' or 'Who's that from?', but he either didn't notice or wasn't interested and I didn't volunteer any information. I was still ambivalent to the extent that I couldn't bring myself to be entirely open about it. I was pretty sure that the other people who knew – Elizabeth, Edward, Georgia, even Rob himself since he professed to like Nico so much – wouldn't say anything. It was down to me to extinguish it.

The sainted Oscar may have talked about each man killing the thing he loves, but he hadn't been through the menopause.

Neither of the poems was about us. One was called 'Default Option' and concerned the expressions people's faces fall into

when not registering anything specific – when they're walking
along, driving the car, riding on the tube, sitting in a waiting
room. It was funny and straightforward and I could see how
he'd perform it live. The other was about his mother – I
wondered whether he'd sent it to me in response to my question that early morning in the garden. He probably thought
I'd be interested, whereas I'd only asked as a way of seeming
interesting to him. The title of that one was 'Look at Me' and
was about the continuing need to win parental attention and
approval. It didn't mess about:

> *Look at me! Get out of there,*
> *Brush the ashes from your hair*
> *Reconstitute and do your duty*
> *You're past the need for brains and beauty,*
> *Look at me! Tell me I'm smart,*
> *And cute enough to waste girls' hearts,*
> *Shrug off that urn, come off the shelf,*
> *Tell me again to be myself.*
> *Don't just sit there,*
> *Look at me.*

Seeing his work on the page made me realize how much
he added in performance. I wasn't even sure whether you'd
call this poetry or verse. The ideas were simple and strong
and the writing had vigour, but perhaps it could only blossom
on a stage. Certainly the flat medium of paper did it no favours.
But of course I had the advantage of seeing him in my mind's
eye, and hearing him in my imagination. I hadn't replied to
the texts – the yes/no thing had got silly anyway – but I did
send a postcard thanking him for the poems.

Then one Sunday evening in October he turned up. It was
six o'clock, the black hole. Nico was dozing in front of the
Antiques Roadshow and I was in the spare bedroom selecting
an outfit for the following day's literary lunch. We'd been
giving the garden its last tidy-up of the season and I'd put on
my dressing gown preparatory to having a bath. When the
doorbell rang I cursed roundly and called down to Nico to
get it. The most likely candidate for doorstepping at this antisocial hour was a neighbour with some grouse or other about
wheelie bins (Monday was rubbish day, focus these days of

more gripes and beefs than any other community activity, and everyone seemed to think I should know).

I stood there with a hat in either hand and listened to Nico grumbling and scratching across the hall. The door opened and I heard him say: 'Well, I never – hallo! What a delightful surprise, come in, come in – Joss!'

When I didn't answer, he said: 'She may be in the bathroom, hang on – JOSS!'

'What?' I affected a distant, preoccupied voice.

'Joss, guess who? It's Rob.'

'Hang on, be down in a tick.'

'Sorry to do this to you!' called Rob, and Nico said: 'Sorry? It'll make her day. Come through and have a drink, I was just about to . . .'

They went into the kitchen. I looked at myself in the long mirror. With Nico there, the dressing gown wouldn't matter, on the other hand it might appear slovenly at this time of day . . . I dropped the hats, hurried into the bedroom and put on leggings, a red sloppy joe and my red tartan slippers. Then I dragged a brush through my hair, washed my hands, and went downstairs.

'Here he is,' said Nico, as if producing him from a hat.

'How nice. Hello, Rob.'

'Hi, Joss.' He came over and kissed me on both cheeks – the double-formal, it would have been better not to kiss me at all. Nico watched approvingly. They had beers and I poured a glass of white wine and we went up to the drawing room. On the way he explained why he was here – he wanted to make a CD at the Yard and had come to talk to the people there about doing the recording.

'I want to get something on YouTube and MySpace as well, so it's pretty important I get it right.'

'And you need to come all the way up here?' asked Nico, putting the obvious question. 'Isn't there anywhere suitable in London?'

'Not that's half as good. The Yard's a really nice space, with good lighting and acoustics. And I'll need a co-operative audience of course.' He grinned.

'Count us in. I've always wanted to cut a disc.'

'Anyway, I thought I'd come and see you.'

'Would you like supper?' I asked.

'No, no, thanks, it's bad enough me turning up.'

'He would,' said Nico firmly. 'I'll make you one of my club sandwiches in due course. Give me an excuse to have one too.'

'You're really kind. This makes the second time I've used your house like a hotel.'

'You want a bed, too?' I didn't intend it to be sarcastic, but that's how it came out.

'No problem if you do,' said Nico.

'Really?'

'No, it was an entirely empty and meaningless offer – of course really.'

'Cheers, that would be so great.'

Nico slapped his knees. 'Stay here and talk to Joss. I'll give you a shout when I've constructed the sarnies.'

He flopped away down the stairs. Rob looked at me.

'You're not pleased to see me.'

I closed my eyes; it was a long time since I'd been completely truthful with anyone, and I badly wanted to be truthful now.

'Since you're here, I am,' I said. 'But I'd rather not be seeing you at all.'

'Why?'

I couldn't make out if he was being disingenuous, or simply didn't get it.

'I'm not comfortable with . . . any of it, any more.'

Downstairs Nico had turned on the radio and a wave of Classic FM's smooth classics rolled up the stairs; the tear-jerking 'Ashoken Farewell' I could have done without.

Rob jerked his head in Nico's general direction. 'He's happy.'

'He's always happy.' It was more or less true but again it came out sour.

'What a gift,' said Rob.

'Look.' I put my glass down. I couldn't have swallowed another mouthful anyway. 'Rob. I'm going to level with you.'

'I wish you would.'

'I've made a mistake. You knew what you were doing – what you are doing – but I didn't.'

'What am I doing?'

'Being charming, flattering me, having a little crush on me . . .'

'Not so little, Joss.'

'I suspect –' I chose my words carefully, not wanting to make trouble for Elizabeth – 'I'm not the first and I won't be the last.'

'Is that what you think?'

'Yes. Yes, it is.'

Now it was the theme from *Dances with Wolves*, carrying with it the smell of frying bacon. Rob was young, he couldn't help turning towards the smell for a moment like a Bisto kid.

'And I haven't dealt with any of this at all gracefully. I've been clumsy, and clumsiness can cause damage. I've been fortunate that so far it hasn't, and I don't want it to.'

He chugged down the rest of his beer and used his wrist to wipe the foam off his lip. 'I don't get it. You've done nothing wrong.'

'I told you, Rob, I'm not comfortable.'

Now he leaned forward, his hands hanging between his knees, shoulders hunched. His voice dropped to an intense whisper.

'But I only want to be allowed my feelings. To adore you from afar. Surely I'm allowed to do that?'

'I can't stop you. Afar is fine. But no more meetings.'

'That's so sad.'

'And no more turning up here. Nico and I—'

'You're great together, I know.'

Suddenly I was cross, and it was no bad thing. I had somewhere to go. How dare he have an opinion on us, on our marriage, on how we 'were' together?

'Rob,' I said, coolly, 'you know absolutely nothing about us.'

'I can see.'

'You see what we choose to show you.'

'I accept that. But you can't help it, you give off a vibe.'

'We wouldn't know a vibe if we tripped over it.'

'I would though. I do.'

'Listen to me,' I said. 'Read my lips.' It felt good to be fierce, to put him in his place, to hurt him a little. To feel powerful, for a change.

'You. Know. Nothing.'

We sat there, both leaning forward, staring at each other, weighing each other up.

'Grub up!' called Nico. 'Come and get it!'

That gave Rob an excuse to blink first. He picked up his empty bottle and ran down the stairs ahead of me, calling. 'On our way!'

I followed at a more sedate pace. No one was going to hurry me. I hadn't felt so calm in years.

He didn't stay the night. After he'd had his sandwich I let Nico drive him to the station. I went to bed and didn't even hear him come in. The next morning was one of those when my entire system protested against exercise, but I pig-headedly dragged my leaden legs out for a short run, and then I took the car in to City Hall and did an hour's paperwork before Reg collected me for the literary lunch.

'No Lady Clarebourne today?' he asked. 'She likes these book do's, doesn't she?'

'She's been very ill, Reg. Not quite up to partying yet.'

'I'm sorry to hear that. Do give her my best, won't you?'

'I will.'

But when we arrived at the Radisson and Reg came round to open the door for me, he said: 'Isn't that her Ladyship there, ma'am?'

'Good heavens, so it is.'

Georgia was standing with Julian just inside the hotel foyer – she would have been conspicuous in any case because she was the only other person wearing a hat. Julian's khaki body warmer and wellies proclaimed unequivocally: only the driver.

'Are you on the top table?' I asked her.

'No, I'm near the door. Ready for a quick exit if the speeches run on.'

'See you later then.' I looked at her. My dear, dear friend, back in circulation – and in a hat! I couldn't help myself, I gave her another kiss.

'Madam Mayor – go!'

I was elated. Like an explorer acclimatizing to harsh conditions I had been preparing myself for Georgia's not being there. Even since the chemo, though she'd been more herself, I'd been aware that the old times might never come back; that things simply wouldn't be the same. But now, suddenly, there was a distinct possibility that they would.

*   *   *

When it was all over, I found Georgia sitting on a padded banquette in the foyer, with a copy of one of the books, a historical novel by a young woman author.

'I liked what I heard,' she said, as I sat down next to her. 'And the reviews were ecstatic.'

'How's it been?' I asked.

'I enjoyed myself. The others on my table were a lot of fun, young things – they all had to dash off to be at the school gate.' She glanced at her watch. 'I'd better make a move, Julian's due in fifteen minutes, and he's always early.'

I went with her into the foyer and we stood by the door. Outside it was a perfect autumn afternoon. The road the hotel was on was like a boulevard, the trees down the centre were a soft haze of amber and gold.

'Lovely day.'

'Isn't it?'

I was sure we were both thinking the same thing – that in other circumstances, if I hadn't been weighted down with the chain of office, and if she weren't being swept away by Julian, we'd have taken off together and walked, looked at shops, and had tea and generally larked about.

'Damn, have you been waiting long?' Julian trotted up the steps. He looked exactly the same as before except that he'd swapped the wellies for desert boots.

'Two minutes,' said Georgia.

'Even stopping round here's a nightmare. We'd better get going. I left the porter keeping an eye.'

We said goodbye, and she took her husband's arm as they went down the steps.

Eighteen

In early November it was Chloe's birthday. It fell on a Saturday this year, so I had arranged well in advance to look in only briefly on Park Street Community Autumn Fair, so Nico and I could drive down with her present – a pair of rollerblades with pink wings on the back, and a twenty-pound note in a card with the legend 'Born to Shop!' – and be back by seven for a Probus dinner.

'What form will these celebrations take?' he asked over breakfast. 'What do ten-year-olds do these days?'

'Whatever it is she's doing it this evening,' I told him. 'We'll be gone by then.'

'Shame.'

In the post, along with Saga Insurance and the Pashmina people I saw a letter with Rob's handwriting and put it in the middle of the ad hoc in-tray, next to the microwave, for later.

I was glad we were able to go together. Nico didn't suffer from my slight guilt-by-association with Cathryn; it was all a grand day out as far as he was concerned. We'd allowed plenty of time for the inevitable hold-ups, and enjoyed the leisurely drive through the home counties.

At twelve we stopped in an especially pretty village for coffee.

'Makes you proud to be English,' said Nico. 'Pity it's so full of prats.'

'Everyone but thee and me?'

'OK – but no, no, it is. A chap couldn't hold his head up in this place unless he had a panama hat on top of it. That's in summer of course. In the winter, what? A Donegal tweed cap?'

'One of those cattle-musterer's things. Harrison Ford.'

'Correct. And what about you?'

'I'd blend in seamlessly.'

We were back at the car and he looked me up and down before unlocking. 'Do you know, I'm very afraid you're right?'

We arrived at Cathryn's at twelve thirty.

'It's quiet,' said Nico. 'Too quiet. Do you think they're out?'

'Of course they're not out.'

As we got to the front door we heard a shout inside of 'They're here!' and a pounding of footsteps. Chloe opened the door and the collie-cross, Bronco, bounded past her. Jed appeared briefly, but only to catch Bronco by the collar, and drag him back to the nether reaches of the house.

'Happy birthday!' we chorused. Chloe offered her cheek.

'Hello, Gran. Hi, Oompa, Mum's in the kitchen.'

'Best place for her,' said Nico.

'Everything I'm wearing is a birthday present,' said Chloe, 'except my knickers.'

I admired the denim and diamanté miniskirt, the fuchsia leggings, black Converse baseball boots and black and pink striped top slipping off one shoulder. 'You look very pretty. Who gave you all those?'

'Dad, from America. No one else will have them.'

'I bet.'

'Damn,' said Nico, clasping my arm theatrically. 'We forgot to buy anything.'

In spite of the huge carrier bag he carried, an expression of terrible complexity flitted across Chloe's face – doubt, avarice and disappointment fought for supremacy with the need, just in case, to be polite. Politeness won.

'That's all right.'

'Nico, don't be so mean!'

'But,' he said, looking at me and then back at Chloe, 'but – we found these lying around at home and thought you might like them.'

He held out the carrier bag.

'Wicked!'

Jed reappeared and submitted to a kiss from me. He and Nico had progressed to something more manly.

'Greetings.'

'Greetings.'

'Mum!'

Cathryn appeared from the direction of the kitchen. 'Joss,

Nico, I'm so sorry, I was in the middle of a tricky manoeuvre with the joint.'

'Who won?' asked Nico.

'No-score draw.'

She took us into the living room. The fire was lit and there were flowers on the side table along with a tray containing white wine, mango juice and Diet Coke, with glasses. Everything shone. You had to hand it to Cathryn, she ran a tight ship. She poured drinks and we watched as Chloe ripped the paper off her present.

'Wow, mega – thanks!'

I rescued the card from the floor. 'There's something in here, too.'

'Wicked!'

Jed had fallen into a minor sulk brought on by seeing his sister with so much booty. 'Can I let the dog in now?'

Cathryn looked at us. 'Do you mind?'

'Of course not – poor Bronco.'

Jed left the room and Cathryn inspected the rollerblades. 'These are state of the art, where on earth did you find them?'

Nico looked at me. 'Where did we find them?'

'In that place on the retail park – Wheels R Us.'

'You did brilliantly.'

Some small non-verbal exchange must have taken place because Chloe came over and gave us both a kiss.

'Thank you. And for the money.'

'Spend it wisely,' said Nico. 'Improving books. That sort of thing.'

The dog came bustling in and we did our best to ignore him. This ignoring was supposed to establish a pecking order and teach him manners, but we had yet to see any sign of either; he was a stranger to boundaries. We all sat down, Jed on the floor with a handful of kettle chips which successfully drew Bronco's fire.

'Are you having a party later on?' I asked.

'We're going bowling – can I go and try these outside?'

'Yes, but stay on the pavement.'

'It's quite cold,' I said, looking at the off-the-shoulder top.

'They don't feel it.'

'How many of you are going?' Nico asked Cathryn.

'Well I'm taking six including Chloe and Jed. But I've got a friend coming along to help. For moral support really.'

'Good idea.'

She peered at the underside of her glass as though it might be sticky. 'His daughter's one of Chloe's best mates.'

'Right . . . Perfect.'

Nico and I noticed the 'his' and tried hard not to look at one another, which was a statement in itself.

'Lucy,' said Jed. 'She sucks.'

'Jed!'

'No, but she does.'

'Why don't you go out and see how Chloe's getting on?'

'No, thanks.' You could see Jed weighing up his options and deciding it was worth a go: 'Can I go on the computer?'

Cathryn glanced at her watch, and asked a second time: 'Do you mind?' We shook our heads vigorously. 'Fifteen minutes only.'

Jed scuttled out before she could change her mind. Bronco nosed around for Kettle-crumbs and then followed. Nico picked up the rollerblades box and studied the small print.

'Cathryn,' I said, 'it's awfully nice of you to cook a special lunch for us when you've got so much on.'

'I wanted to. I like cooking and the kids love a roast. Anyway, Chris is taking us all to the American diner after bowling.'

'Will there be barbecued ribs?' asked Nico. 'Like Center Parcs?'

'And the rest.'

'Can I come?'

'You'd be welcome,' said Cathryn. 'But you'd hate the bowling bit, they play deafening rock music the whole time.'

'He's joking,' I said, 'we shall be long gone by then and I'll be at a very dull dinner.'

There was a short, pregnant pause. We watched intently as Cathryn put a log on the fire. Nico was the first to break cover.

'Tell us about Chris,' he said. 'He sounds a good man.'

'Oh, he is, he really is . . .'

As Cathryn talked about him, we couldn't fail to notice how pretty she became. Her cheeks grew pink, her eyes bright, her whole outline seemed to soften and shimmer. It was nice to see, but I was churning with mixed feelings. She deserved

love, to love and to be loved by a nice man. No one could
have deserved it more. But I couldn't help wishing that it was
our son, the children's father, who'd created this transforma-
tion, who was going to be here, helping with birthday treats
and lighting Cathryn's candle, instead of being on the other
side of the world making money and whoopee. I knew that
in the modern world – in any world – these things happened,
that statistics were against them, and that Cathryn was something of a workaholic. My slightly pampered son must have
found marriage to a social worker, and the consequent
encroachment of other people's problems, hard to deal with.
But I worried that he hadn't tried hard enough, that he didn't
recognize what he'd got and work at keeping it. Till now,
whatever the state of his conscience, he'd still been the children's father; he still was, of course, except that this Chris
was the one on hand and Hal ran the risk of becoming a vague,
sentimentalized irrelevance.

'Absolutely no plans at the moment,' Cathryn was saying.
'It's just nice to have met someone nice, someone the children like, who we can all spend time with.'

She was being so careful, so tactful, it nearly broke my
heart.

'Well,' said Nico, 'I think it's absolutely splendid news,
sweetheart.' He raised his glass. 'Here's to you. Let the toast
be to happiness!'

After lunch, when Nico was watching *Happy Feet* with the
children, Cathryn and I had our coffee in the kitchen.

'Joss,' she said. 'I hope you didn't mind my talking about
Chris. I didn't really mean to launch into it all today, but Nico
asked. Hal is the children's father and always will be.'

'I know,' I said. 'I just wish he deserved it a bit more.'

Cathryn sat back in her chair and folded her arms. 'You
know what? Deserving doesn't come into it. I've felt a lot
more forgiving since I . . . since I met Chris. You can't help
your feelings.'

'But you're entitled, more than entitled, to your new relationship. Hal wasn't in the least entitled to his.'

'It's history. We're all in a different place now. And at least
we've stayed friends, or got back to being friends anyway. He
and Lili are coming over again to spend Christmas in London,

and they're taking the children back with them for two weeks – special dispensation from school.'

My imagination immediately leapt to the next thing to worry about. 'What about coming back? Who will be with them?'

'Oh, there are systems in place for children flying alone. They'll have a brilliant time and I shall be right there at the barrier when they get back, don't you worry, doing the full *Love Actually* bit.'

I vowed to myself that if necessary I would fly to the States and bring them back myself, but there was no point in banging on about it now when Cathryn was so happy.

We left at four. As we left the close, a VW estate turned in. I caught a glimpse of a man at the wheel and a small girl next to him.

'That'll be him then,' said Nico. He put his hand on my knee and gave it a little shake. 'Don't fret. It's all good.'

'I suppose. But poor Hal – I don't know whether to feel sorry or angry.'

'First up, he's not poor anything. He's not the first grown man to make the wrong decision, and he won't be the last. Secondly it's much too late to be angry, and no need whatever to feel sorry, because if this Chris thing takes off it will be a lot better and easier for everyone, including the kids.'

'What if he takes Hal's place?'

'He won't. Hal has his place and he's in it. If it's not the one he wants he has only himself to blame.'

But I was in full-on fret mode. 'We don't even know if he knows yet – about Chris. He may react badly.'

'I don't suppose he'll be overjoyed . . .' Nico paused at a junction and then turned out and accelerated. 'But even in his most arrogant fantasies he can't have imagined Cathryn would live like a nun for the rest of her life.'

For a moment I found myself wondering if Nico still loved Hal.

'I love our errant boy,' he said. 'But I won't take responsibility for him. Not any more.'

'No.'

'No,' he said firmly. 'Fancy *Round the Horne*?'

* * *

That night, on the pretext of getting my next day's clothes ready, I retreated to the spare room to read Rob's poem. Long ago I should have said: 'Oh God, look, another letter from my admirer!' and we could have taken a hey-ho line together. But the moment when that would have been possible was long past; I had allowed it to pass. *Accidie*, as usual, which Paul Simon had written about so well in his song 'Slip-sliding Away'. It was odd the way the spare room had become a sanctuary, a bolt-hole. Nico never came in here. So I was still keeping secrets.

It turned out this wasn't a poem, but a letter. He had odd handwriting, each letter separate like hieroglyphics, but rapidly executed – very labour intensive. The letter wasn't long.

> *Dear Joss,*
>   *I think I may have run out of steam. You were dead right, this is (was) no way to carry on, so I'll stop. But please remember that I never said anything to you that wasn't true, and I never asked you to do anything wrong. So there was no shame in it. I still think you're the business, and I imagine we'll run into each other from time to time, at the christening or something.*
>   *Rob x*
> *PS I've found it a lot harder writing this than a poem. Sorry if it's crap.*

I sat there, trying to analyse my feelings – and told myself that if that was what I was doing then I probably had none to analyse, which was in itself depressing. Perhaps, like the boy in *Equus* I was cured but lobotomized. And 'dead right' was a funny expression . . . And . . . I frowned and looked back at the end of the letter.

What christening?

I retrieved my mobile phone from my bag in the kitchen and texted laboriously: *Wot crisning?* It was akin to writing left-handed and upside down while looking in a mirror, but I was on fire. His turn now to come up with the monosyllabic reply: *Joke?*

The question mark was ambivalent, of course. Did he mean that it might or might not have been a joke? Or that it definitely was, and the question mark was the equivalent of that upward inflection so beloved of the young. I decided it must have been one of those laddish assumptions – marriage, babies, horse and carriage – not to be taken seriously. I didn't reply to the letter, but I didn't throw it away either. I put it with the others in my hatbox.

Two weeks later it was Remembrance Sunday, a three line whip for me and for several other members of the City Council as well, not just those who remembered World War Two but the increasing number who, like the Clarebournes, had sons or daughters in Iraq and Afghanistan. The City boasted a flourishing branch of the British Legion, several Falklands veterans and a sad, troublesome man who was always up before the beak on some drink-related charge or other and who ascribed all his misdemeanours to having been in Desert Storm. Far from remembering, he would be in the Crossed Keys, attempting, equally ritually, to forget.

Like non-punters who only ever bet on the National and the Derby, there were one or two church services Nico and I attended for what might broadly be termed cultural or social reasons, and Remembrance Sunday was one of them. We went for our parents, I think, and our grandparents, and (like the good liberals we were) in the increasingly forlorn hope of peace. Though today was official, and it wasn't necessary for Nico to come, he assured me he'd be there.

'I could do with getting my mind on to higher things.'

'You really don't have to,' I said. 'It's a foul morning.'

'I understand it drizzled a bit on the Somme.'

'Fair point.' I considered the logistics. 'I've got to be on parade with a wreath.'

'I realize that. I'll come under my own steam. And before you mention it I'm not fussed about the official coffee afterwards. I'll come home and get the lunch on.'

'We could go out,' I suggested.

'We could,' he said. 'In fact good idea, why don't we?'

At nine he rang and booked a table at the Carriage House on Market Square.

'No rush,' he said, 'you take your time. Do the business. I'll ensconce myself in a snug corner with the colour supplement.'

It was a raw, grey morning with an unforgiving wind straight off the Steppe, but it wasn't just that which was making me shiver. In spite of a brief rehearsal I was unusually nervous. The sense of occasion weighed heavily on me. The official party, comprising myself, our local MP, the CO from the local army base, representatives of the St John Ambulance, Red Cross and British Legion and the various scouting organizations foregathered at City Hall at ten. One or two people fetched coffee from the machine down the corridor. I'd have loved one myself, but didn't trust my bladder outdoors for an hour in the arctic blast.

A crowd several hundred strong, of all ages, had already gathered by the time we arrived with ten minutes to go. Scanning them briefly I was surprised by how many young people there were – families with children by the hand, teenagers, a couple of dads with toddlers perched on their shoulders – a reminder that though most people's lives had been relatively peaceful since 1945, there had been plenty of blood spilt in distant places in our name. At the humbler memorial in their village Julian and Georgia would be on parade, sending one up for Freddy with the Guards in Basra, and though I couldn't see Nico, it was comforting to know he was there, and could see me.

The Boys' Brigade band was playing 'Nimrod' as we took our places. Two nervous teenage buglers from the base marched out ahead of us and took up position on either side of the war memorial. A squad of young soldiers stood smartly to attention; behind them were lined up the ranks of veterans, men and women, rows of medals displayed on dark coats. Some of the men wore bowlers; none of the women were in hats except the WVS and St John uniform berets. There was one very, very old man, ninety-eight years old, a wisp of life in a wheelchair, the City's sole survivor of the Great War period; I'd met him when I visited Oakdale Retirement Home back in the spring.

My wreath seemed to be getting heavier all the time. There was a handle to make it easier to carry, but its shape and weight gave it a tendency to hang inwards. I had eschewed knee boots in favour of my tried and trusted black courts and sheer black tights, but now, as the lower rim of the wreath tapped against my shins, my general nervousness fixated on the possibility of getting a ladder. I tried to stifle my agitation by concentrating on Nico's 'drizzle on the Somme' remark.

In the end the sheer grave beauty of the occasion, its dignity and solemnity, stilled me. I can't imagine there was a soul there who wasn't similarly affected. The service, as conducted by Charles Pelham and the padre from the base, was less liturgy than meditation – on folly, waste, the living as well as the dead. We were asking, yet again, for the wisdom to learn from experience. Nothing could have been more relevant or less sentimental.

When it was my turn to lay the wreath on behalf of the council, my legs began to shake. For one awful moment I thought I was going to freeze. But there were people out there that I knew, watching – Nico, Hilary, Reg, Charles, my colleagues – and Doctor Theatre came to my aid. I walked forward steadily, leaned, positioned, stepped back, and bowed my head for a count of three. As I backed away my ears were ringing and my heart was in my mouth. But back in my place, humbled and shaky, I was prouder than at any time during my year as mayor.

When the last post died away at the start of the two minutes' silence, the hush was palpable. Over our heads the tops of the trees thrashed and hissed in the wind, but down here our ritual had created its own microclimate. Perhaps that was what was meant by the power of prayer, this great collective thought bubble that bloomed above and around us as we stood there in the icy juddering wind. It wasn't necessary to formulate specific words or well-turned phrases here, just this simple massed focusing of attention. Each one of us became entirely present, and part of the greater whole.

We were recalled by the sharp brazen summons of the reveille. That was then; remember it. This is now; act on it. The expression 'to bear in mind' took on a fresh meaning. This crowd with its diverse memories and its single intention would fragment and disperse and we'd all head off back to our lives – Nico and I to our lunch at the Carriage House. But this brief, cold hour would leave a thumbprint on my consciousness that would take a while to fade.

The Boys' Brigade played 'O God our help in ages past' as we, the official party, processed in silence from the square. When we reached the relative seclusion of the City Hall car park the spell broke. The young representatives of the scouting movement broke ranks and skittered about. We relaxed and began to talk. I confessed to the youthful Akela about my worry over ladders.

'I'd never have known,' she said. 'You did really, really well.'

'And your lot were marvellous. It's a long time to be standing still and in silence at that age. And it was so cold!'

'I warned them about that. Vests and T-shirts. But they don't feel it like we do.' She tweaked her bulging breast pockets, 'This isn't all me, I've got four layers on under here!'

The mayor's parlour wasn't quite big enough for all of us, so refreshments were laid on in one of the downstairs committee rooms. Everydayness seeped back into our systems with the caffeine and carbs. As I sipped my chimps' brew, Hilary came up to me, all smiles and gave me an unprecedented peck on the cheek.

'Very well done, ma'am.'

'Thank you, Hilary.'

'I was just talking to the Colonel – he said you were the smartest mayor he could remember.'

Though I knew Hilary, in her capacity as my de facto agent, would have accepted this compliment as being partly directed at her, I could tell from her face that it was being passed on in a spirit of genuine approval.

'How nice of him.'

'I told him I agreed.'

This was fulsome to the point of gushing on the Hilary scale, and I became quite flustered and moved on. The Beavers' and Cubs' mothers were beginning to arrive, and I told as many of them as I could what stars their children had been. If I had learned one thing in my year in office it was that praise of people's offspring was the simplest and most direct form of public relations.

The MP, a New Labour smoothie called Jim Petherton, had been at school with Hal, a fact with which I still struggled to come to terms. It's other people's children who get older, and not we ourselves; they're the memento mori we could all do without. He greeted me with a kiss – the double/formal, but I still thought it inappropriate.

'Joss . . . Particularly affecting today for some reason.'

'Very.'

He stood back. 'You look positively regal.'

'Is that good?'

'Very good. You lent tone and class to the proceedings.'
Suddenly he was irritating me. 'They had that anyway.'

'True.'

'Bye, Jim.'

Ten minutes later everyone had gone. Hilary set the caterers
to clearing up and went off to check on her roast. On my way
out I encountered ancient Mr Weaver, who remembered the
Great War. He had spent the refreshment break in the Gents,
being loaded into the Oakfield's van by a harassed young carer.

'Are you all right?' I asked. 'Need any help?'

'Wouldn't mind.' She was too preoccupied for niceties. 'Can
you do his seat belt while I get the chair in?'

Mr Weaver looked impossibly frail, like a doll, perched on
the passenger seat. The tartan rug in which he'd been swathed
was still round his legs and posed a problem to the clipping
of the seat belt.

'Excuse me, Mr Weaver, I'm just going to do up your seat
belt.'

'Thank you my dear . . . do . . .'

The van was high; I had to stand on the footplate to reach
the clip on the far side of the seat. The bloody rug was still
in the way and I faffed about, hearing Mr Weaver's agitated
tolerant breathing and feeling his surprisingly piercing blue
eyes on the back of my head as I struggled. The girl loaded
the wheelchair and came round behind me.

'Want me to do it?'

'No, no – there.' I completed the docking manoeuvre and
felt with one foot for the ground.

As I did so I felt, quite distinctly, a hand on my breast.

I say 'a' – it could not possibly have belonged to anyone
but Mr Weaver, but the idea was so preposterous I couldn't
at once believe it. Also, the grasp was strong and – no other
word for it – practised. The hand had found its way under the
lapel of my coat and down the front of my blouse with no
trouble. The palm cupped me nicely, and the thumb was feeling
for my nipple. Mr Weaver knew perfectly well what he was
doing; he was being mischievous.

I froze. The girl appeared on the driver's side and paused
to get out a hankie and blow her nose. The hand was un-
hurriedly removed. She opened the door and climbed in.

'Thanks for that.'

She turned the engine on and sat there with one hand on the wheel and the other on the gear lever, politely waiting for me. Carefully – though heaven knows why I should have tried to protect him – I got out. Mr Weaver looked snug up there on his seat, gazing out of the window with a little smile on his lips. He'd displayed the silky sleight of hand of a pick-pocket; my neckline was scarcely disordered at all. I closed the door and stepped back. As they pulled away the girl stuck her hand out of the window and fluttered her fingers in farewell.

In the bar of the Carriage House I described this incident to Nico and we laughed till we cried though my laughter, it had to be admitted, was slightly hysterical.

'The old bugger,' said Nico. 'I suppose I should be mortally offended, but good for him . . .!'

'He must be what – late nineties? But he hadn't forgotten a thing.'

'I suppose it's like riding a bicycle – sorry, no! Jesus!' He took a swig of his wine and mopped his eyes on his shirt tail. 'Did you say anything?'

'Well, no, I didn't. I didn't want to grass him up today.'

'Grass him up? Come on Joss, I bet he does it all the time. The opportunities for a cheap feel with all those sturdy young women in the care home must be legion. All that winching and lifting and bed-making – an ageing lecher's paradise.'

'Oh, and I thought it was just me . . .'

'Don't flatter yourself.'

Laugh? People were staring at us.

In our slightly hysterical good mood we were bound to get rather plastered over lunch. Our respective bottles of red and white went down at an alarming rate.

'I tell you what though,' said Nico. 'That was a damn fine show at the memorial. Very impressive. I was glad I came. Did you see me? I was over by Barclays Bank.'

'No, but I'm glad you came.'

'I was very proud of you.'

'All I did was stand there.'

'But you did it beautifully. And laid your wreath like a good 'un.'

'How would a bad 'un lay a wreath?'

'I've no idea but not as nicely as that.'

Over coffee and cognac I said: 'I'm pissed, and we don't have Reg. How are we going to get home?'

'Walk. I walked.'

'In these shoes? I don't think so.'

'Then I shall summon a cab.' Nico raised a finger. 'I shall do it now.'

He went off to the reception desk with the exaggeratedly steady gait of the man who feels far from steady. When he came back he moved aside everything on the table – glasses, cutlery, coffee cups, orchid, and held out his hands for mine.

'Joss . . .'

'Yes?'

'This may not be the moment, but may I ask you something?'

'You can ask.'

'Your old Mr Weaver – actually that was rather touching.'

'In every sense.'

'No, seriously. What better tribute to the fallen than such incontrovertible evidence of the life force?'

'I suppose.'

'So I put it to you . . .' He frowned down at my hands and then looked up. 'It's got me thinking. When we get back – would a shag be out of the question?'

The days were shortening. I used to like that – the cosiness, the drawing of curtains and lighting of fires; the big luminous red and gold bauble of Christmas hanging tantalizingly on the horizon.

Now, the closing of curtains and lighting of the lamps at four – three thirty on an overcast day – feels like a hunkering down under siege, a protection against the encroaching dark outside. Without the distractions of the outdoors, the daylight and comings and goings, the freedom of movement invited and allowed by daylight, I was thrown back too much on myself and my thoughts. I remembered my mother when she was old and ill, how she'd fret about something until it assumed gigantic proportions, and then panic would set in and she'd ring in tears, and I'd not always been as patient as I should have been . . . Perhaps the shortening days are like a metaphor for the shortening time ahead.

It's not dark yet, but it's getting there.

In one way my busy mayoral schedule was a good antidote to the seasonal blues; on the other hand it exaggerated that phenomenon with the tyranny of the diary. If you knew to within ten minutes exactly what you would be doing on the third Thursday in February next year, the time in between seemed already used, consumed, not available to you. As for Christmas, with so much on I didn't feel I could plan for it. The year before last we had had Cathryn, her parents and the children, and last year just us, Elizabeth and Hal, home from the States without Lili. Now there was a new dispensation – Cathryn with Chris, Elizabeth with Edward (facing a moving date in mid-January), Hal in London with Lili . . . I wasn't sure what to do.

'When in doubt, nothing,' said Nico. 'You can be quite sure if they want to come, they'll invite themselves. And who knows? Maybe one of them will ask us to their groaning board. Sit tight is my advice.'

I had always thought mail-order shopping, especially for presents, soulless, but this year I kept every catalogue since they'd begun arriving in August, and earmarked two evenings for selection. Hilary told me the Internet was better, and cheaper, but to me surfing wasn't the same as browsing. I liked to be able to keep a finger on the monogrammed picnic rug on page thirty while making a price comparison with the waterproof travel clock on thirty-six. By the end of November I'd done the lot except for Nico and was trying to avoid so much as glancing in shops for fear of changing my mind and buying double.

If I'd ever thought Christmas started too early and went on for too long, then I'd been in a fool's paradise. For the mayor it started much earlier than that and went on interminably and intensively for as far as the eye could see. So many organizations, so much turkey, so little time! That joke about the man lying to his family and having to eat two Christmas dinners . . . it was no joke. I must have eaten twenty at least before mid-December. I began to feel that if I ever saw another sprout nestling up to a dollop of red jam, accompanying two rounds of reconstituted white meat and a ball of khaki stuffing, surrounded by inert gravy, I might very well resign. I tried the vegetarian option, but during the Christmas party season the chefs threw in the towel – flabby quiche and grated carrot, or mass-produced macaroni cheese was the order of the day.

The function that stood out, gastronomically speaking, like a good deed in a naughty world was Diversity Day at the local prison. Happily, it was the function chosen by Georgia for her relaunch as my part-time escort.

'Damn,' said Nico, 'I rather fancied that myself.'

'You'll be working.'

'I could pass it off as work – theatre as therapy. Make music not mayhem. They'd love it.'

'So would Georgia,' I said, rather more firmly than I felt.

'Are you quite sure?' I asked her later. 'It might be quite grim.'

'Trust me,' she said, 'it will be anything but. I used to be a prison visitor, remember, at Hayfield, the sex offenders place? Anything like this is a day out as far as they're concerned. It'll all be very jolly and the food's to die for.'

She was right, especially about the food. Confronted (in mid-afternoon) with samosas, bhajis, chicken tikka sandwiches, naan bread, barbecue chips and a whole panoply of deep-fried, high-carb, spicy goodies, I loaded my plate to capacity. Georgia took only one vegetarian samosa, so I filled up her plate, too. When we sat down at a small table next to the Christmas tree, she watched indulgently as I tucked in.

'Joss, you poor thing . . . I told you the catering was good. It's the post-Jamie Oliver effect.'

'Delicious.' I glanced at my watch. 'It's three thirty. What meal do we call this?'

'Oh, this is just a snack. It's like oil rigs and long-haul flights – eating helps to beat the boredom.' She fixed me with a fascinated expression. 'You're really enjoying that, aren't you?'

I nodded. 'I've done too much turkey.'

'I was hoping for a chocolate digestive,' she said wistfully. 'But I think it's a forlorn hope.'

We left at just after four and took Georgia home first. Reg opened the car door, and she turned to me before getting out. She looked white and tired.

'There's no power on earth that will stop me putting my feet up – but what does the evening hold for you?'

'There is something . . . Reg, what have we got this evening?'

'Evergreens Christmas party at Harold Wilson house, ma'am. Seven o'clock. I'll collect you at six thirty.'

I moaned.

Georgia kissed me and patted my shoulder. It was a sympathetic gesture, but she was laughing. 'Have a lovely time.'

When I got back from the Evergreens, Nico called down from the study.

'I'm in a holding pattern over Hawaii!'

I trudged up the stairs, carrying my shoes and arrived, leaning, in the doorway.

'You look completely banjaxed. Fancy a nightcap?'

I shook my head. 'Alka-Seltzer. And bed.'

'I shall join you as soon as I've landed.' He went back to the screen, and then added: 'Oh – Lizzie rang.'

'Yes?'

They wondered if they could come here tomorrow evening.'

'But it's a weekday,' I said feebly.

'I know. They appreciate you'll probably be out, but they're on their way somewhere and want to spend the night.' He looked at me. 'Why, it's not a problem, is it?'

'No – no, of course not. I'm just wiped.'

'If it makes any difference,' said Nico, 'she was in exceptionally cheery form. She's got a plan for Christmas.'

'Just so long as it doesn't involve turkey.'

Elizabeth was interviewing in Chester the following day and Edward was along for the ride. They arrived at nine thirty, having eaten on the way. We sat round the fire in the drawing room, the men with a scotch, Elizabeth and I with decaf tea. The prevailing mood was unusually peaceful.

'So, what's this idea you've got?' asked Nico.

'It's this,' she said. 'Hal's going to see the kids on Christmas Eve and give them their presents – but they're going to a friend's for Christmas Day.' Nico and I did our not-looking thing. 'So since we'll be in the throes of packing up and you won't feel like being a domestic goddess this year, I've suggested that we – and you if you're up for it – join them at their chic hotel for a festive lunch. Be just grown-ups together for the last time.'

Nico nodded in my direction. 'Just tell your mother she can skip the turkey and you'll have made her day.'

'The place they're staying in is so high end I doubt whether it's even on the menu.'

'It sounds wonderful,' I began, and then sensed they were looking at me – or no, not looking at me, watching me. Watching and smiling, or trying not to smile.

'Hang on,' I said. 'What?'

'Beth,' said Edward, 'she wasn't paying attention.'

'I'm beginning to see that.'

'What?' I said again.

'I think a hint has been dropped, darling,' said Nico. 'A fairly heavy one.'

'What?'

'About being just grown-ups together for the last time?'

At last, I got it.

The baby was due in the spring. We were all very calm and grown-up, in a good way. Even Nico, though delighted, did not become overexcited. A sort of gentleness was in the air, a respect for what was happening to us, and to Elizabeth in particular. I remembered this from Cathryn's first pregnancy, the essential natural dignity of the process that had begun (just as well, since dignity was the first thing to go in nine months' time) – but with my own daughter the feeling was immeasurably more powerful.

We only stayed up another hour, discussing practicalities that were also dreams – the new house, names, who else to tell and when. In bed Nico and I lay in each others arms and heard our daughter and son-in-law still talking softly, and sometimes laughing together in the room that had been hers as a child.

Nineteen

Chloe walked in ahead of her father. She carried a bunch of daffodils and a small paper bag.

'Hi, Gran.'

I stood up and gave her a hug, careful of the flowers. 'Hello, darling!'

'Where's Oompa?'

'He's with Elizabeth.'

'Can we go in?'

'In a minute, let's wait for Dad.'

Hal came over, rubbing antiseptic gel into his hands. He was smart in a dark blue suit, pale blue open-necked shirt, and black shiny loafers.

'Go on, Flo, you'd better do the same.' He took the daffs and the bag off her. 'Just squeeze out a dollop and rub it in.'

'Where's there some water?'

'You don't need water, it's like hand cream.' He watched her go and then turned and stooped slightly to kiss me – my tall, handsome son. 'Hi, Mum.'

'Hello . . .' I patted his shoulder. 'Lovely that you're here. That you were able to be here.'

'You know what? I'd have come anyway. This is huge.'

'Yes.' I thought of Hattie, so frighteningly tiny. 'Yes, it is.'

Chloe returned and took back her package and bouquet. Putting his hand on her shoulder to include her, he said: 'We're the first instalment. We had a meeting with Mum, didn't we, and decided to do it this way round? All of us together would be too much. Cath and Jed will come later, or maybe see her when she's back home.'

'I think that's very sensible.'

Chloe, not to be deflected, had kept her eyes on my face throughout this. 'Can we go and see her now?'

'In just a moment,' I said, 'but remember to be very quiet

and gentle. Elizabeth's quite tired and the baby's brand new and very, very small.'

'Can I hold her?'

'Absolutely not,' said Hal, making a cheerful 'get-her!' face in my direction. At Christmas I'd detected the beginnings of an American twang, but it suited him, as if it had always been there waiting to emerge.

'None of us can hold her at the moment,' I explained, 'she's too little.' I put my hand on her head, but looked at Hal. 'How's Lili?'

'She's good. Working hard. She sent her love, and she's dying for photographs.'

'Any you take now won't show much.'

'They'll give the idea. She wishes she could have come.'

Chloe tugged my hand. 'Can we . . .?'

'Yes!'

Further down the ward, the nurse behind the desk at the nurses' station smiled and motioned us through. As we approached I saw Nico, standing by the glass, gazing. His hands were held, with the palms together, against his mouth. Inside the premature baby unit, Elizabeth was reaching in to touch Hattie in her plastic pod. Neither of them saw us coming. Chloe went and stood next to Nico, her face a bright 'O' of enchantment and naked curiosity. Nico glanced down and said nothing, but he stroked his granddaughter's hair, nodding at me and Hal. His eyes were slightly red.

'Hey . . .' whispered Hal. He clenched his fist. 'Well done, sis.'

Elizabeth looked different. She wore black pyjamas and a short black waffle-cotton kimono, so to that extent she would have stood out anyway in the clinical pastel shades of the unit. But inside the clothes the lines of her body had changed, gravid with the extra weight and purpose of motherhood; and not only that, her body's attitude was altered. In fact – I thought this as I looked at her – for the first time in ages, perhaps ever, it was without attitude. She was softer, more pliant; subject to the biological imperative.

'What's she doing?' asked Chloe.

'She's fixing her hat . . .' said Hal. He held up his thumb. 'A hat that would go on there.'

'Why does she need one?'

'Because she's been inside her mum for quite a while, and it's a lot warmer in there than it is out here.'

'You may say that . . .' Nico took a hankie from his pocket and wiped his brow. 'But they're making a pretty good job of simulating uterine conditions.'

'They have to,' I said.

Nico looked at me as if seeing me for the first time and reached across Chloe's head to place his hand briefly on the back of my neck.

Elizabeth adjusted the tiny hat with careful, unaccustomed fingers. Both the hat and the doll-sized matinee jacket were made of that multicoloured rainbow wool that I'd learned to knit with when I was a child. I felt my stomach contract empathetically, my heart surged into my throat, and my eyes prickled at this sight of my daughter with her daughter.

'I'm going for a coffee,' said Nico. 'See you down there in due course – no rush, take your time. I'll buy a paper.'

I nodded.

'Hal? Hal . . .' He put his arm round Hal and they exchanged a quick hug.

'Cheers, Dad, I might join you in a while.'

Nico moved away, then back again, and kissed me. 'I have so many great women in my life.' He stooped and kissed Chloe. 'Congratulations to us.'

I nearly said, automatically, that we had done nothing. But I didn't, because it wasn't quite true.

'She's tiny.' Chloe moved so that she was standing between me and Hal. 'Was I as small as that?'

'No, you were born at the right time.' I looked at Hal. 'How much did Chloe weigh?' I could remember, but wanted him to say.

'Seven pounds, three ounces.'

'So I was nearly three times as big.'

'Right. Well done.'

'Whoa.'

We pondered this as we watched Elizabeth finish her small, gentle tweakings and strokings. She looked up and saw the three of us standing in a row, staring at her, lifted a hand and mouthed, 'Hi!'

We must all have done the same thing together, because she pointed and laughed, shaking her head. Chloe lifted the flowers and the bag and waggled them. Elizabeth mimed delight and mouthed: 'Coming.'

She came out to us and suggested we go along to the visitors' room at the end of the corridor. Her hair was clean and brushed and she had put on some lipgloss, but in spite of the extra weight she looked tired and fragile. The actual labour, seven weeks early, may have been easier than that of a full-term birth, but the shock and the accompanying emotional tsunami had taken it out of her. I felt for her so much, and I wanted to protect her, to tell her not to worry about us – not to worry about anything, in fact, but simply to concentrate on herself and her tiny daughter, and Edward, because that was all that mattered for now.

Hal and Chloe, though, were buoyant with a sense of occasion, and celebration. We sat down on orange tweed chairs in the visitors' room and Chloe handed over her presents. Elizabeth rhapsodized over both the daffodils and the miniature towelling teddy.

'Her first teddy – she's going to love him because he'll be small enough for her to hold.'

'That's what we thought,' said Chloe.

Hal produced a small box from his pocket and held it out. 'From Lili.'

'Lili . . .? How very sweet of her.'

'For Hattie, when she's older.'

Poor Elizabeth, more expectation, more need to perform. She already had the teddy and the flowers on her lap, and now she opened the box.

'Oh my goodness . . .!'

It contained a seed-pearl ring, the minute pearls arranged in a many-petalled flower shape like a Tudor rose.

Hal leaned forward, as if making a bridge between the two women. 'She says you're to wear it whenever you want in the meantime. It's good for pearls to be worn.'

'Do you like it?' Chloe, in on the whole thing, huddled up close to her to admire it with her.

'I do, I really do, Hal.' She looked at her brother. The water table was high and I half expected her to cry, which would have been a good thing. 'Hal, you must tell Lili . . .'

He covered her hand. 'Don't worry, sis.'

'I'll write.'

'Only if you want to. You've got enough to think about.'

'I do want to.'

Chloe fingered the ring. 'Do you think Hattie will like it?'

'I know she will.' Elizabeth put her arm round her. 'She's going to treasure it. I tell you what, though.'

'What?'

Elizabeth held it up. 'Right now she could wear it as a bracelet.' She put it back in the box and closed the lid. 'I shall keep it somewhere very safe.' She looked at Hal, an endearing look, and he smiled and lifted his chin in acknowledgement.

'Where's Edward?' I asked.

'He's gone to fetch a few things from home. He won't be long, you'll probably see him.'

Chloe got up. 'Can I go back and look at Hattie?'

'Of course you can. There isn't a lot to see, but perhaps . . . soon . . .' The banked-up tears threatened to run over.

I said cheerily, 'Good idea, you go and keep an eye on her for us.'

When she'd gone, Elizabeth took a lump of well-used Kleenex from her pocket. I produced a fresh packet from my handbag.

'Cry away,' I said.

'No, thanks.'

'There's no shame in it. It's the hormones.'

'I don't care what it is, Mum, I don't want to fall apart.'

'Damn right.' Hal raised an eyebrow at me. 'Didn't you realize yet it's only her stress that's holding her together?'

We spoke about Hattie and how she was doing. Which was pretty well, but not out of the wood just yet.

'She can't suck, she's still on a drip. That's the big one.'

'But breathing and so on . . .?'

'She can do that. Breathing, she can do. And heartbeats. Her skin's so fine you can actually see her little heart pumping away at double speed. The machinery's all in place, and working, but she needs to gain strength and – I suppose you could call it will. She needs to hear the message and convert it into action.'

This was pure Elizabeth, the idea that such a tiny mite could behave like the CEO of a multinational. I had to smile, but it was Hal who said: 'You make her sound like Superman.'

'Wonderwoman,' said Elizabeth, 'that's my girl.'

We stayed for another twenty minutes and then left. Elizabeth said goodbye and went back into the unit; the three of us said goodnight to Hattie from outside the glass.

In the lift, it was Hal who put my unspoken thought into words.

'Will she be all right?'

'She will, but it'll be hard,' I said, then realized he might have meant a different 'she', and added: 'And Hattie will too.'

On the ground floor, the hospital had a central 'plaza' – oddly named, like the motorway 'toll plaza' as if locals might regard these as inviting destinations for a night out. Today it was buzzing with an odd mixture of the walking ill with their tubes, trolleys, bottles and plasters, and the visitors in rude health. Edward had joined Nico at a table. He looked exuberantly well and happy – long might it last. I tried to imagine us, two years younger than Edward, confronting all those broken nights, the seeming endlessness of baby-care, the physical and emotional attrition of it all, and I simply couldn't.

'Dear Edward –' I put my arms round his neck – 'Congratulations, she's absolutely beautiful.'

'Isn't she though?'

'I'm not sure you've met our other granddaughter, Chloe?'

'Chloe – gosh. Someone for Hattie to hero-worship.'

Chloe blushed and frowned.

'Hal, nice to see you again. It's so good of you to come over. I know how much it means to Beth.'

'And me,' said Hal. 'It was a no-brainer, frankly.'

'This is my second cappuccino,' said Nico, 'and Edward's on the Darjeeling, so all things are possible.'

Hal and Chloe went to buy our drinks and I sat down. On the floor next to Edward was Elizabeth's Louis Vuitton flight bag.

He saw me looking at it and said: 'Emergency supplies. I hope I've got everything.'

'How long will she stay in for?'

'They're saying she could come out tomorrow, but she wants to be close to Hattie for a while longer, and I must say I agree. The two of them need time together and I know Beth, once she gets home she'll be straight into gear.'

'Dead right, in my limited experience,' said Nico. 'You

know I've got to go back this afternoon, but Joss is staying another day.'

'That's marvellous. Elizabeth will love that, and to be brutally frank it'll give me a chance to see off a few of the jobs that need doing around the house. I have a strong sense of things mounting up. We still have boxes from the move.'

'Is there anything we can do?' asked Nico.

'My dear chap, thanks awfully, but no. I mean I'm sure once Hattie's home in a few weeks' time, Elizabeth would appreciate a bit of, you know, what only a mother can provide . . .'

'Don't worry,' I said. 'I'm there if she'll let me be.'

'Yes.' Edward gave a rueful smile. 'There is always that proviso.'

Hal and Chloe came back with his coffee, my tea and Chloe's Coke. When he'd put them on the table I caught his hand and put it to my cheek for a moment.

'Hey, Mum . . . OK?'

'Yes.'

'Gran?'

'I'm fine.' There's nothing like seeing your emotions reflected on the face of a child to make you realize you're jolting their world and bring you back to yourself. 'Fine!'

'They're powerful ju-ju, babies,' said Nico, squeezing my knee under the table. 'Aren't they? They make you remember stuff.'

He was right. They did make you remember. Seeing Hal, the image of cool, pond-hopping noughties man, with his crisp cuffs, open collar and Ralph Lauren cologne, next to Elizabeth at her most vulnerable, had twisted my heart for both of them. For Hal's self-imposed distance and Elizabeth's new life. For change, and the seasons, and, oh – so much I couldn't or was fearful to put into words. The gift of the pearl ring to Hattie had set my worry sensors quivering. What were its origins? We scarcely knew Lili and she came from another country, another culture; the family that had passed the ring to her spread out behind her like a peacock's tail, strange and brilliant, unknowable. And our Hattie, our tiny Hattie, teetering on the cusp of life up there in her plastic pod, would wear the ring one day and continue to wear it long after we were gone, and Lili, perhaps, had assumed a special place in her life.

Outside the hospital we parted from Hal and Chloe, who were driving back to Cathryn's. We got a cab and asked for the station for Nico, followed by the club, where I was staying. In Hyde Park the crocuses were fading as the daffodils came out, but it was cold out there, and people walking were wearing coats and boots and looked pinched.

'Don't bother turning in,' Nico said to the cabbie. 'I'll jump out here.'

'OK, guv.'

Nico cupped my ear in his hand and drew my face towards his. 'Wonderful,' he said as he kissed me. 'Absolutely bloody wonderful. See you soon.'

At the club I had a goat's cheese salad in the bar and then went to my room and put my feet up. I wanted to go back to the hospital again in the early evening, but I was suddenly worn out and weepy. I cried pathetically for about twenty minutes and then fell asleep.

I woke up at five thirty. It was nearly dark and an unpleasant hard rain was hurling itself at the window. I turned on the television for company made a cup of tea with extra sugar, swigged it down and had another one. At least in a hospital there was no shortage of loos, but I still made a pre-emptive visit before leaving.

At the hospital it felt much later than half-past six. Elizabeth had had her supper, and she and Edward were in the unit, gazing. When they saw me, I indicated that they should stay where they were, but Elizabeth got up and came out to me.

'Hi, Mum. Thanks for coming back.'

'Try and stop me.'

'Edward wants to commune with her a bit longer, but to be honest I'd like to go and put my feet up.'

'I'll come and keep you company.' We waved to Edward.

Elizabeth was in a four-bedded ward, in the corner nearest the door. Her billet was immaculate, the bed made, everything stowed, a book, newspaper, biro and glasses on the bedside cabinet. We'd all been told not to send flowers, but there were roses from Edward, a pink and silver helium balloon with 'All-right!' blazoned on it, and a row of cards on a string

over the bed. One of them, I couldn't help noticing, had Rob's
handwriting: '. . . see her soon, Rob XXXXX'.

'Darling, it's so tidy.'

'I've got nothing else to do, Mum. My life has shrunk,
keeping tidy isn't a problem.'

She got on to the bed and sat with her long legs stretched
out, ankles crossed.

'Chloe was very sweet,' she said. 'She's a nice kid.'

'Isn't she? And Hal and Cathryn seem on genuinely good
terms.'

'It was good to see him. I wish he wasn't so far away.'

'Not far away to him. He's got the money so he can pop
to and fro.'

'Yes, but we can't. Or probably won't.'

I sensed an uncharacteristic melancholy creeping over
Elizabeth, and stepped in to forestall it. 'The children had a
fantastic time when they went over after Christmas.'

'I'm sure they did.' Elizabeth pulled a more familiar sceptical face.

'I don't think it was all spoiling. I hear Lili cooked Korean
food, and they loved it.'

'That was a beautiful ring she gave to Hattie.'

'Exquisite,' I agreed.

'Almost – you know – too much.'

'I don't think so,' I said. 'Accept and enjoy, don't worry
about it. Don't worry about anything.'

Suddenly, explosively, Elizabeth wept, covering her face
and making a soft gasping, wailing sound, her shoulders
shaking, the tears oozing between her fingers. There were one
or two looks from other parts of the ward – all sympathetic,
but even so I drew the curtain a little so she had some privacy.
I moved on to the edge of the bed and put my arm round her
shoulders. Awful, perhaps, to admit it, but I was happy. Glad
she'd given way, glad that I was there when she did, glad to
have her sobbing against my shoulder. This was right. This
was natural.

Two or three minutes passed, and as the sobs died down
she turned her face into my shoulder and put her arm round
my neck. A sweet, sweet moment.

'Oh, Mum, I feel so goddamn useless . . .'

'Darling! You are the most useful person anybody knows.'

'Hmm.' She sniffed, straightened, and felt for her tissues. 'It's a trick of the light.'

'No, it's not. You know it's not. You're so competent and independent, such a high achiever . . .'

'Until now.'

'Everyone feels like that with a new baby. And it must be ten times worse with Hattie because at the moment you can't do anything for her; and you're a doer, so you feel paralysed. Not useless, darling – frustrated.'

'And scared, Mum.' She scrubbed at her face, ran her fingers through her hair. 'Scared shitless. What if after all the watching and waiting, when I'm finally called on to be a mother, I'm crap at it? What if I can't do it?'

'For one thing, you're a mother already, darling. And for another, you will be able to. You'll make a few mistakes, we all do, but you and she will learn together. It's what happens.'

'Really.' It was a comment, but I treated it as a question.

'Yes.'

She looked at me. 'That's what happened with you?'

I cast my mind back to Hal. It was a blur.

'Yes,' I said. 'And we were incredibly young and green.'

'Maybe that's easier.'

She was right. 'You don't worry so much,' I conceded. 'You take it in your stride. But the loss of sleep is worse – we were hardly more than teenagers, and you know what they're like.' When she didn't smile, I added: 'And remember Edward's done all this before. He's an old hand.'

'But, Mum, I can't rely on him! Imagine how you and Dad would feel to have a new baby in the house, right now – yup? He's going to be exhausted – I need, I want to take the pressure off him.'

'I'm sure he'll want to do his bit,' I said, but again I could see hers was a sensible, commendable, point of view. 'It'll be self-regulating, you'll see. You'll do it together.'

'Maybe that's the trouble.' She spread long, well-manicured fingers on her lap and stared down at them. 'I'm not used to doing things together.'

'But you love Edward, and he loves you. That's enough. That'll see you right.'

'I hope so. You and Dad—'

She stopped, frowning to herself. I had the strong sense of

something important coming, and I didn't want to scare it off. Neither, it has to be said, did I particularly look forward to hearing it.

'You were always such a team.'

'I hope so.'

'Take my word for it.'

'So are you two. Or you will be. That's kind of what marriage is.'

The frown was directed at me, now. My shot at greetings-card philosophy, the sort of thing her paper loved, was going to be ignored. Either that or traduced. She chose the second.

'Yours, definitely. No one else could possibly have been on your team.'

'How do you mean?' Why does one always ask that when one knows without a shadow of doubt exactly what is meant, and how?

She looked away, then back down at her hands. 'You had this exclusive thing going on. I don't think you could even help it. I'm sure you didn't intend to exclude anyone, least of all us, but that was the effect.'

This whole exchange was being conducted in a low, tense tone just above a whisper, but even so I got up and drew the curtains the rest of the way. I was keenly conscious, now, of the need to get whatever I said, and however I said it, exactly right. That meant being truthful, shouldering blame, and trans-mitting a message of wholehearted and unconditional love (there must be no 'but', no attempt to apportion responsibility, however justifiably; we had been the adults, the buck stopped with us) – none of them hard in themselves, but a compli-cated and delicate combination.

I took a deep breath. 'I'm sorry.' The words were like two small, hard stones, the bare residue of all I wanted to say.

She was staring at me now. 'Remember that business with Dad,' she said. 'With that dreadful woman, who was always so nice to you. I remember thinking that if I told you about that, got you to fight your corner, it'd be a way to break in to the magic circle, you know?' It was only half a question and when I didn't answer she went on: 'I thought I could get myself a stake in your lives – play a part.'

She paused. Her lips were pressed tightly together.

'Elizabeth . . .'

'Anyway, it didn't work. I went back to college, and you just went off and sorted it all out and when I got back normal service had been resumed. Just like that.'

'Surely,' I said, as calmly as I could, 'that was preferable to the alternative.'

'But, Mum –' her face was contorted, though her voice was still barely above a whisper – 'you never mentioned it to me again! Not once – not even to say thank you!'

'I thought it would be too painful . . .'

'You and Dad closed the circle and I was on the outside of it, as usual.'

'I'm sorry,' I said, lamely. 'I'm truly sorry. That wasn't how it felt to us.'

'What would have happened if I hadn't said anything?'

'I wouldn't have known – well, I might have found out, I suppose . . .'

'And what would you have done?'

'That would have depended.' I heard my voice beginning to rise and brought it under control, saying as gently as possible: 'Look, darling, do we need to be going over all this now? Doing this to ourselves just when we ought to be thinking about Hattie and the future? You and Edward?'

'No.' She looked away. 'I suppose not.' There was a long, long pause. I could hear her breathing. 'I just wanted to explain.'

'Well,' I said. 'You have. And I can see what you're saying. I am terribly, terribly sorry that you felt excluded. Dad would be devastated if he knew.'

'Mum, Dad's never devastated.'

'You might think that, I used to think that . . . But it's not true.'

'OK.'

'Also –' I took her hand; she didn't resist, but didn't respond either – 'this is where we are now. What do they say? We're in a different place, in a good place. And if everything that's gone before has led us to here, then it can't all have been bad.'

'I accept that. And I never said it was all bad.'

'At least,' I said, trying unsuccessfully to catch her eye, to lighten up, 'we were good role models for marriage.'

'Yes . . . Yes, you were.'

'Give or take.'

She gave my hand a small squeeze. 'Are.'

'Thank you. And whatever happened, however we behaved, or seemed to behave, there was never the least doubt, I hope, that we loved you and Hal and you were the most important thing in our lives.'

She raised a finger to correct me, but her mood had changed. 'After each other.'

'I'm not going back there now!' I waved my hands as I got up. 'Now I'm going to go and say goodnight to my son-in-law and my new granddaughter. I'll see you again in the morning.'

I went to the side of the bed and we engaged in a cautious hug.

'Cheers, Mum.'

'Night-night. Sleep tight. We love you.'

She nodded into my neck. I made sure to withdraw from the hug a nanosecond before the little pat that said 'enough'.

Twenty

Certain events provide the punctuation to life. Hattie's arrival was a full stop, the minute but powerful mark that ended one chapter and was the prelude to another.

A month after her birth, in the week that she finally came home, my year as mayor came to an end. I passed the chain of office over to Peter Carroll without regret. This year seemed to have been in parenthesis to the rest of life. I was glad to have had that experience, but I wouldn't miss it. I returned to my bread and butter work on the City Council with a new calmness and focus, a better sense of what – and who – was out there, and what needed to be done. I set myself a time limit of one more year in which to make whatever small difference I was going to. By then Nico would be beginning to think about retirement, or some kind of sideways move, and it would be time for the two of us to establish a new and different pattern.

It would be pleasing to say that my whole futile, foolish, enchanted episode with Rob ended at the same time as the mayorship. That would have been tidy. But nature abhors tidiness as much as she does a straight line, and 'closure' as they say, didn't come until the following December.

By which time a lot of other things had happened to put it in perspective. Doors closed, others opened. Georgia, after a few months of sparkling remission, left us abruptly, almost as if the whole thing had been planned. Only one of their sons was at the funeral. The other, away on active service, was blown up by bomb on a desert roadside only weeks later. Julian displayed true-blue character and cast-iron composure throughout. We, and she, would have expected nothing else. And we took our tone from him. Even I, whom a silly love song could reduce to tears in seconds, stayed dry-eyed at her memorial service, only weeping when we got home, when I thought I might never stop.

'What shall I do without her?' I wailed to Nico. 'Who'll keep me up to the mark?'

'You'll be a credit to her, Joss,' he said. 'And you don't need keeping up to any mark; you stay there perfectly well all by yourself.'

I wished I could believe him.

Denise confounded all expectation by marrying Douglas – but doing so in Australia and letting us know by email, so we couldn't jeer.

Laugh if you must, you rabble, she wrote, *but get it out of your systems before we come back in October. We're keeping separate establishments so everything will be as before. I may be a married mistress, but I'm still a mistress.*

'What a splendid girl she is,' commented Nico, squeezing my bottom. Denise had her usual aphrodisiac effect even from the far side of the world. 'Fancy rolling in the hay with a grandfather of three?'

Cathryn moved in with Chris and there were a few predictable ructions with the children, especially Jed, from which I derived a sneaking, unworthy satisfaction before they blew over. Hal and Lili remained together, though I wasn't holding my breath. And Edward and Elizabeth came through with flying colours – their true colours, I liked to think – displaying more patience and stamina than we'd dared to hope. Hattie remained small, but was a beauty, with a crest of red-gold hair and speedwell blue eyes.

'As soon as it's decent to do so,' said Edward, 'I'm hiring her out to the advertising boys.'

Nico agreed. 'Play your cards right you can have her on the catwalk at twelve.'

Bryony was in the States.

And Rob? Rob was on the road with his poetry. A bird of passage, a troubadour, out there somewhere with a star to follow.

But with all this, I still from time to time felt the butterfly-touch of that sweet, lovely, hopeless feeling. Perhaps it was that – a sort of post-traumatic stress – that brought on an attack of the blues such as I hadn't had in years. As always, I pretended it wasn't happening until the evening when I sat opposite Nico at the kitchen table, unable to stop weeping over my untouched supper.

'Jesus, Joss . . . Darling.' He pushed back his chair, carried it round and sat down next to me, his arm round my shoulders. 'Enough, already.'

'I'm sorry . . . Nico, I'm so sorry!'

'For what? I'm not the one that's unhappy. Or only because you are.'

'I don't want to be like this.'

'Then go to the doc. Not for my sake, for yours.'

'I never thought I'd have to again. It's years since the last time – I thought I was over all this.'

'It comes back,' he said gently, stroking back my damp hair. 'We know that. God knows there's been enough emotional wear and tear over the past couple of years to drive a saint to drink. Go and see the doc, have a talk. You don't have to take anything you don't want to.'

'No,' I said, 'that's true.'

I went to the doctor and he prescribed the latest thing. 'The cheap and cheerful solution,' as he put it, 'for what ails you.' I took two weeks off work, slept a lot, and began, little by little, to emerge from my chrysalis of misery.

It was as the raging unhappiness ebbed that I thought of seeing Rob again. I entertained the thought calmly, almost idly. It was not so much a plan, nor even a wish, just the idea of it spinning slowly in my spaced-out brain like a screen saver.

What if I did? What would happen? What had happened?

And then in late November fate, as they say, stepped in and took a hand. Nico came back from the theatre with the new programme for the Yard.

'Seen this?' He gave it a tap as he held it out. 'Rob's going to be on. Want to go?'

In my imagination, I met with Rob alone, but even I could see that going with Nico was safer. Neither of us suggested meeting him afterwards – I was surprised Nico didn't, but relieved, too. The mere fact that it had been his idea to go at all saved me from myself. But the excitement I felt was the first real, bright feeling to pierce the veil of comforting blahness created by the pills.

That was nothing to the way my heart jumped when he came on stage. I noticed a difference. He had filled out and was no longer a boy – there was even a slight thickening at the waist that might have been due to the beer that accompanied his performances. His hair was longer, curling behind his ears and over his collar. The shadow of stubble around his mouth was darker, cultivated, probably shaped. As to his performance, it had acquired a gloss of professionalism, which was both good and bad. Much of what had been instinct was now expertise. The naturally canny timing was practised, the delivery both more casual and more calculated – I felt I could see the machinery working, but only, I told myself, because I knew him.

There was a lot of new material – less than a quarter of the poems were familiar. There were no rose petals, but he did use 'Let's Stay Sweet As We Are', the one he'd given me in the park, and the fact that he'd kept a copy was another pinprick through the veil.

It was the encore that reached out and got to me. I almost wondered if he'd seen us in our discreet, halfway-back-and-to-the-side seats. The poem was called 'Unfinished Business' and was funny, I supposed, in a dark, biting way. The last lines said it all:

> It's not the ex that threatens sex,
> It's the almost-was and might-have-been,
> Beware the break that isn't clean,
> She'll chew your heart and mess your mind,
> And feed you 'cruel to be kind',
> That one can make you sick for years,
> A nagging pain between the ears.

On the way out, we were silent among the admiring burbles. As we crossed the car park, Nico said: 'Good show. He's on his way, isn't he?'

Back in the car he closed his door but didn't turn on the lights or the engine.

'Joss? Are you OK?'

'Absolutely,' I said. 'A bit sleepy – but then that's how I am at the moment.'

'My poor sedated darling. But you do seem better.'

'I am.'

'I'm really glad we did this.' He put the key in the ignition.

'It's good to keep the connection. Who knows, he and Bryony may be grown-ups, but they could still feel a bit usurped by that young baggage of Lizzie's.'

I couldn't speak, but my silence was covered by the turning on of the engine.

'We should email – say we were here. Will you do that, or shall I?'

'You do it,' I said.

We moved slowly out of the car park, the beam of our headlights trickling over rows of cars, people hurrying in the cold, out into the street.

'Music?'

'Whatever you like.'

'Let's see . . .' He pressed play and on came Dylan with that damn song: 'Not Dark Yet'.

'Bit melancholy?'

'Perhaps.'

He clicked on to the next CD and we had Joni Mitchell strumming and carolling with beach tar on her feet.

'That's better.' He tapped his fingers on the wheel. 'Love her. I used to idolize her, remember?'

I did. I remembered 'Chelsea Morning' and the mention of oranges which always made us fiercely thirsty with our bottle-party and dope hangovers.

'You think you'll grow out of that,' he went on, reflectively, as if talking to himself, 'but you don't. Or I didn't. It was just as well I was laid low for Esther Waring, I'd probably have made a bloody fool of myself.'

'No, you wouldn't.'

'I would. You saved me.' He glanced at me. 'As you so often do.'

'You met her again, though,' I said, 'that time in London.'

'I did.'

'And did you make a fool of yourself?'

'No,' he said. 'No, I didn't. Know why?'

I waited.

'Because though a nice, charming woman, a considerable beauty and no mean actress, my world remained resolutely unrocked.'

'Good,' I said. 'I'm glad.' The relief of speaking the truth was like a headache miraculously lifting.

We drove for a minute in silence.

'I once asked you if I was a buffoon,' he said.

'I remember.'

'When you said I wasn't, at the time I thought you were being kind. Because in spite of everything you seem to love me.' We slowed and turned up the hill towards the north of the city.

'I do,' I said.

'But now,' said Nico, 'I think you were right. I may be more than usually foolish from time to time, and act the giddy goat rather more than I should at my or any other age.' I opened my mouth to speak, and he touched my arm to stop me. 'But I can't be a complete idiot, because I know the difference. And more importantly, so do you.'

We were climbing and criss-crossing the shoulder of town via an ever-changing network of streets, travelling through different periods and different social and architectural zones as distinct as ascending microclimates on a mountainside.

Nico began to recite Christina Rossetti's poetry: 'My heart is like a singing bird'. The poem, and his way of reciting it, was like a lullaby. As we moved upwards, heading towards home, I fell asleep with the soft sound of those words rolling through my head like petals scattered by the wind.